DEAT

MW01133158

DEATH BY THE DROP

Timothy W. Massie

2008

DEATH BY THE DROP

Acknowledgements

The following people deserve special thanks for helping me make this book possible:

Randy, who is always willing to comment on my revisions and provides an endless supply of encouragement;

Laila, Alex, Jake and Nick, all of whom I love dearly and couldn't be more proud of;

Heidi, whose support ranged from late night popcorn delivery, to sharing her much needed editing expertise. I couldn't have done it without her.

For Heidi, my wife and best friend.

Chapter 1

It all started when I walked in on my wife and her psychiatrist. Susan
sought out Dr. Kevin's professional expertise, in hopes of resolving the
long list of issues that have burdened her since childhood. During their
many intense sessions, a unique doctor-patient bond developed. So
overwhelming was this bond that it compelled them to act in a manner
they both knew was wrong, but for some reason, could not resist.

Okay, so that's a bunch of bullshit. Normally it's in my nature to
put a positive spin on my troubles, but screw that. This is still a festering
wound, and to be honest, I'm pretty pissed off about it. Let me take
another shot, but with a more accurate description this time.

It all started when I walked in on my fat-assed alcoholic slut of a
wife and that needle-dick son of a bitch shrink of hers, who really needs
to get his scrawny little ass kicked! He was obviously doing an in-depth
analysis of a lot more than her psyche, and was clearly outside of the
normally accepted boundaries of his profession. I believe that even
Herr Freud would agree this is a much more accurate assessment of the
situation, and if not, then screw him too. It certainly makes me feel
better, and that's what really matters, right?

Assuming you've never been in the situation, you can take my word
for it when I say that no guy wants to catch his wife cheating on him.
It's kind of like having your insides ripped out through your nostrils,
twisted into a huge knot, and then shoved back in through your rectum.
Only worse.

If she's going to cheat and there's absolutely no avoiding it, then you
at least want it to be with someone that everyone would agree is totally
irresistible. You know, someone who's either a movie star, or a rock star,
or even better yet, an international spy, like James Bond. Someone so
suave and ruggedly handsome, that you can shrug it off with a wink and
say to her, "Ah hell, it's all right, honey. I guess I owed him one for that
time I nailed his girlfriend while he was away on a secret mission in
Prague. Just don't let it happen again." It's still not a good scenario, but
at least it'd make a bad situation more palatable.

The last thing you want is to catch the love of your life doing the wild thing with a total loser like Dr. Kevin. It's enough to make you turn into...well, a very bad person, or perhaps I should say a very bad...thing! So, let's put the blame for any misdeeds I might have committed since this unfortunate event where they belong, on my ex-wife Susan and Dr. Kevin, that son of a bitch shrink who needs to get his scrawny little ass kicked!

In an odd twist of fate, it happened on the same day that I began my unplanned early retirement. I'd spent the past twenty-four years in the real estate game, trying to buy, sell, lease, or build something on just about every piece of property on the board, minus the railroads and utilities of course. Perhaps I passed "Go" and collected my two hundred bucks a few too many times, though, because I'd reached a point where I was just putting in time at the office. Somehow during the past couple of years, the same profession that had been the primary focus of almost everything I did in my life, now seemed unbearably routine, impossibly monotonous, and dare I say it, boring! It was probably past time for fate to step in and shake the pillars of my existence a bit, but I certainly never expected to have my perfect little world ripped apart the way it was.

Life might not have been particularly thrilling at the time, but I really didn't have much to complain about. Thanks to the ridiculously lucrative northern California real estate market, I'd made far more money than even an all around swell guy like me deserved. In retrospect, it's obvious that as half-owner of the bustling real estate office I worked in, I could have simply changed my priorities and shifted into more of a cruise mode—maybe taken up golf, ballroom dancing, or just worked on improving my left-handed beer drinking skills. The mid-life crisis that every workingman's entitled to was knockin' at my door; I just wasn't ready to answer its call. Given more time, maybe I'd have realized that I needed a change of pace and gradually eased into a few minor life changes. Fate, though, didn't cut me any slack by simply modifying the life I'd worked so hard to build, it blew my existence to smithereens and made me start all over from scratch.

I'm really not sure why I kept working so hard, especially since I was well past the point of needing more money. A good portion of the profits I'd made over the years had gone back into purchasing more real estate, and as long as a major earthquake didn't cause California to fall off into the Pacific Ocean, I was pretty well set. Perhaps it was guilt over obtaining financial success without believing I was particularly intelligent or gifted. Maybe it was some old fashioned work ethic I'd unwittingly contracted from a stranger's germs. Or maybe I simply didn't know what else to do with myself. Trying to make up for the sense of passion I no longer felt, I kept putting in fifty to sixty hour weeks at the ol' salt mine. Was I trying to maintain a certain image or to trick myself into thinking I still cared? Either way, it seemed to be the best way of proving I was still an important member of the office team and fully engaged in our never-ending quest to stay number one in the local market. Regardless of my attempts to project an image of involvement, those heady days when the continued existence of the civilized world hung on the outcome of every transaction, were now a thing of the past.

I was in my office that morning, furiously surfing the Web to check the local real estate market for any possible leads. To be honest, I was checking the previous day's baseball scores to see if the Yankees had extended their winning streak, but we'll keep that part our little secret. While glancing through the box scores and sipping a cup of my favorite morning pick-me-up (extra hot mocha, double shot, light on the whip), my business partner casually strolled in and sat down. That was my first clue that something was up, since I couldn't recall him ever actually sitting down in my office in all the years we'd been partners. Then, avoiding direct eye contact, he began rambling on about change being healthy, and each person having a destiny or purpose in life. After about three minutes of his pointless psychobabble, I knew something big was up and told him to spit it out. Jeff seldom talks about anything other than real estate, unless it also has something to do with another type of financial gain. Preferably his. When I pressed him on it, he surprised me by blurting out an offer to buy my half of the business.

At first I thought he was kidding; then, for a brief moment I was offended. When I realized Jeff was serious, and his offer was not only reasonable, but actually leaned toward the generous side, I surprised myself by agreeing to sell right there on the spot. Blame it on the Yankees extending their winning streak, too much caffeine in my mocha, or maybe a good hair day. In a move totally uncharacteristic of me, I'd made a major life altering decision on the spur of the moment. In my normally well-organized and meticulously planned life, snap decisions like this just didn't happen. As impossible as it seemed, the same anal-retentive putz (yes, that'd be me), who once spent nearly three hours online researching the cost/benefits of purchasing recycled printer cartridges over new ones, had just decided to sell his business and retire in less than twenty minutes.

It seems that despite my best efforts, Jeff had noticed my fading interest over the last few years. The business had continued to prosper, and though he had no complaints about my contribution, he knew my heart wasn't really in it anymore. After I agreed to sell, he admitted he had some very aggressive plans for steering the business in a new direction. Though he didn't come right out and say it, it was obvious this new venture would require a level of passion and commitment that I no longer possessed. So, we shook hands and agreed to pull the necessary legal and financial documents together over the next few weeks. I walked out the door with my cup of custom-made java still reasonably warm and my head spinning.

Holy smokes! Talk about a life altering change. One moment I was just another working stiff, plodding along in a mental haze with no end in sight. Now, I'd somehow managed to cross the finish line without even knowing I was approaching it. The rat race was over, and from my perspective, I'd won! As I was driving away, the enormity of my decision had only partially sunk in, and though I knew it would be a long while before I could fully comprehend all the consequences, I couldn't resist feeling a bit giddy. Of course, one or two moments of fear, bordering on panic, flashed through me too. When I reminded myself that I was a forty-six year old millionaire who, with just a modicum of self-control, could live the rest of my life as a man of leisure, the feeling of elation returned.

It's odd how things happen in life. Weeks, months, even years can go by without a single significant emotional event touching your life. Then one day you turn a corner and wham, you get your melon rocked by a left hook to the chin, closely followed by a right cross to the solar plexus, and then a kick in the nuts just to make sure you're fully aware that your life as you know it is under siege and about to undergo a major renovation. I'd left for work that fateful morning, wondering just how late I'd have to stay to review a couple of big contracts that I didn't really care about. Less than two hours later, I was headed home early for the first time in about a decade, anxious to spring the big news on Susan, my presumably loving wife of nearly twenty-one years.

Making my second big decision of the day, I decided we were going to take that month-long European vacation we'd always talked about but never found time for. Only after we rediscovered our passion for each other while making love on a moonlit beach in Majorca, would we contemplate the rest of our lives. I couldn't suppress a laugh, knowing that this was all so far out of character for me. Poor Susan would have trouble believing it at first. Springing the big news on her was going to be fun, and I couldn't wait to see her face when she found out that her workaholic husband—make that ex-workaholic husband—was retiring early. After all these years, she was about to find out just how crazy and spontaneous I could be.

I never would have believed that things could fall apart, so fast. Stuff like this is only supposed to happen to bad people, or lowlifes like those idiots you see on reality television shows. With very few exceptions, I don't cheat, steal, litter, or tell offensive jokes. Okay, I may have repeated an insensitive joke or two, but at least I felt guilty about it later. I pay my taxes on time, donate to several worthy causes, vote Republican on almost everything except environmental issues, and have bought at least three boxes of Thin Mint cookies annually from each of the dozen or so Girl Scouts who live in our neighborhood. I must be on their list of easy marks, because every year my freezer's full of the darn things. I've found they're especially good frozen, and then dipped in cold milk and popped whole into your mouth. Hmmm, I may be deliberately changing the subject, though I do believe the Thin Mint cookie issue is a subject worthy of some serious debate. Perhaps if we had more Thin Mint cookies in the world, we'd have less war. All the terrorists would be unable to decide between say, blowing up a mosque or having another cookie. In addition, at least by my reckoning, all the world's armies would have too many fat people to bother with wars, right? It all sounds good, unless there's a milk shortage. Now that could be a whole new issue and I don't have that one resolved yet. You know, the whole cow, methane gas thing. I'm working on it though. Anyway, good things are supposed to happen to good people, so somewhere, somehow, a huge error was made in my case.

I carefully parked my car, a black Mercedes sedan, in its assigned spot in our meticulously arranged, and I'm proud to say, absolutely spotless four-car garage. Entering through the kitchen door, I carefully placed my keys on their assigned hook. By using the cute little "Key's To My Heart" key rack that was mounted on the wall next to the telephone, we always had the peace of mind that comes with knowing our keys would never be misplaced. I quickly looked for Susan downstairs, and noticing her half-empty coffee cup on the sink, took a moment to rinse it out and put it in the dishwasher for her. As I was closing the dishwasher, I heard a noise upstairs. I smiled, realizing the love of my life was probably up there tending to some chore or another, doing whatever it was she did all day. Suddenly, I was hit by another crazy thought. I should have brought her flowers! Oh well, it was too late for that. I'd save that surprise for another day. I practically flew up the familiar curved staircase, with a smile on my face and a song in my heart. In a burst of excitement, I pushed the double doors to our bedroom open wide, ready to break the big news to her. I was free! We were free!

No, she wasn't free. She was bound to our headboard with some fuzzy red handcuffs. Involuntarily taking another step inside, I couldn't believe the scene my eyes were showing me. There was my Susan, naked and spread eagle on our bed. Kneeling in front of her and stroking his manhood, in what I can only assume was some weird type of Rorschach experiment, was good ol' Dr. Kevin. Did I mention that he's also a needle-dick, son of a bitch who needs to have his scrawny little ass kicked? There he was, dressed in this ridiculous black leather and chain outfit, looking like, like, well...a needle-dick, son of a bitch in black leather and chains! Ahhh!

Have you ever noticed that when you really need to come up with a great line the most, it's rarely there for you? Why is that anyway? I've thought of scores of them since then, but at the time the best I could do was to choke out, "What the hell?"

Of course their responses weren't exactly award worthy either. Susan could only manage to scream my name over and over again, "John. John. John." Even in my state of total shock, I noticed that she slid out of the cuffs rather easily, removing any doubt on my part about her being a willing participant.

Dr. Kevin, he of the rapidly shrinking needle-dick, could only managed to stutter, "It's, it's, it's cool man, it's, it's cool."

It's cool? Not to me it wasn't. I stared at them in disbelief for a few more seconds, still too shocked to respond appropriately. Now that some time has passed and my brain doesn't lock up on me when I think about it, I fantasize that I calmly walked over to my dresser drawer and removed a very large caliber pistol. Say, something just slightly smaller than a bazooka. It came with a lifetime guarantee to not only kill whoever I shot with it, but to fill them with several moments of sheer terror prior to delivering its agonizing death blow. After pausing a moment to ensure the sheer terror effect worked as promised in the guarantee, I shot them. First I shot her, right in that double-crossing black heart of hers. Then I shot him, right in that needle-dick of his. It's a lucky thing I'm a good shot in my fantasies, because there wasn't much of a target to shoot at. I now understood why they are called "Shrinks!" Then, satisfied that he'd reached the maximum level of terror a human could withstand without spontaneously exploding, I put a round in his head. Then a few more, just to be sure he got the message. I know, you're thinking I've gone wacko or something, but trust me; this fantasy thing is very therapeutic.

Unfortunately, unlike my fantasy version where I'm as cool as a cucumber, the only thought actually racing through my head at that moment, was that life as I knew it had just ceased to exist. My ears were ringing, my stomach was doing flip-flops, and to top it off, I was having trouble breathing. I heard myself starting to make little wheezing sounds, and knew I was in trouble. Thinking of nothing more intelligent to say than the aforementioned, "What the hell?" I turned and left before I could embarrass myself by either passing out, or puking on our very expensive Berber carpet. To say I was shattered is putting it lightly. How could she, and with that rotten little son of a bitch? I've never been in a fistfight, but I ought to kick his scrawny little ass! And what the hell, they were having a *morner*! A morner, you ask? You know, it's the same thing as a nooner, only sooner! I never got morners. Heck, I never even got nooners. What the hell's going on?

Now that I've bared my soul to the world, or at least shared the most humiliating thing that's ever happened to me, I suppose it would be a good time to tell you a little about myself. My name is John Steele, and if you look in your dictionary under "nice guy," you'll see my picture. Since I'm on an honesty kick here, you can probably find my picture under "anal retentive" and "neat freak" too. However, I can absolutely guarantee you that I'm the type of guy you want living next door to you. I'm courteous, conscientious, and willing to lend my tools out as long as they're returned clean.

I grew up in Fresno, California, which is really not worth mentioning unless you've been there. If that's the case, you'll automatically sympathize with me and that'll come in handy later. Fresno's not really a bad place, if you don't mind crime and aren't particularly fond of fresh air. It's a big flat city with few noticeable landmarks. It stretches from farmland in the north, south and west, to foothills and mountains to the east. In the middle of all this farmland is a whole bunch of houses, most of which are only slightly distinguishable from one another. A bunch of poorly planned stores and strip malls, some schools, and a few other assorted buildings have been thrown into the mix to make it all somewhat functional. Unlike most cities, where development eventually reaches some boundary and they're forced to turn back in and revitalize the older neighborhoods, Fresno seems to have no such boundaries or limits. It just continually spreads, and as new neighborhoods pop up, the older ones are left to fall apart in ruin. For a youngster with the usual overblown teenage dreams of a life filled with adventure and intrigue, it wasn't exactly the best place to start. Rather, it was the kind of place you looked forward to seeing in your rear view mirror at the first available opportunity.

I didn't have much of a family life growing up. My biological parents split up when I was three, then took off in separate directions. Dad headed to San Francisco to join a rock band, and Mom headed to L.A. to become a movie star. Neither was ever seen or heard from again, at least that I know of. I'm sure they probably spent long careers waiting tables at Denny's and wishing they could give me a pony for my birthday. In actuality, I have only vague memories of them, so it really wasn't a huge factor for me growing up. I figure I was the result of two people getting high and being horny one night. Odds are I wasn't the first, nor will I be the last child conceived this way.

I grew up with my maternal grandmother, a bitter little woman who smoked too much and seemed to hate her lot in life. Her one constant was to make sure we were in church every Sunday, come rain or shine. I never figured her out. She wouldn't let us miss a Sunday morning church service, but she never seemed overly religious at home. I never saw her pray or read her Bible, and except for the rare occasion when we had company for dinner, we didn't even give thanks before eating our meals.

Not sure how to raise an energetic young boy after having failed miserably with her only daughter, she tried to keep a fairly tight rein on me. She constantly reminded me of her eternal suffering and of the many sacrifices she made on my behalf. Lacking any real parental instincts or skills, she probably hoped that my weekly attendance in church would provide the guidance and guilt needed to ensure I was raised properly, and to hopefully keep me from a life of crime. I guess her methods worked since I turned out to be a model citizen, though I haven't attended regularly since I left Fresno.

When I turned twelve, my grandmother left me too. She had a better excuse than my biological parents though. She died of lung cancer. Watching her cough herself to death over those last few months of her life was enough to ensure I never became a smoker myself. She was so sick towards the end that I found myself actually wishing she'd hurry up and die for her own sake. Nobody should have to suffer like that, even someone as mean and nasty as her.

After my grandmother passed, I became our church's favorite charity case. The head preacher worked with the local social services, and I got to stay with various families off and on for several months. I hated it and always felt like an unwanted third tit. Most of the homes were simply uncomfortable to be a guest in, but one was really the shits. I was only there for a couple of days, but those days culminated in the scariest experience of my young life. I won't go into great detail, because it's so far in the past and really not worthy of a lot of analysis at this point. I thought I should mention it, though, since it had an impact on some of my thinking later. Unfortunately, I know I'm not the first, nor will I be the last to have to endure the horrific experience of an encounter with a child molester.

The Ramseys always seemed rather strange and were never one of my favorite families at church. I assumed they were just overly religious and hadn't gotten to the chapters in the Bible about joy and happiness yet. I knew the moment I arrived in their home that it was a bad place. I've never been psychic or anything cool like that, but there was something about the place that immediately gave me the creeps. Victor, the man of the house, became very serious as he sat me down and made sure I knew he was, in fact, the man of the house. He looked me directly in the eyes and went to great lengths to ensure that I understood I was now a part of his household. As such, it was my duty to uphold the code of the house, which was to never reveal anything that happened in his house. Up to that point in my life, I'd never lived in a house where anything happened that was worth mentioning, so I said I had no problem with it.

The Ramseys had two kids, both of whom were a lot younger than me. I don't recall their exact ages, but the oldest was a boy of about four, and the youngest was an infant girl. I tried to be friendly and converse with the four year old, but he always kept his head down and wouldn't even look at me. Totally lacking the spunk of a normal four year old, he just quietly played by himself with his few well-worn toys.

Mrs. Ramsey was an odd duck, too, though not totally quackers. She was constantly wringing her hands and always seemed to be in movement. Everything she did seemed kind of jerky. It was like she was trying to do too many things at once and somehow couldn't focus on one thing. The house was clean, and the few meals I had there weren't half bad, so I guess that somehow in all that extra motion, she managed to get things done.

The first night there, I heard Victor come into my room and I sensed him standing over my bed. I figured he was just checking to make sure I'd been able to get to sleep in my new environment, so I lay there as still as could be, pretending to be asleep. Finally, after what seemed an eternity, he left. I didn't know why, I felt a sense of relief when I heard the door close.

The second day was uneventful, but that night, Victor entered my room again. I could hear Mrs. Ramsey sobbing in her room down the hall, so rather than employing my patented fake-sleeping technique, I sat up on one elbow to see what was up. Victor closed the door, and a sense of foreboding came over me. He walked to the edge of my bed and untied his bathrobe. Underneath it, he was naked, and it didn't take a genius to figure out what was up.

"You ever seen anything like this boy?" he asked, indicating his fully erect member. Of course I had, since I had one too. In fact, every time I peed or took a shower, there it was, winking at me. Lately, we'd even taken to becoming better friends. I'm sure now that he was expecting me to be impressed, but being twelve, I simply thought he was an idiot for not knowing all males had one. He was scaring the bajeebers out of me, though, and I was wishing I'd employed my fake-sleeping technique again. When I didn't answer, it seemed to anger him.

"What's a matter boy, you didn't think this was some kind of free ride did you? I'm gonna teach you how to please me in a manly way, and then you're gonna keep your little mouth shut about it. Do you understand me? If you ever even think of telling someone, I'll tell 'em you're making up dirty little lies. Who you think they're gonna believe? A good Christian man like me or some damn orphan kid?" He reeked of alcohol, and I'd seen enough television to know that made the situation even worse.

Though I was scared to death of this drunken pervert in front of me, there was no way I was gonna do what I thought he wanted me to do. My life experiences up to this point hadn't prepared me very well for something like this, but I knew that if I didn't act fast, it was gonna get real nasty, real quick. I threw the covers off of me and tried to dash around him. He caught me by the back of the neck and forced me to my knees. A good smack against the side of my head from one of his man-sized paws had me seeing stars. He waved his "thing" in my face and began telling me what I was going to do to it.

The dirty bastard almost broke me right then and there. I'd have likely been scarred for life and probably would have ended up a Catholic priest or whatever it is that happens to twelve year old boys who are put through this situation. There was one thing in my favor though, well, two things I guess. Victor Ramsey had the balls of an elephant. I'd taken a baseball to the nuts the year before and knew first hand how devastating an injury there could be. In desperation, I reached up and grabbed his sagging old nut sack with both hands and squeezed like my life depended on it.

The response was instantaneous. His knees slammed together,

pinning my little nut grabbers in place, and his big hands grabbed my skinny little arms and tried to rip them loose. Oh, and for the record, he also began to let out a very loud gurgling sound that seemed to emanate from someplace only a doctor should ever see. It may have been unintelligible to most people, but it told me loud and clear that I was achieving my goal.

When he finally fell to the floor, I lost my grip, but I was confident I'd done enough damage to get a decent head start. I ran past him, out the bedroom door, down the hall and through the living room to the front door. It was secured with several different locks, two of which were too confusing to figure out in a hurry. I didn't have time to waste, so I headed through the kitchen for the back door. It was secured in the same manner. A wave of panic swept over me as I realized I was trapped with a drunken pervert, and I was now firmly lodged on top of his shit list. Not good. Not good at all.

Desperate times call for desperate measures, so I focused my attention on finding another way out. The front living room window caught my eye, as it was one big sheet of plate glass. It seemed to provide the best alternative I could come up with after about a second and a half of careful consideration. I picked up what felt like an eighty-pound family Bible that was lying on the coffee table and hurled it at the window. It bounced off. I turned to the next heavy item within reach, which was a half-empty bottle of booze that hadn't been there before I went to bed. It didn't bounce off. I guess for some things, booze is better than the Bible.

As the window broke, Victor von Scramblednutzen stumbled into the living room, still holding his freshly cracked eggs.

"Get back here you little bastard," he croaked as he stumbled forward.

There was no way he was catching this little bastard, not that night anyway. My feet hit the couch and I catapulted out the front window. Fortunately, they lived on a fairly busy street, and I ran down it as fast as I could, screaming for help at the top of my lungs. I got about a hundred yards down the street, when a neighbor opened his door to see what all the commotion was. As soon as I mentioned that I was running from a naked drunk, he and his half-asleep wife pulled me inside their house and called the police.

As you'd expect, the police came, Victor denied, his wife cried, and I got to go stay at the police station for the night. I had lots of doughnuts, my first cup of coffee, and the respect of several of my new police officer friends. A paramedic had to pull a few slivers of glass out of my feet, but it was a small price to pay for getting to stay up all night with the cops.

Finally, after several legal proceedings, which I didn't come close to understanding, I moved in with the Bowmans and found a somewhat permanent home. Mr. and Mrs. Bowman were your prototypical sweet older couple, who'd never had a child of their own and weren't quite sure what to do with a half-grown one. Considering they had no obligation to welcome an unrelated twelve year-old into their home, they were extremely kind and generous. Unfortunately, I didn't fully appreciate it at the time. I have often wished I had shown them more affection, but it just wasn't in my nature then. Living with my grandmother, I hadn't been around affection enough to know how to express it myself. Besides, I wasn't exactly at the age where boys express a lot of affection, unless you happen to be a twelve year-old girl with things starting to pop out on your chest. What I could do for the Bowmans, though, was be extremely helpful around the house and cause the least amount of trouble possible. That set the pattern I followed the rest of my life. Be kind and helpful, don't cause trouble, and maybe you won't be sent away to the Ramsey's. That's me, always Mr. Nice Guy, always Mr. Helpful Guy, and almost always Mr. Stay Out of Trouble Guy.

Immediately after graduation from high school, I joined the Navy. I had the grades to go to college, but not the funds. In the Navy, I was first trained as a Gunner's Mate at the Naval Training Command in Great Lakes, Illinois. If you have a guided missile launcher that needs repair, I'm your man. While there, I applied for and was accepted to the Navy's Second Class Dive School.

At dive school, for the first time in my life, I found something I had a passion for. It was incredibly hard work, but I excelled and graduated at the top of my class. I couldn't believe I was actually getting paid to be a diver. Becoming a Second Class Navy Diver was the absolute coolest thing I could imagine at the time. I was so proud of my accomplishment and the exciting work I did on a daily basis, that I fully intended to become a Navy lifer. In my mind, there was absolutely no doubt that I'd do at least a twenty-year career, maybe even thirty if they'd have me. Ah, the best laid plans...

One Friday afternoon I was helping my mentor, a knurly old Master Chief, Master Diver, carry some equipment out to his pickup. Sitting next to his clunker of an old truck, was a shiny new BMW. We both admired it, and he commented that he wished he'd done something to make more money during his youth. He went on to say that when he retired in a couple of months, he was getting into real estate. What?

Say it ain't so! One of my heroes was considering something other than salvage diving for a living? Didn't he realize he had the greatest job in the world?

I spent an entire weekend wondering how the man with my dream job, a Navy Master Diver, could possibly want to do anything else. So complete was my belief that diving was the only profession worth pursuing, that I couldn't comprehend how someone like the Master Diver could possibly think differently. That Monday, I decided to investigate this real estate thing, just to get some proof that it wasn't as good as salvage diving. I'd get the straight scoop and then enlighten him with the facts.

Having no idea what I was doing, I walked into a local real estate office and asked a salesman sitting behind a desk what the pay scale was for a real estate salesman, and whether or not they were eligible for anything like hazardous duty pay. Fortunately, I got a guy with a sense of humor. He explained how the commission generally works, and that with each piece of property in the area as expensive as they currently were, a good salesperson could make six figures in a short time. On the flip side, a bad one could soon find himself broke in that same short time. He suggested I attend a free seminar, which his fellow salesperson, Donna, was holding that Saturday.

Since it was free, I showed up on Saturday, eager to get the real scoop for the Master Chief. Once I'd straightened him out, he'd get back to focusing on what was really important, like helping me prepare to become a First Class Diver. When Donna greeted me, I fell instantly in lust with her. From the gleam in her eye, I could tell the attraction was mutual. Later, when we hooked up, I liked to tease her that she saw an opportunity to have a professional dive on her, though she never did admit it. Perhaps it was the classy "Diver's Do It Deeper" t-shirt that I wore on special occasions, like real estate seminars, that impressed her. Then again, maybe not!

It turned out that the free seminar was basically an advertisement for the real estate class she was offering, and somehow I managed to get signed up for it. Over the next twelve weeks, she schooled me in real estate taxes, liens, property evaluation, and about thirty sexual positions that as far as I knew, had never in the history of mankind been tried before. She was only ten years older than me age-wise, but light years ahead of me sexually. Though I really wasn't interested in real estate yet, I stuck with the class so I could continue seeing Donna. For some unknown reason, possibly her recommendation, her office offered me a part-time gig after I'd successfully completed the class and passed my test. Understanding that I was still committed to the Navy, it was supposed to offer me an opportunity to learn the real estate sales ropes. The last thing I needed was another job, but since it was my ticket to keep riding the Donnaville express, I accepted.

I still had four months left on my initial enlistment contract when I accidentally made my first sale. I say accidentally, because I wasn't really trying. I was off duty by 4:00 p.m. most days, and I had the majority of my evenings free. So, to be around Donna, I hung out in the office whenever I could. For the most part, I answered the phone, sorted brochures, and drank a lot of their coffee, which was an upgrade over the nasty stuff the Navy served.

I almost didn't go into the office that night, because Donna had gone to Philadelphia to visit her parents. Several others were going to be out too, so I thought it'd be a good night to go in and catch up on some reading. I took a call at the office from a guy interested in buying a house located right there in Alameda. He'd just accepted a new position in Oakland and was only in town that night. He really wanted to see at least a couple of properties in Alameda before he left the area. Since nobody else was available to help him, I hopped in Donna's BMW, which she'd loaned me, and took the guy around to a few houses we were representing. That night, he decided to make an offer on the first house I'd shown him. I almost shit. I was so wet behind the ears that Donna had to help me with the paperwork when she returned. Later, she told me that the guy who bought the house had commented to her about what a nice young man I was and that I took such a relaxed approach with him, that he'd never felt the slightest pressure to buy! He thought I was a natural and guessed I was one of their top salesmen. I made almost as much on that first sale as I had in the past year in the Navy. The possibilities definitely had my attention.

I made my second sale a month before I got out of the Navy and, seeing those dollar signs flash by, pretty much sealed the deal. No reenlistment for me, diving would have to become a hobby. Donna took me under her wing and helped me polish up my act. I leased a big four door Mercedes, bought a snazzy but conservative new wardrobe, and learned to exude both confidence and a muted sexuality in everything I did. As you can probably guess, those were her terms, not mine. I just followed her instructions and, pretty soon, it seemed everyone wanted my help buying their dream home or dumping an albatross. For some reason, when potential clients saw my face on flyers or in the newspaper, I looked like a guy they could trust. Once they met me, they realized that not only was I as trustworthy as my photo appeared, but I was also the original Mr. Nice Guy.

Donna also taught me something about investing. She owned several rentals around the San Francisco Bay Area, including a small apartment complex in Fremont. She hadn't steered me wrong up to that point, so I followed her advice. It paid off. Eight years later, when I turned thirty, I realized I was getting pretty damned rich. By the time I was forty, thanks to the ever-increasing property values, I knew I was worth more money than I had a right to. Some people try to get rich their entire lives without success. I started out in real estate just to get laid and never really set my focus on getting rich. Wealth was simply a by-product of me doing something I really liked and something I had a knack for.

Once I'd made a few sales, I was addicted to the whole process and the possibilities it created. Soon, I lived for moving property in any way I could. It was great to see a young couple buy their first house, a hard working couple move up to accommodate an expanding family, or an older couple free up their time by moving from a labor-intensive monstrosity to a low-maintenance condo. My favorite transaction, though, was for a run-down and neglected piece of property to fall into the hands of my favorite client, a guy who happens to look exactly like me, who'd fix it up and either sell it for a profit or turn it into a revenue generating rental property.

Carrying on a life-long tradition of females in my life, Donna left me too. About two years into our relationship, she moved back home to Philadelphia. Her mother passed away suddenly, and she decided she wanted to take care of her father, whose health was also questionable. I tried to talk her out of it, but she told me she really loved the old guy and wanted to spend his final years with him. This concept was a bit foreign to me, but somewhat understandable given her generous nature. I flew there twice, but it became obvious a long distance arrangement wouldn't work. I realized that I'd never actually been in love with Donna, but she was my security blanket. Once I'd survived a month or so without her, I knew my fragile little world wouldn't come crashing down around me. By gosh, I'd become a man.

I met Susan through a co-worker. First we had a short lunch date to do the compatibility test thing. Next came a romantic dinner in one of San Francisco's finer dining establishments, which also happened to have a very romantic view of the bay. Of course, I plied her with a bottle of expensive wine, a rich chocolate dessert, and best of all, I kept my mouth shut and appeared to listen to everything she said. Having been the perfect date, I figured I had a good shot at jumping her bones that night. She insisted we wait until we were sure it was right and admitted she was a virgin. Somehow that changed things, so wait I did, for almost a year. That's when we got married at her parent's country club. Just like in the old movies, our wedding night was the first time we made love. I wish I could say it was worth the wait, but then again it'd have had to be pretty awesome to live up to a year's worth of pent up frustration.

I always knew I married above myself. Susan was extremely pretty, well educated, came from a prominent local family, and had all the confidence of someone born to succeed. I often felt she was too good for a pretender like me, who had no family, no education, and a confidence level that had a bad habit of wavering just prior to each sale. I vowed to be a good provider, though, and I'm confident now that I was, at least in respect to material things. Obviously, I didn't provide everything she needed. She had to turn to that little butthead shrink for something, and while I'm not cutting her any slack or making any excuses for her, it was probably for more than just the sex. Try as I might, I can't recall a single substantive conversation with her over the last few years of our marriage. I was her wallet, and she was my showcase wife. I still think that out of respect, duty, or something like that, she could have let me down just a little bit easier.

Chapter 2

For nearly four months after catching Susan and Needle Dick playing whatever twisted little game it was they were playing, I was a wreck. I sulked and felt sorry for myself, and my whole life basically went to hell. I moved into an empty townhouse I'd recently purchased, and survived with the bare minimum of furniture or personal belongings. I went weeks at a time without shaving, and often days without showering. Not that it really mattered, since I also went long periods without leaving that dreary little place. The news of our separation got around, and a few people from the office tried to reach out to me. I avoided all contact, though, since I knew nothing could help undo what had been done. Besides, the thought of someone trying to cheer me up actually increased my agony. Even Susan got concerned about me and suggested I visit a psychiatrist. Somehow, that particular suggestion coming from her managed to really piss me off, and almost pushed me over the edge.

I was so mentally down that I actually got physically ill. I'm talking really sick, as in "don't leave the house and stay close to the toilet" kind of sick. I finally went to our family doctor, who was so shocked by the way I looked, that he immediately wanted to run a whole series of tests. I didn't need a medical test to tell me what was wrong with me. I just wanted something to reduce the pain in my gut, so I could focus on the pain in my broken heart. After what seemed an eternity of lying in bed and sleeping for hours on end, I started to gradually feel a little better. One day, I realized I hadn't thought about Susan for almost twenty-four hours. Hallelujah, I was healed!

Okay, not healed, but at least I was turning a corner. I even started to wonder why I was so amazingly distraught over this, and the thought crossed my mind that perhaps I was overreacting just a tad. I couldn't work it out in my normally clear mind, though, so I decided to make some notes. Maybe if I captured and then organized all my thoughts, I'd find an answer? At first, I even had trouble holding a pen for some reason, but after a while I began to write furiously. On the second day of writing, then reading, then writing some more, two words jumped out at me, and I knew they were the keys. Those two words that immediately and repeatedly inflamed my anguish were *virgin* and *pride*.

Though I was an awesome catch, I really hadn't been intimate with many women before Susan. Donna was the only other woman I'd ever had a real relationship with, and since there was no doubt about her having had past experience, it never bothered me in the least. With Susan, I'd always known I was the one and only guy. In fact, she'd only been to two different gynecologists in her life, one in San Francisco and one in Pleasanton, and both were female. To the best of my knowledge, I was the only male to ever explore that one special little piece of real estate, and damn it, I liked it that way. My male pride told me that I somehow "owned" that particular gold mine, and nobody else was supposed to see it, much less mine it. I'm sure that was clearly stated somewhere in our wedding vows.

The realization finally set in, that opposed to the way I might have liked it or thought it was supposed to be, I didn't own Susan or her damned gold mine. She was my wife and not my personal property. As such, she was free to make decisions and choices as she saw fit. I further reasoned that, if Susan giving her body to another man bothered me more than her giving her heart to another, it was pretty clear my reaction had more to do with my pride than the loss of someone I was deeply in love with. The clincher was when I questioned what my reaction would have been if she had asked for a divorce, but there was no other male in the picture. When I answered myself honestly, I knew I'd have not only understood and wished her well, but I might have even secretly welcomed the new freedom a bit. Still, though I was working through my issues and understanding the situation as a whole, I'd never be able to forgive her for going behind my back and breaking my trust the way she did. And with him...

So, being the free-spirited guy that I was, or had decided I was going to become, I determined it was time to cut loose. For the first time in my life, I was going to be a total party animal. I'm talking about being a real wild man, like Casanova or Charlie Sheen. I was going to make up for years of being way too nice and way too boring. I was going to take a tumble with several hot babes, maybe at different times, maybe at the same time. Kinky, huh? Yep, I was going to be the asshole for a change. No more Mr. Nice Guy, no more Mr. Helpful Guy and, for God's sake, no more Mr. Stay Out of Trouble Guy.

I showered, shaved, got my hair cut in a slightly different style than I'd worn it for years, and generally got the physical part of my life back in order. Susan had always been my personal fashion consultant, and with the exception of a few very cool Hawaiian shirts I rarely got to wear, had selected all of my clothes. Rather than returning to my old house and picking up the rest those boring clothes she'd selected for me, I went on a shopping spree and bought a new, more updated wardrobe. I even decided to look for a new place to live, somewhat more befitting a wild womanizer like I'd soon be. The thought of refurbishing a place for my personal use, rather than as another bland rental, really got my juices flowing.

An old golf buddy who'd been married and divorced too many times to count, and who Susan never cared for, invited me to have drinks and dinner at one of my favorite downtown restaurants. Mickey was always a funny guy, and spending some time with him might be good for me. Besides, I knew a night of drinking and carousing with Mickey would piss off Susan if we were still married, and that made it even more enticing.

I was nervous about socializing again in our relatively small town, especially since I still felt more like half of a couple, than a single guy out on his own. Figure that one out. I worried that everyone was going to be pointing at me and saying that I was the guy whose wife was having an affair behind his back...and with some twisted little son of a bitch no less.

As I should have known, my angst was wasted on a concern that simply wasn't valid. My wife's cheating wasn't front-page news after all, or perhaps it had died the quick death that most gossip does. Nobody pointed, stared, giggled, or otherwise indicated I was any different than I'd ever been. Well, at least not that I could see anyway, and I did whip around quickly a few times, just in case. I was amazed to find the world pretty much the way I'd left it. No, in some ways it was better. I was still a reasonably wealthy guy, who was somewhat good looking and had retired early to live a life of ease. Now, I just didn't have the old ball and chain to drag around anymore.

The dinner with Mickey was a huge success and just what the doctor ordered. I hadn't laughed in months, and after my third Chivas and water, he had me in stitches. What really got my attention, though, was when he told me about the experiences he and several other golf buddies had on a trip to New Orleans. They'd partied like college freshmen on their first spring break and stayed out so late that they missed their morning tee times. Looking around to ensure that nobody was paying attention, he produced a small stack of pictures. A few were of the golf gang, obviously hammered and having fun. Most however, were of various women raising their shirts to show off their breasts. I'd heard all the stories before, but had doubts about their accuracy. Now I was holding actual proof in my hands; drunken debauchery was still alive and well in Louisiana. I decided right then and there, that finding a new place to live would just have to wait. I had a trip to make.

Chapter 3

Early the next morning, I booked an open-ended round trip flight to New Orleans. I knew very little about the place, other than what had been covered on the news during Hurricane Katrina and the slower than desired recovery period afterward. The city, and in fact a big chunk of the gulf coast region, was devastated while the world watched, horrified by the images being piped into their living rooms. Tourism, always a huge revenue producer for New Orleans, was almost non-existent for a while. It was said to be on the rebound though, and I was willing to do my part to help the city's economic recovery.

The trip was uneventful, though I sensed a lot of anticipation in the stale airplane air. I wondered how many of my fellow passengers were making this trip for the express purpose of cutting loose. Would I be high-fiving any of these folks on Bourbon Street some night, dancing half naked in the street while slugging down plastic cups of some local libation specifically designed to make tourists lose their inhibitions? Would I be catching a peek of any of the breasts on this plane, in exchange for a few strands of plastic beads? An old woman across the aisle looked at me and, as if reading my mind, flashed me a big crooked toothed grin. Ahhh! My bubble burst at the thought of her antiquated milk duds, and I came screaming back to reality.

Except for the fact that it actually falls within hurricane season, October is a great time to visit New Orleans. I found out that I'd just missed the Mardi Gras festivities, which was when my pal Mickey's pictures had been taken, but only by about a half a year. Hey, give or take six months and I'd have been right in the thick of things. I also discovered that there was a convention in town, and nobody parties like conventioneers, right? Normally yes, but when the convention's actually an old time southern revival featuring not two, but three of television's most popular Bible thumping, sin exposing, cripple healing evangelists, well, let's just say my timing could have been better.

Leaving the nice air conditioned airport with a taxi driver who was clearly in no particular hurry to get anywhere, I found the outside air was warm and humid, but not to the point of being uncomfortable. It just seemed to ask you to move slowly and to take life easy. Shorts were definitely the pants of choice during the daytime, but slacks were bearable in the evening. The sky was clear and the only clouds I saw were an occasional slow moving wisp. The torrential downpours the weather prognosticators had warned of, seemed highly unlikely.

Not wanting to miss out on any of the action, I'd booked a suite in the heart of the French Quarter. Surprisingly, they had plenty of vacancies. The hotel had survived Katrina well, and the hotel manager assured me that it wasn't much different than before those catastrophic events along the gulf coast had taken place those fateful days in August of 2005. The rates were remarkably low for the quality of the room I was given, and the staff treated me like royalty. I knew they'd handle it well when I brought a host of buxom babes to my room over the next few days. Probably speak of me like a legend after I left.

My first night out and about isn't really worth mentioning, though I should say that I enjoyed one of the tastiest meals that I've ever had the pleasure of consuming. It was at a restaurant called Antoine's, and according to them, they created Oysters Rockefeller. Well, that sold me. If their oysters were good enough for the Rockefellers, they were damn sure good enough for me. I won't go into nauseating detail about the meal, since the thought of food right now makes me want to puke up my colon. Let's just say that, at the time, it was scrumptious. The restaurant has quite a unique history too. Since I showed so much interest, the maitre de was kind enough to have a busboy give me a tour of the entire place. It provided a fascinating picture of New Orleans' social history. As for scoring that first night, well I'm sure I could have gotten laid, but I wanted to save my strength. You know, jet lag and all that.

I suppose my second and third days are of no particular interest, either, though I was hitting a lot of pretty cool tourist spots. I spent the daylight hours strolling through the Cabildo, the Presbytery, and other local museums, learning about the local culture and history. I couldn't pass up a ride on a real paddlewheel riverboat, and spent several relaxing hours hunting through the wide variety of shops for nothing in particular. I even took a tour of a couple of the great southern plantations. While all were impressive, in my humble opinion, none compared to Oak Alley. Standing under a centuries old oak tree, sipping a mint julep and looking up at its majestic structure actually moved me, and I'm not just talking bowels here. While impressed with its grandeur and history, I felt a twinge of sadness and wished I had someone to share the experience with. Sometimes, I had to fight to keep thoughts of Susan out of my mind. Twenty plus years of being with someone is a hard habit to break. Alcohol helped ease the pain, and that's one medicine New Orleans will never run short of. By the time I finished drinking my third Hurricane each evening, I had decided that Susan could kiss my big white ass, and I was damned glad she was gone.

On my fourth day in New Orleans, the events that have since changed my life began to unfold. I suppose I'm somewhat to blame in a way, or at least my continually increasing sex drive. The only thing that causes more trouble in the world than the human penis, is organized religion. That's probably because it's run by a bunch of penises. It's amazing the amount of trouble that little, er big, flap of skin can cause. It was early evening, and I'd just finished another wonderful dinner, this time at a place called the "Old N'awlin's Cookery." I decided to walk off my crawfish étouffée by strolling the now familiar streets of The Quarter, and to soak in more of its unique atmosphere. In Jackson Square, just in front of the Saint Louis Cathedral, a pick-up band was playing for the enjoyment of a small gathering of tourists and the dollars they threw into a strategically placed bucket. I stopped and enjoyed a few of the upbeat jazz tunes and dutifully dropped a couple of dollars worth of appreciation into the surprisingly full bucket.

My spirits, buoyed by either the music or the three bottles of Abita beer I'd had with dinner, hadn't been higher in months. Now, if I could just get laid. After three days of checking out the local female population, I'd yet to have even a decent conversation. I was beginning to remember that I'd never been very good at the dating thing, and I'd always hated the bar scene with its always risky pick-up routines. Actually, the dating part isn't really all that difficult. It's the initial approach and asking out part that's hard. It's like making a cold call in sales. Once someone shows interest, you gain confidence. But it's tough when you throw out your best line, and the recipient of this valiant gesture wrinkles her nose and looks at you like you have a world-class booger dangling from your nose. Not that this has ever happened to me, of course. I've just heard that it can happen. Ah, hmmm....

Anyway, as I strolled along pondering my situation, I passed a small boutique. It wasn't the kind of place I'd normally shop, since I preferred to purchase my skirts, blouses, and intimate apparel at the big discount stores where it's much cheaper. Seriously, I would have walked right on past without giving the place a second look, if it hadn't been for a wonderfully intoxicating aroma that drifted out the open door and stopped me in my tracks. First it caressed my olfactory nerves, then it tripped a lever in my brain that turned off my common sense. Finally, it grabbed me by the testicles and pulled me towards the door like some conniving witch's magic love potion. I stepped inside, determined to find out what perfume it was that smelled so wonderful. I might even buy some, perhaps for a future lover. Besides being such a nice guy, I'm basically an optimist by nature. I was sure my soul mate was out there, somewhere. Until I found her, though, I'd settle for a nice long string of sleazy one-nighters.

Immediately upon entering the shop, I noticed the rather shapely backside of a sales clerk, arms overhead as she stretched to put some sweaters on top of an open antique armoire. It had been cleverly converted into a display rack, and several colorful dresses hung inside. She wore a long, sleeveless black dress, which seemed to cling to her generous curves. Her hair, as black as the dress, was long and straight, and had a nice healthy shine to it. What intrigued me the most, though I'm a tad embarrassed to admit it, were her shoes. Or, should I say boots? They were highly polished black boots that appeared to be of the combat variety. Damn, army boots had never looked so good.

I was admiring the back of these boots, when they slowly turned around to let me admire the front of them. The front sides were just as shiny as the backs. Suddenly realizing their owner was now facing in my direction too, I quickly and coolly directed my gaze to the clothes rack on my left. Unfortunately, but befitting my luck, I found myself staring at a display of "sheer but supporting" brassieres.

"May I help you?" the dark-haired beauty in the shiny black boots asked. Her voice was soft, but intriguingly deep. It caused an old joke to pop into my head, the punch line of which had something to do with the Irish version of my name being O'John, and her voice sounding good repeating it over and over again, faster and faster, until, well, you get the picture. Thankful that she couldn't read a dirty old man's thoughts, I couldn't hold back a slightly embarrassed smile.

This dark beauty definitely had my full attention. No doubt, this girl was different from your usual run-of-the-mill women's boutique sales clerk, with long, beautiful hair, a perfect figure, and a sexy voice to match. Yes, she was different all right, in more ways than I could have known. I know I called her a "girl," but in truth I couldn't really pin down her age. Somewhere between twenty and thirty I'd have guessed, though as with most men, I pretty much suck at guessing ages. At my age, anything below thirty constitutes a girl. The realization hit me that I could easily have a daughter in her twenties, and a momentary wave of depression passed through me. I guess age is relative to whom you're comparing yourself to. To this young thing, I was probably old. Maybe even ancient.

Refocusing my attention on her, I decided that the boots were in fact an integral part of the total ensemble. Her skin was as creamy white as any I'd ever seen, and appeared even more so because of her raven black hair and completely black attire. Her eyes were dark brown, almost black, and unwavering. I decided she was doing the Goth thing, but doing it well. I've seen plenty of youngsters back in the San Francisco area attempting to look dark and sinister, but generally they just looked like youngsters attempting to look dark and sinister. No, this girl was different. She was dark, but not really sinister. Or, so I thought.

"May I help you, sir?" she repeated politely.

Snapping out of my reverie, I realized that the generally accepted practice among fully functional adults is to respond when someone asks you a question.

"Uh, me? Oh, no. Well, yes, actually," I stammered. "I'm uh, interested in whatever uh, perfume it is that smelled so good when I uh, was walking by just now. Umm, outside that is. I mean the smell was coming from inside, but I was outside." Yes, I stammered a bit, but it was a cool stammer. I'm sure I had her wondering just what kind of man she was dealing with. Total stud, or at the rate I was going, total dud.

She didn't point to the door and scream for me to get out, or threaten to call the police, which I took as a good sign, though I was probably reaching a bit. Instead, she turned and walked past me to the door and stepped outside. Slowly, she turned and faced me. Lifting her face ever so slightly, she closed her eyes and took a long full whiff of the night air. She opened her eyes and walked back inside, stopping so close to me that I wished I'd popped a breath mint earlier.

"It must be what I'm wearing," she said. Leaning in even closer to me, she pulled her mass of thick dark hair back into a bunch with her left hand, and lowered her right shoulder strap several inches with the right. She tilted her head to the left, offering a clear shot of that long, smooth, beautiful neck to me. "Is this it?" she inquired, leaning so close that her right shoulder was now actually touching my chest.

At this point, she could have been wearing cow dung, and I'd have thought she smelled wonderful. I bent my head down and took a long slow whiff, getting the full effect of her wonderful perfume. It was good. Damn good. It was exactly what I'd smelled walking by.

"Yes," I murmured, not wanting to move away from her neck. "That's it. It smells wonderful. What is it?"

"What's your name?" she asked, stepping back and readjusting her shoulder strap.

Shocked by this sudden change in direction, I said, "O'John, uh, I mean John, just John. What's yours?"

"Emily. Listen, O'John, just John," she said with a concerned look on her face. "I feel bad. The perfume I'm wearing tonight was specially formulated for me, and we don't sell it here. It is made locally, though, right here in The Quarter. If you'd like, I can pick some up for you and have it here tomorrow evening?"

"Tomorrow evening, huh? Well, that would be fine with me, but if it's made especially for you, are you sure you want to share it with someone else? It's really a unique scent."

"Of course, I'd be happy to share it with you. Who's the special lady? Your wife? Girlfriend? Secret lover?" The last she said with a naughty smile and a quick raise of her eyebrows.

Hmmm, good question. I wanted her to know I was single, but then why was I in here shopping for perfume? My pride was still having the occasional internal struggle, telling me that only losers were single at my age. It'd be easy to just say it was for my wife, like I'd done for the last twenty years. But that would pretty much kill any chance I had with Emily. To be honest, though, I didn't see a great chance anyway. She was just being a good sales person. Then again, I did have my fantasy world to support. Tough choice, so I decided to use a little misdirection.

"Oh no, it's for me. Some evenings a fella just likes to smell pretty," I said, strategically holding a straight face for exactly two and one half seconds, then breaking into my best big shit-eating grin. If I couldn't impress her with my stammer, I'd do it with my awesome sense of humor. Any moment now, she'd be like putty in my hands.

She just stared at me. Hard. For what seemed like forever. She wasn't getting my joke. Damn. Now she thought I was gay, which made my chances even slimmer.

"Emily," I said, putting my hands up for emphasis. "I was joking. It's not for me. In fact, I'm going to be totally honest. I really was totally intrigued by the perfume when I was walking by, but now I realize I really don't have anyone to buy it for. My wife and I split up a few months back. I don't have a girlfriend. I do have a lot of secret lovers though. They just don't know about it. That's why they're secret lovers! Ha-ha, you get it? I'm keeping it a secret from them. Ah hell, never mind."

This obviously wasn't going well, and the more I talked, the worse it was getting. Now that she knew I wasn't gay, she thought I was an idiot. I'd have happily gone back to being gay, but I'd blown any chance of pulling that off. My best bet was to quit while I was behind, and just shut up before the damage got worse.

Finally, I saw a hint of a smile, though I couldn't tell yet if I was bringing her over to the dark side, or she was just giving me a mercy smile. "Maybe you weren't meant to buy any perfume tonight? Maybe you were just supposed to come in and meet me?"

My heart did one leap and two bounds. The words sounded right, but her facial expression wasn't giving much away. I decided to throw caution to the wind and go for it. Nodding my head, I said, "Yea, maybe." God, I'm a cool one. James Dean has nothing on me.

We stood there for a few seconds saying nothing. I was rapidly feeling more and more uncomfortable and was ticked off at myself for handling this opportunity so poorly. It was time to take the plunge. All she could do was say no, right? Well, that and she could run a front page article in the *Times-Picayune* about this old loser named either O'John or Just John, who had a speech impediment, wore women's perfume, told bad jokes, and had actually tried to pick her up one evening when he didn't stand a snowball's chance in hell.

"Look Emily, would you maybe like to go out for dinner or a drink tomorrow night? I know I probably seem like an old fart to you, but I sure would enjoy the company."

"I work tomorrow night, but I get off at ten. Why wait until tomorrow night though, unless you have other plans? I'm guessing you don't." She glanced up at an ornate clock on the wall and continued, "Stop by around 10 o'clock, when I close up. Does that work for you?"

I immediately went into my hard to get routine. "Sure, sure, I'll be here at 10 o'clock sharp. Sounds like fun. This'll be great, you'll see. Uh, hey, thanks, Emily," I said, taking her hand and giving it a quick squeeze. She gave me a smile that couldn't hide her amusement at my clumsiness, and I turned to leave before she could change her mind.

"Oh, John?"

For a brief moment, panic set in. I thought she was on to my 'Oh John' joke, until I realized she was just getting my attention. I turned back. "Yes?" I asked, holding my breath.

"Your hotel's close by?" It was more of a statement than a question.

"Uh, yes. Yes, it is."

"Would you do me a big favor?"

"Sure, anything," I answered, more than a bit curious.

"If it's not too much trouble, could you stop by your room and grab a quick shave? My skin's very sensitive, and I'd hate for anything to ruin tonight."

"Of course," I responded before the implications sank in. I wiped my right hand down my cheek and continued, "This old mug will be as smooth as a baby's behind."

I couldn't believe my reply. A baby's behind? Where the hell did that line come from? I never talk like that. At least I hope I don't usually sound that stupid. I needed to sell her a house or a condo, so I could get back into my comfort zone and sound halfway intelligent again. What a young hottie like Emily saw in me I didn't know, but to be honest, I didn't care. Things were really looking up. I left without making a further ass of myself and headed straight back to my hotel.

Though I was tempted to tell the bellboy, the registration clerk, the night manager, and the maid who was pushing her cart down my hallway that I had a date with a hot young thing, I decided not to. They probably already expected it anyway. Once I was back in my room, I popped in the shower for a quick rinse off, even though I'd showered just a few hours earlier. The humidity in New Orleans made me feel as though I needed another shower ten minutes after I'd finished one. I shaved. Twice. I combed my hair and stood back to appraise my naked body in the full-length mirror. It had been conveniently hung on the back of the bathroom door, specifically so people could appraise their naked body when preparing to go out on a date with a hot young shop keeper who wore army boots.

Not bad for a forty-six year old. I'm a tad over six-foot tall, and with my recent weight loss, I'm right around two hundred pounds. Okay, two hundred and ten, but I'm headed in the right direction. Divorce was the best weight loss program I'd ever found. I'd tried to lose weight a dozen times while I was married, but I'd had no luck. Now I was shedding weight without even trying. Perhaps I'd been allergic to Susan and just hadn't realized it.

My hair, though graying a bit on the sides, is still thick, wavy, and very dark brown. I've kept it reasonably short, which I got used to during my four-year adventure in the Navy. As with most things, it has come back into style, and with my recent upgrade on the cut, I'm thinking my hair might just be one of my better features. Other than having decent hair, I suppose I don't have any real distinguishing characteristics, but the overall package isn't half-bad. What I lack in great looks, I make up for in personality.

I poured some Chivas over ice, and sat down to evaluate the situation. I hadn't been out with anyone other than Susan in over twenty years. Of course, I'd done my share of looking, but basically I'd followed the straight and narrow path. Up until the recent disaster, life with Susan had been safe. Boring maybe, now that I thought about it, but safe. Now, in about an hour, I was going out with someone totally different from anything I'd ever experienced.

I toyed with the idea of not going for a moment but quickly decided that I needed to do this. Maybe Emily wasn't as "different" as I was giving her credit for. I didn't recall seeing any bizarre tattoos or major body piercings, and though she seemed to be less than bubbly, she didn't appear to be too morose. She seemed to radiate both confidence and intensity. Yes, intense described her well, but it was a very controlled intensity. Now that I thought about it, I realized that the whole episode at the shop hadn't fazed her in the least. She seemed perfectly comfortable with the fact that I'd walked in off the street and asked her out. Reflecting on it even further, I realized that even though I'd like to take credit for making a date with a beautiful young woman, it was Emily who'd controlled the whole episode. Damn, she was good!

She was one beautiful babe, though. Or was she? Come to think of it, she was nothing like what I saw myself chasing after. Susan was a blonde, Donna was a blonde most of the time, and most of the women I'd fantasized about over the years were blonde. Emily was dark. She had very pale white skin, but those big dark eyes and even darker hair gave me an overall sense of, well, darkness. Somehow she pulled it off though, 'cause the more I thought about her, the more I wanted to experience her and her beautiful darkness. I gave a passing thought to a quick visit from Rosie Palm and her five sisters, but decided against it. I didn't want to work up a sweat. Trying to think positive, I grabbed a condom out of my shaving kit, and headed for the door. As I put my hand on the doorknob, I stopped and smiled to myself. I turned around and headed back to the bathroom and my shaving kit. I grabbed a couple more condoms, and stuffed them into my pocket. I should have been a boy scout.

I must have been excited, because the walk back to the shop took several minutes less than I'd planned. It was about five 'til ten when I walked back in. Emily appeared to be in the process of closing things up. The big smile I received from her as I walked in, relieved my fear that she'd changed her mind while I was gone.

Intent on improving the impression I'd left her with, I walked up and stuck out my hand. "Hi, I'm John Steele. How do you like me so far?"

Smiling, she took my hand and shook it. "So far, I like you very well, Mr. John Steele."

She reached up, and with the back of her hand, gently stroked my now smooth cheeks. Switching to a heavy southern accent, she cooed, "Why, Mr. Steele, I think I like you just fine and dandy."

We both chuckled, but I had the strangest feeling that the joke was on me.

"Can I help you close up?" I offered.

"No, I'm just about done. I just have to turn off the lights, set the alarm, and pull the door shut behind us." She looked at her watch and shrugged. "Let's book. No one else will come in tonight, and I'm hungry."

"You won't get in trouble with your boss will you," I asked?

She shrugged and said, "Not too much, though she can be a real bitch when the mood strikes her."

Seeing the concerned look on my face, she let out a laugh that was surprisingly robust, and said, "Relax John, I own this place. It's fine. I like to sleep late, so I almost always take the evening shift. Besides, you meet more interesting people at night."

I shook my head, knowing I'd been had. "Okay, but I want you to promise to put yourself on report when you come to work tomorrow."

"First thing I walk in the door, I promise," she said with mock sincerity.

I stepped back out into the warm New Orleans air and took a deep breath. This city was looking better by the minute. After turning off the lights and fussing with a little electrical panel by the door, Emily stepped out into the night with me and pulled the door shut. A quick test to ensure it was locked, and we were on our way.

As we walked, I realized how tall she was. Even allowing for the combat boots, she had to be at least five-nine. As we reached the corner, she reached over and took my hand. I didn't want her to think I was a pushover on the first date, but I didn't resist.

We walked along making small talk, and suddenly it hit me that I had no idea where we were going. To remedy this, I queried, "So, Emily, where are we headed? This is your town, so it might be better if you pick the spot. I'm sure all the places I know are tourist traps. "

"Oh, I thought we'd go by my place first. I need to freshen up a little bit, too. You don't mind do you?"

Go to her place? Mind? Hell no, I didn't mind. I could feel the condoms in my pocket begin to vibrate with anticipation, and I worried she'd hear them. "Oh no, that's fine. A shower did feel good."

As we reached the intersection of Ursuline and Chartres, we came upon a group of twenty or so folks listening to a boisterous tour guide. He was wearing a black cape and was waving a cane around theatrically while he expounded on some scary detail or other about the old Ursuline Convent. I'd visited it during the day and had thoroughly enjoyed my tour. A delightful older woman had given me the full treatment, even though I was the only one who'd shown up for the two o'clock tour. It seemed unlikely to me that anything worthy of this type of attention had ever happened there. The group seemed to be enjoying themselves, though.

Motioning towards the group, I said to Emily, "Hey, have you ever taken one of those ghost tours? They sound like a lot of fun, and I hear the ones that stay in The Quarter are pretty safe."

Emily stopped and turned to face me. Far more serious than I'd have expected, she said, "I think they're rather silly, John. A bunch of ridiculous made-up stories, designed to frighten a bunch of innocent people."

Surprised at the emotion in her reply and not wanting to start anything, I simply agreed. "Yea, I suppose they are a little bit silly." I didn't mention the fact that people routinely paid good money to be frightened. The movie industry had made billions off of people who gladly paid their hard-earned cash for the possibility of a really good scare. In fact, I'd been a contributor myself a time or two. Oh well, at least now I knew not to make any Jason or Freddy jokes with Emily.

We walked on, turning left and right and left again. Soon, I was unsure about where we were exactly, but confident she'd get us where we were going. She began to point out houses and tell me a little about their history. She seemed to know her neighborhood and its inhabitants well. We came to an ornate black wrought iron gate in the middle of a brick wall. I expected it to be locked, but a shove from Emily and the gate swung inward. She smiled and said, "When we get inside, look back at the top of the wall. It's covered with broken glass. That's pretty common in the older parts of New Orleans. It helped keep the thieves out, plus it kept more than one young lady's reputation in tact!"

I chuckled at the thought. "We'd never get away with that in California. There, all the criminals are victims. We have to leave milk and cookies for them, or we'll get sued!"

"Yea, well I bet there's a lot of fathers that wish they'd been able to keep you away from their daughters," she teased lightheartedly.

I blushed, and started to give one of my typical smart-ass answers, but decided against it. I was actually getting ready to enter her house, and was not about to chance blowing it this close to victory.

We walked through what appeared to be a small garden for about fifty feet, and then up a short flight of stairs to the porch. I turned to look at the fence, and sure enough, I could see the twinkle of light in the jagged shards of broken glass along the top of the fence. Nasty looking, and though simple in concept, I'm sure it was effective.

Emily inserted a key into the front door and swung it open. I'm not sure what I was expecting, but probably something smaller and less ornate. The place hadn't seemed large from the outside, as the fence and foliage had hidden its true size. I was quickly learning that New Orleans has a remarkable talent for hiding beautiful homes behind uninspiring walls. Stepping into a long central hall, I was immediately impressed. It had to be seventy or eighty feet long, and at least twenty feet wide. The ceiling was nearly fourteen feet high in the atrium portion and was detailed with exquisite crown moldings and two large chandeliers. The woodwork on the lower portion of the walls was the most intricate I'd ever seen, and I couldn't help but think how difficult it would be to recreate that detail today. The upper portions of the walls were covered in dark green felt wallpaper and had several large paintings of ominous looking characters hung on them. A wide cypress staircase started its ascent about half way down the entry hall on the left, leading up to a second floor landing. There were three sets of double doors and another single door at the end of the hall, but all of them were closed. Based on what I had seen so far, I couldn't help but be impressed.

I whistled softly, "Hey, this is nice, Emily."

She shrugged it off. "Yes, I suppose it is. I've lived here on and off for quite a while. It originally belonged to my father, and he left it to me when he passed away. He made a bundle before he died and one of the properties he left me was this house."

"Well, I'm sorry to hear your father died, but I'm glad he was able to leave you something as nice as this house. Was this a recent event, if I may ask?"

My question seemed to affect her deeply, as she turned and stared at one of the paintings on the wall for a long uncomfortable moment. Had I blown it? I noticed a smile slowly come to her face as though she were remembering some happy event in her distant past. She turned to face me. "No, it was a long time ago. I miss my father, but thankfully time heals all emotional wounds. It's been long enough that I can just think of him fondly."

Emily took my hand and began leading me upward. Suddenly, I felt a twinge of guilt. I really didn't want her father's painting to see me sneaking up his old staircase with less than honorable intentions for his daughter. I glanced over to see if he was frowning at me, or possibly giving me the finger, and was surprised to see the painting wasn't her father after all. It was an antique and had to be some old dude from generations past. I breathed a quick sigh of relief. The last thing I needed now was to take a guilt trip.

When we reached the second floor landing, she led me into an extremely large bedroom, which even appeared to have its own private bathroom, something I doubted was common in most of the older homes in the area. The room smelled slightly musty, and all of the furniture appeared to be expensive antiques. Not the dainty little stick variety either, I'm talking about the big, heavy, mahogany stuff. Emily closed the door behind us, and I began to notice a loud pounding noise. Realizing it was just my heart, I took a deep breath and let it out slowly.

"So, Mr. John Steele," Emily taunted, with what I can only describe as a wicked grin on her face, "are you in the mood for love?"

I walked over to a burgundy and gold wing back chair and sat down. It was time to figure out exactly what was going on. I would have loved to think I was such a stud that she just couldn't live without me, but this was so far outside the realm of what my ego told me was possible, it just wasn't making any sense. A beautiful young girl was about to put out for me, and since I hadn't been asked for any money or hadn't had to get her drunk, I wanted to know why.

"Look, Emily, it's probably obvious," I said while motioning in the general direction of my crotch, "that I think you're hot. If it isn't, well, I do. But I have to ask, why me? I mean, think of it from my standpoint. I meet a beautiful girl, who's probably young enough to be my daughter, and a couple of hours later I'm in her room with an offer to do the wild thing. I guess what I'm saying is that I've always believed that there's no such thing as a free lunch, and while I'm not saying I don't want to jump your bones, I would like to know why I'm here with you tonight?"

Emily gave me an impatient look. "Why you? Well, why not you? You're being way too modest, which is a nice quality and fairly rare in men today, but give yourself some credit. John, you're a good-looking man, and I may be a bit older than you realize. You said you're recently divorced, and you probably just haven't re-established your confidence with women yet. You are right that nothing's free, though. I do want something from you, but I don't think it's something you'll mind giving me when I ask."

Assuming she meant a good time, I shrugged and said, "I shall give it my all, ma'am, but I had to ask. Not to sound cliché, but this sort of thing just doesn't happen to me every day."

Emily threw her head back and laughed with more delight than I'd have thought she was capable of. "You are so right, John. In fact, I can promise this sort of thing has never happened to you before. You're in for the time of your life. Now, would you like to talk some more, or do you want to see what you're about to have your way with?"

"Actually, I did have just a few dozen more questions..."

With one quick motion, she grabbed the hem of her dress, and pulled it up over her head.

"....which can wait!"

There she stood in all her glory. Her body was much more voluptuous than I'd realized. I hate to admit it, but I suddenly discovered ol' Mr. Boring has a bit of a kinky side. Seeing that beautiful pale body standing before me in nothing but her boots, well, let's just say I gained a whole new appreciation for black leather boots!

"Mmmmm," I murmured. "Puss-n-boots!"

She put one booted foot in my crotch, and ordered, "Undo me."

I did, and quickly. When both of her feet were fully disrobed, she walked over to the big four-poster bed and slowly crawled to the middle. She patted the spot next to her. " Come now, my love, I'm so hungry for you."

Always the cool comedian in pressure situations, I replied, "Come now? Heck, I'm not even breathing hard!" In all fairness to those who think I'm just too cool for words, I should point out that I was also undressing so fast that it must have looked like my clothes simply jumped off of my body. Suddenly, I found myself wishing I'd followed through on the earlier idea of a visit from Rosie and the crew. Hey, you had to be there. She was hot.

I slid my now naked body next to hers, and our lips met in a hungry embrace. She was delicious. Her body was like silk, so smooth and firm that I couldn't stop moving my hands up, down, and around her various curves and crevices. I'd never felt anything so perfectly smooth. Now, being a gentleman, or somewhat of a gentleman, my purpose here is not to spill the details of our lovemaking. Yes, it was hot, and it was passionate and, of course, it was world-class and all that, but there is a purpose for me telling you all this. It's the dirty trick she played on me as we reached the "point of no return" as they say.

My eyeballs were spinning in their sockets like the wheels on a Las Vegas slot machine, and just as I was about to give her my million-dollar payout, she said, " John? John?"

With much restrained huffing, "Yes, dear?"

Remember that I said I wanted something from you?"

"Yes, dear, what do you want me to do?" Now, I know you're thinking I should have exercised a little self-control here, since you've probably already figured out what she was up to. But you've got to remember the position I was in at the time. I mean, I was clueless that I was boinking one of Buffy's sworn enemies. Besides, nature was against me. I'm a guy. And a very typical guy at that!

"Blood. I want to taste your blood."

I admit I was a bit surprised by this particular request. I might have stopped to think about it, but just as she asked, she put a particularly nice move on me. Besides, I thought maybe it was part of the Goth thing she was obviously into. Hey, if I could get a thrill out of seeing her in nothing but black leather boots, what's wrong with her being turned on by a little taste of blood?

"Argh, that's fine, dear. What do you want me to do?" Wrong answer.

In an instant, her mouth was on my shoulder and she seemed to be taking great warm gulps of something she'd found hiding there. An immediate sensation of pure pleasure nearly overwhelmed me, and at that moment I didn't care what the consequences of her drinking my blood were, as long as she didn't stop. It was as if an electrical current was running straight through my medial forebrain and lateral hypothalamus, then searching out and finding every hidden area of my brain's pleasure center. I was having the world's greatest mind orgasm, and unlike the physical ones I'd lived for throughout of my adult life, this one wasn't stopping.

After making her own special kind of love to my shoulder, she curled up next to me, gently caressing my face and neck. "Oh John, you were wonderful." Looking me in the eyes, she continued, " It's really too bad you must cross over, you're such a sweetheart. I'll be here with you, so don't worry. I'll take good care of you until it's your time to go to the light. I'll try not to drink too deeply of you, so that we can extend your stay as long as possible. And when you do cross over, please know that I loved you to the end."

I wish I could say I made some heroic move here, but I didn't. I couldn't. My body was completely numb and seemed to be useless. The intensity of the pleasure she'd produced in my brain dropped off significantly, almost immediately after she quit drinking my blood. My brain, though still somewhat scrambled from the effects of having a million lightening bolts of pleasure dancing around inside of it, was starting to function again. I realized that Emily thought she was some kind of vampire or something, which of course was impossible. She was just a poor deranged girl, who gave incredible neck. If only I could think straight, I knew I could figure this thing out. I should have probably been pissed at her, but all I really felt for her was an overwhelming love. It quickly became too much to think about, and I fell into a deep chasm somewhere between consciousness and dreamland.

If I was dreaming, it was unlike any dream I'd ever had before. Clear and detailed images of all the happy times in my life began to line up and march past my mind's eye, as though they were on a military parade field performing for my own personal viewing pleasure. I wanted to watch the show, but a nagging voice kept telling me not to give in to it.

A strange pattern began to emerge. I'd be watching my life pass by for review, and then I'd be pulled into a more conscious state, where Emily made love, her special kind of love, to me. Each time was as wonderful as the last, and during these periods I didn't care at all what happened to me, as long as she kept the pleasure coming. I say she made love to me, but it basically consisted of her kissing me for a few minutes, then passionately drinking from what I could only assume was now a mammoth hole in my shoulder. It took all of my energy to lift my hand an inch or so, so I pretty much just lay there, letting her suck the life out of me, swallow by swallow, drop by drop. I know it sounds twisted, but it felt so incredibly good when she was drinking, I just wanted her to continue. After a number of these "love making" sessions, things got even stranger. We had a visitor.

She too was a tall woman, and appeared to be a few years older than Emily. She was really quite regal looking and carried herself like a fashion model. She wore her hair up in one of those tall hairdos you saw a lot of on television shows in the sixties, or come to think of it, all over Texas today. She stood at the end of the bed and looked at me with a warm knowing smile.

"A delightful morsel you've taken, my dear, and I sense that it was just in time," she said to Emily.

"Oh, he's a wonderful man, Jasmyna. It'll be so sad to see him go. Would you care to assist in his crossing over?"

Oddly, when this new woman came in, I stopped feeling the strong urge to lose consciousness between love making sessions. I could even focus enough to feel embarrassed by my nakedness, though I was powerless to do anything about it. Besides, I got the feeling that they didn't really care whether or not I was clothed. It was my blood that turned them on. I still had no control of my extremities, but the ol' brain was definitely on the comeback.

They both fed off me at the same time, and the pleasure was so intense that my body exploded. Okay, it didn't actually explode, but I think it was at least vibrating out of control for a while. Naturally, I did what all males do after a strange encounter of the totally awesome kind; I fell into a deep sleep.

When I woke up, they were on each side of me, and appeared to be dozing. Emily lay with her head on my right shoulder, eyes closed, a smile on her upturned face, and an arm across my waist. It seemed a tender gesture, rather than an attempt to restrain me. Jasmyna, as I'd learned her name was, seemed content with her head on my left shoulder. I could just make her out if I rolled my eyes all the way to that side.

They really were quite lovely, even though they were killing me. Regardless of the pleasure these two beautiful women were providing me, I knew I needed to make a run for it. Unfortunately, my body was still useless. I tried to think of some way out of this, but came up blank. I was beginning to worry that I was a goner. Each time they drank from me, I'd end up weaker. Obviously, they were draining me slowly, and when my body got low enough on blood, I would die. I tried to remember how much blood the human body held. I recalled a pamphlet I'd read that claimed it held approximately six quarts of blood and that the average human heart beats around thirty-five million times per year. Odd, the things you remember in times of stress, but every one of those thirty-five million heartbeats was becoming important to me. So, how much could I afford to lose before I'd die? I'd volunteered to be a donor at a blood bank a few years back, but that was only a pint at a time. The way they'd been drinking, I'd be lucky if I had a full pint left in my tank.

Clear thinking still took a lot of effort, and I knew moving was out of the question. It would have been easy to just give up and just enjoy the pleasure they provided, but I decided that I really didn't want to die yet, at least not like this, not as someone's dinner. As odd as it may sound, the more I thought about it, the more I found I really wanted to live. It wasn't fair for me to go this way. Excepting my current situation, I was healthy, wealthy, and reasonably wise. Boring maybe, but that could be fixed. I had to find some way out. I needed to stop losing blood and gain some strength back.

I was lying there trying to figure a way out of my predicament when Emily awoke. She gave me a long tender kiss on the mouth, and for some reason I couldn't resist kissing her back. "Oh, John, my love. I fear your time is near. I shall miss you so."

"Please. Let me go," I whispered hoarsely.

She looked surprised. "Let you go? Oh, Johnny boy, don't be silly. I couldn't let you die all by yourself. That would be cruel. I want to be there for that last tender kiss. I know you love me, and believe it or not, I love you too. That's why I could never let you die alone. I'll be with you the whole way, helping you cross over to the other side. You're lucky really. So many die horribly and all alone. Your passing will be pure bliss, and soon you'll be with all your loved ones that have crossed over before you. That, I promise you, my darling." She gave me another quick kiss on the lips, then got up and left the room.

Panic was setting in. I had to do something. Jasmyna let out a soft moan and began to nestle up closer to my well-worn left shoulder. That meant she'd give me a few minutes of kissing and caressing, then she'd drain more of my meager reserve. As much as I looked forward to the pleasure that would accompany her drinking, I knew I couldn't afford to lose another drop.

She was on my left, and had been doing most of her damage on that side. I summoned all of my strength and tried to tilt my head to that side, blocking direct access to that particular target area. At first, it seemed useless, but after several minutes of strenuous work, I managed to tilt my head a few inches to the left. Once I hit the halfway point, gravity took over and finished the job. Creating just that small bit of movement made me feel a sense of hope. I know, it wasn't much of a tactic, but it was all I had.

Luck was with me. She briefly opened her eyes, and finding my face pointed directly at her, she gave me a long slow kiss on the mouth. For some reason, when she or Emily had kissed my mouth, it seemed to function normally again, at least for a short time. It felt like I was able to kiss back, and I could only hope I wasn't just slobbering on them like some type of idiot who'd just had major dental work done. If so, my plan was doomed. Finishing the kiss, she slid her tongue tantalizingly across my check to my suddenly ticklish right ear, then positioned herself to drink from the spot Emily had been working on.

It was now or never. Her neck was directly in front of my mouth, and summoning all the strength I could muster, I chomped down on her tender flesh. My teeth sliced through the soft skin on her neck, and blood gushed into my mouth. I had to swallow, or I'd have gagged on it.

The effects of my attack were immediate. She bellowed like a banshee from hell, but I hung on with my teeth. I thought she was going to rip my teeth out of my head, or even my head from my shoulders. She jerked upright trying to get away, and my useless body followed since my teeth were firmly lodged in her neck. My life depended on me hanging on, so I did with all my might. I learned several things quickly. The few quick swallows had an amazing effect on me. I'm not sure what I'd hoped to accomplish, but I got significantly more than I'd expected. Immediately, her blood began to awaken my body and inject my useless limbs with an incredible amount of strength. The more I swallowed, the stronger I became. My arms came back to life and felt like steel girders. I locked them around her a split second before she could break away from my still clenching teeth. We rolled around the bed, eventually falling to the floor as she tried to push me away. But I held on and continued to drink like a man possessed. I drank, and she screamed. The tables had turned.

I felt another set of hands ripping at my head and face, and as they were inflicting what felt like serious damage, I was forced to let go of Jasmyna. She quickly scrambled away from me. I broke lose of these new claws and jumped to my feet. God, it felt good to be alive again. Never again would I listen to the advice of my penis.

We stood there glaring at each other. Emily and Jasmyna were now on one side of the bed, and I on the other. Jasmyna snarled like a beast, and I snarled back. Yes, I snarled back. It felt as if I was on some type of super steroid, or some other strength-enhancing drug. You know, like the ones that Major League Baseball players use, but either don't admit to, or claim it was prescribed for their acne problems. I could have kicked ass on King Kong at that precise moment. I felt so good and they looked so pissed, that I started to laugh.

"You have no idea what you've done, you damned fool!" Jasmyna spat at me.

"What I've done? What the hell, are you talking about? Just what did I do that's wrong? Set myself free from your death trap! Surprised, huh? How many other poor slobs have you coaxed in here with offers to have sex? Dozens? What's the matter, none of them ever bit you back?"

"You're a damn fool if you think that just because you got a taste of my strength, you can take us on? You're no match for us. You think you can just take our gift? You think you can steal it? No, it must first be offered, and only then can it be accepted. Only a few make the transition successfully, and you won't be one of them. I'd sooner burn in hell than see you become one of us!"

"Too late, you, you June Cleaver-lookin' bitch. I took it!" I shot back at her. Not that I knew what "it" was, but it sounded like the right response at the time. Don't ask about the June Cleaver comment, because I have no idea where it came from and don't really want to know.

"Ha," I continued, since I was on a roll and making such good sense, at least to me. "You murdering bitches, you have no right taking innocent lives. I think maybe the police will be very interested in the little games you two whores have been playing."

For the first time since the fracas began, Emily spoke up, and in her calm sexy voice, said, "He doesn't understand Jasmyna. He has no clue what he's done. In fact, I'm not exactly sure what he's done. I can't sense him like the others of our kind. Is he one of us now?" I had to look away from Emily, because I knew that despite everything that had just happened, I still loved her.

Jasmyna looked at me more carefully for a moment, as if somehow studying my whole being. Appearing to calm down significantly, she shook her head. "No, he's not whole. He's like an empty shell. I've never heard of someone reacting the way he did, but I'm sure he's not whole. Part of the ritual took place when he drank my blood, but not the key components. I've attempted to change four, but only you and Virgil came back to me. In his condition, he should be dead now. He may well be dead soon. His strength will fade quickly without food, and his body hasn't gone through the required physical changes yet. Besides, there's no way he can change without making The Choice."

I'd heard enough of their unintelligible ravings and began easing my way towards my clothes. They were still on the floor, right where I'd dropped them. Housekeepers these ladies weren't. "Look, you two kooks. I'm getting dressed, and then I'm getting the hell out of here. If you try to stop me, I'm not taking any chances. I'm going to seriously hurt you. I'm talking broken bones if necessary. Got it?"

They didn't look very scared, but they didn't move to stop me.

Jasmyna let out a heavy sigh and seemed to have had a change of heart, "I hate you for what you did. I swore after Virgil that I'd never make another. But, I have to give you credit. You have more will to live than anyone I've met in the last two hundred years. Live, you won't though, not now. You're dying, Johnny boy. I'm not sure what happened here, but now, at least as long as you survive this strange occurrence, you're my child. You have my blood in you, just like Emily. You'll have to stay here with us. There's much to do if we're to prepare you for making your Choice."

"Yea right," I said as I slipped on my second topsider. "You're nuts, lady. Geez, you two are loony tunes, you know? You need some serious help. I'm sure you'll get it in prison."

"John, don't be ridiculous. Don't you feel my strength flowing through your veins? That's not human. You're in our world now, or at least you're partly one of us. Your only hope is to stay with us and see if we can complete the change. You won't survive in the middle, that much I can guarantee you."

I was finished dressing. "You should know that I'm going straight to the police. I'd suggest that you take care of whatever business you need to. Perhaps call a lawyer?"

Jasmyna shrugged and said in an irritated voice, "Cut the police crap, John. You just raped a seventeen-year-old girl. How will your police like that? Emily dear, would you kindly show John your identification?"

"Seventeen? Seventeen? There's no way she's seventeen." I was in a panic now. "Even if she is seventeen, what about attempted murder?"

"No, you're right. Emily's not seventeen. In fact, Emily's over a hundred and fifty years old."

"Jasmyna, please!" Emily exclaimed. Obviously she was not pleased at her age being revealed, even at a time like this. I guess some things never change with women.

Jasmyna ignored her and continued, "One of the identity's she's currently living under is that of a seventeen-year-old, and it's foolproof. And what attempted murder John? Where's your proof? You look fine to me."

"Yea, well how about this?" I asked, pointing to my shoulder. As I did so, I glanced in the mirror over the dresser. My shoulder looked as good as new. Damn.

"You have an improved capacity for healing now, John. Look where you bit me. It's almost totally healed already."

Oddly enough, her neck looked fine, though just minutes ago, I'd severely damaged it with my chompers. Double damn. Things weren't looking good for the home team. I didn't want to hang around and argue with them because I was leery of their tricks. On the other hand, they had what appeared to be some valid points. I was sure most of it could easily be explained, but this was not the place to sit around and noodle it out.

Emily stepped forward. "John, you can't go now. Stay with us for a while. There's so much to do if we're to have any chance of making you whole. We're of no threat to you now. I promise..."

"Give me a break, you freakin' whacko," I screeched in a voice that sounded oddly familiar, though hardly man enough to be mine. I was amazed that after everything that had just happened, they would even bother with trying to talk me into staying. Unless they wanted another shot at killing me, perhaps.

"I'm not staying here another minute. I'm outta here." I spun and headed out the bedroom door and down to the first floor, taking the stairs two at a time. As I reached the front door, Jasmyna called out to me.

"John, wait. There are things you must know. You'll need our blood to sustain you now, not solid food. And your body needs to change. Oh, there's so much that needs to happen, you just can't leave..."

"Are you crazy, lady?" I gasped. "Blood? I'm not drinking blood. I'm not entering your demented world. Just stay away from me, or next time there'll be real trouble."

"John," she said, more calmly now. "I forgot how difficult it is to accept the change, and you really weren't seeking it. And of course we never know what will happen when it comes to making The Choice. Go if you must, but you'll be back. When you can stand it no longer, come home, back to us. Then, if you make The Choice to become one of us, we'll teach you and attempt to make you whole. You'll always be welcome here, in your birth place." Emily, looking sad but beautiful, stood behind her and nodded her agreement.

I looked up at them and felt more pity than anger. I shook my head and walked out into a light but steady drizzle.

Chapter 4

Returning to my hotel, I decided I'd had enough of New Orleans to last me a lifetime and booked the next available flight back to the Bay Area. I was amazed to find that only one day had passed in the company of those two beasts; it had seemed so much longer. I jumped in the shower and scrubbed myself from head to toe. I wanted to wash this experience from me as thoroughly as possible.

Exiting the shower and toweling myself off, I was amazed to see several obvious changes in my body. My muscles were as hard as rocks. As I combed my hair, I noticed that the streaks of gray, which I had been unsuccessfully trying to convince myself were distinguished looking, were nowhere to be seen. I thought I'd seen everything, until I grabbed my razor. My face was still as smooth as the night I'd left to see Emily. This was getting too weird.

The trip home was uneventful, except for my vomiting that is. Playing a small joke on myself in an effort to maintain my sanity, I ordered a Bloody Mary. The first few gulps went down fine, and then I began to feel a fire burning somewhere deep down below. Luckily, I made it to the restroom in time, where I proceeded to power vomit. I'd taken maybe two or three swallows. What seemed like a gallon and a half came out of me. My gut felt like it was on fire. I returned to my seat and put a blanket over me. It wasn't that I was cold; I just didn't want anyone to see me shaking.

The thirty-minute drive from the Oakland airport to Pleasanton seemed to take forever. When I got back to my crummy little townhouse, I skipped checking the answering machine or looking at the mail that had accumulated. I swallowed a handful of antacid capsules and some aspirin, and went straight to bed. Sleep is what I was craving, and I felt like I could sleep for a month. Hopefully, I'd wake up, and everything would be right with the world again.

No such luck.

That was the first time I had what I now consider "The Dream." I guess I should call it a nightmare, but I don't wake up from it afraid of what's happening in the dream. It's only after I'm fully awake and realize the implications of the dream that I become afraid. Afraid of what you ask? For the first time in my life, I was afraid of myself.

The Dream was always the same as far as the events that took place, but the intensity seemed to grow each time. I'm back in Emily's bed. It's soft and warm, and I'm lying naked on top of the bed covers. Her and Jasmyna are at the foot of the bed, one on each side. They're resting on their haunches, like a couple of sphinxes, and they have their eyes closed, as though sleeping. I'm happy and comfortable and safe with them there to protect me. Then the bed begins to swallow me. It just opens up, and I begin to be sucked inside. I fight and struggle but to no avail. I realize that I'm sliding into a pool of warm water. I'm in up to my chest and still clawing at the bed covers. No one hears my screams, or at least no one cares. Jasmyna and Emily have their eyes open now and they're watching, knowing smiles on their faces, totally unconcerned about what's happening to me. I'm pulled in deeper and deeper. Finally, I can no longer hold on and I'm pulled completely under. I'm afraid I won't be able to get back to the surface in time to take another breath of air. I know I'm going to drown. I close my eyes and hold my breath until I feel my lungs will burst.

When I can take it no longer, I open my eyes, prepared to breathe in the warm water and drown. I open my mouth, knowing that death will come soon after I fill my lungs with this liquid. A short uncontrolled exhale and I involuntarily inhale, filling my aching lungs to their capacity. Surely, I'll die soon. I relax, waiting for the inevitable, and slowly take in another lung-full of death.

Oddly enough, I find I can breathe the warm water. It fills my lungs more completely than they ever had been filled with air. It satisfies a need deep within my chest that I never even knew I had. Amazingly, the thought of breathing air now seems somewhat hollow or empty. If I'd known it felt this good to breathe water, I'd have started long ago.

Then I realize its not water I'm breathing, it's blood. Human blood, and I'm greedily sucking it into my lungs like a man possessed. I know it's horribly wrong for me to use it to satisfy this need deep within me, and somehow I must fight it. It'd be better to die than to continue under the blood's magic spell.

I stop breathing, holding my breath as long as I can.

I know I can do it if I try hard enough.

But I want more.

I know it's wrong.

I'm ashamed of my craving.

But the blood is so satisfying, so very satisfying.

It fills a void, a deep inner need I never knew existed.

Suddenly, it all becomes clear to me, and I make a decision. I simply don't have the strength of character to fight it, so I give in, knowing I have made a major life altering decision. I open my mouth to breathe in huge quantities of this deeply satisfying, life giving elixir...and then I wake up.

I wake up thirsty for blood. I can taste Jasmyna's blood in my mouth, and I want to fill my belly, my lungs, my entire being, with her blood. When the realization that it was only a dream begins to set in, I actually burst into tears. I need more! Only when I return to full consciousness, do I realize what's happening to me. I'm repulsed by it, and by me. It doesn't take a rocket scientist to realize my desire to breathe blood rather than air, is really an incredibly deep desire to drink blood. To consume it until it consumes me. I'm becoming something that's no better than Emily and Jasmyna. I've got to fight it.

After two days, my strength withered away, too. At first it wasn't noticeable, but soon I looked worse than I did before I left for New Orleans. My face looked drawn and my cheeks seemed to be sunken in. Food stayed down only in the smallest of quantities, and I had to shift to a liquid diet. I sipped at small cans of a high calorie chocolate shake, generally reserved for old folks with digestive issues. I was afraid to go to a doctor; afraid of what he might find. My gut hurt constantly and I had no strength to speak of. I could live with the physical pain, and I was even prepared to die from it. But I couldn't live with The Dream. It made me think things in my saner moments that I knew only a mad man would dream.

Hoping some fresh air might clear the fog from my brain, I went for a short stumble around the townhouse complex. I ran into an elderly neighbor lady who was also out walking, and doing better at it than me I might add. I'm sure she thought I was either drunk or physically impaired. Most likely in her late-sixties, she was no peach by any standard. She struck up a light conversation, I'm sure out of politeness. Attempting to reciprocate, I acknowledged her chatter, and smiled and nodded. Little did she know, how badly I wanted her, I needed her. No, not like you're thinking. I wanted to hold her plump white body next to mine, and I wanted to bite into her the same way Emily had bitten into me. Then I wanted to suck that fat bitch's life out of her veins, pint-by-pint, drop by drop. I even found myself wondering if it was better to have the fat ones. Was there more blood, or just more fat? How about taste? Did taste vary by nationality or maybe by sex? Or perhaps by what they'd eaten, like corn-fed beef or free-range chicken?

Then there's the mailman. Ah, yes the mailman. I sat in my townhouse each morning, and as he came up the walk, I could hear his heart beat. Walking must be healthy for him, because his heart pounded like the bass drum in a marching band. With each resounding beat, my body tensed tighter and tighter. I tried putting my hands over my ears, but it was useless. The pounding was in my brain, not my ears. And notice, I said mailman. What the hell did I want to suck on a man's neck for? I'm not gay, or at least I wasn't the last time I checked. Now, I found myself fantasizing about luring my rather rotund and balding mailman into my apartment, and sucking the life out of him.

There's only one logical answer to all of this insanity. I'm sick, I'm twisted, and I'm a vampire! No damn it, I am not a vampire. I refuse to be a freakin' vampire. They only exist in books and movies, not real life. They couldn't possibly be real. Emily and Jasmyna had somehow managed to pull me very deeply into their demented fantasy world, and I needed to figure out how to get out of it.

Finally, after five days of hell, I couldn't take it any more. I decided they were just going to have to fix me. I wanted my stomach to quit burning, I wanted The Dream to go away, and oddly enough I still wanted to jump Emily's bones a time or ten. More than anything, if it was at all possible, I wanted my boring old life back.

Chapter 5

I sat back in the wide leather seat and tried to focus on the airline ticket in my shaking hand. Row two, seat C, the last first class aisle seat that had been available. I flipped the ticket over to see if the small print said anything about there being a layover in Hell for certain unlucky passengers. There wasn't, but I had a feeling that's where I was headed regardless of what the ticket said.

I was doing it; I was actually going back to New Orleans, just like they said I would. More than likely, those two beautiful women were going to finish the job they started and kill me. I pictured my tombstone and the possible epitaphs. I was sure I deserved something like:

Here lies the idiot, John Steele
He went to New Orleans to cop a feel
He did his best to get a woman in bed
Instead, he managed to end up dead

I groaned out loud at the thought. Could it get any worse? If they didn't kill me, they were probably going to make me into...a vampire? I guess that's what they'd be called since they drank blood, though I don't recall any fangs or bats anywhere. If that happened, I might not go straight to hell, but when I did, there'd probably be a special fire pot with my name on it. This was all too depressing for my battered psyche, so I decided to look on the bright side. Hey, if I was in fact going to Hell, at least I was going first class!

The ride back to New Orleans quickly turned into a nightmare, starting at the point where they closed the door. Being trapped in an airborne smorgasbord with 150 pounding hearts, pushing gallons of priceless antidote through all those beautiful circulatory systems was nearly too much for me. I fantasized about killing them all, except for the pilot of course. Maybe I was going completely Looney Tunes, but I wasn't stupid! No, the pilot could wait until we landed. The door would pop open and the ground crew would be in for the surprise of their lives.

They'd find a hundred and fifty or so bodies strapped to their seats, and totally drained of blood. In the back, they'd find me engorged with all of my fellow passengers' blood, looking like a very satisfied Jabba the Hutt. Belching and picking flesh out of my teeth, while trying to hide the scraps of evidence, I'd say something like, "Who me? Why, I have no idea what happened to all these in-flight meals, uh, I mean, to my fellow passengers."

I wanted to drift off and sleep to make the time pass faster, but I dared not. The Dream would surely return and I still had just enough pride left in me not to want to put on a screaming exhibition for the rest of the people on the plane. The looks on the other passengers' faces spoke volumes about my appearance. The flight attendant asked me numerous times if there was anything she could get me. What I needed, she couldn't give. I needed a month of dreamless sleep, and I needed sustenance of a kind not generally found on an airline menu, regardless of how progressive they are. I needed Emily and Jasmyna. They knew this would happen and had tried to warn me. I should have taken their warning more seriously, but at the time I just couldn't comprehend that what had happened was actually real. Stuff like this just didn't happen to me.

Once on the ground, I grabbed a cab back to the French Quarter and got out in front of Jackson Square. The driver of a horse drawn carriage wanted to give me a one time special deal on a tour of the sites. I wanted to give him a one time special deal on a trip to hell. Luckily for him, I knew I was now very close to the only possibility I had of ever finding relief from my pain, and while I felt no strong urge to let him keep living his pathetic little life, I had just enough sanity to know I needed to push on.

Stumbling through the square like the village drunk, I threw General Jackson's statue a quick salute. Just as when I left, he was still sitting on his trusty steed, forever tipping his hat to Micaela Almonester, the Baroness de Pontalba. Some things never change, and probably never should. On the far side of the park, I had to sit and rest for a few minutes. Dusk was settling in, and the rich, sweet smells of New Orleans cuisine assaulted my nasal passages to the point of making me want to vomit. I got up and wiped the sweat from my face. I had to keep moving.

I found the boutique and paused briefly outside the door. There'd be no coming back from this point on. A sharp pang in my stomach threatened to bring me to my knees. Decision made, I went inside.

Emily was showing some jewelry to a customer and barely seemed to notice me as I entered the shop and closed the door behind me. It was not exactly the warm reception I'd expected, and I had a sudden fear that she wouldn't remember having nearly sucked the life out of me. Maybe to her I was nothing more than a meal gone bad? As the customer finished a comment, she politely excused herself and to my relief, came over to me.

In a loud voice, she announced, "Your package is in the back, sir. Please come with me." Taking me by the elbow, she quickly led me through a heavy black curtain and into a small space that looked to be part office and part lounge. She unceremoniously pushed me onto a worn wing-backed chair, which sported a snazzy floral print. Just the kind of chair a macho guy like me would pick to die in.

"You look like hell, John," she scolded. "Why did you wait so long to come back?"

I was feeling delirious, and the room was beginning to spin. She propped me up, and I watched as she took her right thumbnail and made a small slice in her left forearm. She pressed the narrow cut to my mouth and moved around behind me, holding the top of my head. I didn't need to be told what to do.

I can't tell you how wonderful she was. As her blood flowed through my lips, down my throat and into my eager belly, I felt as though I knew true love for the first time. I was just settling in for a deliciously warm liquid feast, when she tried to pull her arm away. I'm embarrassed to say that I wasn't a very polite diner. Not knowing the danger involved, I was reluctant to give back her arm, which she'd so freely shared with me. Luckily, Emily has guessed this would happen, and had positioned herself in such a manner that she could wrench her arm free and pull my head back at the same time.

Before I could say anything, she gave me a meaningful poke in the chest with her index finger and commanded, "Stay here and stay quiet. I'll be back in a few minutes." With that, she spun and left through the black curtain, ensuring it was completely closed behind her.

It was amazing, but I felt great. I was having a little trouble focusing my thoughts, but compared to a few minutes ago, I felt...great, really great! I stood up and suddenly felt compelled to dance a quick jig. Now trust me on this one, not only am I not a dancer, but I'm not even sure what a jig is! The joy I felt had to be expressed in some physical manner though, so I invented my version right there on the spot. I was back, and I was bad. I loved Emily, and she loved me. She had to love me. At that moment, if I knew one thing, I knew that there was no way somebody could make someone else feel that good without truly loving them. No way.

I heard her conversing with the customer and then the click of the door closing. I was sure she'd return to me at any moment, but then I heard her talking again. Damn, must be another customer. She needed to get her priorities straightened out. The man who loved her more than anything else in the world was waiting for her. After another minute or two, the love of my life came back through the curtain. She looked more beautiful than ever.

She stepped in front of me and took my face into her hands, tilting it back and forth as though examining me. She lifted my eyelids, obviously looking for something of some importance to her, but I could have cared less. I felt great! So great in fact, that I couldn't contain myself any longer. I crossed my eyes, stuck my tongue out to the side and rocked my head back and forth like I was crazy. For added effect, I began to make my body twitch and jerk all over.

She pulled back for a second and audibly gasped. Obviously, she thought I was losing it big time. Where's the Oscar nominating committee when you need them?

Instead of going into the massive convulsions I'd tricked her into believing were just around the next loony bend, I returned to my normal charming self, grabbed her around the waist and pulled her into my once again powerful arms. I kissed her hard, leaving no doubt that I loved her madly.

Emily pushed me away and looked at me as though I'd gone totally berserk. As I started laughing hysterically at my own little prank, she asked way too seriously, "John, have you gone crazy? What are you doing?"

I was a man on a mission. I would not be swayed from expressing my true feelings, so I took her hand and dropped to a knee. "Emily, I love you. I want to be with you forever. No, I don't just want to be with you, I need to be with you forever. Will you marry me?"

Her response wasn't exactly what I expected. It was her turn to burst into a hysterical fit of laughter. "Oh my God, you silly man. My blood has you higher than a kite. Sharing the blood of another vampire always affects us more than human blood. It's a special bond we generally only share with those we trust. Obviously, my blood has made you my instant lover. Oh my, how fun could this be? Now, I have to get you home though. What I gave you won't last long, and Jasmyna doesn't think you can survive much longer like you are. Come on, I've closed up early and called Jasmyna. She's waiting for us. We must go quickly."

I stood up, disappointed, and in fact a little pissed. "Are you saying you don't love me? I can't believe that. I won't believe that." I felt like a spoiled brat and knew I sounded like one, but for some reason I just couldn't control my emotions. All my life I'd been a master at controlling my emotions, and now they were going totally bonkers on me. Next thing you know, I might start crying. Sheesh.

Emily took my face in her hands and looked me in the eyes. She shook her head. "You have it bad, boy. Listen. I love you more than, than, well, I love you more than life. How's that?"

Unconvinced, I continued to pout. I crossed my arms over my chest and looked away. Sounding remarkably similar to a four year old in need of some serious disciplining, I said, "I don't believe you."

She gave me a wicked grin and, leaning over so that I had a clear view down her top, purred, " How would you like to take me home and show me just how much you love me?"

This was more like it. My emotional dial spun from sad to gleeful in less than a second. "Yes, yes, let's go home. I want to show you how much I love you, and I just knew you love me too. I can feel it." I had a new fire burning down below. One that I was sure only Emily could extinguish.

She led me out the door like a puppy dog. I was so happy to be alive and walking with my Emily again. The walk to her house was like being in another world. Not like having too many Hurricanes where your brain is totally numb and you just stumble along in a drunken stupor, but more like being on some totally awesome drug that takes all your troubles away and leaves you so totally happy and carefree that you don't need to be able to focus on anything. I was on another plane for that brief period, and it was a pretty nice place to be, especially after the days of pure hell I'd just endured.

The door opened when we reached the porch, and Jasmyna quickly ushered us in.

"Hi, Mom," I chirped. "Guess what? Emily and I are in love, and we're going to get married. Is that cool, or what?"

Jasmyna raised an eyebrow at my comment, but wasn't amused. She turned to Emily. "How much did you give him? I told you, he's sick and our blood is far too rich for him to subsist on while he's human."

"A couple of swallows at most. I hardly felt the drain. If he chooses to turn, he's going to be a strong one, Jasmyna. His ability to recuperate is incredible. He was nearly dead when he stumbled into the shop and within seconds of feeding, he was lifting me up and proposing to me."

"As you know, we really won't know anything about him until he turns, Emily. I guess I should say "if" he turns. He's still far too human. He may be in love with you now, dear, but later he may end up despising both you and me. Look how Virgil turned out. He was such a sweet boy when he was human. Once we've turned, there's nothing holding us to our old human values. I seem to remember that a certain promiscuous young lady used to be a nun."

"I was only in training. You know that. But please don't let him turn out like Virgil. This world isn't big enough for two Virgils. I know you're right about him being different if and when he turns, but he's got so much potential. It would be nice to have him around when Virgil comes back."

"Yes, it would be nice to have someone put Virgil in his place. But even if this boy is the one to eventually do it, it could be years, maybe even decades before he could possibly be ready to stand up to Virgil. Of course, there's no way to tell what his strengths will be prior to him turning. He may lack great physical strength, but have other gifts that are far more valuable. You need to be able to deal with Virgil on your own. Use your brain, dear. Your intellect and guile are your greatest weapons."

I was still in my happy place, and while I could listen and somewhat comprehend their conversation, I didn't really care about it. None of it made enough sense to bother focusing on, especially since focusing was so darn difficult for some reason. I'd made my decision to return, and so far it seemed to be the right one. I was happy, and in a few minutes, Emily and I would probably sneak upstairs and do the wild thing. I gave her a big loving smile, and she snarled at me. I looked hurt and she laughed. She looked deep into my eyes, and though her mouth didn't move, I heard her say, "I love you too, John. Sit tight just a short while longer and Emily will take care of you." I smiled, and this time she smiled back. Ah, love is such a beautiful thing. But how the hell did she just talk to me without moving her mouth? It was too much to think about, so I decided I'd take a nap.

I wanted to go upstairs to stretch out on Emily's big comfortable bed, but she and Jasmyna led me down into the basement instead. Somehow, in the back of my mind it registered that while I was in the house's basement, I was probably only at, or near, street level. To get to the main floor of their house, we'd had to go up some stairs to the front porch. The high water table in New Orleans makes having a real basement difficult, unless you want an indoor swimming pool. Why notice or care about a detail like this, especially at a time like this? I have no clue. Sometimes my brain works in mysterious ways that even I can't comprehend.

Even in my diminished mental state, I was surprised at the size of the basement, and even more surprised to find the floors and walls made of a white marble. Emily gave me a tender kiss, and then she easily lifted me up and laid me down on what appeared to me a large marble altar of some sort. Whoa, my lover girl is strong! She began to remove my clothes, and when I began to help, she stopped me. "Let me, my love."

God, how I love that woman.

Jasmyna snorted. "Come on, Emily, he doesn't have much time left. Don't forget what I said upstairs. He'll most likely remember how you're screwing with him later if he decides to return. He'll get his revenge for it someday, one way or another."

"But he's so cute like this and it's nice having someone adore me this much. He actually proposed to me. That's so sweet. I wish I'd thought to record it. A girl never knows when she'll be proposed to again. It could be centuries!"

They gently took my arms and laid them by my sides on the granite slab. I lay on the table, naked as a jaybird and grinning like an idiot. I was clueless as to what was about to happen. I mean, I thought I knew what was going to happen. After all, I was naked wasn't I? Any time now they'd start taking off their clothes, and join me. Little did I know, I was only moments away from my human death.

Chapter 6

I won't go into great detail about the ritual that was performed to make me what I am today. For one thing, I'm not absolutely sure that the ritual is all that important, or whether it's even necessary for that matter. My fear is that some poor disillusioned fool may actually think they can become one of us by replicating the ritual I experienced. Unfortunately, they'll only be halfway successful; they won't become a vampire, but they will end up dead. Then, everyone will blame me for putting ideas in their head, instead of blaming them for being stupid. It's always the same old story, whenever possible, blame it on the poor innocent vampire. So, in an effort to dissuade any halfwits from making this fatal mistake, I'm intentionally leaving out several parts of the ritual. Not to worry though, as there should be plenty of gory parts to keep you squeamish, like the part where they let cockroaches eat my brain. No, they didn't really do that, but if you're going to die and become a vampire, you can't make the journey sound pleasant, right? After all, not many people get to tell the tale of their own demise, so why not adjust it to my liking?

Now that I'm intimately involved in the whole vampire thing, I've learned that many people think being one of us would be really cool to experience, at least for a while. First of all, it's very much a permanent condition. And remember, we're dead from a human standpoint. Yep, we're dead. As in, no longer living. There's no going back. I'll never be able to fully resume my life as a human being. I can mix with humans, and I'll share more on that later, but I can't be human.

We gain some pretty neat capabilities, like increased strength, significantly improved senses, and the ability to live for a very long time. We lose a lot too. We can't produce children, at least not in the fun way. We have an extremely limited diet. We're loathed by most humans and hunted by others. As if that weren't enough, we're also the subjects of envy by many who are jealous of our oversized genitalia. After considerable thought, I believe one of the worst things about being a vampire, is that we know why you're here on Earth. It's the great mystery of life, and believe it or not, most of you need that mystery to keep you going. The only great mysteries left for me are figuring out who shot J. F. K. and why I just lied about vampires having oversized genitalia.

For us, dealing with you is pretty easy. For you, dealing with us isn't so easy. More often than not, an encounter with one of us means death to you. Hey, it's what we do! To us it's perfectly normal, and often even delightful to feed off of you; however, it's not usually such a positive experience from your standpoint. So, to those of you who think being a vampire might be cool, please keep in mind that human death surrounds us. We leave a trail of human sorrow and sadness in our wake. If you need more convincing, look in the obituaries section of your local newspaper for funeral notices and pick one out. Go to it, appropriately attired of course, and look into the faces of those that loved the dearly departed. There's real pain there, and it's not a game. Remember, the usual outcome of becoming a midnight snack for a vampire is death for you and a satisfied belch for us.

As I said, though, I will share with you the parts of the ritual that are relevant to this account, in hopes that it may give you a better understanding of what I am now. To understand the ritual, you need to understand what we really are. Forget about most of what you think you know about us, because it's highly inaccurate. We have the potential to be much worse than you could ever imagine, but fortunately for you, our numbers are few. Most importantly, nobody has ever become a vampire without wanting to. You see, there's a choice involved.

What I've become is a species similar in appearance to humans, but quite different physiologically. From your standpoint, I'm probably best thought of as a beast that must consume substantial quantities of blood to continue to exist. As with most living entities, my continued existence is important to me and I'll do whatever is necessary to avoid ending my existence. I feel about as much guilt and sympathy feeding off of you, as a lion might feel if it stumbled across you wandering alone on the plains of the Serengeti in Tanzania. Better yet, how often do you feel sympathy for, or even think about the poor little moo-cow, whose life came to a tragic and premature end, just so you could scarf down a hamburger?

Though I may appear like you in many ways, trust me, I'm no longer human. To you, I am this mysterious creature, commonly known as a vampire. To me, you are a walking thermos bottle waiting to be tapped into. I don't hate your species, but I don't hold you in the same regard as I do my own. Think of it in the context of having a pet, say a cat or a dog. You may be fond of cats or dogs, and may even become emotionally attached to one. You still recognize that they're not human, though, and typically wouldn't value their life over another humans.

Still confused? Me too, since it's not an easy thing to explain. A short while ago, I didn't even believe in vampires, and now I am one! Try thinking of it this way. There are beasts on this Earth, which most humans choose to discount as fictional creatures created by the vivid imagination of Bram Stoker. It looks like a human. It talks like a human. In fact, it easily passes for human. But it's not human. There are many other beasts on this planet, like lions and tigers and bears. (Oh my!) You know they exist, and that they're physically more powerful than you, a human. Weapons aside, if you're smart, you stay away from them because they will kill you and eat you, right? Well, so will we! But, unlike the other beasts I mentioned, we're as intelligent as humans, have mastered the concept of opposable digits, and we've got great natural camouflage since we appear to be human. Cool for us, bad for you.

Okay, back to the ritual. Since my existence is dependent on large quantities of blood, you could probably guess that the ritual involved a lot of this life giving substance. Mostly mine unfortunately, but also the blood of others of my kind. Jasmyna hadn't attempted the ritual in over a hundred years, which might have concerned me if I was thinking straight. I never could remember my ex-wife's birthday from year to year, and now I was trusting Jasmyna's memory on something she hadn't tried since Ulysses S. Grant was president. Luckily, in my state of blissfulness, I totally trusted her and my beautiful Emily. It was probably better that way, since there was no fear factor to deal with. I was surprised and a bit confused, though, to see many familiar religious artifacts around. My brain, still functioning at less than full capacity, had made an assumption that I was about to enter some kind of pact with the devil. I'd already decided that if I was "goin' on down to the crossroads" to sell my eternal soul to Satan, there better be a little kinky three-way with Emily and Jasmyna in the deal somewhere.

Alas, it was not to be. Just my luck, I was the only one who got naked at the ritual and it didn't involve anything remotely sexual, unless seeing a naked middle-aged man lying on a table and grinning like an idiot is your bag. I really should talk to somebody about fixing that part of the ritual. There should definitely be some naked dancing women and cool music involved. Passing a rather ornate dagger back and forth, Emily and Jasmyna took turns poking small holes under my arms, down my sides, and on the insides of my legs. None of them were critical wounds in and of themselves, but they got my blood draining at a pretty good rate. Not that I cared much, but I assumed I was making a decent sized mess on the floor. Then I noticed it wasn't flowing over the edge at all. It was running into a small groove carved into the marble near the top surface's edge. Letting gravity do the work, it drained into the groove, and then flowed down towards my feet and finally off the table by way of an ornately carved downspout. From there, I assumed it was going into a bucket or something, but I couldn't see past the edge of the table and I was getting too weak to sit up and look at it. I had a vague recollection of seeing this set-up before, and couldn't suppress a weak smile when I realized it was very similar to my old electric pancake griddle back home. So, I was to die the death of a pancake. Better that than a waffle, I told myself as I began to lose consciousness.

Jasmyna had mixed a potion, which consisted of a large portion of Emily's blood and hers, as well as a few mystery ingredients that Jasmyna still won't tell me about. I'm not ready according to her, but I think it has something to do with some old vampires. They held my head up so I could choke some of this down, and as had happened before, I immediately began to feel my strength returning. Before this new burst of energy could fully take effect, with great ceremony and mumbling in what sounded like Latin, they killed me. That's right, the bitches killed me. They stuck the ornate dagger into my heart, and killed me.

Take it from me, the getting killed part isn't much fun. As I mentioned, Jasmyna and Emily stood on each side of me. I watched them put their hands together around the dagger and lift it high over my chest, an action that made me only slightly uncomfortable, at least until I got a glimpse of the accompanying psycho look on their faces, and then pure panic set in. Nobody had to tell me what was coming next. I had a sudden moment of clarity and screamed, though it came out more like a gasp, "Noooooo!"

Of course they didn't listen to me, they never do. I felt the dagger enter my chest and pain instantly shot throughout by body, then almost as quickly it began to fade away. I felt them give the dagger a sharp twist for good measure, but by that time, I found I didn't really care anymore.

We always talk about life and death like there's some great jumping off point. Oddly enough, I found out that you never really die. Oh sure, the human body dies, but not the soul. One moment I was a human in intense pain, and then I was neither human or in any pain whatsoever. Though watching my body during my death would probably tell a different story, I can assure you that I never left consciousness, or went to sleep or anything like that. I felt myself drift up out of my body, just like all the near-death experiences you read about. I saw Jasmyna and

Emily very clearly as they stood over a rather handsome man's naked body. I knew it was my own, but in truth, I didn't necessarily feel an attachment to it. A bright but comforting light enveloped me, and I felt compelled to float up a slightly inclined ramp towards it. Actually, it was all very peaceful.

At the top of the ramp, the light got slightly brighter and even more inviting. I was naturally drawn towards its warmth, which wasn't really physical warmth, but more like a comforting spiritual warmth. I also had a strange feeling like I was returning to a place I knew. To my surprise, a huge black Lab ran out of the light to greet me. It nearly knocked me down and I recognized it as Asta, a dog the Bowman's had owned, and the only pet I'd ever really been around. When I was in my early teens, Asta and I had been pretty tight buddies. I dropped to a knee, and she gave me one of her specially patented doggie kisses, which consisted of a wonderfully wet tongue schwack across my cheek as a greeting. A bunch of people I recognized from my past began to come forward as if to greet me, and I stood up anxious to see them. I had the most wonderful feeling of coming home. They were all smiling and their faces were full of love. If this was death, it wasn't bad at all.

Suddenly, just a short distance from me, they all stopped. The expressions of love never left their faces, but something was holding them back. Asta hung her head and stepped back slowly. Out of the brightness, I suddenly sensed a new and important presence. Though I never actually saw anything but light, I fell to my knees and bowed my head. I knew I was in the presence of The Creator, the greatest power in existence. Trust me when I say you know it when you're around it. There is absolutely no doubt in your mind.

Though the great presence remained in front of me, another being suddenly appeared at my side. Somehow, I knew his name was Saul and that he was my spirit guide. He'd watched over me my entire life and we had a special bond. Like running into an old friend, I felt a great sense of comfort in seeing him. He placed a hand on my shoulder in a gesture obviously meant to put me at ease. "Do not be afraid," he said. "You're in God's good grace. We have much to talk about and you must make a decision about the next path in your ongoing quest for knowledge."

"Am I in Heaven?" I asked, though somehow I knew immediately that I wasn't.

He gave me a very comforting smile, "No, though you may be in Heaven, as you've learned to call it, very soon if you so choose. Since your memory of your time here has not been returned to you yet, let us just say that you are at the Gates of Heaven."

This place was without a doubt the most comforting place I'd ever been, and yet I still felt a bit lost and confused, like I wasn't quite able to remember something that I should be able to. I knew I was supposed to know what was happening, but it was just outside my memory's grasp.

"Your journey has come to a fork in the road," he said. He spoke in ancient Aramaic and, amazingly, I understood him perfectly. It was almost like it was my native tongue, though I couldn't recall knowing it even existed while on earth. He gestured towards a pathway to my right and we began to walk, side by side.

He continued, "Your current time on Earth is over, and you can stay here and enter Heaven, as you called it, if you so choose. You've accomplished most of what you set out to do during this current venture on Earth, and we know you're weary."

"I don't understand. You said that my current life as a human is over? That would seem to indicate I've had other lives as a human. And what do you mean when you say that I've accomplished most of what I set out to do? Did I miss something or do something wrong?"

Saul smiled and put his arm around my shoulder. It gave me a warm tingle that was both comforting and energizing. "Yes, you've had several other lives as a human on Earth, and each provided an excellent opportunity to gain knowledge that's unattainable here. If you choose to cross over now, all will be made clear to you, and I can promise you'll understand everything completely once your memory is returned to you."

I can't explain how I knew this, but I had no doubt the smart play was to simply cash in my chips, say I was done, and that I wanted to cross over. Something was keeping me from jumping at that choice though. I felt compelled to learn more, so I asked, "I have to choose to come here? I always thought I had to pass some kind of test to be allowed to come here! You know, Saint Peter's supposed to be waiting at the pearly gates with a big book of all my sins?"

He smiled and raised his eyebrows a tad, "Peter? No, Peter has more important things to do than sit around with a book of earthly sins that really don't matter here. Their value was on earth, though records are of course kept for learning purposes. That's not relevant to your current situation, though."

We continued down the path, and he seemed to be deep in thought. He stopped and turned to face me. It was hard to look at him and concentrate, because he emitted an essence of beauty and love that I couldn't recall having experienced before. "On very rare occasions," he began, "some of us are allowed to make a choice to return to the plane you just left and know as Earth. You would return to Earth in a different form, without returning here first. This is necessary, because you would pick up where you left off as a human, with all the same knowledge, memories, and experiences, though as a significantly different entity. You would go back as an entity more commonly known to you on Earth as a vampire. Have no doubt though, they too are God's creatures and just like humans, are capable of both positive and negative, or good and evil, as you'd call them. As with your recent human existence, your goal would be to experience the things that are not possible on this side, though in a significantly different manner than the human life you just left. Though you do not recall planning the human life you've just returned from, I can assure you that working together, you and I planned every major event. As a vampire, you would be able to experience extremes that are not possible as a human. Your unique existence will make you capable of accomplishing some very good deeds, or conversely, evil at a level few humans are capable of. As with your human lives, your daily choices will be up to you."

I was so in awe of where I was, that I'd temporarily forgotten the whole vampire thing. "Saul, tell me why I would want to go back? This place just 'feels' so good, and I've got so many questions, and somehow I know all the answers are right here. Yet for some crazy reason, I find myself considering this vampire thing."

Once again, he smiled at me and continued on patiently. "Negativity does not exist here, in any form. To fully understand and appreciate what good is, you must understand what bad is. To fully understand and appreciate negativity, or evil, or pain and suffering, you must experience them firsthand. For us to do so, we must become human and live briefly on Earth. That is why you went to Earth in the first place, and now, if you decide to return, you will be able to experience it in a way that's much different than as a human."

It was gradually making some sense to me, and I risked another question, "So I invested forty-six years on Earth, for the simple purpose of making myself better understand what bad stuff is?"

"Think of it this way," he responded. "On the Earth plane, your natural body temperature was 98.6 degrees. If you lived in a world where everything was at exactly that same temperature, how would you know what hot and cold are? You could study temperature variations forever, but until you experienced them, you really don't understand. As for the forty-six Earth years you invested, they are of no significance here. Time as you currently understand it is irrelevant. Here, we have no such restrictions."

"What do I do, Saul? What would you do? Help me make a decision," I said, knowing a decision needed to be made, but having no idea which way to turn.

"It is not my decision to make. If you return, you will be welcomed with open arms. If you choose to stay on Earth, I will be with you every moment."

"You said I'd accomplished nearly everything I'd set out to do. That means I didn't accomplish everything, which also means I failed at something," I said, more thinking out loud than actually looking for a response. I had no idea what it was that I hadn't accomplished, but something told me there was a significant amount of unfinished business left. Thinking back on the life I'd just left, I felt I'd been wasting my time on Earth. My life had been empty and boring. The only reason it had ended early, was because I'd gone out and tried to get laid after my wife had cheated on me. What a loser! Though Saul said I had accomplished enough, I knew I was coming up short of the expectations I'd set prior to beginning my earthly life. I'd left this place for a life on Earth, to experience things impossible to experience here. Instead of experiencing life on Earth to the fullest, I'd simply existed. I hadn't done enough. I knew I could have done so much more if I'd only tried.

Home was close and I knew I would be welcomed with open arms as he'd said. Once I officially crossed over, if everything is positive like Saul said, I couldn't feel a sense of failure or guilt. Since negative feelings simply didn't exist on the other side, I could leave these "human" burdens, like guilt and disappointment, behind. But I was still on this side of the fence, or gate, and I felt the guilt and disappointment. I was overwhelmed with a tremendous sense of failure. I felt that I'd be letting someone down if I didn't go back, as well as myself.

Saul had remained quiet while I was working things out in my head. Though we'd walked in what seemed to be a straight line, we were suddenly returning to the place we'd started from. The great presence was still there in front of me, waiting for my decision. I looked at Saul, and asked, "You promise you'll be with me all the time?" It's hard to explain to those of you that haven't crossed over yet, but we all have a spirit guide. Basically, it's someone you trust on the other side that helps you get through your time on Earth. Knowing he'd always been with me was a great sense of comfort now, though when I'd actually been alive on Earth, I didn't even know that he existed.

"Yes," he said with a reassuring smile, "though I'll be assisted by others. Your existence will be much more complex if you go back. You'll become somewhat of a special case."

Special case? That sounded like me all right.

"You see," he continued, "you'll now have the power over the life and death of humans. Most humans are conditioned to believe this is God's domain, and it is. Nothing happens that is not His will or plan. Your natural resistance to taking human life will be lowered, though your innate knowledge of right and wrong will still be with you. What you do will always be part of His and your plan."

I was somewhat confused, but thought I had the jist of it. I may kill, but God was one step ahead of me and my victim was meant to die. I needn't feel guilt for simply doing what vampires do.

"Of course we'll still be watching you every step of the way, just as we did when you were in human form," he continued.

I let out a heavy sigh and lowered my head. "I'll go back." This may have sounded like an easy decision, but believe me, it wasn't. I've spent a lot of time thinking about it since then, but the key to my decision at the time was my strong sense of having failed to accomplish anything special in my human life.

Saul touched my shoulder and I felt a great strength. "You'll be fine, and remember, we'll always be with you. You may also be comforted to know that several angels will be with you too. Do not discount their ability to help when called upon."

Suddenly the great presence moved closer towards me, and I was enveloped in a tremendous wave of warmth and love. Instead of bowing this time, I closed my eyes and tilted my head back, spreading my arms wide to receive this blessing. In that brief moment, when I was enveloped in God's pure love, I knew I would in fact be all right. The light, though still present, receded a bit. I turned to look for Saul, to tell him everything would be okay now, but I could no longer see him.

I saw another figure walk out of the light, and as she approached, I recognized her as my earthly grandmother. Her face radiated a love and joyfulness that I'd never seen on Earth.

"We're proud of you, John," she said. "Follow your heart, and don't be afraid."

I was shocked but happy to see her. "Grandma!" I blurted out.

I went to reach for her, but I felt myself being whisked backwards and, suddenly, I found myself back in the basement. I wasn't back in my body, though, I was floating above it. I saw Emily and Jasmyna fussing over my carcass, all the while chanting their Latin sounding phrases. I suppose the polite thing to do would have been to jump back into my body and let them off the hook. I wasn't in the mood for polite, though. I floated there for a few moments, watching them sew up the hole they'd so willingly put in my earthly body's chest, and contemplating the decision I'd just made. I wasn't sure I wanted to get back into that thing. Now that I was no longer in the presence of a superior being, my normal smart-ass attitude began to return in full force. In fact, I was a bit bummed out and totally confused about the situation. Vampires were supposed to be from hell, not from heaven. What had I gotten myself into?

Saul had said I'd be capable of both good and evil, but I assumed I was supposed to try to be good. What was I supposed to come back as, a religious vampire or something? How do you eat people and still be a good little vampire at the same time? The least they could have done was fill in a few blank spots, or perhaps told me the rules. An instruction manual would have been a nice parting gift. The whole thing had happened so fast that I had no idea what I'd agreed to. Excuse me, but I think somebody screwed up here!

Emily stopped chanting, and looked up at me. She smiled and said in mock disgust, "So, you're back, huh? I guess that means you've decided that being one of us isn't so bad after all. Quit screwing around up there and get back in your body."

Here I was enjoying the last few moments of my out-of-body experience, and somehow she saw me. I was a ghost, spirit, or some other invisible thing, but somehow she could see me. I tried to answer her, but found she couldn't seem to hear my voice. There was no use putting off the inevitable, so I decided it was time to climb back into my shell. I wasn't sure how to re-enter it, since I only vaguely remembered leaving it. So, lacking a better idea, I just lay down on top of it, and whoosh, I was back in. I couldn't believe how cold and heavy it felt. It was so confining that I felt a twinge of claustrophobia, and my first few breaths were more like the gasps of a dying man than those of someone recently reborn.

I open my eyes and blinked. They felt dry. My mouth felt like I'd just licked an ashtray clean. Emily lifted my head and, holding a silver goblet to my mouth, gave me a long drink of that delicious red nectar that I knew I was about to become extremely reliant on. Immediately, my body began to tingle, and I felt a powerful new energy surge through my limbs. Slowly the combination of body and soul began to feel comfortable again, though for the next few days I had to put up with the constant feeling of my internal organs shifting around.

I suppose I'll always question my decision to come back. You don't stand at the gates of heaven every day, and you tend to rethink an experience like that a few million times. I knew that I'd been so close to the total mental and physical relief that one has on the other side, that at times I want to kick myself for passing it up. Then again, since I didn't feel I'd accomplished enough here on Earth, I couldn't very well stay there and cross over, now could I? To make matters worse, I somehow know that if I'd decided to stay and had officially crossed over, I wouldn't feel as though I'd come up short. Confused? Me too, that's why I spend so much time thinking about it. Maybe there's more to it than what I currently know, but for now I'll just have to accept that I'm back and make the best of it.

My human death was a little tough to get used to, but the knowledge that I hadn't accomplished anything important in my human life was the real killer. It's kind of embarrassing in a way. Although I wasn't really being judged in the sense you'd normally think of when arriving at the Pearly Gates, I'd been allowed to judge my own life. You can't lie to yourself in that situation, and I knew I had come up short of my own expectations. Sure, I'd had a few successes. I'd made millions of dollars in real estate, and I'd always given to charity, at least to the extent my accountant told me to. In general, I was always a nice guy. I'm not saying I should have spent my life solving world hunger or finding cures for the incurable. That's not the stuff I'm talking about. I'm saying that I hadn't really lived. I never took risks, especially emotional ones. I never really invested much of myself in other people. I know nothing about art or religion. I know next to nothing about history or geography. I'd never really traveled much. I'd always fantasized about having an affair with a hot-blooded redhead, but never did anything about it. I'd never really lived. This time around, it was going to be different.

I'm sure you're curious about how I changed, so I'll share the basics. On the outside, I look very similar to the original model. Most of my old friends or acquaintances would probably think I'd just spent a couple of months in a health spa. The internal changes from a skeletal and muscular density standpoint are major, though, and could probably fill a medical textbook or two. The physical transformation is only a part of the overall change, as I also changed dramatically from a mental standpoint. For all my newfound physical abilities, it's the improvements in my psychic capabilities that are the most important to me.

The first few days as a vampire were the worst. As I mentioned, my strength had greatly increased and all my senses were much more acute. Learning to use them was like learning to walk all over again. First, I over compensated, then I under compensated. The ladies had to "baby proof" the house, because I became somewhat of a klutz. Emily and Jasmyna stayed with me constantly, patiently teaching me what they considered basic survival functions, like listening to the faintest sounds with my enhanced hearing, seeing into the darkest corners with my greatly improved eyesight, and smelling the most minute of odors with my enlarged nose. Gotcha! No, my nose didn't grow larger, though my olfactory senses did increase dramatically. While difficult, frustrating, and sometimes downright irritating, dealing with these physical changes was not the hardest part.

The mental aspects of dealing with the new me nearly drove me crazy. I had to learn to control my new psychic and telepathic abilities. It's much more difficult than you'd think. I now sympathize with human psychics and the issues they have to deal with. One minute I'd be chatting with Emily, and then I'd get a flash picture in my brain. The first time it happened, it scared the hell out of me. I relayed the image I'd seen to Emily, and she explained that what I had seen was a true picture of an event in her life that she'd been thinking about. I've learned the obvious value of these flashes or pictures, but at the time I wanted them to go the hell away. Needless to say, they weren't all pretty pictures.

Additionally, I had to learn to accept what I'd become. When you're human, you take certain rules of life for granted, like what's food and what's not. Sure, some cultures eat some pretty strange stuff. I'd learned this first hand while traveling through the Philippines during my Navy days. But, unless your last name is Donner or Dahlmer, you typically don't consider humans as part of the food chain. I had to learn to think of humans as food, which wasn't easy. At least, when I wasn't hungry. I wish I could say I was excited about the possibilities that my new and physically improved funky self could look forward to, but initially I wasn't. I just wanted to regain some control of my faculties.

I'd like to leave this part out, but I'm sure someone out there wants to know about my first "kill." It's not like scoring your first touchdown or getting laid for the first time. Someone dies because you're hungry. At first, this was tough to swallow. Yes, the pun is intended and yes, I do crack myself up sometimes. Back to my first kill though, and yes, I'll never forget her.

The first few days after my rebirth, Emily and Jasmyna let me feed off of them. My appetite wasn't that great, so it was manageable between the two of them. Finally, Emily told me that it was time for me to feed on someone else. Of course, being a gentleman of high moral standards, I initially refused. That lasted about two days. The hunger pangs became excruciating, and I begged them for nourishment. Like good parents, they refused me.

I lay curled up on my bed, wishing I were alive, so I could go ahead and die. Jasmyna came to me, and led me into Emily's room. There, naked on the bed, lay a beautiful older woman, who I'd guess was well into her eighties. Beautiful in her eighties you ask? Get your mind out of the gutter. She was beautiful in the way a twenty-six pound turkey is beautiful on Thanksgiving Day. I was weak from lack of food, so Jasmyna sat me down in a chair. It was the same chair I'd sat in the night I met Emily.

The woman's eyes were closed and she looked incredibly peaceful. I asked, "is she dead?"

"No silly, probe her mind," Jasmyna admonished. Emily has put her into a state of bliss. She's totally happy and content.

"How do I probe her mind," I asked, intrigued even through my hunger?

"Just do it," she insisted. "Relax and let your natural telepathic abilities flow. Picture yourself listening to her thoughts."

At first it sounded so simple, that I thought the idea ludicrous. I let out a heavy sigh and began to "probe," though all that came into my mind was the image of me trying to probe someone's mind. Suddenly, I heard someone else's voice. Not spoken aloud, but an inner voice. Then, like adjusting a radio, I began to focus in on her thoughts. That breakthrough nearly did me in. Once I could hear her clearly, I couldn't turn her off. I felt stuck in her thoughts. I must have expressed my distress outwardly, because Jasmyna slapped my face and the woman's thoughts leapt from my brain. Wow, talk about intense!

"Well, what did you hear?"

Embarrassed, I stammered, "She seems to be imagining herself at a party."

"John," Jasmyna laughed, "she's imagining herself at the Revels. It's a carnival ball that's part of Mardi Gras here in New Orleans. She probably attended a few in her younger days."

"This is too weird," I said. "What in the hell is going on? Why is she naked?"

"How did Emily hook you? Surely you remember? It was an invitation to make love, or in your case, John, simply to 'do the wild thing' as you like to say."

I rolled my eyes to let her know her teasing didn't affect me and made a mental note not to use that phrase again any time soon. Besides,

I preferred the term *boinking* anyway! From now on, I'd refrain from doing the wild thing with her, and boink instead. Problem solved.

"Most humans," she continued, "find great pleasure in the act of making love. Many vampires do too. I'm closing in on three hundred years old, and I still get cranky if I go more than a few weeks without it. All vampires take their prey in different ways, but this is how Emily and I prefer to do it. For us, at least for now, it's a comfortable way to exist."

"Lucky victims, huh," I joked, and then suddenly realized that not long ago I was one of those lucky victims.

"Remember, John, sex is different when you're a vampire. You can drop all the silly human hang-ups. We don't marry, and we don't have children. So, there's no need to be faithful to anyone, or any expectations that you will be. Just enjoy whatever feels good. Personally, I happen to like making others feel good, even humans. There's a feeling of power that I suppose I get off on, having complete control of another's level of pleasure. You can take them to places that will have their whole being alive with pleasure, and they're totally in your control. I was considered a pretty good lover in my days as a human, but I'm much better now, having had a few centuries to perfect the art. And the best part, at least for a former church going girl like me, is that there's no such thing as sin for us. Human morality laws don't apply to us!"

"Uh huh, so let me get this straight," I asked, giving her a puzzled grin. "You two screw all of your victims to death?"

Jasmyna gave me a wicked smile. "No, silly, we suck them to death. The sex is just for mutual pleasure before they pass over to the other side. We've provided scores of humans with the best sexual experiences of their lives. And we almost always try to stretch it out for them. For the strong ones, we can make their passing, and thus their pleasure, last for hours and hours. Of course that requires restraint on our part."

"But what about an old hag like this? There's no way she was lookin' for love in all the wrong places," I said.

"She's a woman, John, not an old hag. Hey, everybody needs to be loved, or at least the false sense of love that we provide them. It's the old "perception is reality" thing. They perceive they're loved, and therefore they are loved. Some need it differently though. In her case, she just needs to be held and caressed. The feel of another body up against hers is quite enough." With that, Jasmyna dropped her robe and climbed up onto the bed next to the woman. Slowly, she caressed the old woman's face, neck, shoulders, and breasts. Tenderly, she brushed her hair back out of her face, and gave her a small kiss on the cheek. "I'm going to take a small taste of her now, and I want you to probe her mind while I do it."

I tried once again to clear my mind, but it was more difficult because I was finding myself aroused by the site of Jasmyna in front of me. I closed my eyes, relaxed, and tried to tune in her thoughts. Once I locked on, I was amazed. The old woman was in sheer ecstasy. As Jasmyna gently extracted her life through a small hole in her neck, the woman actually shuttered in delight. I nearly did too.

"Come and give her some pleasure, John," Jasmyna coaxed. "You need her and she needs you." She patted the bed next to her.

I stood up and walked to the edge of the bed.

"John?"

"What?"

"Your clothes."

"Oh, yeah." I undressed quickly and mechanically. Taking a deep breath (yes, vampires can breathe), I laid down close to the old woman. I felt kind of creepy, so while I was technically next to her, I ensured I wasn't actually touching her. Being this close to her malodorous old body was overwhelming my sense of smell. I could see that she was reasonably clean, but the natural odors emanating from her were quite nauseating. I knew I'd have to get used to the way humans smell, or I'd be a very thin vampire.

Jasmyna took my hand, and began to nibble on my fingers, all the while looking deeply into my eyes. She was so damn hot that I couldn't repress a smile. "Taste her, John," she cooed in between nibbles. "Just a swallow, though. Bite down gently, just until your teeth break through her skin. The blood will flow freely enough without biting deep."

I closed my eyes and tried not to think about what I was about to do. A sharp hunger pang urged me on. I leaned over the woman's neck and, picking a spot that was similar to Jasmyna's, I opened my mouth and pressed down on her neck. Her skin was softer than I'd expected and tasted of strong perfume at first. I was sure I'd bite down incorrectly or screw it up somehow. Nope. Like a duck to water, my incisors sliced through her skin and the blood began to fill my mouth. It was only a trickle at first, and then a steady flow of her life nectar began to fill my empty tank. My mind melded with hers, and I sensed her joy at making love to such a wonderful and caring man. Though all I did was drink, she shuddered in ecstasy again. Lucky old hag, er, woman!

"Easy boy, don't drain her all at once."

I released my hold, and rolled over. Power surged through my body. No longer grossed out by her, I felt nothing but gratitude for this woman's generous contribution to my diet. She took a deep breath and drifted back to sleep. Now that was a familiar scenario, and I could easily relate to her situation. I got up and walked around to the other side of the bed.

Lying down next to Jasmyna, I took her hungrily into my arms. Our mouths locked in an eager embrace. I could taste the old woman's blood mixed in with Jasmyna's warm breath. Never had I felt so powerful and passionate. I was hot for some wild vampire love. I was shocked when right in the middle of a wicked tongue twister of a kiss Jasmyna stopped me.

She pushed me away, and got up from the bed. Walking towards the door and struggling to suppress a giggle, "Not now, John. There's still much for you to learn here today, and no time for 'doin the wild thing' right now." On this last part, she lowered her voice in an obvious attempt to mimic me. "Emily will be in, and she'll assist you with finishing this poor dear."

I was crushed. The ol' flagpole quickly bent like a willow. Rejection and humiliation, all delivered in one swift blow. Damn, I hate rejection. Humiliation too. I'd had a couple lifetimes worth of the two in the twenty years I was married to Susan. I abhorred them then, and I abhorred them now. I quickly got redressed, and giving my lunch a last quick look, headed for the door. As I was opening it, Emily walked in.

"Hey, where are you off to, sailor," she asked, obviously surprised to see me leaving.

"I think I'm done here," I said with just the slightest bit of attitude.

"Oh no you're not." Nodding towards the bed, she continued, "She's not very strong and her time is near. It's time to help her cross over.

"Screw her, I got what I needed," I said, the bitterness of Jasmyna's rejection and teasing bubbling up inside me.

"What's the matter, John, why the attitude?"

"Nothing's the matter," I said and started to turn away. Suddenly, I felt Emily in my head. I hadn't yet mastered the ability to keep others out of my thoughts. If she was in my thoughts, she knew exactly what I was pissed about.

"John," she said, "let it go. Jasmyna was only teasing you, and if you're going to survive for centuries, you're going to have to grow some very thick skin. Remember, it's like you're ah...oh, I know. It's like you're a freshman in high school again. Yea, you're supposed to get teased!

Tease her back, for God's sake. Hit her with an age joke or something. Usually you're good at that."

I realized she was right, and I knew better than to let teasing get to me. Growing up as I had as a human, thick skin and the ability to turn a joke had been part of my survival kit. I knew it wasn't the teasing that had me so pissed off, it was Jasmyna's refusal to have sex.

Still reading my mind, Emily continued, "Jasmyna wasn't rejecting you, she simply wanted you to finish this lesson first. She knew I was coming in, and that time is of the essence. This poor woman has only a few minutes left."

Her words helped take the edge off a little, but anger is never easy to drop, even for a vampire.

She walked to the side of the bed Jasmyna had been on, and quickly dropped her gown. Seeing my hesitation, she barked, "Now, John."

Grudgingly, I walked back over to the bed. "I'm not getting undressed again," I said, as though that were some kind of triumph.

Emily looked at me strangely, and said, "Suit yourself. Lie down next to her though, and take another drink. Do it very, very slowly though."

I didn't really feel hungry, and her neck was looking much older than when I'd been starving. I let out one of my trademark heavy sighs, lay down in my previous spot, and clamped down on her neck with my mouth. I'm ashamed to say that I was none too gentle.

"Easy, John. Drink slowly and probe her mind. I'll taste of her too, so that I can take the journey with you. It's a special moment in the human existence, and we're privileged to share it with her."

I had no idea what Emily was talking about, but I closed my eyes and probed. I still had to work at it, but soon I was focused in on her thoughts. She was obviously reliving some of the special events of her life, and while I became fascinated as each scene was revealed, I surprised myself by finding that I didn't feel any sorrow for her. She was pretty darn happy at the moment.

I felt the beat of her heart slow down, then come to a stop. Instinctively, I stopped drinking as her thoughts faded away. I realized my eyes had been closed, probably a natural reaction to help me focus, and when I opened them, I saw the form of a much younger girl rise up out of the body and float a few feet above the bed. The form turned and looked at us, as though puzzled, then looked towards a light that began to glow across the room. She smiled and headed for the light. This scene was all too familiar to me, since I'd just experienced something similar. I found myself apprehensive and worried that she too might be found wanting. Instead, I saw her rush towards a throng of people that had gathered to meet her. From all accounts, it looked like a joyous occasion to me. A twinge of jealousy passed through me, but I was too happy and relieved for her sake to dwell on it long. Slowly, the light faded and I found myself back in the room with Emily and the dear old woman's corpse. I was too much in awe to speak.

Emily reached across the body and took my hand. "Pretty awesome isn't it?"

"Yea, it was," I said with a newly found reverence for what I'd just witnessed. "What's out there Emily? Did she go to heaven? Will we ever get the opportunity to go back?" I hadn't spoken to either of my fellow vampires about my own experience.

Emily just shrugged and smiled. "'I don't know, John. I suppose you could call it Heaven, though I prefer to think of it simply as the Other Side. I have no idea whether or not we'll ever go there. I should tell you, though, not everyone does. I wanted your first experience to be a positive one, so I picked this dear woman especially for it. I knew her crossing would be good. Her life was a good and meaningful one."

Once again, I felt a twinge of regret for not crossing over and secretly wondered how much Emily knew about the reasons for my decision to return when offered "The Choice." Did she too come up short during her human existence, or did she choose to come back because she liked to kill? "What happens to bad people?" I asked, though I knew she could only give me her opinion.

"We'll deal with that one later. I don't want to overwhelm you with things you really don't need to be too concerned about just yet. I know that if you slide back into your human frame of mind, it seems more humane to feed on bad people. After all, they deserve it, right? Well, it's not as simple as that."

A thought occurred to me. "When I came back, you could see me before I re-entered my body. Is this how?"

She smiled, "Yes. I didn't see you rise up out of your body, but I sensed the light and when I turned to look, you were headed towards it. As I recall, a dog greeted you and then you disappeared into the light. A short time later, I sensed you were back, and when I looked up, there you were. To be honest, I was a bit surprised. I didn't expect you to return. Anyway, the sun's almost up now, so go and get some sleep. We'll continue your lessons tomorrow night."

As I got up to leave, she called after me.

I turned. "Yes?"

"Not all vampires can see the spirits leave the body like you and

I. Jasmyna can too, of course, but many can't. Humans are just food to them. I believe that the ability to see their spirits is a special gift and I'm glad you have it."

Not sure what to make of this, I nodded and sauntered off to my room. I had a lot to think about, having successfully fed and killed for the first time. Oddly enough, I didn't feel like a lion or some other wild beast that had stalked then bested their first victim. I felt more like a vulture who'd swept in on their prey when they were already near death. At least the hunger pangs were gone. Temporarily.

I guess it's also time to clear up a few more details about vampires. If you're still living under the impression that we're anything like you see in the movies, you've got it wrong. Perhaps a few general tidbits about vampires will aid in the understanding of what we are. I've only seen a few vampire movies, but based on what I recall, I'll attempt to set the record straight.

First off, vampires are flesh and blood. The laws of nature apply to us too, just with a few different twists. Yes, we can die, but I think it takes a lot to do us in. Jasmyna nodded in the affirmative when I asked this question, but quickly changed the subject. We're not truly immortal, though Jasmyna also claims to know of a vampire that's over two thousand years old. That's getting pretty close to immortal in my book. So, I guess we can at least say that we have a slight longevity edge on most humans, the only exception being my eighth grade English teacher who I've always believed to be older than dirt. For some odd reason, we tend to look ten to fifteen years younger than we were at the age we died our human death, but we seldom look younger than eighteen to twenty. I was forty-six and could probably pass for being in my early thirties. Emily was only twenty-two, and I still have a hard time figuring out how old she looks. Sometimes she could pass for eighteen, other times she looks nearly thirty. Odd. Maybe it's a female thing.

Our ability to heal quickly is phenomenal, though we do feel pain. As you might expect, we're actually well designed killing machines. We're much stronger and faster than humans from a physical standpoint, though the more energy we expend, the more we must feed.

Most vampires have enhanced psychic abilities. Interestingly enough, all vampires seem to have different gifts. I suppose this would be expected, since most humans have different gifts too. One human has an ear for music, while another has natural mechanical abilities, and yet another is athletic. Thought of in this manner, I guess it makes sense. I've yet to really discover what my gifts or talents are. I think it may have something to do with being an unstoppable sex machine. I thought I was horny when I was human, but this is nuts. My libido has gone through the roof. I'd offer to be Viagra's poster boy, but I don't need that stuff anymore. Not that I ever did, of course. I meant to say *if* I'd ever needed it. You know what I mean? Ah, hmmm.

We are also creatures of the night. Yep, this is one place the books and movies are partially right, since we are generally nocturnal. Fortunately, it is possible for us to shift our sleep patterns so we can exist in much the same manner as humans, sleeping at night and being awake during the daylight hours. Emily has explained to me that our modern world is now a nine-to five-world, and if you want to fit in as a vampire, you have to stay awake during the day. She and Jasmyna only have to sleep for about ten hours every four to five days. Since they live together, they always sleep at different times. They do like to nap or doze with victims while feeding, but this isn't really necessary; just part of the enjoyment they take in the fine dining experience.

Changing one's sleep pattern is an acquired skill for us, and of course I haven't mastered it yet. Don't worry, though, Emily assured me it only took her about thirty years. For me, as a novice vampire, I'm stuck existing in the dark hours. As soon as the first rays of sunlight emerge from the eastern horizon each morning, my eyelids slam shut. As the sun sets in the west, my eyes pop back open again. It's odd, but at least to date, I haven't dreamed while sleeping. I fall asleep almost immediately after I first sense daylight coming, and I wake fully refreshed and full of energy. Controlling my sleep patterns is one of the first vampire tricks I want to master. Knowing I'm limited to operating during the hours of darkness makes me feel incredibly vulnerable.

Another myth that I can dispel is the one about us turning into bats with a puff of smoke and flying away. Remember the laws of nature thing I mentioned? Now, having cleared up that crazy notion, let me explain what we can do. This is so cool that it often sends my mischievous mind into overdrive. We, or at least the vampires with the proper psychic skill set, can leave a victim with the impression that we shape-shifted after feeding on them. On occasion, vampires will have victims that they string along and feed off of on a regular basis. Theoretically, they could enter the person's room at night, dine, make love, play trivial pursuit or whatever, then leave the person's mind with an imprint of something totally different. The person would swear they saw a bat fly away, or a snake slither away, or whatever. Why would someone want to go to all this trouble? Beats me, but it still sounds cool. I want to master this too.

Another cool option found on those of us who are the more advanced models, is an ability to speak to each other telepathically. Since we have an enhanced psychic ability, all we have to do is send someone a signal, and if they so desire, they respond. I mastered this almost immediately. I call it speaking in silent voices, which makes the ladies laugh. They've done it for so long, they take the ability for granted.

Garlic doesn't affect us, nor does holy water. Crosses, though, are a different story. If you aim the long end carefully, and catch us in an unsuspecting moment, you might be able to poke us in the eye. Not that it would do any real damage and would probably have the added effect of pissing us off, but I thought it only fair to point out that crosses aren't totally useless. So, what can be used to fight off vampires? Bullets and knives are basically worthless, though I suppose a small, well-placed bomb might do the trick. The bottom line is that a human stands little chance against us. Not only are we physically superior, but we also have the added advantage of being able to mess with your minds.

Oh yeah, I almost forgot about the mirror thing. Care to guess? No, silly, of course we're not invisible in mirrors. I already told you that we're flesh and blood. How else would I comb my full head of thick brown hair each morning, er, uh, evening?

After a couple of weeks, I still hadn't ventured out of the house. I was beginning to get an acute case of cabin fever. Emily sensed this and suggested one evening that we take a stroll down to Jackson Square. I only made it as far as the front gate. It was completely dark when I stepped outside onto the front porch, but I could see perfectly. First, I was nearly overwhelmed with the multitude of sounds that pelted my overly sensitive eardrums. It was quite discombobulating, and I had to go back and sit on the top step to get my bearings. I'd been able to master the various sounds inside the house, but outside it was a different story.

To make matters worse, the air around me smelled so bad that I'd have sworn it had been professionally designed to assault my heightened olfactory senses. My God, the stench was all over. I caught whiffs of everything from the Gumbo cooking a block away, to fuel burning on a tugboat in the Mississippi a half-mile away, and rat shit in the gutter across the street. It was overwhelming and I had to put my head down and close my eyes for a few minutes.

Emily, bless her heart, just sat there with me and helped me sort it all out. She'd forgotten how shocking these things could be to a new vampire and told me a humorous story of how she'd hated the piles of horse manure that dotted the roads in her day, because it took her months to be able to pass one without getting nauseous. We sat for several hours and, after a while, I noticed that I could turn down or tune out the excesses if I tried hard enough. She assured me that I would quickly master this and likened it to learning how to use a volume control. Basically, the rule was to keep the volume on my various senses on low, until they were needed. We decided that this was important enough that we'd venture out a little more each evening until I was completely comfortable and in control. Besides, I liked spending time with Emily. I liked it a lot.

Chapter 7

I knew the minute I saw him that he was Trouble with a capital T. It was nearing midnight, and the ladies and I were in the parlor enjoying a quiet evening of reading and exchanging idle chitchat. Simultaneously, they both stiffened and I didn't need enhanced abilities to know something was up. A moment later the front door opened, and immediately my new vampire senses kicked in and alerted me to the fact that there was another of our kind close by. The fact that Emily and Jasmyna had sensed it first didn't escape me. In fact, my fragile male ego was sufficiently damaged that it pissed me off a bit. I jumped to my feet, ready to redeem myself by investigating, but Jasmyna grabbed my wrist.

"Sit down, John," she commanded in her silent voice. "It's Virgil. You need to be on your best behavior, and whatever you do, don't act threatening. He's immature, even for a male, and he tends to overreact to even the slightest things."

Over the past few weeks we'd talked about this Virgil character enough for me to know she was serious. Unhappy but compliant, I sat back down and waited. I didn't fully understand why I should act subservient to this guy, no matter who he was. I was a male vampire too, and for that reason alone, I felt I was worthy of equal respect. Silly me. Fortunately, it wasn't too long before I learned that a vampire's gender has little to do with their status or power. Emily's crack on males should have told me something.

When Virgil barged into the room, I'd swear that every hair on the back of my neck stood straight up. Never had I known such a strong sense of imminent danger. He looked to be five-foot, nine-inches tall at best, but wide and stocky. His arms seemed to be longer than normal, which combined with their exaggerated swing when he walked, gave him a kind of gorilla like appearance. I noticed that he seemed to move quickly, in jerky, almost spastic movements. From the ill-fitting clothes he wore and his dirty brown uncombed hair, he reeked of white trash. His complexion was ruddy, and his teeth? Yuck! Let's just say he looked like he could eat corn-on-the-cob through a chain link fence with no problem. His eyes were what bothered me the most, though. The irises and pupils were both black as coal, and the whites weren't white at all, they were almost completely red. I'd never seen anything quite like it. He looked and smelled like he'd been on a weeklong drinking binge. Now I knew why she wanted me to behave. There was little doubt this guy could kick my ass right now. Probably even with one hairy hand tied behind his back.

"Who the hell are you?" he growled at me, ignoring my two female companions.

"Virgil, I'd like you to meet Mr. John Steele," Jasmyna said in a formal voice, as she stood up and gestured towards me. "John has joined our little family."

"What?" he spat in disbelief. "You made 'im? I thought you was done with that crap. The last thing we need is some damned young blood screwin' things up for us. What's the matter?" he asked, glaring at me. "You ain't got no mouth to speak up with?"

I wanted to ask what the hell "you ain't got no" meant, or at least confirm he knew it was a double negative, but I wisely bit my lip.

"Oh yes," I said giving him my best 100 watt smile instead, "I do have a mouth to speak with. In fact, you'll find I have a very intelligent one. And don't worry about me being too young, I'm actually forty-six years old and seldom screw things up." I turned up the wattage on my smile another notch.

"Forty-six? Shit man, I'm over a hundred and forty-six and I'm still a pup." He turned to address the ladies, "I don't like it. I don't like it a'tall. We been doin' fine jes as we are. Don't need some wiseass, city slicker dude, comin' round here and screwin' things up. I say we get rid of 'em now, 'fore he does any damage."

"Nonsense," said Jasmyna with a tone of finality in her voice. "He's one of us now, and I'll deal with any trouble he causes. I taught both of you, didn't I?" she asked while indicating both Virgil and Emily. "I don't want to hear any more about this." With that, she returned to her chair and sat down. I was impressed by her composure in the face of such obvious danger.

Virgil stared at me for a few seconds and said to no one in particular, " No sir, I jes don't like it. He smells funny and I know he's gonna be trouble. I ain't likin' it, but I'll let 'im live for your sake, Miss Jasmyna. Don't 'spect me ta like 'im though."

With that, he spun and left the room as quickly as he'd entered it. A few seconds later, we heard the front door slam. The moment he left the house, the air seemed to lighten up.

"Nice chap," I said.

"Shush now," Jasmyna hissed at me, switching to her silent voice to emphasize the danger. "Virgil isn't someone to trifle with. He's got a mean streak a mile long. You must learn to watch your back, John. Never trust that...thing."

"No worries there," I responded, also switching to silent voice. It never hurts to be careful when discussing a homicidal monster who's recently offered to "get rid of 'em," especially when the person he's talking about getting rid of happens to be you!

"I don't see me and ol' Virg hangin' out together anytime soon."

"You have a very intelligent mouth?" Jasmyna queried, looking at me as though I'd lost my marbles. "What was that all about?"

"Well, you two ladies are constantly telling me I have a 'smart' mouth," I replied, grinning with pride at my juvenile little play on words. "Generally, right before you punch me, and way too hard I might add."

"Thin ice," Jasmyna said, shaking her head. "You've got to be more careful with Virgil. He's not very bright and he knows it. It's a sensitive spot, and if he figures out you're making fun of him, he won't take kindly to it."

"Now tell me again, just why was it you made that 'thing' a vampire?" I asked. "I thought it was a somewhat selective process?"

"It's like I said before, everyone's personality seems to change. Virgil was the sweetest boy you ever met. He was one of our stable boys, and was as faithful to me as the day is long. He was never very bright, but he wouldn't have hurt a flea. One day a horse reared up and kicked him in the head. Well, in a momentary lapse of judgment, wanting to keep my faithful stable boy around, I took his dying body down to the basement. This was just a few years after the Great War, and good male help was hard to find. In truth, I actually cared a great deal for that poor dimwitted boy when he was human."

"The Great War?" I asked. "Do you mean World War I or II?"

"No, silly boy. The Great War between the states—The Civil War, as you'd probably call it, though I promise you there was nothing civil about it. I believe the year was 1868, or maybe it was 1869? Anyway, I didn't actually think he'd make The Choice to come back. I assumed he'd pass through to the light and stay, because he was always such a good boy. In a selfish act, I guess I hoped he'd come back to me as he had been. I hate to say it, but if I'd known what evil I was creating, I never would have made him. We all feed and I've never had any qualms about it. That's part of our existence. But Virgil kills for the fun of it. To him, it's a sport." She looked at me with true concern in her eyes, "Do be careful around him, John."

I was touched by her sincere concern. "Don't worry about me," I said in a reassuring voice. "Any idea how long he'll stay?"

I turned to look at Emily, who'd been mostly quiet through the whole episode. She seemed to be staring off into space.

"Emily, dear," I called. "Earth to Emily. Come in please."

She turned to look at me, and I noticed tears in her eyes. "God, I hate him. I wish he'd just stay away."

Shocked by the emotion she displayed, I asked again, "How long does he usually stay? I thought he only popped in occasionally, at least based on our past conversations."

"Oh," Emily said, shaking her head and shuddering all over, like she was trying to rid her brain of some gruesome thought. "He's seldom here for more than two or three days a year. Thank God. He's a bastard, John, and physically strong as hell. Jasmyna's right, watch out for him. He tolerates us because he thinks we're his only family, but I could tell he really didn't like you. It's probably some petty male jealousy thing. He thinks we belong to him, or at least that he can bully us around when he's here. The bastard."

"But Jasmyna made him..." I started.

"That doesn't mean anything," Jasmyna cut in. "Look at you. Emily and I made you, and I'll bet you've given considerable thought to getting rid of us, if you knew how."

I was more than a little bit shocked. "What?" I exclaimed.

"It's all right, John, I understand. You had a wonderful life as a human, and we ended it. If you hadn't somehow found a way to drink my blood, your existence here on Earth would have ended. You were close to death when you managed to bite me. I still don't know how you knew to do that," she said as more of a statement than a question.

"Jasmyna, I'm shocked," I said with conviction. "Why would I want to get rid of you two? You and Emily were just doing what us little ol' vampires do to survive, feed and kill. I don't hold that against you now."

She smiled at me, but I could tell she wasn't in the least convinced. "Come now, John, if you could go back in time to the night you came home with Emily, knowing what you know now, would you still have come to the house with her?"

She had me. I hesitated a moment, then looking down, I said, "I honestly don't know. My life wasn't really all that wonderful. I hated my job, so I quit. Well, let's just say I retired earlier than I should have. My wife was screwing her damned shrink, which probably explains why she never had time to screw me. Do you know, and this is pathetic, I came to New Orleans just looking to get laid? My sex life had been a dud for the last twenty years. I realized, after Susan and I broke up, that I'd never really been very satisfied. She used sex to get me to do what she wanted, and I was whipped enough to go along with it. I always wanted kids, and she pretended to try a few times, but she never had her heart into it. Then one day we were too old. She was always more interested in which country club we belonged to." I realized I was rambling and had said much more than I'd intended. Feeling like I needed to finish making my point, but not realizing I was leaving a huge question unanswered, I concluded, "I guess I don't know if I'm happy being a vampire yet. I still feel like an infant in so many ways, but I do know this: I wasn't all that happy in my other life. So don't think I blame you or hold anything against you."

"That's sweet, dear," Jasmyna said with a smile. "But don't hold it against me, if I reserve judgment for awhile."

"Look," I said to Jasmyna, belaboring the point. "I don't know what happened when you two died, but since you've always talked about 'The Choice,' I assume you two had an option presented to you. I did, and I chose this existence. You had no influence on that decision."

I realized this was turning into a heated discussion and that I wasn't going to win. If Jasmyna really wanted to believe I'd turn on her, so be it. It was time to lighten the mood though. "Now, Emily, on the other hand, I suppose if anyone's to blame, she'd be the one."

"Me?" she asked, surprised by the turn in the conversation.

I got up and walked around behind her chair. Bending over and grabbing one of her ample breasts in each hand, I continued, "Yep, I was presented with two choices: Heaven or Emily's breasts. Well, it wasn't even a fair contest. Emily's breasts are heaven to me. Why, I'd die a thousand deaths just to hold these major league casabas in my unworthy paws."

It worked. Slapping my hands away but giggling, Emily replied, "By my count then, you need to die another nine hundred and ninety-nine times before you get to caress my casabas, as you so eloquently called them. John, you're such a horn dog. Just another example of someone not turning out like you'd think. I thought you might actually be a real gentleman."

I leaned over the chair again, this time kissing her on the head. "I don't know much about this existence, yet, but you know what I do like about being a vampire?" Not waiting for an answer, I continued, "The sexual freedom. I guess I had some hang-ups as a human. I was into that monogamous relationship thing, and I'd have suffered another thirty years with my wife and our pitiful excuse of a sex life, rather than cheat and get some on the side. Say, what was it like in your days as a human, Emily? Did you have any sexual freedom at all? I always assumed the people back in your day just did it to have kids. You know, business instead of pleasure."

"Silly man, of course we had sex for the fun of it. As long as you didn't mind being publicly labeled a whore, that is. Once, I just said the word 'penis' out loud in public, and I was shackled and chained in the public stocks for two whole days. They branded my arm with the sign of a whore too, I might add."

"Really?" I asked, amazed at this bit of real life history.

Seeming even more animated, she leaned forward and continued, "Yes, and I still have the scar. It's an erect penis inside a red circle, with a slash through it."

As the image she described unfolded in my head, I knew I'd been had.

Emily saw my look of embarrassment at having been suckered in and broke into a grin. "No, silly, I was a student at the Ursaline Convent, which you said you toured once. Then I became a nurse because the man I became engaged to marry was too busy schlepping his slave girls to pay much attention to me. I realized later he had quite a thing for the young dark skinned girls, and boys I might add. I was smart enough to know he wouldn't grow out of it, and I'm glad I decided not to marry him. Even if I was considered a frigid old maid later on."

I put aside the momentary flash of irritation at having been made to look so damn naïve, and realized this was part of what endeared Emily to me. Her sense of humor was amazing. I wanted to know more about her human life and urged her to continue her story.

"No," she replied. "I haven't talked about this in years, and it's better left buried in the past. I, too, didn't have a perfect life as a human, John. I'd just as soon forget about it."

Jasmyna had been quiet, but now she piped in. "He was a worthless peace of human flesh, Emily. You did the right thing by killing him."

I burst out laughing and couldn't help myself. "You killed him? You killed your fiancée and fed on him?"

"Ex-fiancée," Emily said indignantly, sitting up straight and thrusting back her shoulders. "Besides, he made me mad. He embarrassed me in front of the whole city. Everyone knew we were to be wed. It was in all the papers. When it was cancelled, I was ruined. No man in his right mind would have wanted me then, since it was assumed he'd had his way with me. He hadn't, but that didn't matter. Remember, things were much different in the 1840's. In fact, they were different in the 1940's. Only recently have men not expected to marry a virgin."

I couldn't stop laughing. "Jeez, Emily, remind me never to piss you off. I don't want you to kill me too. Wait a minute…you already did!"

Now even Jasmyna saw the humor and started to shake her head and chuckle. "See, I said he'd hold it against us. You kill a man and you'd think it's the end of the world or something. It's not like there aren't plenty more out there someplace."

I smiled at her. "Now, Jasmyna, you're not still hanging on to that bone are you? I wasn't kidding when I said I don't hold a grudge against you." This vampire stuff never ceases to amaze me. I was getting excited just looking at her. I reached down and rubbed my crotch through my slacks. "There is something I'd like to hold against you though."

"Damn you, John," Emily spit. "Is that all you ever think about? Don't even think about it with Virgil back in town."

I was shocked by Emily's outburst. If anything, lately she'd matched my sexual aggression, stroke for stroke. "Is someone jealous?" I asked, though I knew she wasn't. The three of us had romped in every way imaginable, and never had any sense of attachment been even hinted at.

She just looked away.

"So," I said, changing the subject. "Just how old are you Emily? You were around in the 1840's?"

"It's not polite to ask a lady her age, John. I guess you're family now, though, so I might as well tell you the gory details. I was born in 1830. My mother was Spanish and my father was French. They were married and seven months later left Europe for Louisiana. I was born two weeks out to sea, so I think a little hanky-panky was happening before they wed. Good for them. They ended up owning a small plantation on a Caribbean island, as well as a significant amount of property throughout the Gulf Coast. As far as I know, the only thing they ever fought about was my education. My father, who was a dear man, didn't want to let his oldest daughter leave. My mother, who was fiercely independent for the times, demanded that I receive a proper education. Since the island was no place to properly educate a young lady, I was sent to New Orleans at the ripe old age of eleven. The rest is pretty boring. I went to school at the convent, was taught to be a young lady, and was 'selected' by the aforementioned idiot to be his wife and the mother of his children. It didn't work out, at least not for him."

"Amazing," I said, trying to imagine Emily as a young girl growing up on an island plantation. "Simply amazing. How 'bout you?" I asked, turning to Jasmyna.

"Oh, I was a Coffin Girl."

"A Coughing Girl? What the hell's that? Were you part of a whooping cough epidemic or something?"

She chuckled. "No, silly boy. That's coffin, as in casket. Since we're having a history lesson here, let me see if I can explain it. I was born in France, in 1725. My family's fortune was dwindling, so my father sent me to the New World. I was a young teenager, and it was a great adventure. First we went to Quebec, where the Bishop determined who'd be sent south to help populate New Orleans. It was a wild place then, and there was a severe shortage of 'good and virtuous' young woman for the local gentry to marry. There were plenty of whores, native Indians, and women of color around to satisfy their male urges, but nowhere near enough of us prissy little white girls to produce their legitimate Catholic offspring. The church was very interested in expanding here and wanted to tap into the vast wealth being created. What better way to sink their hooks into these men than to supply a good Catholic wife? Of course the ultimate motivation was a large Catholic population. They wanted us to make lots of little Catholic babies.

"When we left Quebec for New Orleans, we were each issued a box shaped like a coffin to carry our belongings in. After we arrived, and our belongings were brought ashore, the locals took it as though we were so sure we'd die here, we'd brought our coffins with us. It was a bit of a joke, of course, but there are families in New Orleans to this day that are proud to tie their heritage to a coffin girl."

I was amazed. These two incredible women had lived so much history. I felt like I'd missed out on something. "So, did you kill a potential husband too?"

She looked up and a smile slowly crossed her face, as she seemed to think back to another place and time. "Oh no, I married a wonderful man. I was very much in love with him and we had a fantastic couple of years together. Unfortunately, he died of yellow fever, just as so many others did back then. It was a terrible time for diseases. I was crushed and had thoughts of taking my own life, but then I met a very special man."

"Let me guess," I asked, "The vampire who turned you?"

She smiled again. "Yes. He's very special. You'll meet him one day, when the time is right. I think you'll like him. In fact, I think you two will hit it off just fine."

"My grandfather," I mussed, picturing a wise old gentleman. "So, what's he think of Virgil?"

They both got quiet for a moment and then Jasmyna spoke up, "Not much, really. He's tried to educate Virgil. In fact, he made a significant effort to change him for the better, but Virgil just seemed to resent it. We don't speak of it, but I think he threw in the towel after what Virgil did to Emily."

"What did he do?" I asked.

"Nothing," Emily said, looking away.

"Tell him," Jasmyna said to Emily.

"No."

"He needs to know."

"No."

"There's nothing to be ashamed of, dear. Besides, John's family now."

"Jasmyna, I said no!"

Tired of the back and forth conversation, which seemed to be going nowhere, I urged, "Tell me what?"

Emily looked away.

"Virgil raped Emily. It was about seventy years ago."

"It was sixty-four years ago," Emily cut in, but made no further attempt to stop Jasmyna.

"Anyway," Jasmyna continued, "sixty-four years ago, Virgil brutally raped Emily."

It sounds odd to hear of a vampire being taken advantage of, but as with any society, some individuals are physically stronger than others and use it to their benefit. I was shocked and confused. The thing I liked best about being a vampire, so far anyway, was the sexual freedom. The concept of rape seemed foreign.

"But we're so sexually free..." I began.

"Some things never change, "Jasmyna interrupted. "Rape is seldom about sex, John. Someone like you, 'who's self-confident and a gentleman, probably wouldn't understand that. In this case, it was about exerting power over someone else. By raping Emily, he was making sure she and I knew he was physically more powerful. He was making a statement that he's the alpha dog and can take what he wants and do what he pleases."

All this was pissing me off. "Someone needs to teach him a lesson."

"Not you," Jasmyna shot back at me. "Not now, anyway. He knows how to hurt people John, including vampires. We're not the only vampires he's crossed. He's well known and generally disliked throughout our world."

"But..." I started to protest.

"He's constantly on the move, but we like to stay put. If we started anything and didn't finish it, he'd have no problem finding us. Besides, we like it here in New Orleans. It's just not worth a war that we're not sure we can win. So, we dare not do anything rash. He's simply a problem that pops up a couple of days a year, that's all. We've dealt with it for over a century now."

"Okay, one last question," I said. "I can easily see he's stronger than any of us physically, but what about mentally? Couldn't you simply overpower his mind, and then thrash him physically?"

The ladies looked at each other for a moment, then Jasmyna answered, "That would seem to be the most likely way to beat Virgil in a confrontation. However, we'd only try it as a last resort. Nobody is really sure how strong his mental powers are. There's a difference between mental strength and intelligence. Once someone attempted to overpower his mind, it'd be a clear declaration of war against him. If you didn't succeed the first time, I doubt you'd get a second chance. It'd be an all or nothing gamble, which we're not willing to take at this point. There are those in our world who have the mental power to defeat him though. Of that we're sure."

I was clueless about the politics in the vampire community, but it seemed unjust that an idiot like him should be allowed to exist. They were right about him being physically powerful, though. That much I could sense. My anger made me want to go out and thump the jerk, but logic told me Jasmyna and Emily were right. I wasn't even in his league. I'd bide my time and see what developed. He obviously wasn't real bright, so maybe an opportunity would present itself. It wasn't like I was going to run out of time anytime soon.

"I'm going to bed," I said, and got up. They sat there, lost in their own thoughts. I walked out of the room, and I doubt they even noticed my departure.

In my room, I undressed and carefully hung up my clothes. The thought of Virgil's wrinkled and dirty attire crossed my mind. This wasn't good. Not good at all. There wasn't much I could do about it this visit, but I could definitely be better prepared on his next visit. They said he only stayed a few days each year. Perhaps he'd be gone in the next day or so, and things could get back to normal. As I climbed into bed, I realized how much I cared about Emily. Jasmyna too, of course, but I felt a special bond with Emily. They had carefully explained that vampires weren't capable of true love with one individual, as in the human sense. So by their logic, I couldn't be in love with Emily. Whatever it was though, it sure felt strong. With her on my mind, I fell into my usual deep sleep.

For the first time since my existence as a vampire, I had a dream. I dreamed of Emily.

Chapter 8

I sensed his presence the moment he put his hand on my bedroom doorknob.
I opened my eyes as the door was thrust open.

"Let's go boy, we're burnin' moonlight. It's time to make sure you can hunt. I don't want you bein' a burden to the women folk."

"Good evening, Virgil," I said in a calm voice, not wanting him to know he'd startled me. "What's this about a hunt? Jasmyna has asked me not to go out for a while. She said it'd be safer for everyone. At least, until I've received more training."

"To hell with her. She's nursemaidin' ya. Ya ain't a man if'n ya can't hunt. Git dressed. We're a goin' out huntin'."

It didn't look like I had much choice in the matter, so I obliged by quickly putting on a pair of black jeans, a black polo shirt, and some Rockport sneakers. It helped that Emily was in the clothing business, as she'd had no problem picking up an adequate supply of clothing and toiletries for me. I didn't need to shave, but I splashed some water on my face and combed my hair back. I glanced at the window and could see around the edge of the shade that the sun was just setting. Interesting. This was the earliest I'd ever been up.

All the while I was dressing, Virgil stood and stared at me. I paid no attention to him, not wanting any fear to show. "All right, Virgil, I'm ready to rock and roll."

"Hmmf," he snorted, "Rock and roll, huh? Let's go, Slick."

I half hoped Emily or Jasmyna would stop us before we got to the front door and demand that I stay in. I knew going out with Virgil was going to be dangerous. I have to admit, though, that a small part of me wanted to go. I hadn't really been out and about since my untimely demise, other than my nightly excursions with Emily. We'd stuck to walking the darker streets and focused on getting my overactive senses under control. I felt I was ready to adventure out farther, but Emily always urged caution.

I knew if I could somehow survive an evening with "The Virg," I might actually learn something of interest about him. Somehow, he'd survived for a century and a half with the mental capacity of an empty shoebox, so I knew he must have something working for him.

We made it to the front door without being stopped by the ladies, and before I could come up with a reason not to continue, we were out on the sidewalk headed towards the French Quarter. Company aside, it was a beautiful evening. The warmth of the day lingered, but the sleep inducing rays of the sun had passed. My heightened senses were almost overloaded at first, but I slowly gained control. I could smell many different things, some as if for the first time. It was a mixture of flowers, food, the Mississippi, people, urine and a hundred other assorted smells. Amazingly, I could smell them all at once, yet I could identify them all individually. What a night to be alive. Or, dead in my case. Maybe this wouldn't be so bad after all.

Virgil eyed me suspiciously. "First time outside, huh?"

I decided not to let him know I'd been practicing, hoping he'd think I was at more of a disadvantage than I was. Also, I figured I could win him over by asking questions and making him feel like the expert. Everybody likes to be the expert, even an idiot.

"Yea, this is really something! I feel like my senses are a little bit overloaded. Wow, it's great though. I can smell all kinds of things. And my vision, it's nearly dark and I can see better than I used to be able to during the day. Everything looks so vivid and bright. Do you ever get used to this?"

He seemed to think a minute. "Yea, you git used to it. "Ya gotta learn to use it to yer advantage, though, so you best be appreciatin' what you got. All of us git different abilities, and it sounds like you got the vision and the smellin'. How's your hearin'?"

"Seems fine," I said. "I don't notice much difference though. Not as dramatic as my vision and sense of smell."

He looked across the street at a two-story building. "There's some folks a talkin' in there. What are they sayin'?"

I focused on the building, and sure enough, I could make out a male and a female voice taking about something on the television. I decided to keep this to myself, though, since I wasn't too sure about Virgil. "Nope, I don't hear anything. Maybe I'm not doing it right, or maybe it'll come to me later."

I'm not sure, but I thought I saw a small smile pass over his face. "Yea, it'll probably come to ya. Maybe, maybe not. Me, now I got great eyes and ears. My nose don't work so well though. Not that it's a weakness," he quickly threw in. "Besides, it's what's up here that counts," he said as he tapped his head.

"Can you read people's thoughts too?" I asked innocently.

"Course I can," he snapped. "Make 'em jump through hoops if I wanted to. That's the key to huntin'. Ya find the right one, then ya reel em' in."

I wanted to say that it sounded more like fishing, but we seemed to be rapidly becoming buddies, and besides I didn't want to accidentally hook myself in the foot. I decided it was time for a compliment. "Emily and Jasmyna said you are a great hunter. You can always catch the biggest fish in the pond." Okay, I couldn't help being just a bit of a smart-ass, but I figured the odds were in my favor that he'd miss my little joke.

He didn't let me down, as he responded with pride, "They said that, huh?"

"Oh yeah. They said that when it came to hunting, no one could bait them and reel them in like Virgil. When it comes to baiting the hook, you're the master."

"Damn straits, I'm the master," he said with a genuine smile. "Them women are purdy damn smart sometimes."

As we turned to walk towards The Quarter, I mumbled, "I guess that would make you a master-baiter."

"What's that?" he asked.

"I said, we'd better go before it gets any later."

"Yep, dinner's a waitin'."

Chapter 9

In retrospect, my night on the town with Virgil initiated a whole new chapter in what I now hope will be a long and successful existence as a vampire. It was the beginning of my real education as to what I had become, what I was now capable of, and the choices I'd have to make. Most lessons worth learning come at a price. As is typical of me, I paid the full tuition and then some. The lessons I learned over the next several months were physically painful and mentally exhausting. I believe, however, that successfully navigating the labyrinth of challenges I encountered has made me a significantly stronger and imminently wiser vampire.

Though I didn't realize it at the time, I was ridiculously naïve about the complexities involved with being one of everybody's favorite blood sucking creatures of the night. I suspected that going out alone with Virgil could be hazardous to my health, but I had no idea that it would come close to bringing my story to a very premature conclusion. I saw first hand the unfettered evil my new species is capable of and quickly established that it was not a path I was capable of pursuing. While I can readily accept that my kind has no qualms about killing humans to sustain our existence, I now know that there are those among us who do it for the sheer pleasure of inflicting pain. I learned the hard way that despite my new talents, things can turn ugly in half a human heartbeat. If I wanted my story to be more than a brief essay on what not to do as a new vampire, I'd have to keep my head about me.

Up until that point, all I'd seen was the mostly serene lifestyle that Jasmyna and Emily had fabricated for themselves. Don't get me wrong; the bottom line is that they are two extremely proficient human-killers, as is evidenced by the fact that they seldom miss a meal. As I'd experienced first-hand, though, they attempted to treat the taking of each life with a certain degree of dignity and respect. Helping a human cross over while feeling engulfed in the sensation of the love they craved, whether physical, emotional, or spiritual, was the least they could do for the sustenance they received from the victim. While not exactly a perfect situation for the human since they were still going to die, I now realized that it sure as hell beat a run in with Virgil.

We hit Bourbon Street and Virgil began to morph into someone, or some thing, totally different from what I'd seen in my brief exposure to him. His normal demeanor was something akin to that of an agitated rattlesnake, ready to strike at the slightest provocation. Now, he appeared to be almost normal, by which I mean he could easily have been taken for a somewhat affable young man, simply taking life easy and enjoying the sites like any other tourist. His mood perked up perceptibly, to the point that he appeared almost giddy with the anticipation of the hunt. I made a mental note that Mr. Virgil, despite his rough edges, had mastered the skills of the chameleon. We strolled along slowly, trying to blend in with the still somewhat sober early evening crowd.

When we reached Lafitte's Blacksmith Shop, we made our first stop of the evening. Lafitte's is a fun little bar that's housed in a decrepit little building. According to local lore, it was once the great pirate Jean Lafitte's blacksmith shop, though it was far more likely he used it to trade booty. Perhaps I should say he traded pirated goods, though a little booty may have shaken its way through on occasion. From the outside, it looks like the wrong place to be if a stiff wind picks up, or someone sneezes too hard. Somehow, it's managed to withstand the ravages normally associated with the passing of a significant number of years, and being in close proximity to large numbers of drunks smoking cigarettes. Now, it provides a great place for both locals and tourists to partake of their favorite libation. Amazingly, after all these years, people still go to Lafitte's trying to score a little booty. Hell, even I was guilty, since I'd been trying to score there once too!

I'd stumbled across Lafitte's in my days as a horny tourist, so I was familiar with the intricacies of its layout. Let's see, big room with bar, small room with piano, men's room with pee trough. Yep, that about covers it. Unfortunately, I'd become all too familiar with the aptly named Hurricanes they served and the damage they left in their wake the next morning. They may not be as dangerous as a hungry vampire lurking about, but they're close.

To our advantage, the bar was very dark inside. How dark was it? Well, according to the official standards established and published for dark bars each year by '*Blind Drunk*' magazine, this place was well past the safe limit for drunks to be stumbling around after a sixth beer or third Hurricane. No, of course there's no such magazine, but if there were, Lafitte's would surely be on the list of America's oldest and darkest bars.

There were some rickety wooden tables and chairs scattered about, no doubt left over from that famous night when Jean Lafitte's older brother Pierre planned a private party for his personal posse of petulant pirates and panderers, who partook of purloined pork posterior, pepperoni pizza and according to legend, a really good after dinner port. Pierre's posse was pondering the possibility of purchasing pornography, until their persuasive parish priest threatened to have their peckers pickled. There is a long held belief that pirates of old were not very well educated, perhaps because of their odd speech habits or preference for outlandish apparel. Many years of exhaustive research has produced evidence to the contrary. Those blustering old buccaneers with their bristly brown beards and bulging bags of ill begotten bullion were in fact alliterate, not illiterate. Poetry was also a favorite hobby, right behind murdering, thieving, whoring and jay walking.

Enough of the historical perspective, the bar's current management had thoughtfully left a candle on each of the tables to provide a little mood lighting. Unfortunately, the mood mustn't have been too good on this particular night, as only a few candles were actually burning. Never fear, Virgil and I were there and were sure to bring the party to life. Hey, who blew out those few remaining candles?

We passed on several prime tables and the opportunity to sit close to the night's entertainment, a Billy Joel wanna be, as Virgil headed to an empty table in a corner. Of course, I could see perfectly well, so sitting in the darkest spot in the bar didn't matter. My imagination took over, though, and I had to resist the urge to squint and look cagey. I felt like an international spy waiting to rendezvous with a dangerous enemy agent. Queue the James Bond theme and a British accent. "The name's Steel, John Steele. I'd like a liter of A-positive, shaken, not stirred. Please hurry, dear girl, before it starts to coagulate you know…"

We sat, we watched, and we waited. After what felt like a millennium given my present company, the waitress made her way over to our table. Virgil surprised me by ordering a couple of the Hurricane's I'd grown to respect, if not fear. He seemed more the watered-down beer type, but I guess you never know about us crazy vampires. Next, he might surprise me by suggesting we stop for sushi. We both sat quietly and surveyed the crowd. I was doing an excellent job of it, though I had no idea what we were looking for and I damn sure wasn't going to ask.

Actually, this "stalker" approach was fine with me, since the experience of being around so many people was new and kind of fun. I found to my great amusement, that my enhanced hearing could be more directional than I'd realized. That is, by focusing in on a particular table, I was able to increase the volume at that location, while toning down the surrounding chatter. Of course, like every other enhancement and upgrade I'd gained over my old human form, I'd need a lot more practice before I mastered it.

I focused in on a table with two middle-aged geeks and an overly expressive woman. Using my supernatural powers of deduction, I was able to determine they were part of a convention, perhaps having something to do with computer systems or software. The ID badges for a software convention, which they wore alongside several strands of cheap Mardi Gras beads might have helped guide me to that conclusion, but I can't be sure. I'd prefer to believe that I now have the power to just know things, kind of like male intuition on steroids. This would have come in quite handy in Ms. Wallace's seventh-grade Geography class, perhaps saving me the embarrassment of announcing to the class that New England replaced Old England.

The woman, who was somewhat attractive in a "lift up her skirt and bang her on the desk like a cheap whore" sort of way, was about a decade or two younger than either of the geeks. Clearly, she was dominating the conversation, and I was fascinated by how much she used her hands and arms while conversing. She was gesticulating so wildly that, for a minute, I wondered if she was demonstrating the process for landing a jet on an aircraft carrier. Intrigued, I couldn't resist eavesdropping...I mean, uh...practicing my focused listening skills from across the room. I soon realized why the two propeller heads sharing the table with her looked like they were sucking on lemons. It became painfully evident that she was their boss, and she was a major bee with an itch!

"Now, Paul," she commanded in a surprisingly nasal tone that reeked of too many years spent in the greater Boston area, "I want you to buddy up with their web development team. Find out exactly what they're up to and when they think they'll be fully functional. And you, Bill," she continued, directing her attention to the other neutered male, "I need to know exactly what this venture is costing them. Whatever it is, we'll undercut it by twenty percent."

"But, Sue," the one she'd addressed as Bill whined. "There's no way we can web enable them for less than they can do it internally. Hector Ramirez is one of the best project coordinators around, and..."

"Nonsense, Bill," she interrupted. "It doesn't matter that we can't do it for less. It just matters that we get that contract and our foot in the door. Once we're far enough along, we'll simply increase our billable hours and blame it on 'scope creep' as usual. Of course, we'll ensure that their requirements aren't well defined, which will provide ample wiggle room and make the inevitable cost over-runs appear to be their own fault. You know how the game works. Let me remind you two, I plan on making partner off of this deal, and if either of you blows it for me, I can guarantee you that your career is finished at..."

I'd heard enough. I wanted to walk over to their table and politely tell these guys I was a friendly neighborhood vampire. If they'd like, I'd suck the life out of the self-serving bitch they worked for. In fact, I'd even let them watch the show as long as they didn't start cheering too loudly. I couldn't suppress a smile when I imagined these two corporate prisoners joyfully doing "the wave" as they watched their boss get the life sucked out of her. Of course, the fact that I'd overheard her name was Sue, the same as my ex-wife, had nothing to do with my desire to rip the bitch's neck open and watch her life slowly ebb away. Really. Okay, I wonder if there's such a thing as a vampire psychologist?

My little fantasy was interrupted when our waitress, Joy, who looked less than joyful to be working on this fine evening, brought our drinks. Virgil tossed a couple of bills on her drink tray, and grinning like an idiot, told her to keep the change. The tip briefly brought what might be considered a smile to her lips, and she did us the courtesy of letting us know that if we wanted anything else, just to get her attention. Obviously, Virgil's generous gesture had elevated us to her A-List.

I picked up my cup and took a nice big gulp, then immediately experienced my own little hurricane. Maybe it was just a remnant of human habit, but clearly I acted without thinking this simple action through. Undoubtedly, I'd made a major mistake. My mouth, throat, belly, rectum, and something else down there all began to burn at once. My body went into wild convulsions, something that sounded like a train whistle blew, my eyeballs flew out of my head and bounced around like they were on springs, and then I spontaneously combusted. Okay, so maybe I'm exaggerating a little bit, but it really did a number on me for a few minutes. There was no doubt that my new vampire body was not at all happy with me.

If things weren't bad enough with my body now threatening to boycott any further decisions made by my brain, Virgil had witnessed my distress and was now hee-hawing like a donkey who'd overdosed on crack cocaine. The possibility that he'd planned the whole episode didn't escape me, especially when he suddenly got serious again and made a big show of slowly pressing his cup up to his mouth and taking a long deep slug of the icy pink death in his cup.

"Ahhh," he sighed with an exaggerated gesture, "that there hits the spot. What's a matter boy, the sauce burnin' yer belly a little bit? Are you stupid or somethin'? Ya dumb shit, yer a vampire now. Ya can't be a drinkin' human food."

It still burned too much for me to say that I'd never intended to drink human food. I decided it was best to let him have his fun and do what I do best, play stupid.

"How come you can drink it, Virgil? It doesn't seem to have any effect on you," I finally choked out.

"Cause I'm a hell of a lot strong'r vampire than you and I been 'round damn near fer ever. Ya gotta learn what you can and can't do. "Ya can't be drinkin' human food yet, ya dumb shit."

He picked up my glass, and with a quick look around to ensure nobody was watching, dumped half of it on the floor under the empty table next to us. "Ya gotta learn to make it look like yer drinkin', but not to be really drinkin' when yer lookin' like yer drinkin'. Got it?"

"Got it," I assured him, more than a bit concerned because I actually had understood him.

"So what exactly are we looking for, Virgil?" I queried, looking around, and anxious to change the subject.

"Dinner," my new teacher answered. He looked carefully at me to see if I got his joke. Satisfied from my smile and forced chuckle that I knew he was one funny guy, he continued more seriously, "I likes to just kinda scope things out fer a while. Mingle with the enemy so's to speak. There's lots a ways to take 'em. Kinda depends on how long it's been since I done fed last. If'n I'm real hungry like, I don't mess around like this here stuff what we're doin' now. No sirree, when I gets to hungerin' real bad in a big ol' place like this here New Orleans, or any other place with a river fer that matter, I jus' go fer it. See, ya jus' hang by the river 'till some damned fool comes 'long all by 'is lonesome. Then 'pow', ya jump 'em and ya eat 'em. Then ya chuck the body way out in the river and nobody's the wiser. Maybe rip the belly open a bit and stuff a coupla rocks way up inside to weight 'em down some if'n the river ain't flowin' real strong and if'n you got the time. Sometimes I do, 'n sometimes I don't. Keep it simple's my number one rule. At least when I'm hungerin' real bad."

He'd brought up an interesting point. "But what about the marks on the body? Isn't it a dead give away that a vampire fed on the victim?" I asked.

Emily and Jasmyna had what amounted to a shallow well in their basement. It probably wasn't very deep, given the high water table in the city, but it led to an underground river or canal. They'd shown me how they simply dropped their weighted victims into the well, and an underground current carried them away within a few hours. Occasionally, they'd float up in the Mississippi, but it usually took many months, and the remains that floated up were always extremely deteriorated. I'd realized with some trepidation when I first saw their nifty little body disposal system, that it had nearly been my own fate.

"That's the whole point of the game, boy. Hell, killin's the easy part. If ya wanna stay put fer a piece, ya don't wanna draw no extra 'ttention to yerself. Ya gotta learn to do away with the evidence of yer feedin' so's to speak. Not that no damn police could ever take on a vampire worth 'is salt, but the last thing ya want is ta draw that there 'ttention I's jes talkin' 'bout to our kind. Makin' a body disappear ain't that tough though, once ya get the knack fer it. Fire's good, or a nasty car wreck. If'n ya can't do nothin' else, jus' mess up the body real good like so's it ain't obvious it's been fed on. Jus' hang with ol' Virg an' I'll show ya how it's done."

As one could probably guess, I was totally thrilled at the prospect of "hangin' with ol' Virg." I'd sooner chew on broken glass than to have to spend an extra minute with this loon. Part of me knew that there was probably value in the lessons he could teach, but another part, the wiser part I'm sure, knew I'd be better off far away from him.

Keeping him answering questions seemed to be working, so I ventured another. "The ladies said you're only in New Orleans for a short period of time, then you move on. Do you travel a circuit or something, or do you have a main place you stay elsewhere?"

Virgil glared at me and hissed, "Why do you wanna know where I'm a stayin' at? Ya thinking you can track ol' Virg and sneak up on 'im sometime?"

"What?" I asked, genuinely shocked. "I was simply trying to figure out what a vampire's life is supposed to be like. Emily and Jasmyna seem to stay put. You seem to travel, not that it's any of my business of course. I was just curious because I need to think about my own future. I can't stay with the ladies forever."

He glared at me a moment more, then looked back across the room. "This here place ain't no good fer huntin' tonight. Let's get on outta here." I noticed he hadn't answered my question, but I figured it was wise to let the subject drop. We maintained our cover by taking the remaining vampire poison he'd purchased, now innocently camouflaged in red plastic cups, and proceeding to amble along Bourbon Street like a couple of somewhat normal Joe's. I fought the urge to hold the cup way away from me, like some deadly radiation experiment gone awry. Instead, I focused on all the things around me that had always been there, but now, it was as if I were seeing them for the very first time. I'd finally gained enough control over my enhanced senses to be able to appreciate how they brought a new degree of clarity to my surroundings.

I began to focus in on the people around me, and soon I was so entranced by the details I'd never noticed before. The ages old game of People Watching now had a whole new set of possibilities. I could see the minutest details in people's facial expressions and eye movements. I could listen to any conversation that I desired to tap into, and every once in a while I even picked up a random thought someone had. Unfortunately, I could also smell their many scents, which seemed to go from sweaty to over-perfumed, with nothing in the middle. Let me tell you, most humans smell pretty horrible!

We stopped near a small crowd that was boisterously urging an inebriated young blond to lift her top and flash her breasts, even though they appeared to be on the smallish side. Judging by the quantity of beads she had around her neck, their continued urging would likely pay off. I quickly calculated that a normal human male would stop and watch for a bit, and not wanting to blow my cover, I paused long enough to feign interest. Sure enough, the top went up and the cheers and beads began to fly.

Not that I was really paying attention, since I was on a more important mission, but they were actually bigger than you'd have expected from the top she was wearing. They had a wonderful shape, and were in perfect proportion to the rest of her slim body. She'd obviously spent a significant amount of time in the sun, because she had dark tan lines that formed the triangular shape generally associated with a bikini top The inside lines ran within a quarter of an inch from her ample areolas, which were a particularly nice shade of dark, reddish-brown. The combination of darkly tanned skin, surrounding a tender white triangle of smooth breast skin, which further surrounded a perfectly round areola with the nipples firm and erect, could be considered somewhat appealing, I suppose. I'm sure the three small moles on her left breast, as well as the nearly undetectable freckling of her skin in general, would be viewed as assets by many. As I said, though, I only gave the scene a passing glance to maintain my cover.

The peepshow now over, I began to admire the unique architecture surrounding me. My attention was suddenly drawn to a building on my left. It was a beautiful three-story brick building. Its ornate wrought iron balconies were packed with thriving plants, and sported the usual downward tilt toward the street. Something had caught my eye, and it took a moment to realize what it was. I'd found a ghost. I did a double take. I saw it, or I guess I should say saw him, as clearly as I saw everything else around me. He was pacing back and forth on the top floor balcony and seemed to be contemplating some critical issue. So intense was his focus, he appeared to be oblivious to everything else going on around him, including young women flashing their breasts for plastic beads. Back and forth he paced, never looking anywhere but down towards the wooden planks a few feet in front of him. I thought about pointing him out to Virgil, but decided against it. I'd have to ask Emily about it when I got back.

Virgil brought me back to reality and our purpose, by pointing to a corner bar and drawling, "Let's go get us some fags."

"Excuse me?" I asked, not sure I'd heard him correctly.

"What's a matter boy?" he growled, obviously having fun at my expense. "Ya worried if ya feed on a fag, ya might become one?"

"Well, no," I responded carefully. "I guess I'm just surprised that you'd choose to target the gay community specifically. Then again, they have just as much blood as anyone else. I suppose all humans, regardless of sexual preference, are fair game, aren't they?"

He stopped and turned to face me. Raising one bushy eyebrow, while leaning slightly towards me, he asked, "You a queer, boy?"

It was time to tread lightly, I decided, and proceeded to carefully choose my words. "No, I'm about as straight as you can be. In fact, I'm so straight that...well what I mean is that I totally dig chicks and all. I guess I've just never really concerned myself with other people's sexual orientation or preferences. Maybe it's a California thing or something, but I suppose you could say that I really don't care what happens in other people's bedrooms. I'm really only concerned about what happens in mine."

Trying to lighten the mood with some self-deprecating humor, I continued, "To be honest, I suppose I'm really only concerned that 'something' happens in mine, at least occasionally! Hey, for over twenty years I was married to a woman who suffered from untimely 'headaches,' if you know what I mean!" I finished with a weak laugh and a silly grin.

He paused a few moments and stared at me, as if he was still trying to figure me out. I maintained my silly grin in case it was helping my cause.

"Well, ya do what ya wanna do when yer a vampire. Ya wanna hump 'em before or after ya kill 'em, that's yer choice. Rip their head off and fuck their throat hole if'n that's what ya feel like," Virgil hissed. "Not that I ever done that," he added quickly.

Realizing he might have said too much and I'd be reading into it, he continued as though he were trying to convince me of something, "I kin have any bitch I want and you'd better believe it. I'z jus teachin' ya how to feed here. It ain't like I like faggots er somethin'. Food's food, and it's just that generally speakin,' they're some easy huntin'."

"Virgil, my man," I assured him, realizing he might have a better chance of getting a man to leave a bar with him than a woman, "I know you're not one of *them*. You sure don't have to prove anything to me."

"Ya just be rememberin'," he said as we approached the entrance. "What happens in here is jus' an act. It's huntin' and nothin' else, ya hear?"

"Loud and clear, big guy. Now let's go suck down a few. Er, uh, beers that is."

To simply say Virgil changed when we went entered the club, just doesn't do the situation justice. It's like saying the Sahara has some sand, or Canadians like beer. Better yet, it's like saying my ex-wife only has a few minor faults. My new best friend, formerly the ape man from the southern swamplands, turned into the Gay Pride poster boy. If I hadn't been so shocked by the change, I would have laughed out loud.

Virgil swished, yes I said swished, his way up to the bar and ordered a couple of Cosmopolitans. I wouldn't drink one when I was alive, and I'll be damned if I was going to drink one when I'm dead. Then again, given my recent close call with surviving a Hurricane, I wasn't willing to risk even a small taste of any liquid concoction designed for human consumption. I guess it didn't matter which drink I held in my hand, since I couldn't drink it anyway. Instead of looking for a table, he seemed content to mingle at the bar. Ever the faithful student, I hung close so I could learn from the Master. Baiter.

The exaggerated use of his hands when he coyly talked to our fellow bar patrons, the complete change in his speech and voice, and the way he managed to make eye-to-eye contact last for several seconds before looking down in an attempt to be seductive, actually amazed me. This couldn't be the Virgil I'd grown to know and hate. He was a completely different animal, and I started to wonder how much of this was an acting job. Could it be? Naw, no way...

After a few minutes of chatting with the boys at the bar, I began to lose interest. Instead of focusing on the people around me, I practiced listening in on conversations around the room. Yes, I was snooping, but it was for a good cause: my curiosity. Being my first visit to a gay bar, I'm not sure what I expected to hear. Perhaps some fantastic secrets about the gay world or something I'd never have guessed, but all I heard was a lot of conversation about mundane things like sports, movies, interest rates and, of course, the usual work related chit-chat.

Virgil came up from behind me, put his arm around my waist, and winked at me. It had to be the most evil wink in the history of all Winkdom. "Come on, let's go. We've been invited to a party with some new friends."

Invited to a party? Someone had actually invited Virgil to a party? I was right; this guy *is* a master baiter! I was so amazed that, for a moment, I didn't know what to say. Fortunately, being as cool as I am, I made up for it with a snappy recovery. "A party? Uh, that sounds great. Let's go uh...party!"

Virgil kept smiling, but having noticed that the evil glint stayed in his eye, I knew things were about to pick up, and my earlier suspicions about his sexual preferences were probably unfounded. It also reminded me that this was business. Deadly business.

We walked outside with a small group and, once we were in the middle of the street, I took stock of our new found friends. Not counting Virgil and myself, there were four fairly normal looking guys in our newly formed party pack. Normal in the sense that they were all male humans, in their late twenties to mid-thirties, clean shaven, reasonably well dressed, and all more than a bit hammered. In the French Quarter, this trait alone was enough to qualify one as being fairly normal. Of course, I recognized them from the general area we'd been standing in, but I had no idea how Virgil had conned them all into leaving and inviting us along. Okay, so I missed one teensy little part of the lesson. I have forever to pick it up though, right?

A quick round of introductions revealed our new friends to be Robert, Richard, Randal, and Raymond. I was a tad bit envious, because I'd always wanted a name like any one of theirs. There wasn't much you could do with my name, John. My birth certificate reads simply, John Steele. Not Jonathon, Johnny, Johan or Juan. Nope, nothing exotic for me, just plain old John. Not even a middle initial, much less a middle name. I can't ever be J. R., or J. T., or any other cool combination of letters. All I can be is J. Hell, that's no better than John, so what's the use? When I was a kid, I used to lie and say my middle name was Wayne. Sounds pretty cool, right? Try it. John Wayne Steele...Man of Action! Wait a minute. It sounded cool when I was a kid. Now it sounds like either a mass murderer, or an idiot who gets his penis chopped off by his own wife. Never mind, guess I'll just stick with plain ol' John.

Anyway, these were guys with options. They could be Bob, Dick, Randy, and Ray. I was about to mention this, and the oddity that their names all started with the letter R, when Virgil introduced us as Ronald and Ralph. I'm not sure what was wrong with Virgil and John, but Virgil obviously felt a need to use aliases. Guess who was Ralph? Once again I had a name that couldn't be modified. Damn the bad luck.

It turned out we were heading to Richard and Robert's house, and I fell in with them as we merrily walked along; one big happy group of vampires and unknowing victims. Actually, Richard and Robert, who'd both passed up the available options on their names, were pretty nice guys. I soon picked up that the two of them were very much in love with each other. Richard was a local chef of some repute, and Robert was a high school science teacher. Virgil's voice seemed strangely absent from the group in the rear, and I assumed he was just letting the conversation flow. The walk wasn't long, as it turned out that they only lived a few blocks away. In no time we were entering a very neat little two-story house.

Obviously experienced hosts, Robert made sure everybody was comfortable while Richard fetched a round of drinks. We sat in the cozy little living room, sipping our drinks, laughing at jokes, and enjoying the easy conversation. Most of my drink accidentally spilled into a nearby palm tree though nobody noticed. I was getting pretty good at making drinks magically disappear. I'd been out of touch for a while, and these were all bright, intelligent guys, whose company I found quite enjoyable. I hardly noticed when Virgil excused himself to go to the restroom, but we all noticed his return. Either Virgil was a closet nudist or the shit was about to hit the fan. My new best buddy was bare-assed naked and he had his game face on.

The room instantly fell silent, and I'm sure everyone else was as shocked as I was. I noticed Virgil's swagger was back as he made his way to the middle of the room. He threw back his head and appeared to flex his neck muscles as he twisted the enlarged melon he uses for a head from side to side. All the while a slow rumbling sound seemed to emerge from someplace deep down inside of his massive chest. When he lowered his head, he let out the most God-awful growl I've ever heard. A split second later, I felt my head get slammed by some type of pulse, and found myself frozen in fear for an instant. As if Virgil's normal mug wasn't ugly enough, it had transformed into something straight out of hell.

In a lightening quick move, Virgil grabbed Randal by the hair and stood him up. He snapped his head back and I heard the unmistakable crack of his neck breaking. With a savage bite he tore into his carotid artery and buried his face deeper and deeper into his neck. Randal's mouth was open as if to scream, but only the guttural sounds of Virgil feasting could be heard. I saw Randal's spirit leave his body, float up a few feet, and then drift away without looking back.

The initial shock passed, and I stood up and quickly scanned the room. The remaining three humans sat trembling, totally absorbed in the horror before them. I realized that Virgil was somehow controlling their minds and that was likely the pulse I'd felt. The hellish image of him I'd seen when I felt the pulse was no longer visible to me; however, I knew the others still saw him as he desired, a blood-thirsty animal from the pits of hell. My vampire abilities had kept me from staying under his control for long, but I made a quick mental note that it had stunned me temporarily. I let my thoughts merge with the others for a brief instant, and was horrified and sickened by the terror they were being put through.

Whereas Jasmyna and Emily had killed gently and with compassion, if there is such a thing while killing, Virgil was purposely making the event as horrifying as possible. I wanted to stop him but knew that it was impossible. Pride aside, I knew I was no match for the beast in front of me. Finished with Randal, he lifted his body up and hurled it across the room.

He grabbed Robert next and, standing him up, tilted his head back with a savage pull of his hair. Before ripping into his neck, he turned and glared at me. Blood and flesh spitting from his mouth, he growled, "Feed."

My appetite was nearly gone from the horror I'd just witnessed, but the smell of the fresh blood made my vampire senses tingle. I looked at the remaining two, Richard and Raymond, and made a quick decision. I'd give Richard credit for the few minutes we'd spent walking together, and see if I could ease his passing. They were going to die no matter what, but maybe they didn't all have to go Virgil's way. If any good could come out of this scene from hell, it was my only chance.

Richard was mesmerized, watching his lover being torn apart. I could sense his heart breaking with despair. I sat next to him and, taking his face in my hands, turned it toward me. Virgil's grip on his mind was strong, but my close proximity and the physical contact allowed me to break it. He looked at me and blinked, as if waking from a bad dream. I tilted his head slightly, and when his eyes focused on mine, I let my thoughts meld with his. I sensed the panic, but gently reassured him that everything was all right. I forced an image of Robert into his mind, and I felt him relax.

"Are you an angel," he asked?

I didn't answer, but smiled as warmly as I could at him. It wasn't that I wanted to deliberately mislead him, but I felt the truth might have sent him over the edge. I wanted to make his passing as painless as possible and, given the circumstances, not scare the bajeebers out of him. It felt odd to be asked something so ridiculous, though, and the question would haunt me for a long time.

Conscious of the fact that Virgil was now starting in on Raymond, I tilted Richard's head back quickly and gently bit into the tender flesh on the left side of his neck to begin the now familiar process of draining the life out of him. I mentally assured him that everything was going to be all right and that he and Robert would be together and happy again soon. I heard him sigh and relax, gradually giving in to the image I was placing in his mind.

Out of respect for the situation, I tried not to notice how wonderful his blood tasted as it flowed steadily down into my greedy belly, or the feeling of increased strength I felt as his life force began to flow into me. The overwhelming smell of all the blood flowing so freely in the room made something stir deep down inside me, growing with each breath and each swallow, until I thought the beast within me would explode through my chest and demand to be set free. No, I can't say I really noticed these feelings at all.

One of the things Emily taught me to appreciate was that magical moment when the spirit leaves the body. Fortunately, for me, I can clearly see it rising up out of the body and floating up a few feet. Sometimes the spirit takes a moment to look around, generally with a puzzled look on its face, but more often than not it simply heads for the light. It always seems similar to my own experience, with the bright light and the ramp and all. I must admit, seeing these spirits head off up the ramp and knowing that they are going someplace better than here, makes taking their lives much, much easier. Hell, maybe they ought to thank me for helping them along.

I felt the last bit of life ebbing out of Richard, and was waiting to watch his soul take that special trip, when he was ripped out of my arms. Virgil gave him a quick shake and growled into his face. Poor Richard's peaceful image of Robert disappeared in the blink of an eye, and the horror of his present surroundings returned to him in full force. Holding the dying man upright with one hand, Virgil thrust his other into Richard's chest and with a lightening fast twist, pulled the poor guy's heart from his body. Holding it up for him to see, Virgil took a huge bite out of it. Of course, Richard's soul left his earthly body seconds afterward, but I knew the last moments of his life were filled with terror.

Virgil unceremoniously dropped the body and, stepping into the middle of the pile of corpses littering the floor, tilted his head back and let out another tremendous roar. He held his arms out, palms skyward, and growled in a way that I can only describe as horrifyingly primal. Then his shoulders lowered and he slowly turned to face me.

"What the fuck were ya doin' there boy? Ya ain't no God damned vampire, that's fer sure. Ya some kinda pussy? When it's time to feed, ya don't screw 'round makin' nicey nice. Ya rip the bastards open and feed."

I'm sure one of my smarter moves that night, was keeping my mouth shut and not saying how disgusting he was. I wanted to kill that ugly bastard with every ounce of my existence, but his recent display of brute strength left no doubt in my mind that I was no match for him. I hung my head and shrugged. "That's the way Emily and Jasmyna taught me," I offered meekly, hoping he'd accept it as an excuse this time.

"Well, they taught ya wrong. What am I gonna do with ya now? Look at yer clothes. Ya got yer dinner all over 'em."

I looked down and, indeed, I was covered in blood. Then again, the whole room looked like it had been sprayed red. Suddenly, the whole naked Virgil scene made total sense. Sure enough, shaking his head, he turned and walked out of the room. Seconds later I heard a shower start up.

I sat for a few minutes looking at the carnage we were responsible for, and wondered if this was really something I could do for, well, forever. I really hadn't spent much time pondering the killing aspect of being a vampire, other than to have become comfortable with the fact that humans were now the primary element on my food pyramid. I didn't mind too much that I was drinking their blood, or the fact that doing so was taking their earthly life from them. But this scene I'd witnessed tonight wasn't something I'd bargained for. Was this what being a vampire was all about?

As a human, I'd enjoyed many a good steak though I'd seldom, if ever, given a thought to the death of the cow. I assumed they were killed in a humane manner, though I can't say I knew for sure. I do know that I never attacked a cow with an insane vengeance, killing it brutally by burying my face in it to feed. Nor had I ever ripped a steer's heart out and eaten it in front of it while it was dying. I decided then and there that Virgil's method of feeding would never work for me.

Virgil reemerged, dressed and free of any traces of blood. He methodically went through the house looking for valuables or cash that would fit in his pockets. One by one, he went through the victims' wallets, removing the cash and chucking the rest back down on the floor. Next, he removed any rings, watches, or other jewelry they were wearing. I realized that this was probably his only means of income, and was sorry I'd accepted the drinks from him earlier. Although I knew these four fine gentlemen had no further need of their earthly money or possessions, stealing it seemed like a rather cheesy final insult.

I rinsed my face, hands, and arms in the kitchen sink and then wiped them on a kitchen towel, which hung neatly on the oven-door handle. I then replaced the towel where it had been and, as a small sign of respect, I made sure it was hung as neatly as when I'd found it. I returned to the sitting room and found Virgil there with a lightweight tan jacket in his hand.

"Here," he said, thrusting the jacket at me. "Put this on fer now. It'll cover the blood until we git ya some where's else."

Numbly, I put the jacket on and headed for the door. I was reaching for the doorknob, when I realized we were leaving behind a hell of a mess. I turned to question Virgil about it, just in time to see him walk into the kitchen. I heard him fussing with the stove, and a moment later, he emerged with a grin on his face.

"Let's git. I done turned on the gas full blast, and lit the kitchen curtains on fire. In a coupla minutes this joint'll blow sky high."

Realizing that the place was now a time bomb ready to explode, I hastened out into the still night air. Virgil was right behind me and, as we hit the street, he grabbed my arm and pulled me toward the left.

"Come on," he urged. "We ain't got much time left 'till the sun comes up. I don't wanna be carryin' ya 'round cuz ya done fell to sleep on me."

I hadn't realized that it had gotten so late, and the thought of falling asleep outside with Virgil didn't thrill me. For a new vampire, it's not like you yawn and get drowsy. One second you're fine and the next you drop off to Lala Land, not to be heard from again until the sun sets the following evening. If I dropped, I was reasonably sure he wouldn't carry me far, perhaps only to the nearest garbage bin. Worried about the rising sun, I hustled along with him, only slowing once when I heard a loud explosion behind us. I glanced back over my shoulder, and saw flames shooting skyward. For some reason I thought of Richard asking me if I was an angel, and a wave of guilt passed over me for having let him down at his special moment. Am I an angel? No, I'm about as far from being an angel as one can get.

Virgil stopped suddenly, and said, "We ain't gonna make it." He looked across the street and, with a nod of his head, indicated his intentions. "Come on now, we'll spend us the daylight hours like real vampires suppose' to."

Seeing where he was indicating, I took a deep breath and let it out slowly. To my utter dismay, we stood across the street from one of New Orleans oldest and creepiest cemeteries. While I can appreciate traditions and all, I'm more the 'Simmons-Beautyrest-with-six-hundred-thread-count-combed-Egyptian-cotton-sheets' type of vampire. Surely, the whole coffin thing was an old wives tale or a Hollywood invention. It sounded neither comfortable nor sanitary. Then again, I'd failed Virgil once tonight and I might not have many screw-ups left. Besides, in the back of my mind, I truly was worried about being caught out in the sun with him.

Without voicing any of the hundred and one arguments knocking around inside my brain, I followed Virgil across the street and through the gate. If you've never seen a New Orleans cemetery up close, you're missing out. They call them "cities of the dead," because all the tombs are built above ground. There are rows and rows of ornate tombs, statues, and mausoleums, and when viewed in totality, they appear like city streets lined with small buildings. He seemed to know where he was going, so I just followed and made sure I didn't lose him. Funny, I'm a vampire, and I was nervous in a cemetery at night. I guess it'd take a while to get used to being one of the bad guys.

We stopped at a rather distressed looking tomb, and Virgil said, "Here ya go, Junior. This here one'll do just fine. Give ol'Virg a hand with the lid, will ya."

With that, he put his enormous hairy paws against the stone covering the top of the tomb and began to push it sideways. Due to our increased strength, the heavy stone slid open easily. In fact, we had to be careful not to push it too far, lest it fall to the ground and break. Hiding in a tomb is bad enough, but hiding in one with no lid would be downright silly. We turned the lid on a slight angle and finally had an opening large enough for me to crawl through.

"Go on, get in" he urged, indicating the narrow gap we'd opened. "I ain't sleepin' with ya. I got me another spot all picked out that I kin get in-n-out of real easy like."

I peered into the opening, and saw nothing but a small pile of ashes. There didn't appear to be any critters or skeletons inside, so I weaseled my way through the narrow opening. It seemed plenty wide inside but could have been a little longer. If I lay at a slight angle, with my right knee bent a bit to the left, and my left knee angled a tad to the right, and my head slightly twisted, and if I didn't need to breath on a regular basis, it'd do just fine. I was just about to ask Virgil if he'd be by the following evening, when the side of beef he had for a hand reached through the opening and grabbed me by the throat.

I was of course shocked by this turn of events and instantly in a dire state of distress. This was most likely a natural reaction to getting my windpipe crushed like a wet paper straw. I grabbed his wrist with both of my hands, but it was like grabbing an iron girder, and it was instantly obvious that my two average hands were not going to be a match for the neck-crusher on the end of his forearm. The cramped space my body was in prevented me from getting any leverage, though I doubt it would have helped my cause if I had an acre of room and a crowbar. He pulled my face close to his, and let out a low hiss.

"Dear God," I prayed, suddenly remembering how natural his swish had been, "please don't let him kiss me with that stinky breath and those crooked teeth!"

As it turned out, I'd have been better off with a stinky kiss. Spittle sprayed from the hellhole located just south of his flaring nostrils. "The last thing we need is another vampire 'round these parts. 'Specially a smart-ass no good loser like you. Jasmyna may have made ya, but I'm a gonna end yer pitiful existence right here-n-now. Good-bye, brother John."

With that, he brandished what appeared to be a kitchen carving knife, probably from the fine set of expensive Wusthof cutlery I'd noticed in Richard and Robert's kitchen. He reached in and proceeded to cut my head off.

Yes, the rotten bastard cut my head off. No, not with one swift cut like you'd expect to get from a certified professional executioner. Oh no, I had to get my head hacked off with a stolen kitchen knife by a moron who never learned to properly handle the utensil. Though he made a mess of severing my head from its home atop my shoulders, at least I could take comfort in knowing the knife was reasonably clean, based on the location from where I'm assuming he stole it. Then again, when you get your melon sawed off, what do a few germs really matter?

Trust me on this little tidbit; there is nothing more painful than having your central nervous system brutally disconnected with a kitchen knife, wielded by a moron with little manual dexterity. Pretty scary stuff too, when you don't die right away. I recall reading an article about rampant executions during the French Revolution, and the preferred method of dishing out punishment was a quick trip to the guillotine.

According to observers, for a few seconds after their beheading, their eyes could be seen blinking and their mouths formed words that never came out. Yech!

I knew I was going to die any moment, and prepared myself for another trip to the great white light. Time suddenly seemed to stand still. I heard Virgil laughing as he slid the lid back into place on what now really would be my tomb. I lay in the darkness, waiting to die, but nothing seemed to be happening. The pain was overwhelming, and I began to fear that I'd spend the rest of eternity like this. What if I couldn't die? That thought became more frightening than dying. Given that option, I really wanted to die, and die soon. I began to realize that I'd very likely go mad if I didn't die soon. I wanted to yell and scream, but it's hard to do when your lungs are no longer connected to your vocal chords. Finally, after what seemed an eternity, the bright white light once again began to appear before me.

Chapter 10

The bright light was definitely back, but this time it didn't seem to emanate the same love and warmth that I'd experienced during my first death. Rather, it seemed to be more like, well, more like just a very bright light. Something else seemed to be missing, and it didn't take long to realize that I didn't feel myself rising up out of my body. Something was very wrong here, and panic started to seep in again. Where was that loving feeling? Why wasn't I floating around peacefully, and where was the damn ramp I was supposed to float up? And the greeting committee, where were they? The least they could have done was send the dog again. Where was good ol' Asta, my ever-faithful dog who'd greeted me last time? The rotten bitch was supposed to be here to greet me with a wagging tail and copious doggie kisses.

"Aw shit," I thought, as a deep layer of dread rolled into my detached heart, "if I'm not headed back to the Other Side, I must be headed somewhere else."

Somehow, I hadn't made the cut this time around and now I was headed to the other "Other Side" which Emily had so deftly avoided telling me about. I had to face the fact that I was now firmly on the "Highway to Hell." Damn, somehow I'd blown it.

Close, but no cigar. Actually, I was on my way back to sunny California. As one might suspect of someone in my slightly diminished physical capacity, I was pretty much out of it. In fact, shortly after I saw the bright light and determined I'd been selected for a quick trip on the down elevator, I decided that a short nap might do me some good.

Emily still claims I fainted and, considering what I'd gone through, passing out would probably be a justifiable reaction. My male vampire pride, which all too often is similar to male human pride, forces me to argue the issue with Emily. I've tried to point out to her that it was time for all new vampires to be sleeping. She counters with the fact that there were actually several hours of darkness left, which I'd have known had I bothered to look at my watch prior to entering the cemetery with Virgil. Therefore, I had to have passed out. She clearly doesn't buy the fact that my watch was on the fritz at the time, or I'd never have followed Virgil into the cemetery. Yes, it does seem to be working now, but I swear there was a problem at the time. On and on the argument goes...

Unfortunately, I'll have to relate what happened after I passed out, er, uh, fell asleep, second hand. I believe it's reasonably accurate, or at least close enough for our purposes. Trust me, my impaired physical state at the time more than justifies any short-term lapse in my journalistic accuracy. Luckily for me, while I was painting the town blood red with Virgil, events outside of my knowledge were rapidly unfolding.

It seems that Virgil's sudden appearance had made Jasmyna and Emily feel a call to Adrian was warranted. Adrian sired Jasmyna, who in turn sired yours truly. In vampire genealogy, that makes him my grandfather. I always wanted one of those. Although I knew nothing about him at the time, he knew all about yours truly. Seems the ladies had been keeping him up to date on my progress without my knowledge. While the possibility of Virgil showing up had always existed, they hadn't anticipated him making an appearance so soon. It seems he was usually very predictable and shouldn't have made his annual trek to New Orleans for several more months.

Hearing Virgil had made an early appearance, Adrian quickly boarded his private jet and headed for New Orleans. While the V-man was stopping by my room, inviting me out for a night on the town, Adrian and his flight crew were somewhere over Texas. By the time he landed, I was well into my thrilling night of bar hopping, blood drinking, and apartment burning with my new best buddy. Emily was assigned the task of tailing us and had seen everything that transpired. She witnessed us hitting the bars, picking up the guys, burning down their house, and later entering the cemetery. Uniquely aware of Virgil's ability to inflict physical damage of the serious variety, she had to wait until he left the cemetery to enter herself. Luckily, it hadn't taken her long to sniff me out. A quick call back to the house with her cell phone brought Adrian and Jasmyna to the rescue. They arrived about ten minutes after I lost my head.

The bright light I saw wasn't the Other Side; it was just a nearby street lamp that my noggin happened to be pointed towards. They carefully slid the top of the tomb open and found me lying there in my nearly decapitated condition. Oddly enough, Virgil hadn't done a very thorough job. He'd cut through about eighty percent of my neck, but hadn't completely cut through my spine. Adrian theorizes that given the limited space and the size of his hands, he couldn't effectively execute a slicing motion. This may have saved my existence or, at the very least, ensured that my head wasn't reattached backwards. Needless to say, even for one with enhanced healing abilities, I was in pretty bad shape.

Adrian's blood was by far the most powerful of the group, so he sliced his forearm and quickly spilled some across my wound. He realigned my head to my shoulders, and had Jasmyna hold it in place while he ran a few loops of duct tape around it. My clothes were quickly removed and left in the tomb. Finally, he cut off a few small chunks of my flesh and left these inside the tomb to cover a casual sniff test by Virgil. Carefully, he carried me to the back of his waiting limo and we were off. The part that still blows me away is the duct tape, which fortunately there'd been a spare roll of in the trunk. The stuff works miracles. Think of the endorsement I could give them!

A quick trip to the airport, where I was carefully carried aboard his jet, and Adrian and I were off to sunny California. The ladies stayed behind to ensure that Virgil didn't suspect I'd been rescued. En route, Adrian performed crude but adequate surgery on my wound, sewing as much back together as possible and leaving the rest up to my natural healing abilities. When he finished, he bound the wound with sterile bandages and placed me in a coffin. The rest was up to me.

I guess I could lie and say that my healing powers are so fantastic that I was able walk off the plane whistling Dixie a few hours later, but I won't. I'm just satisfied that I did eventually recover from what would have easily killed a human. It took several months. Several very long months of pain, frustration, anger, and eventually, healing.

The first week was the worst. Adrian owns a large vineyard and winery in Napa Valley, which is where I was taken from the airport. I was placed in the basement of the estate house, which I was later to learn had been specially constructed to suit Adrian's unique vampire needs. To ensure privacy and total darkness, I was left in the ornate cypress coffin that I'd been placed in aboard the plane. It was quite comfortable, actually, and when the lid was down, I could sleep undisturbed for long periods of time.

The challenge was to find a way to speed up my recovery. For proper healing, it was essential that I regain the ability to drink blood. Receiving it intravenously helped some, and I'd been hooked to an IV almost immediately upon boarding his plane. For some reason, though, IV's just don't work well on vampires. Consuming nutrition orally is far better. Blood is our life force, and a nice big dose of oxygen-enriched blood does wonders for our healing powers. The sooner I could drink, the sooner I'd get better. Until my central nervous system and the various muscles used in the swallowing process reconstructed themselves, my healing was stuck in low gear. Even though I was healing, it was at a snail's pace, at least for a vampire.

Finally, tired of my struggle to breathe, much less feed, Adrian acquired a special plastic tube from a physician friend. He unceremoniously inserted it up my nose, and twisting it back and forth, fed it down into my stomach. Luckily, for me, I was still too far out of it to complain, but I do remember it hurt like hell when he pushed it through my sinus cavity. Once it was satisfactorily in place, Adrian removed a thin stabilizing wire from the inside of the tube, and I was left with a nifty little passageway for funneling blood to my starving belly. I didn't need to swallow, just lie there and absorb as much as I could. A small electrical pump allowed Adrian to administer what he determined were the correct doses, on a schedule he designed. Of course, blood tends to clot, so he had to occasionally cleanse the tube with a blood thinner, Heparin, to ensure this handy little lifeline stayed clear. Even though I couldn't taste the blood thinner, I could always sense this foreign substance entering my belly.

Once I began receiving nutrition in this new manner, the healing process was greatly accelerated. At two weeks, I opened my eyes and felt fully conscious for the first time. I recognized that I was looking at a ceiling, and knew I'd undergone some major ordeal but couldn't piece it all together. Suddenly, the face of a stranger was looking down at me. It was a handsome yet rugged mug, and he looked to be roughly the same age as me. Except for the eyes, that is, which seemed to contain a timeless wisdom, with just a hint of mischief thrown in for good measure. The warmth emitted by this gentleman's smile caused me to relax almost immediately, and I knew without him having spoken a word that I was in good hands.

"Well, hello there, John. Welcome back to the living dead. I'm Adrian, and you're safe here with me." His lips hadn't moved, and I knew he was speaking to me in his silent voice. "You just relax. You've been through quite an ordeal, but you'll be just fine. We'll have you back on the dance floor in no time."

"What...happened...to...me," I stammered back in my silent voice.

He looked at me puzzled for a minute, then smiled. "You will have difficulty speaking out loud for a while, but I think you'll find your "silent voice" as Jasmyna says you like to call it, works just fine. "Let's try it again now."

I quickly realized he was right. I was being overly dramatic, probably a reaction born from watching too many late night movies. "Oh, yeah, I guess you're right. Sorry about that," I replied back to him, minus the stammer. "So, what happened to me?"

"Close your eyes and think back. I'll try to assist you."

I closed my eyes, which wasn't all that easy, and tried to focus. I heard his silent voice telling me to relax and picture New Orleans. Slowly, it began to fall together. With his help, I remembered the bright light, then thinking I was headed to the big plantation down south where they harvest fireballs for fun. I slowly put together an image of Virgil reaching towards me. I was in a hole; no, it was a tomb. I was in a tomb and Virgil was reaching in with a carving knife. Hey, it's one of those nice Wusthof knives like Susan and I had. He probably stole it from the kitchen of...

Suddenly, it all came back in a flash. I had been decapitated. Yet, somehow, I was still alive. I wanted to sit up and scream, but my body didn't respond. Oh God, I had no body. I was just a head!

"Relax," Adrian's calming inner voice came back to me. "Remember that you're a vampire now and many new and different things are possible. Your injury is really nothing at all. In fact, I've had much worse on numerous occasions. This is nothing to be concerned about, hardly a scratch, really."

His smile was very reassuring, and I instantly felt better. I began to wonder just who he was and why he was helping me.

"I hope you don't mind," he said, "but I've placed you in a coffin for now. Don't read anything into it, my boy; it's just that it allows me to control your environment a little easier. Once you're up and around, you're welcome to one of the big fluffy beds upstairs. Personally, I'm a bit of a traditionalist and I still prefer to sleep in a coffin myself. Why, I have dozens of them, all over the world, but there'll be time to discuss all that at a later date. Now we just need to focus on getting you back into shape."

I had no way of knowing that my wound was about as serious as it gets for a vampire, and that he was lying to me to put my mind at ease. I knew so little about being a vampire, and he was so convincing, that I naturally believed him and forced myself to relax. His yammering on about coffins actually seemed quite natural. Like talking about which deodorant you prefer. Oddly enough, I found I didn't mind being in one at all. Perhaps I felt it fitting.

"I suppose it's my fault, really," he apologized, as though my predicament were truly his doing. "I knew Virgil wouldn't take a liking to you, though I had no idea he'd react so violently, or so quickly. Killing another vampire is a very serious matter, which is not taken lightly within our small community. Truthfully, I never would have guessed that Virgil could muster the courage to act so brazenly."

Adrian stared off into the distance and seemed to slip deep into thought, as though trying to resolve a real brain twister. He continued talking, but I wasn't sure whether he was still talking to me or simply vocalizing his thoughts. "Oh, he's a bully, all right, and he can be downright mean when he wants to. A strong fear of the unknown, that which his simple mind's incapable of understanding or comprehending, usually keeps him in line. This is very bold behavior for our dear friend Virgil. Very bold, indeed."

The mention of Virgil's name would normally have sent a chill down my spine but, unfortunately, I didn't have one at the time. Technically, I guess you'd have to say that I did have one, it just wasn't fully connected and working yet. This minor detail wasn't lost on me, bringing into full focus my current inability to protect myself or run like hell. Not being able to control myself, I once again mentally leaned on the alarm button. Before I could self-combust from an out-of-control panic attack, this gentle stranger took note of my rising distress and managed to put me at ease.

"No need to worry about Virgil anymore, my boy. You're absolutely safe here with me. We're in California, now, which is a long ways from the New Orleans cemetery he left you in. Besides, he thinks you're dead, or at least dying a slow death. He never came back to the house and there have been no reported deaths of the type normally associated with Virgil. More than likely he's moved on. Oh, I'm sure that the next time he's in New Orleans he'll go back to the tomb where he left you and sniff around a bit. We left your clothes and several hunks of your flesh in there, as well as the rather large quantity of blood you lost. Even with his crude and limited skills, he should detect the scent of your remains easily enough. The temperature gets so hot in those above ground tombs during the summer months that bodies can actually bake in them. Hopefully, all that'll be left when he comes snooping around will be some ashes, the clothes you were wearing, and enough of a scent to convince him his handy work was successful. I'm confident that'll do the trick, at least until you're back on your feet and able to take care of yourself."

Once again, his words calmed me down, though the "hunks of flesh" thing hadn't gone unnoticed. I wondered just which hunks he was talking about. Maybe I was better off not feeling my body for a while. I wanted to carry on our conversation, but my eyes were growing heavy and my focus was rapidly fading. There was so much I wanted to ask, though, so many answers that I needed. Who was he? Where exactly was I? Where were Emily and Jasmyna? Were they in danger?

"All in good time, my boy," he said, reading my thoughts. "All in good time. Sleep now. That's what the doctor orders. Lots of sleep and nourishment."

His words seemed to push my eyelids closed, and I wasn't up to fighting it. I faded into a deep dreamless sleep, and when I awoke, he was again at my side.

"Ah, back from the dead, are you? Hmmm, probably not the wisest choice of words, given that we're vampires and all," he chuckled, as though embarrassed by his choice of words. This time he was speaking aloud and smiled down at me. He seemed so relaxed and confident that I was immediately put at ease again. Whoever he was, he had a knack for making me feel comfortable. Something in his easy going, yet dignified, manner impressed me. I knew nothing about him, yet I couldn't help but feel that he was someone I wanted to befriend and someone I wanted to impress. No, impress isn't quite right. Rather, he seemed like someone I wanted to be proud of me, like a teacher or mentor, or maybe even a parent.

I tried to smile back at my new best friend, but from his startled reaction I knew something wasn't right. I couldn't control my facial muscles yet, and my heartfelt attempt at a smile came out more like some kind of twisted and contorted goober-face. It got worse when I tried to stop smiling. I felt half of my facial muscles lock up, and the other half go completely slack, as though they'd undergone a sudden attack of Bell's palsy. I was stuck with a twisted goober-face that wouldn't go away. Graciously, Adrian reached into the coffin and massaged my face until the muscles relaxed and I got my normal handsome mug back. I wouldn't try that smiling crap again any time soon. Yep, so far I'd impressed the hell out of this guy. Trying to keep up with a face that seemed to contort and spasm out of control whenever it felt like it was rather exhausting, so once again I drifted off.

The next time I awoke, it was totally dark. I didn't mind, though, because it gave me time to collect my thoughts. I had no idea how long I'd been wherever I was, but I seemed to be safe and in good hands. I felt like crap, but that was to be expected given what I'd been through. I knew I was seriously damaged, but I might just survive if I played my cards right. This guy seemed pretty cool, but I couldn't help but wonder what he was up to and why he was doing all this for me.

The lid on my coffin opened, and I instantly realized why it had seemed so dark. A soft light illuminated the room I was in, and though I couldn't see the whole room around me, judging by the scalloped ceiling and thick crown molding, it seemed to be well appointed. Once again, Adrian's face appeared. Instead of smiling this time, he had a concerned look. Suddenly his face twisted and contorted, and I thought he was having an attack of some kind. Slowly it dawned on me that he was making the same goober-face that I'd accidentally made earlier. The son of a bitch was making fun of me. Given my rather bizarre sense of humor, I found this funny as hell but I couldn't laugh yet. I felt my eyes bulge with the effort and I broke into an involuntary goober-face similar to the last one. I immediately swore an oath that nice guy or not, some form of payback was in Mr. Adrian's future. I was pleased to note that, this time, my face returned to normal when I finally managed to relax. Regardless of my pleasure at this slight progress, I vowed that the aforementioned payback would be hell.

"Ah hah," he exclaimed, "Now we're making progress! " He left for a moment, and from what I could tell by his body motion, he must have pulled up a stool or tall chair. He sat down and was now leaning on the side of my coffin.

"You seem to be making excellent progress, my boy. I've got a nifty little thing called a NG tube hooked up to you now. That's a special tube that allows us to by-pass the whole swallowing process, and to continually feed you from this handy little pouch of blood here. It runs up your nose, does a u-turn in the nasal passage, passes through the throat and proceeds on down to your stomach. Of course, I wish I could get you to actually drink some blood. It'd be good for the throat and neck area. Can you try swallowing?"

I tried, but nothing happened.

"All in good time, my boy. All in good time," he said, patting my shoulder.

He must have sensed my feeling of helplessness, because next he suggested I try blinking. I couldn't really blink, but I could slowly ease my eyes shut and back open again. It was sort of a 'slow-motion' blink, if you will.

"Okay, now we're getting somewhere," he said with such obvious pleasure, that I actually felt a sense of accomplishment. "I know it's difficult not to be able to speak out loud, but just like gas, this too will pass. In no time, you'll be talking up a storm. For now, let's see if we can develop an alternative form of communication. Blink once for yes, and twice for no. Can you do that?"

I slowly blinked twice.

He laughed and, shaking his head, he said, "The ladies warned me you're a real wise guy. I think you'll find I'm up to the challenge, however. For now, you'd better be on your best behavior, or I'll wake you each evening with that hideously contorted face thing you call a smile.

He couldn't leave well enough alone. Oh no, the rat had to start making grotesquely contorted faces at me, all of which managed to contain some semblance of a smile.

I tried with all my might and even closed my eyes, but the image of how stupid my face must have looked when it had contorted so violently popped back into my mind. I couldn't keep my face from contorting again. Damn, this guy was good. Of course, not letting an opportunity pass, he immediately made the same face back at me when I reopened my eyes for a peek. Which, of course, in turn made my face twist even harder. He was killing me. God, what I wouldn't have given for a good belly laugh at that moment.

I celebrated my three-week anniversary with Adrian by swallowing a tiny bit of blood he placed in my mouth with a dropper. It wasn't easy, but he'd promised that once I could swallow, he'd remove the tube from my nose. I'd grown to hate the damn thing so much that this promise provided a real incentive. True to his word, he gave it one long pull, nearly gagging me, and out it came. He made a quick slice in his forearm and holding me upright, instructed me to drink. It wasn't pretty, but I managed several more swallows. His blood was so powerful, that it nearly inebriated me.

Within days, I began to regain the feeling in my fingers and toes. It started with what felt like little electric jolts. They became more and more intense, until my extremities felt like they were on fire. The delicate network of nerves interwoven throughout my body was beginning to reattach and come back to life. Even though it hurt like hell at times, this was a pain I could live with. It felt good just to feel something again. I still couldn't talk, but I could grunt with the best of 'em.

Chapter 11

In celebration of my tremendous progress after a month with Adrian, I got to go outside. He helped me into a wheelchair and rolled me out onto the pool deck behind his house. It was the first time I'd been out in the night air in what seemed like forever, and the moment was so special to me that I actually felt myself tearing up. I held my face up to that big beautiful full moon, closed my eyes, and basked in its warmth. Actually, it was pretty damn cold outside, but on that night, it didn't matter. As far as John Steele was concerned, it was one of life's perfect moments. I was alive, or as alive as a vampire can be, and for the first time I knew I was going to make it.

By the end of the second month, I was going on nightly jogs and lifting weights. Nothing too impressive to be sure, but I felt it was a significant accomplishment. Adrian began to train me in the martial arts, more for the flexibility it provided than for its usual combatant purposes. It provided discipline and physical exercise, and I loved every minute of it. When I'd shower, I'd look at the quickly fading scar around my neck in amazement. Somehow, I'd survived having my head chopped almost completely off. Unbelievable. Absolutely unbelievable.

During those first two months, and the months that followed, I grew to love Adrian like I've never loved another being. No, we didn't become lovers in the physical sense. I don't think that's possible with me, and I sure never got any indication from Adrian that he wanted our relationship to head in that direction, thank goodness. Perhaps it was my near miss with Victor Ramsey when I was a kid, but while I've never been homophobic in the least, I have no tendencies in that direction myself. Like most men, I have no problem with two females goin' at it, which really is no different, I guess. Hell, when I look at the male body, it's so...gross and...hairy that I wonder why females even bother with us. They must have tougher stomachs. I guess it's just my wiring, but it takes a woman to trip my trigger.

Adrian and I were more like father and son, best friends, and blood brothers all rolled up into one. Of course, he'd carefully explained that he was the maker of my maker, but the lack of a significant age difference in our physical appearance kept me from really feeling like he was my grandfather. I needed him, but strangely enough, he also needed me. By nature, he was a teacher, and teachers need students. I made sure that I was a darn good student.

I asked a million questions, and he provided a million answers. He taught me how to maximize my potential as a vampire and to appreciate the many gifts vampires have. He taught me about our weaknesses and how to avoid many of the pitfalls that lay in our path. In that all too short period of learning, he even taught me to read, write, and speak Spanish reasonably well. Most importantly, he taught me to have fun again.

Adrian is an extraordinary being, and his existence, if for no other reason than its length, is fascinating. It seems he's been everywhere and done everything. Of course, he says he's just scratched the surface, which is one of the reasons I admire him so much. He's pretty amazing for a guy who's almost six hundred years old.

Adrian taught me that the life of a vampire is getting more and more difficult, thanks to, of all things, technology. We have to feed to live, and it's easiest to live amongst the herd, so to speak. To live in today's society, it's nearly impossible to remain totally anonymous. You have to have an identity to purchase property, acquire credit cards, rent a car, or stay in a decent hotel. You can't maintain the same identity forever, because the people you associate with begin to wonder why they look like old farts and you still look like you're in your thirties. Keeping up with all this was becoming more and more difficult for many vampires. Instead of inhabiting cities in the developed nations, they were heading to remote areas of South America, Africa, and even the Australian outback. There, life was much simpler, and far fewer questions were asked.

We decided I could maintain my current identity for at least ten more years. As a precaution, I would immediately start the process of creating several new ones, though. (Secretly, I vowed that any new identity I created would have a very cool name.) If I kept my current identity after the next ten years, I'd have to stay away from most of the people I knew. Once I was ready to move on, I'd simply pass away and take up life under a new identity. It sounds simple, and I know thousands of people do it every year to escape paying taxes or alimony, but its actually very detailed work if you want to do it right. We have a lot at stake (no pun intended), and getting caught isn't an option. For a

---

vampire to exist as openly as Adrian, controlling a few good law firms comes in handy too.

Bless his heart, Adrian offered to bankroll me for a while. He's a very wealthy man, and he explained to me the importance of money to a vampire. With enough money, you can buy privacy. I thanked him but explained that I was relatively well off as a human. I saw no reason I couldn't regain access to my own funds. It was this conversation that sparked me into going back out in public.

As a last bit of recognition for Adrian's true genius, I should note that he made great progress teaching me to stay awake during the daylight hours. Undoubtedly, this is the greatest hurdle for new vampires. The only way I can describe it is to compare it to narcolepsy. One minute you're wide-awake, and the next you're out cold. It's as if someone had flipped a switch. I'd grown to hate this fact of my existence more than any other, and I didn't want to wait decades to overcome it.

Knowing my irritation at needing to sleep while the sun was up, Adrian developed an ingenious method for overcoming this need based on his many years of observing our kind. Instead of having me fight to stay awake as the sun rose each morning, Adrian had me fall asleep as I was naturally inclined to do. However, instead of allowing me to sleep through an entire day, he woke me five to ten minutes earlier each day. Eventually, I was waking up an hour after I'd fallen asleep and could take short naps when I felt like it. It was when I hit this point that I realized I wasn't just conking out anymore. Instead, I felt myself getting sleepy and could fight off falling asleep for ten to fifteen minutes. Then, an hour or so after I did fall asleep, I could wake myself up. This made me quite happy, and I felt much less vulnerable. According to Adrian, he still feels the pull to sleep as the sun rises, so I'm guessing it's something I'll never totally shake.

My diet still consisted of whole human blood and occasionally a little of Adrian's powerful vampire blood. I didn't really need his blood anymore, and though he claimed it was to help speed up the healing process, I figured it was more of a gift to increase my core strength. Adrian has an unlimited supply of blood readily available, so I was well fortified on the human blood front. One of his many ventures includes a medical research facility, which as you could probably guess, studies human blood diseases. Blood donors gladly line up either to help the research cause or to collect the few dollars offered for their contribution.

Adrian, being a significantly more developed vampire than I, will occasionally enjoy a dinner fit for human royalty. He said that while he doesn't particularly enjoy it, being able to eat human food has its advantages. His weakness though, is wine. He has a cellar full of his own "special" wine, carefully mixed with blood in his private laboratory, and he savors it on a regular basis. In fact, he can consume several bottles in a day, and it never seems to have any intoxicating effect on him. However, I have noticed a glint in his eye, and a small smile cross his lips, when he's consumed a particularly palatable vintage.

When it's out of the human body, blood is a difficult thing to keep around for long periods of time. Freezing it is one possibility, but Adrian has found a way of extending its life span at room temperature by mixing it with wine. I'm not sure how this works chemically, and he hasn't volunteered the information. I do know he owns multiple vineyards, even as far away as Australia and South America, and I'm guessing his research goes on in those locations too. It dawned on me one day that Adrian could survive for years, as long as he had an ample supply of his special wine. Adrian's a pretty smart vampire. I, on the other hand, am a pretty stupid vampire; I tried a sip of his special wine and immediately puked it up, along with my liver, my lungs, and my left testicle.

My first experience venturing out on my own was totally awesome. Like, totally. I killed three southern California valley girls and sucked them like totally dry, you know? Unfortunately, now I'm like totally stuck talking like them, you know? It must be like in their blood or something, you know? Okay, I'm like totally bullshitting you, but I'm like an asshole sometimes, you know? In truth, I'm just now realizing that my first solo flight wasn't exactly the stuff adventure movies are made from and maybe it could benefit from a little embellishment here or there. I'm sure a BS story about doing battle against three naked valley girls with satanic nipple rings and cleft tongues who wanted to kung-fu me to death would be cooler; but hey, it's my story, so I'll stick to the facts, boring as they may be.

Okay, so we've established that nothing really spectacular happened my first time venturing out, but for the first time in what seemed like forever, I was free. Anyone who's been away from mingling with the general public for a long time will understand how this in itself can be exciting. A criminal who's been in jail, a sailor returning from a long cruise, or an inexperienced vampire who managed to lose his head in New Orleans, could all appreciate how good it can feel to be free to do as you please. From a mental perspective, the experience of being on my own, even if only for a few hours, was truly exhilarating.

Chapter 12

Goal numero uno, as established by Adrian and I, was really quite simple. I just needed to be able to be John Steele again. Confused? Well, as I mentioned earlier, I wanted to reclaim my money and my property. To do so, I needed to be able to pass myself off as that ultra-stud, formerly known across the free world as John Steele. Yes, I needed to work at being me again.

The physical changes in my appearance were not so drastic that I couldn't simply claim to be living a good healthy life. I looked several years younger than I had when I disappeared, but humans are always pulling off that trick thanks to health spas, cosmetic surgery, and Botox. No, the hardest part was not to act differently. Somehow I needed to acquire the ability to be your basic, average, somewhat boring guy, who nobody pays any special attention to. Okay, I guess in my case I needed to "re-acquire" that ability.

I learned a handy lesson from Adrian. It's natural for certain "special" humans to draw attention to themselves. It's in the way they move and the way they carry themselves. They're so self-assured that people are automatically drawn to them. Look at movie stars, musicians, and professional athletes for example. Many strut into room and all eyes are upon them. Well, I'm also somewhat special now and when it comes to dealing with humans, it'd be easy to get overly self-confident. The difference is, I don't want to draw attention to myself. I need to be able to move around freely and preferably to have nobody pay the least bit of attention to me. It's difficult when you're this charming, but possible with practice. Adrian assured me I shouldn't worry too much about acquiring this skill, and he promised I'd be able to master it in no time. I think he was having some fun at my expense.

When the time was right, I borrowed a Mercedes from Adrian and drove to Santa Rosa for my first big night out on my own. Parking in the handicapped vampires only section of a public lot, I got out and walked a few blocks, soaking up the smells and atmosphere. Spying an establishment designed for humans who'd survived on Earth a minimum of twenty-one years to consume certain fermented beverages, I went in. I'd been drawn to the loud music and soon realized it was a country and western bar. Yee-ha! I'd never been a big fan of country or western, but tonight it didn't matter. I sat at the bar, pretending to sip a beer and chatted with some fairly interesting urban cowboys and cowgirls. I had a good time mingling even though I didn't eat anybody, and I was proud of the fact that I hadn't drawn too much attention to my bad self.

I ventured back outside and strolled down the street a few blocks, enjoying the crisp night air. Once again, the beat of some overly loud music got my attention; this time it was coming from what appeared to be a Latino bar. I saw this as an excellent opportunity to try out the Spanish that Adrian had been teaching me. Turns out, I'm not as good at Spanish as I'd hoped, although I'd be a whole lot better if everybody in there would have just slowed the heck down. There's absolutely no reason to talk so darn fast.

I noticed an interesting thing, which I doubt I'd have noticed in my pre-vampire days, especially since I probably wouldn't have gone to either establishment as a human. The décor of the two bars was similar, the music was slightly different but equally loud and, as deduced from my keen observational powers, the most common brew they both served seemed to be beer. Oddly enough, the Cowboys seemed to enjoy a substantial amount of imported Mexican beer, usually with a slice of lime. My new Latino friends seemed to prefer a popular U. S. Domestic brew. Sexual tension ran equally high at both places. So why two separate bars?

I'm sure you're wondering where I'm going with this, so I'll get to the point. Although I used to be one of you, I find that now I can't help but wonder why humans have all the stupid racial, sexual, political, and religious disagreements. Who cares? You're all humans, and to us, you're all food! Band together. Be brothers. Save yourselves from yourselves. Perhaps if I was hungry I'd offer different advice, but my God, I never realized how stupid your "important" issues really are.

I know, I should stop here, but I'm on a roll. Why does there have to be a white bar, a black bar, a straight bar, or a gay bar? You're all so much more alike than different, yet you focus on the differences. Trust me, you all taste pretty much the same. Like chicken. Just kidding. It's more like turkey. Yes, I'm kidding again.

I guess I'm an equal opportunity feeder these days, since I don't really care whom I feed on now. Old, young, male, female, gay, straight, or bisexual, all of you get an equal opportunity to be my dinner. Hell, I don't care if you're into shaved squirrels and mayonnaise for your kicks.

You all like to think you're so different, but to us vampires you're just food. Color does matter though. Black, white, yellow, brown or red; all of these are fine with my palate. Green is not good though. It means you're either a Martian or you're a rotting corpse.

I think what the human race needs is a good common enemy. Remember the old *War of the Worlds* movie? Maybe if aliens attack Earth, you'll realize you need each other and band together for the common good of all humanity. Oddly enough, a creature that is alien to most of you has been attacking at will for years, and you've done nothing about it. They're known as vampires. Comprende? Okay, sermon over.

As I said, my first night out was nothing to get too excited about, but it'll always be special to me. Remember the first time you got to drive all by yourself after getting your license? It was kind of like that. At Adrian's request, I hadn't "dined out." Blood was plentiful at his place, but then again, there's nothing like milk fresh from the cow, so to speak. Still, there was always the body to deal with, and I was far from an expert on hunting yet. No use in making a mess of things this close to Adrian's home. My experience over the last several months had taught me patience, and I could wait until I was properly trained to dine out. Besides, I have all the time in the world now, right?

My second big adventure was far more exciting and did entail some good ol' vampire blood sucking and slurping. Adrian and I headed into San Francisco for a few days of fun, and to do some shopping. So I could sleep when necessary, we took the presidential suite at a plush hotel on the Embarcadero. Adrian could survive for days at a time without sleep, but I still needed my beauty rest. While I slumbered, he read or futzed with his ever-present laptop. The man, I mean vampire, consumes more books and information in a week than I did in my entire human life. Anyway, any discomfort I felt about sleeping in a new place was put to rest knowing he was watching over me.

Dressed quite sharply in black trousers, shirt, and coat, I ventured out with Adrian to take advantage of a local vampire club. Of course, we were the only real vampires in the joint, and had any of the patrons known the truth about us, they'd have stayed as far away as possible. Adrian explained that these places have become popular again in many major cities and provide an excellent place to feed. A bunch of silly humans go to extreme lengths to become "vampires" for a night. Some of these idiots actually file their teeth until they're sharp little points. Others rely on sharply pointed caps that provide the necessary look, avoiding the permanent damage to their teeth. Either way, they're silly. Vampires do not have fangs. Our teeth are extremely hard and sharp enough to bite through human skin like it's softened butter, but we don't have fangs. Our saliva contains a chemical that numbs the general area we bite and stops the flow of blood as soon as we quit drinking. This is far more useful than a pair of fangs that would make you a dead giveaway every time you opened your mouth and undoubtedly make you talk with a serious lisp.

Adrian explained that many vampires like to visit a victim multiple times. They drink from an area not generally visible to the victim, like under a shoulder blade, then stop short of draining the donor. The wound closes up, leaving only a small mark and no pain. I realized that this had probably happened to me during my initial encounter with Emily and Jasmyna. Although they hadn't bothered to hide the wounds they were making, I had felt no pain in the area. When Emily and Jasmyna had stopped drinking, I had stopped bleeding. Of course, since some of us can press visions and ideas into the minds of humans, I suppose we could leave someone with the impression that we have huge fangs. I can think of a few better impressions to leave than large fangs. Just call me...Big John!

The club we visited on our first evening was called The Coffin Club. It occupied the second floor of an old warehouse and was designed to be dark and spooky. I got a kick out of all these folks pretending to be vampires, and it was obvious that Adrian did too as he pointed out a few of the over-the-top nutcases. He explained to me that these types of clubs had existed in various forms for hundreds of years. Bram Stoker had popularized the concept of vampires when he wrote Dracula in the late 1800's, but prior to that there were plenty of wannabe witches, demons and other dark creatures of the night. Adrian theorized that it all boiled down to sex, which is usually the driving force with humans, especially human males. Most religions teach that sex is bad, unless it's being used to produce children. These various dark creatures are also bad from a religious standpoint. Therefore, if you become some evil creature, even if it is just an evening of role-playing, having wild and crazy sex is now normal since the two go hand in hand. Become a monster for a night, and you can fulfill your wildest sexual fantasies. Ever wondered why nobody pretends to be an angel? There's not much fun in that, unless you have a thing for harps, that is.

He also explained that there were typically two types of role players in a vampire club. Blood drinkers and blood donors. Why someone would want to be food for another is beyond me, but who am I to complain about a free meal? With the abundance of blood related diseases floating around, there's no way I'd have participated in something like this when I was human. I was afraid to sit on a public toilet seat, much less swap blood with someone I didn't know. But once again, why complain now?

The place was designed for maximum privacy. There was a small dance floor, and a few black clad figures were swaying to an old Black Sabbath tune I'm happy to say I recognized. The majority of the space was filled with high-backed booths, many of which could almost be called private rooms, except for the narrow opening for guests and wait staff to pass through. We picked a booth that provided plenty of privacy but a decent view of the main floor and ordered Bloody Marks. They were a twist on Bloody Marys, and came highly recommended by our waif-like waitress. While we waited for our drinks, Adrian and I scanned the room. We listened in on bits of conversation and generally got a feel for the crowd. He indicated a character across the room that was short but fairly buffed. Wearing black leather pants, and a tight sleeveless black T-shirt, he seemed to be engaged in wooing two similarly clad women, both of whom were taller and heavier than him.

"He's a policeman," Adrian said calmly.

I didn't panic, but he had my attention. "Should we leave?" I asked.

"No. There's no need. He's here looking for illegal drugs. He thinks all this vampire stuff is a bunch of crap. He's right."

I smiled. "Yes, he is. So how did you know? I'm sure he didn't announce it to those two lovely ladies he's with."

"I probed his mind. Try it, John. Focus on him until you can pick his voice out of the crowd. Then ride his voice back into his mind. It's similar to placing a thought in his head, only this time you're just listening."

I'd done this to a degree while feeding, but had never tried it long distance, so to speak. I focused on the cop for several minutes, first picking his voice up, and then trying to follow a path back into his thoughts. It was difficult, since I didn't know what to expect. Suddenly, I had a very clear image of him humping one of the fat girls. It wasn't my idea, so it must have been his. I focused harder and realized I was in. He wanted to hook up with either of these women, but he was afraid of what his buddies back at the station would think. They'd teased him about being with "large" women before, and he didn't want a repeat offense. He was undercover, and while acting out a come-on with them to get information was acceptable, he knew he'd better draw a line before it went too far. Yep, he'd never hear the end of it back at the station. He'd already asked them if they wanted to get high, but they wanted to stick with alcohol. No crime there. Better to break off the conversation and move on. Perhaps he could risk getting a phone number. If he saw them off duty, maybe nobody would know.

Pleased with this newfound skill, I said to Adrian, "It's almost unfair. We're like gods among mortals. We're faster and stronger, we can hear, smell, and see better. Now I find out we that not only can put images into their minds, but we can read them too. We are invincible!"

He didn't smile, but slowly turned to face me. "I can't believe I just heard that from such an invincible super hero, that he managed to get his head chopped off a few months ago. A super hero whom I've also noticed still falls asleep at the crack of dawn and is utterly defenseless during that minor of part of the day when, oh, the sun happens to be shining! No, John, I'd hardly call you invincible. I'm much stronger and more experienced than you, and I don't consider myself invincible. Just lucky."

Properly put in my place, I bowed my head. "Yes, master. I have been stupid yet again and failed to snatch the pebble from your hand. Can you ever forgive me, oh wise one?"

Adrian lightened up and chuckled. "The point is a serious one, John. We live in a human world. No matter what, we live in their world, not them in ours. We do have a few advantages, but don't underestimate mankind. There are many who know about us and have made hunting us down their life's work. More than a few vampires have met their match in a human."

Shocked, I asked, "There are humans who hunt us down? I've never heard that before. I thought our existence was a secret."

Adrian smiled and casually replied, "You've been kept in the dark about a good many things, my boy. You'll be brought up to speed when the time is right, and that time is soon. It was more important that I get you healed physically than to burden you with a bunch of other crap."

"Other crap? There are people out there hunting for me and you call it 'crap'? Adrian, I need to know these things!"

Still calm, he replied, "Don't make too big of a thing out of it. You're so new that they probably don't even know of your existence. Let's plan on keeping it that way. If you don't draw attention to yourself, it could be years, even decades, before they know about you. In the mean time, you'll have developed other identities and safe havens, and you'll know better how to defend yourself. But enough of this talk, we're here to have fun."

I was shook up but respected him enough to drop the subject, at least for the time being anyway. For a brief moment I'd felt like the hunted instead of the hunter, and I didn't like it. I didn't like it one bit.

"Ah, here comes some fun now!" exclaimed Adrian.

As if on command, a young lady approached our booth. Adrian stood up and silently offered her a spot on the bench. She looked at it for a moment, her eyes glassy and vacant, then sat down.

"So, what are you two dudes doin' tonight?" she asked.

She looked to be in her early twenties, at best, and had a round face with fairly nondescript features. Her hair was an odd mixture of purple, blonde, and black streaks, and I'd bet none of them were her original color. Her complexion was ruddy, and across her cheeks she had a trail of acne scars. As witnessed through her blackened lips, orthodontia had either not been a family priority or wasn't within their budget. She wore the required black ensemble, and though her breasts weren't large, her tank top exposed them to their best advantage.

Doing a terrific impression of Count Dracula, Adrian arched his eyebrows and said, "We have just come from our crypts, and 'the hunger' is upon us. As we emerged to the brilliance of a beautiful moonlit night, we heard the baying cry of our wolf brothers summoning us to this fine establishment. Their melodious voices were carried to us on a warm southerly wind and told of beautiful women filled with the nectar of life that we need so desperately."

Looking her up and down hungrily, he added, "I see that the children of the night did not lie on this evening, for your beauty is certainly something to behold." With that, he took her hand in his and kissed it slowly.

I couldn't resist smiling as it was obvious he was having fun playing vampire.

"Now, my child," he continued, "We're a couple of very powerful vampires, but we're in need of sustenance. We need to feed, and we need to do it soon. By chance, you wouldn't know anyone who would be willing to help a couple of nice blood-suckers like us would you?"

She looked around the room suspiciously, and once satisfied nobody was showing interest, she exposed her crooked teeth with a grin and said, "Yea, I might be able to help you two old freaks out. It's gonna cost you though. Fifty bucks each for two minutes on my arm. I make the cut. Anywhere else, the price goes up."

I wanted to burst out laughing. She was a blood whore. The little bitch was selling her blood! Part of me wanted to rip her neck open and drain her, and part of me wanted to stand up and applaud her. A blood whore! I never would have guessed.

Adrian made a one hundred-dollar bill appear out of nowhere and leaned close to her. "Okay, sweetie, here's the deal. My friend and I will each take an arm. We make our own cuts though. They won't be deep, in fact they'll be smaller than the cuts you'd make with that little razor blade you've got tucked away."

She hesitated for a moment, but the sight of that crisp hundred-dollar bill was too much. "They better not be deep cuts," she warned. Figuring us as easy marks, she added, "For another fifty, I'll pull my top down."

Adrian magically made another hundred-dollar bill appear out of nowhere. "With breasts as beautiful as yours, I'd say they're worth fifty dollars a piece."

That bought us another big crooked-tooth grin, "Slide together, boys."

She came around the table, and doing a little magic trick of her own, made her top drop. We slid a little closer together, and she straddled our laps. She placed a hand behind each of our heads and brought them to her breasts. I may be naive, but I think she'd done this before. Feeling both a tad silly and naughty at the same time, I gave her breast what I thought was a respectable amount of attention, then turned to look at Adrian. He smiled and nodded, and simultaneously we bit into her arms just inside of the biceps. The warm rich taste of her blood flowed into me and I yearned to drink deeply, until the ache in my belly was satisfied.

Before I could do any real damage, Adrian stopped me. He gently pulled my head back, and with a smile more commonly found on the mug of a very satisfied fat cat, he cautioned in his silent voice, "We don't want to kill her. We just want to taste. Don't worry, before the night is through, your belly will be full."

He took her puffy face in his hands and looked directly into her eyes. She was totally under his control. "What's your name sweetheart?"

"Sheila."

"Okay, Sheila, you've been a very good girl. Now I want you to walk around the club and find all the other girls who like to either sell or give their blood. Find them all, Sheila. The girls that charge, and the girls that just like to be fed upon. Tell them that there are two really cool guys over here and that we have lots of money. Send the girls our way Sheila, but do it quietly. Do you understand me?"

Unblinking, she responded in the vacant voice of one deeply hypnotized, "Yes, I understand. Bring the other girls to you. Please, drink more of my blood. It feels...so good when you drink my blood."

"We'll drink more of your blood if you're a good girl and do as I say, Sheila. Now its time to get properly dressed again and go find us more girls."

With that, Sheila slowly pulled her top back up and left. I turned to Adrian. "Isn't this a bit risky, getting rid of all these girls?"

He shrugged. "Yes, I suppose it's a tad risky, but it's a great way to sample lots of blood in a short period of time. Since we're doing it in a public place, I suppose there's a higher element of danger involved, but not so much that we can't afford to have a little fun. I have to admit that I find it fun to pay for it. We can and do take blood from our victims at will. I've been doing it for centuries. Ah, but paying for it, that's different. I suppose that's why so many humans go to prostitutes. There's that certain little element of risk and, of course, there's the unknown component. The thrill of doing something different, with someone different, can be intoxicating."

Adrian looked off into the distance; from the smile on his face, I could tell he was reliving a juicy memory. I let him have his moment, wishing I had a few more juicy moments to reflect on. I'd never had the balls to visit a prostitute when I was traveling around in the Navy, and the closest I came to cheating on Susan was whacking off in the shower when I knew she wouldn't catch me. I'm pathetic. No, I *was* pathetic. I have to remember, I have a second chance now.

He refocused on the present and suddenly gave me a scowl. "Get rid of all these girls? Why on earth would we do that? Where'd you ever get that idea? I once kept a housemaid that I fed off of for forty years. It was mutually enjoyable. She had a crippled leg, but thoroughly enjoyed sex. I simply treated her like the woman she was, and she provided me with a steady supply of blood. If we kill these girls, we'll set off exactly the kind of incident we need to avoid."

I was a bit embarrassed. The thought of not finishing off a victim was foreign to me. Emily and Jasmyna had led me to believe that while a victim could be strung along over multiple feedings, once bitten, all victims were doomed. It was our responsibility to ease them across life's finish line, so to speak. I didn't want to admit this major blunder, so I changed the subject. "You made love to a crippled woman for forty years?"

Adrian slowly shook his head, obviously on to my misdirection ploy, but not wanting to admonish me now. "Yes, for forty years. Well, we took a few breaks now and then," he said, raising his eyebrows up and down for effect.

He continued seriously, "Yes, I did, and she was wonderful. Would have made a great wife for someone, but it was the early eighteenth century and she was considered an outcast. No man in his right mind would have her, since there was a possibility that his children would come out crippled too. I accepted her for what she was, and she accepted me for what I was. We were quite happy together and I've never had my house as clean since I might add."

"Wait a minute. She consciously knew you are a vampire?"

"Oh, heavens yes. It was her leg that was bad, not her brain. She had me figured out right away. She'd been in my employ for less than a week when she asked for a few minutes of my time. Laid it all out, nice and simple like. If I'd make her feel like a woman, she'd do my bidding. Talking about her really makes me miss her. When she died, I lost a great friend and lover. I was tempted to allow her to make The Choice, but out of respect for her, I let her go. Besides, she was at the end of her life and she deserved to cross over quietly. We generally make it a policy not to try to turn anyone who's at the very end of his or her human life. Virgil was an exception, and you see how that turned out."

This revelation was interesting, but our second course had arrived. I tucked it away and enjoyed the banquet. We dined seven times through the course of the evening and, true to his word, my belly was full. Nobody was dead, and the only damage was the fact that seven young ladies would forever be fuzzy about what had happened that evening. They'd likely just chalk it up to having had too much alcohol to drink, again.

I napped a bit the next day but was ready to hit the town shortly after noon. We did what all good vampires do while in San Francisco. We took advantage of the shopping. Adrian took me to his tailor, who measured me for several snappy new ensembles. He also recorded these measurements for future use. Now all I have to do is ring him up on the telephone or log on to his web site, and I can order all the custom made shirts, pants, and coats I'll ever need. I've decided this is a cool way to buy clothes and that Adrian lives very well.

That night, we hit two more clubs, and just like the first night, I left with a very full belly. Though I'd lived in the Bay Area for many years, I never knew how much fun San Francisco can be. It has long been known for its fine dining establishments, though, so I guess I shouldn't be too surprised!

Chapter 13

Back in Napa, sitting with Adrian on the patio next to the pool, waiting for the sun to show its ugly face, I broached the subject of his crippled maid again. "Did you love her, or did you just mean that it was a real convenient thing?"

He looked at me for a long time, then asked one of his impossible rhetorical questions, "Ah, love. What is love?"

I knew better than to respond. He was all primed and loaded for one of his prolonged assaults on the various philosophical angles that could be applied to such a simple question, thus turning it into an unanswerable riddle I'd need to solve over the next millennium.

He sighed and looked up at the slowly brightening sky. Likely taking into account my propensity for falling asleep at dawn, he answered more directly than I'd anticipated. "I suppose I loved her, as much as a vampire can love a human. We're all unique individuals, John. Even vampires. Most vampires see humans only as food. I know I did for many years. Now, I don't know. I guess I feel for humans. I mean, as with all vampires, I was human once, a long, long time ago." He looked at the now fading stars overhead, but I could tell his mind was miles and years away.

My mind was buzzing, and I couldn't contain myself any longer. "I'm confused about so much, Adrian. Humans for instance. Should I be ripping them to shreds, like Virgil? Should I be doing it under some false pretense, such as 'helping them cross over,' like Emily and Jasmyna? On the other hand, should I be like you, who come to think of it, I've never seen actually kill a human. In all these months, you've always had an ample supply of blood, but you never seem to feed in an animalistic way. Now I find out you had a forty-year relationship with a human."

Adrian smiled at me. "There are some things you'll just have to figure out for yourself, John. I don't think the Virgil mold fits you very well, although it's perfectly within your right to kill brutally and as often as you wish. It's our nature to kill and feed off humans, so how can it be wrong? As for Jasmyna and Emily, well, since they only kill dying humans, they may have gone too far in the opposite direction from Virgil. Are they too civil? Who's to say, but they would probably starve before killing a healthy human. As for me, I do believe that's my business."

"So butt out, huh? Nice and subtle, Adrian. Why don't you tell me how you really feel?"

He just smiled back, letting me know it was a closed subject. I'd caught all he said, but was confused at the part about Jasmyna and Emily and thought I'd pursue that angle. "What do you mean Emily and Jasmyna only kill dying people? They fed on me, and I was as healthy as a horse."

Adrian shrugged, and obviously didn't want to continue down this path of conversation either. He suggested I take it up with them. I hadn't talked to the ladies since my beheading as a security precaution. Not that I'd admit it to anyone, but I still dreamt of Emily. Often. It couldn't be love, since I'd pretty much convinced myself that us cold-blooded killing machines weren't capable of love. Now I was more confused than ever.

"Can I communicate with Emily and Jasmyna yet?" I asked.

"Of course. I think they'd love to hear from you. They've been very concerned, but I've kept them up to speed on the major events in your recovery."

"How do I contact them?" I asked, still not sure it was good idea.

"Oh, John," he said, sounding a bit exasperated and shaking his head. "I know you've mastered this skill. Think back."

I thought through the many lessons he'd taught me, but came up empty. "I can't remember," I finally said, giving up. "My silent voice only works in close proximity."

He shook his head again, sighed heavily, and handed me his cell phone. "It doesn't always have to be complex or difficult. They're listed in the speed dial menu."

I chuckled. He'd gotten me for the millionth time. "Smart-ass," I muttered under my breath.

"I heard that. Be kind to your elders, Junior."

I handed the cell phone back. "I'll call them later. I think I'll head in for a quick nap. I feel the pull of the sun already. I am tired, and I've got a lot to process."

I tried to act like everything was normal, but my head was spinning. Surely he was wrong. The ladies killed just as indiscriminately as Virgil, they just made the experience easier on their victims. While I genuinely liked the ladies, especially Emily, I'd always accepted that they were a force to be reckoned with. Although they appeared to be just a little bit loony tunes at times, at least in my humble opinion, they could kill with the best of 'em.

He smiled, "Take your time, John. There's no rush. I'll see you later." With that, he ambled off to check on the vineyard, the rising sun seeming to have no effect on him whatsoever. Lucky schmuck.

Chapter 14

I'm not sure why I was hesitant to call Emily and Jasmyna, but when I finally felt comfortable enough to dial them up, I was a nervous wreck. My mouth went dry when I heard Emily's soft and sexy voice answer their phone. I immediately decided to take the safe route and act like my normal smart-assed self. "Hey, Emily, I thought I'd call and let you tell me how much you miss me."

"Hello, John. How are you?" she said, after a moment's hesitation.

I immediately sensed a coolness that didn't require enhanced vampire skills. A bit flustered at this, I tried the light-hearted approach. "I'm fine. Kind of lost my head for a while there, but my gracious host has me all patched back together. I'm a few inches shorter, but what the heck. So, how's Jasmyna?"

"Why?"

"Why? What do you mean, why?"

"Why do you want to know about Jasmyna, John?"

"What kind of question is that? What the hell's going on Emily? Did I do something wrong that I don't know about?"

"No, John, you've done nothing wrong. I just wondered why you wanted to know about Jasmyna?" Her voice sounded almost mechanical and was devoid of even the slightest hint of emotion.

This was all beyond bizarre until an inkling of an idea began to form in the back of my brain. As absurd as it seemed, I realized it might be the most likely reason for this frigid reception. I pleaded with her, "Please tell me you two haven't been sitting out there building on that silly notion of Jasmyna's that I'm going to turn on you like Virgil."

Silence.

"Damn it, Emily, what do I have to do to prove myself to you?" I was getting more worked up than I should have, and I knew it was because I wasn't getting the warm response from Emily that I'd hoped for. Warm, hell. I wanted Emily to be as hot for me as I was for her.

"Time will tell, John, and the one thing we all have is lots of time. Is that right, John?" She had that far off, detached sound in her voice again.

Now I was past the irritation phase and was pretty much flat out pissed off. Not having a clue what I could say to get through to her, I began to spit out whatever came to mind, "I don't know shit about how much time we've got, Emily. I do know that I had strong feelings for you and it's quite obvious they are not mutual. For six months I've gone to sleep each morning thinking about you and wishing I could fall asleep with my arms around you, exhausted from a night of passionate lovemaking. Now, after all this time and after all I've been through, I get this damn cold shoulder treatment. You know what Emily? I've got your time hangin'. I really don't give a damn about you anymore."

More silence. I let out a heavy sigh and continued far less passionately, "Emily, my childish side would like to hang up on you right now, but I've got an important question I'd like you to answer honestly."

"What is it, John?" Her voice still sounded distant, but there was a bit of a tremor that hadn't been present before.

"Adrian seems to be under the impression that you and Jasmyna only take victims that are already dying. If that's accurate, then why'd you take me? I was healthier than I'd ever been in my life, or at least in the last twenty years. Why me, Emily?"

Now it was her turn to sigh. "I'd always planned to tell you this, John, but the time just never presented itself. Then Virgil came, and well, you know the rest."

"Tell me what?"

"Heart disease. John, your heart was in pretty bad shape. In fact, your arteries were almost completely clogged."

Shocked, I asked, "No way, you mean to tell me I was sick enough to actually die?"

"Oh yes, John, you were dying. If not, I'd have never paid any attention to you when you entered my store. I took one look at you, recognized what a dear sweet man you are, and I knew I wanted to make your passing peaceful and blissful."

"So, that's it then," I said, dazed at this piece of information. "You took pity on me because I had heart problems."

"Uh, John? Actually, there's more. I want to be totally honest with you, so I need to tell you everything."

I was confused. How could there be more? I'd been dying for God's sake. "What else can there be," I queried?

"You were also HIV positive. I don't believe you'd have lived long enough for the HIV to turn into AIDS, but I'm sure it wasn't helping matters. Your heart problems were too severe. You were a massive stroke waiting to happen. Jasmyna and I have developed a keen sense for knowing when people are ailing, and you reeked of eminent death when you walked into my store. There are plenty of diseases I can't pinpoint, but the big ones like cancer, heart disease, and HIV are easy."

"That's bullshit!" I spat, knowing she was lying now. A heart problem I could deal with, but there was no way I was HIV positive. "I wasn't homosexual, and I never had any blood transfusions or operations. Hell, I hadn't even been to a doctor's office in years. There's no way I had frickin' AIDS."

"I'm sorry, John, but it's true," Emily said softly. She paused a few seconds, then continued, "Nobody knows your sexual preferences better than me, John, but I swear you had it. No, you weren't on your deathbed from the HIV, and you might have lasted for many more years if not for the heart complications. Nevertheless, you had it, John, and if your heart had held out, it would have worn you down until something, maybe a simple virus, killed you. Think back, were there any signs or symptoms you can remember? I know it must be hard, John, since all humans want to think they'll live forever. I know I did."

I wanted to cuss and scream at her, but something held me back. Flashes of reality were coming into my head. I'd been under the weather a lot those last few months, though I'd chalked it up to grief over my ruined marriage. It seemed I was constantly fighting a flu bug, and when the weakness went away, I had some severe headaches and a nasty rash I could never explain. In addition, there was the weight loss, which had come far too easy. It was killing me to admit it, but inside I knew she was right. In my grief, I'd ignored the symptoms.

"Oh, God," I said, feeling numb all over. "I hate to admit it, but you could be right. But how...?" The question hung in mid-air for a moment as the answer hit me like a tidal wave.

"Susan?" I asked numbly.

"That would be my guess, John. You told me how you caught her cheating on you. I'm afraid she probably contracted the disease and passed it on to you. I'm sorry you had to find out this way."

"So, I was just another dead man walking, and you were just there doing what comes naturally," I surmised.

The implications were sinking in quickly. I started talking aloud as I was thinking, "I would have died in the next few months, or years, or whatever. Either I'd have had a stroke, or the HIV would have gotten me?"

"More than likely the stroke, John. Your arteries were in bad shape. Do you remember that we fed off your shoulders instead of your neck?

It's natural for us to feed where the blood flows the easiest. Your neck arteries were too blocked for us to bother trying to feed off of them."

Ignoring her comments for the moment, I continued talking as I reasoned it out in my head. "That means that per the blueprint of my life, I had almost accomplished everything I'd set out to do. If I'd have known that, I might not have felt like such a failure when it came to making The Choice. When confronted with the decision of staying on the other side or returning as a vampire, I might have chosen differently if I'd known I was only a short time from dying anyway. Damn, I was overwhelmed with such a sense of failure when I stood before the Supreme Being, that I felt I needed more time to accomplish what I'd come to Earth for."

"You were never supposed to have been in the position you were in, John. Biting Jasmyna like you did was just such a fluke thing. The rest of us made The Choice mid-life, so we knew we had a long way to go when making our decision. As I'm sure Adrian's told you, someone who's close to death would never be considered as a candidate for becoming one of us, for the very reasons we're discussing." A short silence, then what sounded like an admission of guilt from her, "You're right, John. If we hadn't done our thing to you, you'd probably be living happily on the other side now, or you would be in the very near future."

Now it was my turn to be silent for a moment. Finally, I started, "Emily..."

"Yes, John?"

"Were you there when I made The Choice?"

"No, of course not. You know that's a private thing between you and the Supreme Being. We simply carried out a small part of the ritual, which was more for tradition's sake than anything else. I saw your spirit leave, then come back. I think I've told you before, I was surprised you actually came back."

"Okay, then let me clue you in on something. I made my decision. Not you, and not Jasmyna, certainly not Virgil or anyone else. I made the decision to come back. Me. John Steele. Got it? Good. If not, get it, and get it soon. Last question. How tough is the skin on Jasmyna's neck?"

"What do you mean?"

"I've thought about this a lot. Our skin appears normal, but it's tough as hell compared to a human's skin. How did I manage to bite through her skin deep enough to draw even a single drop of blood, much less a quantity significant enough to strengthen me the way it did, especially in the condition I was in? Think about it, I could hardly even move my head."

It was her turn to be silent again. "You know, I've never really thought about that, John. Of course her skin is normal for a vampire. Smooth, but tough. She could use a bit more moisturizer, but she never listens to me. I'd think it would be extremely difficult for a human to pierce it as easily as you seemed to that day. Of course, you were obviously motivated to survive, but what are you getting at, John?"

"Divine intervention, Emily. Yes indeed, divine intervention. I think that exactly what was supposed to happen...happened. I was supposed to be given The Choice. Don't ask me why, because I don't know. At least not yet that is. Maybe I never will. I don't want to get into a lot of philosophical bullshit right now, but I think it's safe to say that my being here had less to do with you and Jasmyna than you've been giving yourselves credit for. You were simply a means to an end. Hey, the Supreme Being and I, we were just using you!"

For the first time, Emily sounded upbeat, "Do you really think so, John? So, then you're really not upset with us?"

"Argh, girl, woman, old lady, whatever the hell you are. For the last time, I'm not upset with you two. Well, actually I am sort of pissed off, but not for the reasons you think. I'm pissed that you're treating me like an unwanted third tit. I'm pissed that you're always suspicious of me. I mean, I can understand you being wary of me at first due to the whole Virgil ordeal and all, but I'm not him."

"I think about you every day, too, John."

It popped out of her so quickly I wasn't sure I'd heard her correctly. She'd just done an unexpected one-eighty on me and I needed clarification that my ears weren't deceiving me. "I'm sorry, what did you just say?"

"Oh, John, I hope what you've said is all true. I miss you terribly, and the thought that you might be unhappy with us, enough so to make us your enemies, well, it's been tearing me up inside."

Hallelujah! Now she was singing my tune. She did have feelings for me after all and the possibility that there was hot vampire sex in my future had just increased significantly.

"Oh," I said, "I'm sorry, I thought you said something about wearing out your vibrator thinking about how much you miss riding the ol' John Steele love train! "

A third voice spoke up, which I immediately recognized as Jasmyna's, "Well, I suppose you two youngsters have a lot to talk about, so I'll say goodbye for now. Oh, and by the way Emily dear, I *do not* need a moisturizer. Goodbye!" Click.

I was speechless. The old broad had been listening in on our whole conversation. Damn her. I was so embarrassed for a moment that I actually blushed.

Emily chuckled. "I think that means she's okay with you now, John. She's known how I feel about you since the beginning and has been working hard to get you out of my system. She was afraid I'd be hurt. Emotionally hurt."

I wanted to be angry with Jasmyna for working against me, but I was far too happy hearing that Emily had similar feelings for me. In fact, I was happier than I'd been in a very long time.

Chuckling, I said, "That was a pretty dirty trick she just played on us, or should I say on me? Tell her I'll let her slide this time, but next time she wants to hear some phone sex, she'll need to make an appointment and pay my usual fee."

Emily laughed so loud that it startled me. She normally had a rather dry sense of humor, and I'd learned that a chuckle from her equated to a hearty belly laugh from most people. I knew it was more of an exclamation of her happiness, than a response to my weak attempt at humor. "You're still the same, John. All you think about is sex. That's what I like about you."

"You bring out the best in me, Emily, or should I say the worst? I need to go now, but I have one favor to ask."

"For you, anything."

"Next time we get together, I want you to wear those black boots again. They really must have turned me on, because I think about you in them all the time."

"Why you horribly perverted man, you. I was thinking you'd want me in virginal white, and instead you want me in my black leather boots. Well, what you want is what you get, so I'll dig them out and polish them up for you, my love."

Chapter 15

Adrian and I sat across from each other, elbows propped up on the glass top of a black wrought iron table next to his swimming pool. We watched, and waited. Slowly the suns first rays began to rise in the East. I felt the familiar weight on my eyelids, but now, with considerable focus and effort on my part, I was able to fight it. He watched me closely, and began to ask me difficult questions, rapidly changing between Spanish and English. It wasn't good enough for him that I didn't fall asleep; I needed to be able to remain sharp.

Adrian: "You have emergency funds in several places. Name three."

Me: "I put a hundred grand in a vault in the Von Schilling Mausoleum at Mountain View Cemetery. I buried another hundred grand in a waterproof container near Rock City on top of Mount Diablo, and I put an additional hundred grand under the brick floor in the cellar of a home I purchased in Bodega Bay and am having renovated to be a beach rental."

Adrian: "What's my cell phone number?"

Me: "(707) 555-1959."

Adrian: "Now backwards."

Me: "Damn. Let's see, 9591-555 (707)."

Adrian: "Who succeeded Harry Truman as president of the United States, and in what year did he take office?"

Me: "Who cares? Okay, that would be President Dwight David Eisenhower. Elected in 1952, but of course he wasn't sworn in until January '53, if you were trying to trick me. He was re-elected for second term in '56, and turned the reins over to J. F. K. in January 1961"

Adrian: "What's the capital of Venezuela?"

Me: "Caracas."

Adrian: "Who's 'The Man'?"

Me: "I am. Oops, I mean you are."

"Well," he said approvingly, "You were pretty good up until that last one. Not too shabby."

"Come on, Adrian, you've got to admit, your method worked. The sun's fully up and I'm wide...ZZZZZzzzzz," I dropped my head to the table and feigned sleeping.

"Ah ha," he exclaimed, playing along with my silliness!

I popped my head up, and pretending confusion, said, "Where am I? Where'd all the dancing girls go? Waiter, two more Bloody Marys over here!"

"Bloody Mary, my ass. More like Bloody John Steele is what I'm worried about. I know, you've passed every test I've cooked up for you, but I'm still not comfortable that you're ready to venture out on your own."

I had a major case of cabin fever, even though I was free to come and go as I pleased. Adrian had been a most gracious host for over a year now, but I had the itch to be on my own. Although I knew he enjoyed my company, and I had yet to wear out my welcome, I needed to do this for me.

"I'll be back, Adrian," I promised. "I just want to spread my wings a bit. You've told me the importance of establishing multiple identities and safe havens. I need to start that process."

He grunted but gave in. "Okay, you win. Tonight I'll have a nice going away dinner for us. There are still a few things I haven't told you, but I don't expect they'll change your mind. Now, get some rest, John, you may need it." With that, he stood up.

I stood up, too, the excitement of having finally graduated his training flowing through me. I turned to go to my room, but he called after me.

"John?"

"Sir?"

"I'm proud of you. It seems impossible that only a little over a year ago, we carried you in here with your head hanging on by a thread. Not only have you transformed yourself into a remarkable physical specimen, even by vampire standards, but also you've maintained a sense of humor throughout what I know was a painful ordeal. You've attacked every lesson I've offered with vigor and determination. In a short time, you've gained the tools to become a powerful vampire in your own right. I wish you well."

I was stunned at his unbridled display of pride and affection. He was a reasonably warm individual, but he typically handled these types of emotional things the same way I did, with a smart-ass comment, or nothing at all.

"I love you too, Adrian," I said, and turned back towards my room, quickly walking away. No use turning it into a big hug fest or something.

Chapter 16

That evening we dined on several excellent varieties of blood. Adrian, as was his custom, drank his wine and blood mixture, and had even opened a special bottle for the occasion. I'll trust his word that it was exquisite. He seemed relaxed and in no hurry to impart any last minute tidbits to me, so I too relaxed and enjoyed his company.

Holding his large wine glass of dark red nourishment up to the light and giving it a swirl, he said poetically, "Ah, the sweet red elixir of life, where would we be without it?"

I couldn't resist a smile. Where would we be, indeed? Not many people would give us a second thought if we survived off of some other liquid, say root beer or creme soda. Nope, vampires and blood go hand in hand. Or neck in mouth? Oh hell, you get the point.

Finally, over coffee, the only human beverage I could hold down in very limited quantities, he began to talk seriously. "I told you once that we have something in common."

"Yes," I said. "I assumed you meant our bloodline?"

"Yes, of course. We have that, too, but there's something else. To my knowledge, you and I are the only vampires who actually took vampire blood, and thereby forced our way into being given The Choice."

"No kidding? So, tell me about it."

"We haven't time to go into my life history, now, but I would like to share it with you someday. As an added enticement to get you back here in the near future, I'll give you one small appetizer. My story involves none other than that infamous historical character, Vlad Dracula."

I sat up straight. "No way. I thought he was just a figment of Bram Stoker's imagination? He was a real vampire? This is unbelievable."

"Don't jump to conclusions, John. I said my story involves Prince Dracula. That's all I'll say for now. You'll just have to come back to hear the rest. What I want to share now is of greater importance. As I may have mentioned, I lived in Europe for several centuries, and in fact didn't visit the United States for the first time until the early 1700's. At the time, it was still a collection of colonies, and independence wouldn't come until later in the century. I fought in the Revolutionary War, and in fact held the rank of Colonel. Those were good years, contributing to a cause I believed in and drinking English blood by the barrel full. After the war, it was decades before I wanted to dine on English blood again."

"In the early 1800's, I gave in to a sense of homesickness and returned to Europe. I taught at various universities in Austria and what's now Germany, and even authored a couple of pretty decent textbooks, which saw limited use for a number of years. To do so now would seem reckless for one of our kind, but you must remember this was before the age of electronic communications, computers, and the Internet."

"I returned to the States in the mid 1800's and assumed the persona of a young European gentleman attempting to establish himself abroad. I'd acquired a significant amount of property during my first visit and took advantage of this on my second trip. After a decade or so, I once again found myself confronted with a war. Since most of my holdings were in the South, you can guess where I ended up! We Southerners lost, of course, but I swear I gained twenty pounds feeding on Yankees. Wars are a great way for a vampire to fatten up. Remember that."

"Anyway, I'm telling you all this to set the framework for what I was doing during this period. What I really want to talk about is the period when I was back in Europe. As I said, I was teaching in Germany, Hamburg to be exact. I stumbled across a group, a kind of secret society if you will, that's grown very powerful over the years. Now, they seem to be very powerful indeed, John. Unfortunately, they think of anyone else with power as one of their enemies. To them, the more power you have, the bigger the threat you represent."

Intrigued, I urged him to continue.

"Have you heard of the Knights Templar?" He asked.

Once again embarrassed by my lack of historical knowledge, I confessed, "Yes, I've heard of them, but I don't know much about them. As I recall, they fought in the Crusades, right? They were kind of mythical or secretive, and now people use them as the bad guys in books and movies. Oh, and Simon Templar from the television series, *The Saint*, took his last name from the Templars, right?"

He smiled, but it wasn't an amused smile. "You'd be smart to learn everything you can about their history, John. Your survival could depend on it."

"But aren't they one of those groups that have lodges all over the world, now?" I asked. "Basically they run social clubs for old men to drink at, from what I've heard."

"No, they don't have public lodges set up, but one of their closely associated organizations does. You're thinking about the Masons, who have hundreds of Masonic Lodges set up across the states and around the world."

Adrian closed his eyes for a moment, and from experience I knew that he was ready to go on a long roll. He began, "The Templars were indeed formed during the Crusades, and from the humblest of beginnings became a grand organization. In fact, it became the most powerful organization in all of Europe during the Crusades. The only organization whose power rivaled theirs was The Catholic Church. They were the first organization to establish international banks, and they held huge amounts of property all over the world. Most European kingdoms of the period were in debt to them in some way or another."

I nodded to show I was tracking with him.

"As with any large and successful organization," he continued, "outsiders became jealous and began to take shots at them. Even though they were always a secretive organization as far as their rituals went, they found it necessary to go completely underground around 1314. Their Grand Master, Jacques de Molay, was executed and that was pretty much the end of the Knights Templar."

"Wait a minute," I queried. "You mean to tell me they were this huge organization, with all this money and power, and they just disappeared because this De Molay guy was executed? That doesn't seem possible, unless he was the glue that held absolutely everything together."

"Ah, you're catching on," he said, obviously pleased with me. "After a well orchestrated, though totally fabricated abolishment of the Order, most of their members miraculously resurfaced with the Masons or the Rosicrucians. The Masons played a key role in most of the political activities that took place throughout the western world for several centuries, including the establishment of the United States. You may not realize it, but George Washington, Patrick Henry, Nathan Hale, John Paul Jones, Benjamin Franklin, Paul Revere, Alexander Hamilton, and many of the other founding fathers were all Masons. The list goes on and on, and several times has included yours truly, of course."

I was feeling a bit overwhelmed at this point but urged him to continue. "I feel like I should know all this Adrian, and it kind of pisses me off that I don't. I guess I have some research to do, huh?"

"Yes, you do need to educate yourself on many things," he continued. "Don't beat yourself up, though, you're just the product of a public school system and a society where most people care little about things that don't impact their daily lives, and that's always worked in these types of secret organizations' favor. Once again, I've gotten off track though. The Mason's impact on history is pretty well documented, and I'd suggest you educate yourself on it as soon as possible. I have some excellent books I'll loan you, but you may find it valuable to actually join them at some point to get a look under the hood, so to speak. You'll learn a lot, but keep in mind that the average Mason is a pretty good guy, as far as humans go. In general, they are not the problem.

"Of concern to us though, is a special organization that I believe was formed out of the original Knights Templar group when they disbanded back in the fourteenth century. Their focus seems to be on religious phenomena and artifacts of any consequence. Of course, it includes all religions and belief systems throughout history, not just those related to Christianity. So, be it witches, magic, the suspected powers of certain artifacts, or whatever, they're all of interest to this group and are worth pursuing."

I nodded again, but this time in a much more exaggerated fashion. Combined with the "Ah yes, but of course" look on my face, I hoped he'd believe I was totally tracking with his purpose for telling me all this stuff. The biggest problem with being an only student is that you always get called on.

"Well," he continued, obviously satisfied with my performance, "inevitably they found out about us. Their overall goal has always been a quest for power, and to them we represent a significant form of power. If they can't control a power, they typically want to eliminate it. How much they know about us, nobody knows for sure. Most of our kind chooses to ignore them, likening them to an irritating gnat on a hot summer day. As for myself, being a cautious individual by nature, I have investigated them on and off through the years and have found them to be a most formidable opponent."

"How so?"

"Well, for one thing, I believe they've worked hard to identify and track as many of us as possible. I know they've managed to kill a few unsuspecting vampires over the years, but they've learned from experience that most altercations end badly for them. They launched a failed attack against an old friend of mine, and we determined that a statement needed to be made. We tracked down and killed not only the attackers, but also every single living relative of theirs that we could find. Obviously, this scared the organization badly, since they haven't attempted an outright attack now in over a hundred years."

"Additionally, they've developed some limited psychic abilities. How limited I don't know for sure, but it allows them to put up a reasonably effective mental barrier to our mind control powers. Our abilities really aren't much different than a powerful form of hypnosis. Watch any hypnotist perform and you'll find that some people are easily hypnotized, but others have a very difficult time being hypnotized."

"Now that you mention it," I interjected, "I did see a stage hypnotist perform once at the county fair. I wasn't sure if it was all a put on or not, but it was highly entertaining. As I recall, some of the people in the audience actually ended up hypnotized, while some of the volunteers who'd gone up on the stage never went under."

"Exactly my point," Adrian exclaimed, clapping his hands together. There was no stopping him now. "Why this is, I'm not really sure. Books on the subject suggest that some people are just more susceptible than others, but I'd venture to guess that their minds are simply too active at the time to allow them to go into a hypnotic state. Therefore, taking this guess a step further, I believe our Templar friends developed a method of forcing a thought into their minds, and repeating it over and over again. This repeated thought requires such a conscious effort, there's almost no way for our thoughts to enter theirs and have any impact. At least that's my current theory, and until proven false, I'm sticking to it."

I acknowledged his attempt at humor with a smile, but urged him to continue.

"Anyway," he said, complying, " I personally experienced this a few years ago. I was in Toronto and sensed I was being watched. I circled back around my tracker, and cornered him easily enough. I thought I'd put a scare into him, and maybe let him take a confusing story back to his superiors. Plant a little 'disinformation', if you will. When I tried to implant an image in his mind, however, he was able to successfully block it. Somehow, he sensed my presence, and immediately began forcing a thought through his mind over and over again. It wasn't anything fancy, and if I hadn't been on my way to dine with a certain beautiful young woman, I might have spent more time trying to break down his defenses. As I said, though, the basis of this defense mechanism seemed to be the relatively simply act of forcing a specific thought through his mind over and over again. Simple, but effective."

I was fascinated now that we were past the history lesson, especially since this could actually apply to me someday. "What thought was he repeating?"

"Let's just say that he wasn't a very civil chap. His dialogue was like something straight out of a cheap horror flick. To the best of my recollection, he said, 'Back, you servant of the devil, I command you in the name of the one and only true God.' If he hadn't been so serious, I'd have laughed in his face. There were several important facts revealed to me in the words he chose to repeat, however."

"Such as?" I prompted.

"Well, for starters he thought we are from Satan. That suggests that he, and by extension his organization, couldn't know too much about our true origin. Also, he seemed to think I'd shirk away at the mention of God, or at least obey him because he'd invoked His name. I'm surprised he didn't try to throw holy water on me or hold up a cross. Finally, he kept repeating the same line, over and over again. He was extremely scared, but to his credit he kept his wits about him enough to focus on repeating his mantra. That's why I think it was a practiced response."

"This is very interesting, Adrian. What was the final outcome of this meeting?"

"Well, since I couldn't exert my mental powers on him, I resorted to my physical superiority."

"Ah ha, you ripped his throat open and sucked the life out of him," I cried, warming to the task.

"Oh heavens no, John. There was no call for that kind of cruelty, especially since we were in a public place. Besides, I wanted to study this individual more at a later date and that would have been difficult to do if I'd mangled him in the manner you suggest. No, I simply vanished into thin air. Poof! I disappeared."

"Poof? You disappeared? Okay, Adrian," I restated his response, my enthusiasm slightly squelched for the moment. "Well, I guess that really showed him who he was messing with, huh Adrian? Poof, you're a freakin' magician! Bet he'd be on the lookout for your disappearing coin trick next time!"

He rolled his eyes in a manner that expressed total exasperation. He'd perfected this look over many centuries, though he'd only had an opportunity to use it on a daily basis since he'd met me. He continued, "Yes, I temporarily disappeared, but I followed him on and off for several days. Finally, he returned to what I assume was his home base, in Salt Lake City, Utah. At least he kept an apartment and an automobile there."

"Damn, now we're getting some place," I exclaimed, while pounding my fist on the table. My original fire had been stoked back to life. "So, it's those dirty Mormons is it? I should have known they were up to no good. Peddling around neighborhoods in their white shirts and ties, looking all clean-cut and innocent while knocking on doors and pretending to look for converts. I'll bet it's all an elaborate scheme to secretly search every domicile in the country to see if vampires live there. My God, this is huge, Adrian!"

He held up both hands to indicate that either I needed to slow down or he wanted to play patty cake. "Once again, my boy, don't jump to conclusions. I never made any connection whatsoever to the Mormon Church. In fact, I now believe that the group he was part of was located there to investigate the Mormons, too. Investigating me was likely just a side trip for him. Remember, they're interested in anything that has to do with religion and/or power, and certainly the Mormon Church has continued to grow and gain power over the last century."

For the hundredth time, I'd discovered it was best to keep my yap shut around Adrian. I decided that even if he threw me a question with a fifty-fifty chance next time, I wasn't biting.

"I did make contact with him," Adrian continued, a smile growing on his face. "After I'd played a few childish pranks on him, that is."

Curiosity was killing me, but I wasn't going to ask. Whatever I said would be wrong, so why bother.

"Well, aren't you curious about what I did to him?" he asked, a mischievous twinkle in his eyes. "Care to make a few guesses?"

I responded with an extra heavy sigh, which was intended to indicate I wasn't responding seriously, "Let's see, you pooped in a brown bag and put it on his doorstep. Then you lit it on fire, rang the doorbell, and ran away. He opened the door, saw the fire, and began to stomp on your bag of vampire poop. You jumped out from behind a bush, gave him the finger, and then did your cool vanishing trick again."

Adrian looked at me like I was the bag of vampire poop. Calmly stroking his chin between his thumb and index finger, while raising one eyebrow to complete the puzzled look on his face, he said very slowly, "No, not exactly. While that's an interesting idea you have there, John, I'm afraid that's not it."

"Okay, I give up. How 'bout you tell me what you did to him," I said. Damn, I wished I'd never mentioned the burning bag of poop trick. Now if I do it to him, he'll have a pretty good idea it's me. I'd better wait a decade or two and hope he forgets.

Adrian shrugged, and I could tell he was pleased with himself. "Oh, at first I had a little harmless fun with the chap, just to get him feeling like his life was out of control. I suppose the worst thing was canceling all of his credit cards, since they're so hard to replace. Or maybe it was placing drugs in his car and tipping off the local police. Let me tell you, that one really had him up in arms and confused. The silliest prank was when I mixed a diarrhea-inducing drug into some of the food in his apartment. I guess that was a pretty shitty thing to do, huh?"

So, Adrian wasn't above playing poopy tricks after all. I'd better keep an eye on this guy and what he was feeding me. "You're an animal, Adrian. So what happened next?" I asked.

"Oh, after a week or so of these silly pranks, which had him wondering what the hell was going on with his life, I made a point of sitting behind him in church one evening. It was the last place he expected to run into me. I'd decided to play along with their games, and I put on a theatrical performance worthy of an Oscar, I must say."

"Best actress in a church killing?" I queried.

Ignoring me, he continued, " I sat behind him for a while and eavesdropped on his thoughts. As I recall, he didn't like the Minister and thought he was a blowhard. Oh, he also thought a particular female choir member with dark brown hair would be an animal in the sack. I agreed on both accounts, by the way. Anyway, I'd found out enough from his thoughts to know this guy wasn't a religious zealot and was in fact capable of rational thought. So, I decided to try popping into his consciousness by using my silent voice. Sure enough, he was one of those rare humans who can hear us. I began whispering to him before he could begin to put up his defenses. Being so close physically, I could be extra forceful to the point where it must have seemed as though I were right inside of his head with him. I told him that my father, Satan, had his eye on him, and wanted him to become one of his followers. His judgment day was upon him and since he'd been personally chosen for our team, he was doomed to an eternity in hell regardless of what he tried to do. I promised I'd return in the very near future to take his soul. Needless to say, I think I scared the poor boy nearly to death. I noticed a rather strong urine odor shortly thereafter."

"Adrian, you never cease to amaze me," I chuckled. "It sounds like an absolutely excellent adventure."

"Ah, but let me finish the tale. The next day, I went by the poor lad's apartment with the intention of picking his brain for information. To my surprise, he'd been murdered. I believe his organization did it out of fear that he'd become one of us and would turn on them."

I quit smiling. "That's some pretty serious stuff, Adrian."

He nodded. "Indeed it is, and you'd be well served to keep it in mind. I've prepared a dossier on this group and I'll send it with you. It has everything that I've discovered over the years."

"Thank you, I'll study it at the first available opportunity."

"Unfortunately, there's another organization that also I need to warn you about. My gut tells me they're in cahoots with the first. I just haven't found the link yet. This second group is actually within the United States government, though, John."

Somehow, this didn't surprise me.

"Even though I personally thought vampires were a myth until I became one, I'm not at all surprised to hear that the government has been looking into our existence. Then again, maybe I've seen too many reruns of *The X-Files*," I said. "The issue I'm always thinking about is all the missing people that have piled up over the years. Surely not every vampire is as tidy as you and the ladies seem to be. Some of the bodies have to turn up sometime."

Adrian nodded. "I believe they often find what some of our sloppier brothers and sisters leave behind, but cover it up for fear of panicking the general public. No government wants a full-scale vampire scare on their hands. That happened centuries ago, and people everywhere were digging up graves to make sure their dead relatives and friends were actually dead. God, what a mess that was, and talk about a stench..."

He put a hand on my shoulder and looked so intently at me that I almost felt nervous. "I suppose some local law officials might go out on a limb occasionally and chalk one of our victims up to a vampire wanna-be, but that'd be about as far as they got. At the federal level, it's a different story, John. I'm absolutely positive there are some true believers there, since they spend a significant amount of money researching us."

"So, now we know that the U. S. Government also knows about us, and at the very least attempts to track us. Be leery of them, John. Nobody has your best interest at heart, except yourself. You represent unlimited power, and human nature is to either control it or eliminate it. I've also included information on this group, though it's more limited."

Adrian had just dumped a lot on me. I'd thought our actual existence was much more of a secret, though that was probably just a remnant of my own personal human naïveté. I'd have to be more careful than I thought, and now many of Adrian's concerns seemed warranted. I was still determined to head out on my own, though.

I looked down for a moment as I carefully planned my words, then it was my turn to look at him intently. I said, "Thanks to you, I understand the risks out there much better now, Adrian, but I still need to go. Please trust that you've prepared me well. I just need some experience under my belt and I think I'll make a first rate vampire who hangs around for a long, long time. Thank you for sharing all this with me, and I promise I'll be back soon. Besides, I can't wait to hear that Dracula story!"

He smiled. "Yes, I know. I've come to the realization that the time is right for you to spread your wings a bit. Go on and see the world and all it has to offer. Experience it like you never could before. See Emily. Hold her close, and let your emotions for her flow freely. Take all the time you need, John, but you must promise to come back to me someday. You'll be sorely missed."

We hugged, and I headed out to the black Corvette convertible he'd bought me as a going away present. In my entire human life, I'd never owned anything other than a four-door family sedan. I'd owned some nice ones to be sure, but never anything sporty or cutting edge. This was his reminder to me that it was a new day, and I was a new creature. I was a vampire, now, and I had the whole world in front of me.

The top was down and as I climbed in and turned over the powerful engine. I felt my spirits surge along with its throaty roar. I put the car in gear and aimed it towards my destiny. Settling back with the wind in my hair, I reached up and turned on the radio to a local rock station. Bob Seger's *"Night Moves"* was playing, and it seemed so appropriate that I cranked the volume. I was planning a few 'night moves' of my own. Looking up at that big beautiful full moon, I got swept up in the moment and couldn't constrain my emotions any longer. I tilted my head back and howled like the wild beast I am.

Chapter 17

My first stop was Vintage Oaks. It's an upscale, gated community, nestled among some new vineyards at the edge of the foothills east of Pleasanton, California. I'm not sure where it got its name, since there were at best four oak trees worth taking note of in the vicinity. Then again, based on some of the folks that reside there, a misleading name seemed appropriate. I should confess that I'm somewhat familiar with the place, given that I lived there for the last ten years of my human life. I had a little unfinished business with Susan, my HIV infected whore of an ex-wife. I'm sure a psychiatrist would say that I needed closure. I'd be inclined to agree with them, as long as the definition of closure includes plenty of suffering on Susan's part.

I pulled up to the gate and stopped. I didn't recognize the guard, who seemed more interested in my car than me, and casually leaned out to greet me. It was 2:00 a.m., but he was used to guests in nice cars coming through the gate at all hours. He never got a word out. No, I didn't kill him. I simply planted a thought in his brain. He politely waved me through the gate and would never remember having seen me.

I pulled into the familiar driveway and stopped a few feet from the garage door. The house looked dark, but my keen hearing picked up the sound of a television. I'd intended to make a grand entrance through the front door, but changed my mind and quietly went around to the back of the house. The sound was coming from my old study, so I walked up to the window and looked in through an opening in the blinds.

Susan sat on my brown leather couch, a drink in her hand, staring at the television. I didn't need any special gifts to tell that her mind was elsewhere. I tried the handle on one of the French doors and wasn't surprised to find it unlocked. I silently slipped in and was standing behind her before she knew there was anybody else in the room.

"Hello, Susan," I said, trying to keep the bitterness out of my voice.

She dropped the glass in her hand, and sprang up off of the couch. Her eyes were wide as saucers, and she was too shocked to speak at first. I guess I got my grand entrance after all.

"John? Oh my god, it's you. Thank heaven, it's really you!"

To be perfectly honest, I'd come back to kill Susan and that asshole, Dr. Kevin. I didn't know what type of vampire I was going to be yet, a nice one like Adrian or a monster like Virgil. Nobody would begrudge me this one extravagance though. After all, I was now a killing machine, and they were food. I was going to scare the living hell out of them, ala Virgil, then slowly suck them dry. Now though, I looked into her face, and into her heart, and almost felt sympathy for her. The disease was doing my job far better than I ever could. She was dying a slow and painful death.

"How are you, Susan? It's been a long time."

She ran to me and buried her head in my chest, sobbing. "Oh John, I've missed you so much. Where have you been? I was so worried about you."

This was not the reception I'd expected. I forced myself to put my arms around her and pat her bony back. To this point, I'd used none of my newly developed talents on her. "How about a cup of coffee for an old friend?" I asked, thinking of nothing better to say and anxious to be out of her arms.

"Yes. Yes, please come into the kitchen. We have so much to talk about," she said, while quickly tying to straighten up the tangled mess of a mop that was her hair.

I picked up the glass she'd dropped and followed her into my old familiar kitchen. I sat the empty glass in the sink with a bunch of other dirty dishes, then walked over and sat in my old spot. The same seat where I'd eaten countless breakfasts, lunches, and dinners, back when I ate breakfast, lunch, and dinner. She busied herself with a teapot and scooped instant coffee into two large mugs that I recognized. Water heating, and nothing else to do but wait, she came back and sat down across from me at the table. Her hands trembled, and she folded them in her lap to quiet them.

Her eyes were puffy, and I realized she'd been crying. With true concern in her heart, she asked, "How are you, John? Seriously, how's your health? Are you okay?"

I knew, or thought I knew where she was heading, but I didn't let on. It would have been fun to say that I'd died last year and become a vampire, but I was pretty sure it'd ruin the moment. Months with Adrian had taught me to resist the urge to say the first thing that popped into my mind. "I'm fine, Susan. Never better."

She looked at me hard and seemed to see me for the first time. "Life after our divorce has obviously been good to you, John. You were always so handsome, but you look fantastic, like you're thirty years old again." She lowered her head, "I look like I'm sixty."

"You look fine, Susan," I lied. She looked seventy. I couldn't believe I'd once found her attractive.

She looked me in the eye and placed her hand over mine. "I buried Kevin last week, John."

I wanted to ask if he was dead first, or at the least, to crack a big smile. I didn't, though. I just held her gaze. One of my better moments, I do believe.

She continued, "I've been so afraid for you, John." She took a deep breath and continued, "You see, he had AIDS."

I feigned shock. "He did?"

She covered her face with both hands and began to weep. "I have it too, John. I'm so ashamed of what I did, and I've been so afraid that I've given it to you. If I have, I just don't know what I'll do."

Hmmm, decisions, decisions. I'd come as an angel of death, eager to extract my revenge. Now, I was sitting there feeling sorry for her. I was also surprised that she was so obviously concerned about my health.

"I'm fine, Susan, as healthy as a horse. Just had a complete physical a few weeks back, and there was no sign of anything like HIV. But how about you, really?"

She shrugged, just as the teapot began to scream. Getting up with noticeable difficulty, she moved to the counter. While pouring hot water into the cups, she said. "I'm taking my medications, and they're keeping the worst of it at bay for now. It's only temporary though. My days are numbered, John, but I'm okay with it. Really, I am. I could last for years, yet; many people do, you know. Every day they're working on new cures, and the longer I last, the better my chances."

I searched her feelings and realized she was lying. The lies weren't really intentional any more, or even specifically meant for me. Rather it was simply a story she'd gotten so used to telling, it felt natural. She was skipping her medications and was drinking herself to death. She'd already given up on life.

She paused for a moment, and then looked directly into my eyes, "I was just so concerned about you, John. I didn't want my stupidity to have hurt you in any way."

I looked away. So far, I'd been on my best behavior, but there are limits. Softly, I said, "Oh, you hurt me, Susan. You definitely hurt me."

Walking back over to me, she took my face in her hands and turned it towards her. In all the years I'd known her, I'd never seen such a sorrowful look on her face. "I'm so sorry, John. I really am. Surely you've figured out by now that you're much better off without me. You're such a special person, a true gentleman, and I always knew you were too good for me. I did love you, John, but I got tired of waiting for you to figure out that you deserved better."

"Come on, Susan..." I started, but she politely cut me off.

"John, when you know your time on Earth is limited, honesty comes much easier. In fact, it becomes essential. No more lies or deceit. I was a lousy wife. The only reason you didn't divorce me years ago is because you were too honorable. You're that rare type of person who honors their commitments, regardless of how unhappy it makes them. Instead of living the life full of adventure and intrigue that you were meant for, you settled for 'comfortable' just to honor your commitment to our marriage. Instead of having fun, you focused on making sure I had everything I desired. I know you loved me, John, but not with the unbridled passion you're so capable of. That's what you deserve and need to find."

I was too shocked to say anything. In a handful of words she'd summed up our marriage perfectly, though I'd never allowed myself to think in terms this direct or painful. How'd she do that so easily?

" Now," she said with a heavy sigh, "I'm a dying drunk, and I'm reaping what I sowed in the petty life I lived. Nevertheless, John, you have the rest of your life ahead of you to do it right. You've got to forget about the years you spent shackled to me and let go of any anger or resentment that's festering inside you. Don't let some bad memories of our marriage and my shortcomings taint your future. You'll just be cheating yourself of the happiness you deserve. You're a good man, John Steele, a damn good man"

I was surprised at the depth of her emotions. Susan had certainly changed in the time I had been gone. I'd come here intent on being a cold-hearted killer, and now I was sitting here having coffee with my intended victim and feeling sorry for her. I realized her words had brought me to a point of closure that killing her never could. The realization that my old life wasn't so good hit me full force, and I felt a new appreciation for the opportunity to "do it right" as she said.

She sighed and broke the silence, "I'm so glad I found you, or I guess I should say, you found me. There are some loose ends that I wanted to tie up. I've left everything to you in my will. It was all yours, anyway."

"That's sweet Susan, but you didn't have to do that." Now I was progressing from sadness to feeling some major guilt. I'd come to kill her and Dr. Asshole. He was already dead and she was leaving me everything she had. At this rate, the whole thing would be my fault pretty soon. "Is there anything I can do for you, Susan?"

She brightened a bit. "Yes there is, John. It's a lot to ask, but what the hell, you only die once, right?"

I thought of correcting her, but nodded slowly instead. "What can I do for you, Susan?"

"Would you mind seeing to my funeral and burial, John? As you know, most of my family's gone now. Besides, I know you'll do it with class. I'm not talking about anything fancy, I just want a simple send-off."

She blushed, at least as much as her condition would allow. "I would like some flowers though, John. I've made all the arrangements as far as the cemetery and the mortuary go. I've even picked out my casket. Everything's already paid for, of course. The only thing missing is some flowers. I started to contact a florist, but then I realized how tacky that would be. Flowers should come from others, not yourself."

I stood up, knowing I couldn't handle much more of this. "I need to go now, Susan. Thanks for the coffee."

She nodded and stood up too. "Your welcome, John, and thanks so much for coming to see me. I feel so relieved knowing you're okay."

She looked so frail and weak that I could hardly look at her. I'd come to kill her for what she'd done to me, and now I realized that killing her would probably be a blessing in disguise. In fact, I'd likely be doing her a favor since I'd be saving her from a lot of pain. I found my sudden lack of hatred for her only went so far, though. I'd let nature run its course and consider any revenge I needed to satisfy my ego as having been served. I turned to walk back out the way I'd come, but stopped and turned back around.

"Susan?"

"Yes, John?"

"Don't worry about the flowers, or the...the other arrangements. I've got you covered."

She smiled up at me, and I pulled my only vampire trick of the night. I left her with the impression that I'd walked back and held her tight for a few minutes while she softly cried on my shoulder, then gently kissed her forehead and told her everything would be okay before vanishing into the night. Hey, it was a vampire trick. Really. What do you think; I'm some kind of softy or something?

Chapter 18

A rather handsome vampire, who happens to look exactly like me, boarded a plane from San Francisco to Cabo San Lucas. For those who are geographically challenged, Cabo sits on the very southern tip of Baja California in Mexico. Anyway, this particular vampire was pretty pumped up and eager to begin a well-deserved vacation far away from the nightly grind. To top it off, he was going to finally get to spend some time with another of his kind, a vampire who he had special feelings for by the name of Emily. If all went according to plan, I, er...HE was just hours from doing the wild thing again for the first time in ages. Okay, okay, I'm talking about me. I was just trying to be polite, and not to brag or make anyone jealous. I'm so happy for me!

I figured a beach resort was the last place anyone would expect a couple of vampires to be hanging out. Few people think of us playing volleyball on a sunny beach, body surfing, or deep-sea fishing all day in a sun drenched fishing boat. Not that I intended to do any of these things, but they're the primary reasons people typically go to places like Cabo. As vampires, we're supposed to be lurking around the foggy back streets of London or traipsing about the Carpathian Mountains, anywhere but a beach town.

If you like riding on roller coasters and you're the adventurous type, I highly recommend flying into Cabo. If dropping out of the sky like a rock makes you want to puke, you might look to vacation elsewhere, or at least plan to arrive by land or sea. One minute you're flying over some pretty serious mountains, then the pilot spots a postage stamp size piece of flat land and decides to land on it. Yes, I'm probably exaggerating, but I tend to do that when I've had the poop scared out of me. Thankfully, I wasn't the only guy who screamed. Hey, I'm just kidding, but I had a pretty darn good reason for wanting to survive this particular flight. This was my much-anticipated rendezvous with Emily and her black boots, and I was planning to be a very naughty vampire!

Emily was supposed to arrive a couple of hours after me, but had caught an earlier flight to surprise me. As I passed through customs quickly, thanks to a slight mental nudge I gave the customs agent, I was surprised and pleased to find her already waiting for me. We embraced tenderly, and I'm sure we looked no different than any other young couple in love. I think it's safe to say that nobody in that airport knew that Death, in an oversized Hawaiian shirt and flip-flops, stood amongst them.

We headed straight for the Hacienda Hotel and were each greeted at the entrance with a huge Margarita. Nice touch, though it was wasted on me. I did notice that Emily took a sip, and appeared to enjoy it. Damn. After a quick check-in, an attendant showed us to our townhouse. Within minutes of his departure, we were rolling around the bed like a couple of sex-starved animals, which of course we were.

For three days, we stayed in the room. We ordered room service and flushed the food down the toilet. Emily could go for fairly long periods without feeding, but I could only last a few days. I nibbled on her, but that had a draining effect on her reserves and made me feel like a freeloader. I realized that we needed to hunt soon, and since she would only take a dying person, our options were limited. She'd assured me before the trip that they were everywhere and expressed the same opinion during our three-day romp.

We walked into town the fourth evening as the sun slowly sank behind the mountains to the west, letting her sniff out a likely victim. Amazingly, she had no luck. "Everyone's healthy down here, drunk, but healthy," she mused.

I pointed out a guy who was smoking and suggested that those things were going to get to him sooner or later. Why not make it sooner? She wasn't having any of it.

I didn't tell her I had almost no experience at hunting, having been fed by Adrian's supply the last year. Somehow, it didn't seem manly.

I needed to feed, but we weren't near the point of needing to take desperate measures yet. We decided to take a walk along the beach, knowing that we, of all people, were safe. We were strolling along, hand-in-hand, making plans for another rendezvous, when both of our senses picked up danger ahead. Sure enough, two fairly large males were walking towards us. They began talking animatedly, laughing too loud and pretending not to notice us, sure signs they were up to something nefarious. We looked at each other and smiled. They had no clue that they'd selected the two worst possible robbery targets in all of Baja California.

As our paths crossed, just a few feet from each other, one of them whipped out a small handgun. Aiming it at us, he said, "Keep your mouths shut and hand over your wallets and jewelry, gringos." His accent was more East L. A. than Mexico.

I couldn't suppress a chuckle.

"You think this is a fuckin' joke, man," he said as he waved his gun under my nose. Faster than his eyes could capture my movement, I rammed my right index and middle fingers into the left side of his chest, just under the rib cage. They pierced the skin, passed through layers of fat and muscle, and ended up just inside of his heart. He dropped the gun, and I caught it with my left hand. The look on his face was more astonishment than fear. I shoved him towards Emily and said, "I'm no expert, honey, but I think this man's dying."

She nodded and, without a word, latched onto his neck as she lowered him to the sand.

I turned to his friend, whose eyes were now bulging out of their sockets and gave him a big shit-eating grin. Imitating the dying man's East L.A. accent to the best of my ability, I said, "No, this ain't no fuckin' joke, man!"

"You're crazy, hombre," he said, pulling his own handgun from his waistband and leveling it at me. I saw his trigger finger begin to move, and I quickly slapped the gun out of his hand. He could have run when he saw his partner go down, but he'd decided to shoot me instead. This guy was a killer. I judged and sentenced him on the spot.

My bandito friend's imminent demise was only a few hearty slugs away, when Emily lightly touched my shoulder. I stopped and looked at her. Her eyes weren't pleading with me, but they were asking politely. I handed the thug over to her, and she saw him home. Is she an angel of mercy, or what?

I carried the bodies toward a road that ran parallel to the water line on the far side of the beach. A few hundred feet down the road I saw a car parked all by itself, and it had a guilty look on its grill. Walking up to it, I sniffed hard. Sure enough, I could smell their stench on the car. I carried them over to it and quickly placed one behind the wheel and one in the passenger seat. I gave a passing thought to keeping their guns, but realized they weren't needed. I placed them on their laps, and took a rag out of the back seat. Opening the gas tank, I stuffed the rag down as far as I could, and once it was soaked, I pulled about half of it back out. I'd seen it done this way on television, and I hoped it really worked.

I stared at my near perfect set-up for a few seconds, wondering if I'd missed anything. Suddenly, it dawned on me that I had no matches. I quickly searched the car and my two dead friends. No matches. No lighters. It figured that the only two non-smoking thieves in all of Mexico would mug us. They were probably on "the patch" or something.

My dilemma worsened when I heard voices coming in the distance. If I'd just heard them, they were probably still a fairly long ways off. I needed to move fast. I grabbed the keys and opened the trunk, thinking that maybe I'd find a large stash of illegal matches hidden there. No such luck. The trunk was empty except for a spare tire and a set of jumper cables.

Every once in a while I absolutely amaze myself as to how smart I can be. I grabbed the cables and slammed the trunk lid. As fast as I could, I popped the hood and hooked the cables to the battery. Running them back to the gasoline soaked rag, I began tapping the negative and positive leads together next to the rag, hoping a spark would ignite my homemade wick. It did. The damn thing caught on the third tap, and the car nearly exploded into flames. Every once in a while I absolutely amaze myself as to how stupid I can be.

Though I'd nearly incinerated myself, I'd accomplished my mission. There was no time to admire my handiwork, as the voices were getting louder and I needed to beat feet. So, like a flickering flame, I disappeared into the night.

I met Emily back in the room.

"Did everything go all right?" She asked.

"Yea, sure. No problemo, Senorita. They're in their car becoming Tostitos."

"Tostitos?"

"Sure," I said, anxious to deliver the punch line. "Toasted banditos. Tostitos!"

She just stared at me. No polite giggle. No role of the eyes. Nothing. Just that damned deadpan stare. God, I hated that stare. Talk about feeling stupid.

Finally, she took a whiff of me, and ignoring the genius of my "Tostito" joke, asked, "What'd you do, climb in there and keep 'em company for awhile?"

"Yuck, yuck, yuck. You don't know if they sell eyebrows around here do you?"

She looked puzzled. "What on Earth are you talking about?"

"Oh nothing. I was just goofing around. You okay?"

"I'm fine, but you know, John, looking for people who are dying typically means they're dying from natural causes. That doesn't include people you happen to be in the process of killing."

"Awe, come on, Emily, they deserved it. You know that. They tried to rob us at gunpoint and probably would have killed us if they'd been given the chance. Moreover, I'll bet they would have raped you if they'd had the opportunity. Uh huh, and worst of all, I think I saw one of them checking out my tight little booty. For God's sake, Emily, they came close to having their way with me! Them were some bad hombres Senorita, and I was only trying to protect your life and my dignity."

Emily couldn't keep a straight face any longer, and she broke into a big grin and started shaking her head. "You are the silliest man I've ever met. Yes, I know they were bad, John, and we probably did society a favor by eliminating them from the mix. I just don't want you to think you'd found an easy way of feeding me."

She started making exaggerated stabbing motions with her index finger, and said in a deep voice that was supposed to imitate me, "Oops, here's another dying one, honey, better finish 'em off!"

I chuckled at her antics and took her into my arms. "Okay, okay, you're on to me. I planned to kill everyone in Cabo just to keep you here with me."

We fell onto the bed, and I kissed her long and hard. Though I'd been joking about killing everyone in Cabo to keep her with me, holding her close made the thought a lot less ridiculous. She rolled me over on my back and straddled my hips.

"Do you love me?" she asked, rolling her shoulders back and thrusting her ample breasts forward.

I smiled, still amazed at how sexy she was. "Of course I do. You know that."

"How much?"

"How much?" I asked. "Well, I guess as much as is possible. Are you teasing me?"

"Enough to marry me?" she asked, as she fell forward and caught herself with her arms. Her long, dark hair formed a sort of tunnel between our faces and she slowly lowered herself down to where our lips were nearly touching.

"Marry you? Uh, I guess so. I mean, sure I do. Do vampires get married?"

Emily rolled off of me and slid down far enough to rest her head on my chest. "No John, vampires don't get married."

"Okay, now I'm really confused," I said, since I was really confused.

"We need to talk about us. First I want you to listen to me say something and I need to know you understand it and believe it before I continue."

"Uh huh..."

I love you, John, more than any male I've ever known. Being over a century and a half old, I've known a lot of men. I've never felt the same connection to any of them that I feel with you."

"You've got nice hooters for a hundred and fifty year old. They don't look a day over a hundred."

"Thank you. Now I know that your initial feelings for me were brought on because I fed off of you. You were human and this is natural, but it wouldn't explain your continued affection for me since you made The Choice."

I was still really confused, but it was obvious I'd somehow escaped getting married again. This was obviously important to her, so I could afford to go with it for a while.

"Are you saying that there's some doubt about my feelings for you," I asked?

"No, I know you love me. I feel it as strongly as I've ever felt anything during my existence. What I'm asking is if you truly believe I love you?"

I thought about it for a minute. "That's a tough question. I thought Susan loved me. Boy, was I wrong. Well, I guess she did, but not in the right way. She and I never shared the level of passion that you and I do. It's scary to answer this since things change over time. Feelings change. I'm comfortable saying that at this point in time, I believe you do love me."

"Good enough," she said. "The reason I wanted to make sure you know that I love you is because I want to talk about us, our relationship, and I don't want the remnants of your human ego bruised."

I was wary of where this was going, but nodded for her to continue.

"John, we'll never get married. We'll never settle down somewhere and make babies. It's not what we do. We're vampires."

"Wait a minute, you asked me if I loved you enough to marry you. I didn't bring it up."

"John, the point is, you were willing to hitch your wagon to mine. It's a lovely thought, but it's not realistic. It's a human concept. The whole marrying and remaining monogamous thing works well for humans, because they need to preserve the family unit to survive. To be honest, I'm surprised that The Supreme Being gave us a sex drive. Frankly, we don't need it since we don't produce offspring."

"Okay, Emily, so what's your point?"

She sighed and continued, "The point is, you and I can have a special bond and love each other all we want. However, it's not going to be a monogamous relationship. I'm going to occasionally help males and females cross over that need physical comfort, much as you did. I'm also not going to lie to you about it, since I intend to enjoy the experiences. Being with you is a different kind of feeling, though. A much more complete feeling. I just don't want you hurt in any way. Don't take this wrong, but you're still an infant when it comes to being a vampire and understanding what living forever, or at least a very, very long time entails. I hope in a hundred years we can still get away together and be this passionate, but by then I think you'd understand what I'm trying to say and actually agree with me."

It was my turn to sigh, "Lighten up, Sweetie. I think I'm catching your drift. We're going to be around for a long, long time, and while we can maintain this special relationship, it's not going any further. For us, monogamous equals monotonous. Though I hate to admit it, I did feel a twinge of jealousy when you mentioned being with other men. Mentioning other women just got me horny, but the other men part definitely pissed me off."

"Is that all you ever think about?" she said, breaking into a grin.

"No. There's feeding and sleeping too. But yes, mostly sex."

She climbed back up on top of me. "Sometimes I wonder if you really died. You still have the three key human male needs. You want sex, food, and sleep, and other than that, you're generally pretty easy to please!"

"Hey, don't forget sports. I still like to watch sports, too!"

"Okay," she laughed, "the four key human male attributes!" Turning serious, she asked, "Are we okay, John? Do you still love me?"

Opening my mind up to places it had never dared go before, I replied, "Emily, we are just fine and I probably love you even more now for being so honest with me. You were right, of course. It'll take some time to totally reprogram my brain, but what guy would complain about having someone as special as you to hook up with, and to still be able to go out and get all 'the strange' he can get, guilt free?"

She put a serious expression on her face. "Oh, were you under the impression that you could fool around, too?"

I must have looked seriously shocked, because she couldn't maintain the straight face. She kissed me hard on the lips. "Yes my love, you have permission to get all 'the strange' you can get your hands on. In fact, it's an order. Just don't forget who loves you the most, baby."

Chapter 19

After three wonderful weeks in Cabo, it was time to return to the real world. I saw Emily off at the airport, and my heart was never heavier than watching her board her plane. My flight was a few hours later, so I decided to grab a cup of coffee. Both sips I took tasted pretty disgusting, so I had no problem stretching it out.

Sitting in the waiting area, I began to sense that I was being watched. I forced myself to remain calm and casually scanned the room as I pulled the old yawn and stretch routine. On my second pass, I picked her out—a red head dressed a little too properly and trying a little too hard to look like a tourist. She'd been looking at me intently, and now she was doing everything she could to avoid looking at me. She could just be a smart babe who knew a good thing when she saw it, but my male intuition told me I shouldn't count on it and that I should keep a close eye on her. For the time being, however, there wasn't much else I could do but maintain my cover as a simple tourist heading home after a long and well-deserved vacation.

My flight was back to San Francisco, of course, and I noticed my red headed friend just happened to be on the same flight. Arriving at SFO, I once again passed through customs easily enough thanks to a mental nudge I gave the passport inspector. I grabbed the shuttle to long-term parking and, having recovered my now filthy Corvette, I headed for the local Hyatt Regency hotel. I left my bags in the car but checked into the hotel. Once in my room, I turned down the lights and waited.

Focusing all my attention on the hallway outside the door, I could hear other guests passing by on the way to their rooms, the ice machine, the downstairs bar, or wherever else legitimate guests go. I made note of the various footsteps and was gradually able to pick out a distinctively feminine walk that seemed to be paced slower than the rest. The third time I heard it, I knew it wasn't a coincidence and decided the next time this set of footsteps passed I'd make my move.

I closed my eyes and strained my hearing to its maximum range. Sure enough, I heard my mysterious hall-walker coming by again. If it turned out to be some poor innocent cleaning woman, I'd have a lot of explaining to do. I waited until the steps were right in front of my door, then I whipped the door open and grabbed the woman by the arm, yanked her unceremoniously into my darkened room and quietly closed the door. The whole thing had taken about a second and a half. She didn't even have time to scream.

Now I held her, pressed against the backside of the door, feeling her heart beat rapidly. Her mind was in a state of confusion, but not as much as someone who wasn't already alert. I could see perfectly in the dark, and she was no cleaning lady. It was my red head all right, and I'll be damned if she didn't smell good for a human.

"What do you want?" I growled in as menacing a voice as I could muster.

She struggled to break my grip, but quickly realized it was useless. "I'm, I'm a federal agent. Let me go. Let me go right now, or you'll be in a lot of trouble." Her breath smelled good too. Minty fresh.

I laughed what I hoped was a sinister laugh, "A government agent, huh? We'll just see about that."

I probed her mind and was surprised when she blocked my initial probe. She was forcing the image of a tree into her mind, and repeating the word, "tree," silently to herself, over and over again.

I was amused when her focus began to slip and she suddenly switched to the image of a dog, and kept repeating the word "dog" over and over to herself. Hmm, I wonder how a dog and a tree fit together? Let me think about it while I go take a leak.

This was similar to what Adrian had described, though she wasn't calling me a son of the devil or anything cool like that. Figuring it would be a good idea to see just how good these mind-control blocking tactics were, I decided to try a little experiment on my redheaded captive. Making a slight adjustment to a theory I'd been mulling over, I tilted her head back and kissed her. I'm not talking about your normal little tight-lipped grandma smack, mind you. No, this was the granddaddy of all big wet sloppy tongued kisses. I let out a low moan and pressed my body fully up against hers.

It worked. The unexpected physical stimulation caused her to forget about dogs and wonder what the hell I was doing kissing her and why she was kissing me back. This lapse of focus was enough to let me into her head. I should point out that I was actually improvising on my original theory a bit. For some reason, I'd figured that if I encountered someone following me, it'd be a male. It was a silly mistake on my part, and one that wouldn't happen again anytime soon. Anyway, my original plan was simply to knee some jerk in the nuts, which I figured should be an ample distraction for anybody with a pair. Drastic times call for drastic measures, though. To prove I'm not a total cad, I should also report that once my mind was locked in with hers, I ceased the physical contact.

"Sit down," I commanded her, testing to ensure that she was totally under my control.

She walked to the edge of the bed and sat. It's difficult to explain how this psychic connection works, but I'll try. Basically, it's similar to having them hypnotized. I can ask any question, and they'll usually respond. Everyone's different, though, and it's not just words that come out of their mouths, but pictures or images that kind of jump from their minds to mine. If I asked who their mother is, I'd probably get a name, but also an image. The cool part is that sometimes, depending on the person, I can insert pictures and information, too. If I want them to think they see a monster, I just push the image into their mind. I can also insert simple commands, like telling the gate guard back in Pleasanton to let me pass, and that he never saw me. Life goes on normally for the person, there's just a brief moment erased from their memory.

Now that I had Red, I had to figure out what to do with her. I started simple, "What's your name, sweetheart?"

"Leslie Denise Poole," she replied, and I got several images of her, though interestingly, none were nearly as attractive as the real thing.

"Leslie, and just whom is it you work for?"

"The Federal Bureau of Investigation, Paranormal & Psychic Investigations Department, specializing in vampire activity." This time I got images of a tidy little cubicle and what I assumed were some co-workers.

"Why are you following me?"

"You are the subject, John, no middle name, Steele. Originally reported as having been turned, then killed shortly thereafter by the vampire Virgil Walker in a New Orleans cemetery a little over a year ago. The subject John Steele disappeared for an extended period of time and was assumed dead as reported. A few months ago, a significant amount of activity was detected on subject's finances. Bank photo records and fingerprints lifted from financial documents at said financial institutions indicate the person manipulating John Steele's finances was in fact the subject himself. Since the subject was alive but not a vampire, his record was re-opened."

"Go on," I encouraged, amazed that I'd been tracked so thoroughly.

Approximately one week ago, it was determined through airline records that subject had traveled to Cabo San Lucas. Upon further investigation, it was determined that subject was residing in the same hotel room as the known vampire Emily Durant. Subject is now suspected of aiding vampires, possibly for promise of being made a vampire in the future."

I was a bit shocked. The information she was giving me wasn't exactly accurate, but proved that someone was keeping tabs on me. The images I was getting were filling in the gaps. The only reason she was following me by herself was because I wasn't considered dangerous.

"What makes you so certain I'm not a vampire?"

"Impossible. Subject John Steele has been seen and photographed in daylight several times. This makes his being a vampire impossible, since it's well documented that it takes several decades for new vampires to be able to function normally in daylight."

So that was it. Adrian's trick may have saved me in a way I'd never dreamed of. I grilled her for another ten minutes or so, then decided to plant a few suggestions. "Okay, Leslie Denise Poole, here's the deal. I'm not a vampire, nor do I cavort with vampires. I'm not worth watching. Do you understand?"

"Yes, I understand."

I couldn't resist a little fun. "This meeting never took place, Leslie, but every time my name is mentioned in your office, you're going to feel incredibly horny. You're going to feel so strongly about me that you won't trust anyone who suspects me of being a vampire. Do you understand me, Leslie?"

"Yes."

All indications were that this was one hell of a nice girl. A real straight shooter, so I decided to do her a favor. "On the first Monday of the month of June next year, you'll have the sudden realization that you're pursuing the wrong career. You'll have an incredible urge to teach underprivileged children. You'll quit the FBI, obtain a teaching credential, and you'll be happy doing that for the rest of your life. Do you understand Leslie?"

"Yes, I understand"

"Good, now leave here and forget we ever met. I'm just a boring guy, not worth the effort of trailing. Put that in your report. Now, goodbye Leslie Denise Poole."

"Goodbye, John Steele," she said as she got up, ready to leave the room.

"Wait a minute, Leslie," I said, needing satisfy one more bit of curiosity. "What's the significance of the tree and the dog, are they special images that help you block our mind influencing techniques?"

There is no special significance," she responded robotically. "They were just the first things that popped into my mind. I was supposed to say 'Back away, servant of the devil. I command you in the name of the one and only true God', but you grabbed me so fast I made a mistake and forgot what to say."

I wanted to laugh, but didn't. Now I knew how their technique worked. She had rehearsed lines, but when she failed to remember them, she'd simply plugged in a strong image and repeated it over and over again as a back-up plan. Simple, and more than likely it would have been effective against a vampire less charming or creative than myself.

"Goodbye, Ms. Poole."

"Goodbye, John Steele."

Once she'd gone, I allowed myself a good laugh. I knew it wasn't right to make her get hot when my name was mentioned, but it seemed relatively harmless. I may have screwed up her life in the short term with the career change scheduled for next year, but probably saved it in the long run. I'd spent long enough probing her mind to know she wasn't a bad person and actually thought she was doing a good thing. It was also clear that Leslie Denise Poole was a mere foot soldier in this war and knew only what her superiors wanted her to know.

I mulled over what I'd learned, as I left the hotel. She seemed to know quite a bit about Virgil, including that his last name was Walker. That was something I'd never heard before, though I hadn't really asked, either. There was definitely a high fear factor there, and his hideous image had popped into her mind when she mentioned his name. She must have had more than a little contact with him, or someone had told her plenty of horror stories about his nasty little deeds. I was anxious to talk to Adrian again and decided to make the drive north to his place.

Chapter 20

Two hours later, I was sitting comfortably in his family room, or parlor, as he liked to call it. Slugging down a pint of warm Canadian, I quickly filled him in on the events that had taken place. When I told him about Susan, he closed his eyes and nodded slowly, sharing in my pain as though it were his own. He promised to send flowers, too, and I knew he'd do it up right. When I told him about Emily, he lightened up considerably and informed me that Jasmyna had already called. Evidently, Emily had returned happier than she'd seen her in decades. I blushed, but my chest puffed out a bit. He was most interested, however, in my encounter with the red headed FBI agent, Ms. Leslie Denise Poole.

After I'd finished covering everything of importance that I could remember having happened over the past month, Adrian smiled and, folding his arms across his chest, said, "I'm pleased that my training has benefited you. Of course I should have known you'd do fine on your own. Please pardon me if I've acted like an overprotective parent at times."

I looked him in the eye. "I wouldn't have it any other way."

He gave a single nod of appreciation, then changed the subject. "I'm amazed at the depth of their knowledge about you. I find it of great interest that they have acquired so much detail and so fast."

He wasn't saying everything that was on his mind. "Come on, Adrian, give..."

"Well," he said, shifting uncomfortably in his chair. "It has occurred to me that perhaps one of our kind is providing them with information."

"One of us? But who would do that, and why?"

"Well, it's been bothering me that Virgil made such a bold move in New Orleans. I'm talking about his attempt to kill you, of course. I've known Virgil for a long time. He's not a terribly bright lad, and he's always been afraid of that which he can't comprehend. His skills are extremely limited, with the exception of his physical strength, which is unparalleled as far as I've seen."

I shuddered just thinking about Virgil and couldn't resist reaching up and gently touching the line on my neck where he'd nearly decapitated me.

"He's learned to survive using his brute strength and well practiced hunting techniques. Perhaps our friend began feeling the pressures of surviving in the modern information age and decided he needed an edge. What could he do to acquire an increased degree of protection from all that he doesn't fully comprehend?"

"Rat us out to the government for protection, maybe?" I asked, catching on.

"Mmmm, yes, that's part of what I'm thinking. Thinking it through, there's also the fact that he'd be the center of their attention. The star witness, so to speak. That'd be a first for him. That fool could give away many of our secrets without even knowing it."

"But why would he do this?" I asked. "Who does he need protection from, and why?"

"My guess, at least in part, is that he's trading information about vampires in general for detailed information about Jasmyna, Emily, and me. I believe he's planning to get rid of all of us, John, and he's acquiring a back-up plan in case he fails. I'm not sure how he plans to do it, but the indicators are there."

"Are you serious?"

"Quite, I'm afraid."

Baffled, I asked, "But why would he want to get rid of all of you? You're his family."

"I'm afraid that's not the way Virgil sees it, and to be truthful, we don't either. You see, in our world, you have a certain responsibility for those you turn. Virgil has become a liability and though we never indicated it to him, he's been on a short leash. If it's determined that he's out of control and has become a danger to our way of life, it's our responsibility to eliminate him. I should say it's Jasmyna's responsibility, but of course she can enlist our aid."

"So, let me get this right," I said. "Virgil's been screwing up with his heavy handed ways, and you were contemplating ending his days as a vampire? Does he know this?"

Adrian responded thoughtfully. "It's been building for years and he's been warned multiple times. Maybe he's got a gut instinct that his time's run out, and he's decided to act first. I just don't know, but we'll have to be cautious."

"He knows where Jasmyna and Emily live, Adrian. You don't think he gave them up, do you? Do you think that's why they were trailing Emily?" Panic was starting to set in.

"I'm afraid so, though it'd simply be a high probability guess at this point. We need more facts to know for sure. Just to be on the safe side, though, I think I'll suggest the ladies go into hiding for a while."

"Please, Adrian, call them now. If he does anything to them…"

Adrian pulled out his cell phone and punched up the number. His conversation was short and totally unrelated to what we'd just talked about. I thought for a moment that he was losing it.

He hung up and turned his attention back to me. "Okay, I talked to Jasmyna. Emily is at the shop, but they'll leave for a secret location as soon as she returns. It seems that she's been concerned about Virgil's behavior, too. Jasmyna has a sense about these things that can be downright uncanny at times. She's a very bright woman, you know?"

"You got all that out of the conversation you just had?"

He smiled. "Anyone can listen in on a cell phone call these days. Encrypted lines are a pain, and I never felt they were safe from Uncle Sam, anyway. It's easier to use whatever line's available and to simply talk in code. I see you need another lesson!"

I pretended to bow down to him. "Teach me, great master, even though I'm such an unworthy student."

He picked up a pillow from the sofa he was sitting on and hurled it at me.

"You know, Adrian, I never knew how boring my life was until I died. Now, I'm learning new stuff every day, and I feel like I'm living in some kind of constant adventure movie. I still don't feel totally comfortable with the new and improved me, but the good thing is I'm starting to feel like I'll actually get there someday."

He nodded. "There's a lot to learn in your first few decades as a vampire, and in these insane times, you'll have to learn quicker than most of us old farts did. Back in the day, we could take our time developing. There were no computers, cell phones, or any of the modern conveniences that can aid those who are against us today. As I've said many times, you're progressing just fine. For someone so mentally and physically challenged, that is."

I threw the pillow back at him.

Chapter 21

I was deep into a dream, which decorum prohibits me from recounting the details of here. Suffice it to say that it involved Emily and me, and large quantities of blood. Suddenly, my vampire senses picked up someone in the room and I was instantly awake. For a brief moment, I lay in the darkness of my coffin and caught my bearings. I was at Adrian's house and probably safe, so there was no reason to panic. I focused my energy and realized it was Adrian outside my coffin.

I opened the lid and sat up, fully alert. He had me hooked on sleeping in a coffin now. It's really quite comfortable, and the isolation is very calming on my enhanced senses, particularly my hearing and smelling. I figured I'd stick to beds when I traveled, but it would be nice to know there was a nice soft coffin waiting for me at home.

"What's up," I asked, knowing he'd never interrupt my sleep for something that wasn't important?

"Emily's missing."

"What? What the hell's going on?" I choked, not only awake now, but on my feet.

"Please remain calm, John," he said, but I could tell he was deeply concerned. "I just received a call from Jasmyna. It seems we called just in time to save her. After I called, she tried to contact Emily at the shop. An unknown male voice answered, which shouldn't have happened since there are no males working there. As she hung up, Virgil showed up at her house with half a dozen humans. They were all wearing some type of helmet that seemed to protect them from her telepathic signals. Perhaps it's an improvement on their simple thought blocking techniques. Luckily, she had a secret way out of the house and escaped to one of her hideaways. I think she'll be fine there for a while. The ladies were careful to ensure that Virgil only knew about that one house in New Orleans."

"I'll kill that dirty SOB if anything happens to Emily," I said, feeling my blood pressure rising fast.

"Jasmyna has a very strong psychic connection to Emily. She can sense that she's unharmed, but trapped somewhere; most likely, she's being held as a prisoner. We need to find her and free her as quickly as possible. In all my days, I've never seen any group take such a bold move against us. Humans have killed vampires to be sure, but they've never had the audacity or guts to try to trap and hold one of us. Killing a vampire for survival or from fear is one thing, capturing and holding one is another."

"And they'll be sorry," I hissed. "I'm going to New Orleans, Adrian. I've got to find her."

He frowned. "Haven't I taught you better than that? I doubt there's anything left in New Orleans to see now anyway. We need to develop a logical plan of attack and then execute it. Rushing off half-cocked won't get us where we need to be."

Unfortunately, I didn't have his patience. "I just want to kill someone, Adrian. Someone's going to pay," I choked out through clenched teeth.

"I'm sure there'll be a time for that, John, but first we need to figure out where they took Emily and how they managed it. Physically, she's a match for a dozen humans. Hell, maybe two dozen."

"But not for one Virgil."

He nodded. "I think you're right. Virgil could overpower her, and perhaps force her into some type of containment vessel. If the humans around her were able to resist her telepathic signals, she'd be helpless to use them to do her will."

The pictures that were forming in my mind weren't pleasant ones, but I wanted to sound more positive after my previously overemotional outburst, "Emily's bright and resourceful, and never once have I seen her lose her calm demeanor. If there's a way to break free or trick them, she'll find it. But we can't just wait and depend on that to eventually happen. Where do we go first, Adrian?"

He smiled slowly, though I'd hardly call it a happy smile, "Washington, D. C."

I nodded, catching on quickly, "FBI Headquarters, Paranormal & Psychic Investigations Department."

Chapter 22

Eight hours later, Adrian's private jet landed at Thurgood Marshall Airport in Baltimore. We were moving quickly, but we hoped with reasonable care. We didn't want to do anything too obvious, like fly directly into Washington Dulles in case "they" were tracking Adrian's plane. We grabbed two nondescript rental cars, each booked under a fictitious name, and headed for the nation's capital. Fighting traffic, the roughly thirty-five-mile drive took almost an hour and a half. We met up at a predetermined motel along the beltway, not far from Bolling Air Force Base. I'm sure it wasn't popular amongst the D. C. Elite, but it was clean and obscure. We checked in under the same fictitious names we rented the cars under, but planted different images of ourselves in the desk clerk's mind, just in case someone came asking about us later.

We met in Adrian's room and finalized our plan. He was going to touch base with some old acquaintances to see what he could learn, and I was going to try to reconnect with Miss Leslie Denise Poole. We'd meet back at the hotel in a few hours.

I spent a few moments trying to decide the best way to locate her. I could do an Internet search, or maybe sneak my way past FBI security somehow. After pondering my options for a few moments, I decided to try it Adrian's way. I flipped through my room's handy phone book and sure enough, she was listed under L. D. Poole. How did I know it was my new redheaded friend? Well, I didn't. But how many L. D. Pooles could there be in the Washington, D. C., area?

I parked a couple of blocks away from the street address given in the phone directory and quickly walked the short distance to the house. It was a small red brick house with white trim. It was in a rather rundown neighborhood, which makes me figure that FBI agents aren't in it for the money. I casually glanced up and down the street, and seeing nobody paying attention to me, I walked up to the front door. My senses immediately told me that nobody was home.

I quickly moved around to the back of the house and, seeing no signs of an alarm system, let myself in through the kitchen door.

Highly trained professional that I am, I did a quick look around the joint to get my bearings. I immediately noticed several interesting and important clues. Miss Poole was a decent housekeeper, but definitely not anal about it. Her refrigerator contained mostly healthy human food, though there was a half-eaten box of Bonbons in the freezer. Her bedroom smelled very good (I recognized the perfume) and only half the bed looked slept in. Most importantly, the toilet paper roll in both bathrooms was installed correctly, with the paper feeding over the top from the back. Though she was technically the enemy, her home gave off a warm and comfortable feel.

It was a little after five o'clock, so I assumed she'd be home before too long unless she was pulling a late shift. I decided to make the best of my time and do some real high-quality snooping. The first twenty minutes only confirmed my earlier conclusion that she wasn't anal about her housekeeping. Everything was picked up, but she wasn't the type to dust behind or under her knick-knacks. The house was small, so there really wasn't much to cover beyond what I'd seen in my first walk through.

I was standing in her living room, which doubled as an office on one end, wondering where I'd hide if I were a clue. There was a computer on her desk, but I'm not much of a hacker and it seemed too obvious and time consuming. Besides, I was relatively sure any FBI agent worth their salt would know better than to use a home computer for anything this sensitive. Suddenly, I realized I was staring at a bookcase. I moved closer, rapidly glancing through the titles. They were all about vampires, ghosts, werewolves, the occult, and there were even several dedicated to the art of magic.

One book in particular caught my eye, not because I'm psychic, but because it was the only one with a bookmark sticking out of it. I pulled it out and, opening the front cover, was surprised to find that it was an autographed copy. The inscription said, "Keep the faith, Leslie, and I'm sure we'll rid the world of this plague with the help of dedicated individuals like yourself." The title of the book was *The Plague's Upon Us*, written by one Dr. Peter Sedgewick. The jacket cover quickly told me that this guy had a major hard-on for vampires, and he often worked as a consultant to the FBI.

I was starting the third chapter of Mr. Sedgewick's book, when I heard a car pull up in front of the house. I didn't need the lights on in the house to see, so I'd never bothered to turn them on. I just sat quietly and waited for her to enter. When she was still thirty feet from the front door, I confirmed it was Leslie by her scent, which was still very nice by the way. Having a super sniffer can be great as long as you're surrounded by good smells. Accidentally step in a pile of dog poop, and it can be a long day! As she put the key in the front door, I reminded myself to be cool. More than likely, she hadn't personally abducted Emily, and might not even know anything about it.

She instinctively turned on a light as she entered and shut the door behind her. I let her turn and see me before I entered her mind. For my own sake, I needed to feel the fear in her. I expected the initial moment of pure panic, but was surprised at her response.

Rather than feeling afraid, Ms. Leslie Denise Poole was instantly turned on just by the sight of me. Though she'd been momentarily startled, instead of panicking, she let out a deep sigh. She rolled her head to the side and began slowly walking to me, trying her hardest to look sexy. It was my turn to lose focus due to shock, but just before my thing began to spring, my brain kicked back into gear.

I'd forgotten the reaction I'd placed in her head, which made her get hot whenever my name was mentioned. This time, the joke was on me. Evidently, seeing me was the same as hearing about me. Now, per my previous hypnotic instructions, she was getting worked up at the sight of me. Too bad I didn't know this trick when I was human.

I spent the next hour learning everything she knew about vampires. Had she been talking, it could have taken days, maybe weeks. Being inside her head, though, I was able to "download" big chunks at a time. I couldn't necessarily process it all at once, but I could acquire it for deciphering at a later date.

I put special effort into learning everything I could about this Dr. Peter Sedgewick fellow. It seemed that for all intents and purposes, he ran her department. Not officially, of course, since he wasn't a member of the FBI. He had a lot of pull from somewhere very high up, however, and he knew more about vampires than anyone else. Nobody she knew of questioned his orders. She looked up to him but had a healthy fear of him too. Outwardly, she thought the world of him, but deep inside, she feared he wanted her for purposes other than work. It was my first experience seeing a lecherous old man from a young woman's point of view, and it wasn't pretty. Good thing I intended to stay a lecherous young man.

Of the greatest interest, however, was a video that was firmly stuck in her memory. Sedgewick had played it for the department recently. It was designed to show them what heartless murdering animals we vampires are. Supposedly, he just happened to catch this scene on tape, but I knew differently almost immediately. It was odd watching it from

Leslie Poole's memory, but there was no mistake. The star was my old friend Virgil. Suffice it to say, acting is not one of his vampire gifts.

The tape was supposedly taken from a liquor store's surveillance video. It showed him walk into the small store and brutally attack and kill the poor night clerk. This tape did indeed show a brutal murder, but it was obvious to me it was a staged murder. Virgil even looked at the camera once and growled. He made sure the killing happened center stage, and made it far more brutal than it needed to be. The thought occurred to me that they'd ruthlessly murdered a human, just to make a training video. Who are the real monsters here, anyway?

I left Miss Poole in much the same manner as before my visit. She'd never know I'd visited, but she'd never find her signed copy of Dr. Peter Sedgewick's book, either. It was now tucked carefully in the back of my jeans, under my coat. I walked slowly back to my rental car, running through all the information I'd just absorbed. My hand was on the door handle of my car, when a distant shout caught my attention. I was anxious to get back to Adrian with what I'd found, but I was drawn to the emotion emanating from the raised voices.

I quickly moved to the front of a small house, roughly the same size and shape as Ms. Poole's, but not nearly as well maintained. My senses almost went on overload. There was an incredible amount of anger being generated, and an even larger amount of fear. The street remained empty and quiet; so obviously, this type of domestic dispute was a common occurrence around here.

As a human, other than my encounter with Victor Ramsey when I was twelve, I'd always had a relatively tranquil home life. It may have been devoid of love, but it hadn't been a threatening place. Of course, I'd read about domestic violence in the papers and seen it on the news, but I had little actual experience with it. As a human, I'd have probably steered clear of this confrontation, figuring it was clearly none of my business. Well, that was then, and now I'm a vampire, so I decided to make it my business. Maybe there was another Victor Ramsey in there who needed to be taught a lesson. I went to the door and, without hesitating, stepped inside.

I was standing behind a very large, dark-skinned man, and he was definitely the one generating all the anger. He was yelling, but the words were irrational. Hunched down in a corner was a young black woman, her body shielding two small crying boys. I was amazed at how clear her silent voice came through to me. She was pleading with God not to let this man hurt her babies again.

She must have suddenly realized I was in the room, because

she stopped praying in her silent voice and stared at me in disbelief. Her mouth never moved, but I clearly heard her say, "Help us please. Whoever you are, please help us."

"No problem," I responded in silent voice. I mentally slapped the big blabbering idiot's brain, and he fell to his knees. The silence was almost deafening. The only remaining sound in the room was the soft whimpering of the boys.

"Are you an angel,?" she asked in silent voice.

I smiled my most reassuring smile. "Hardly, many think I'm exactly the opposite."

She tensed. "You're not here to hurt us are you?"

I continued smiling and shook my head. "No ma'am, I promise I won't hurt you or your children."

"How is it you can talk to me without speaking out loud?"

"I'm not sure. I can do this with others of my kind, but I've never done it with a human before. You must be special."

"Your kind? Are you from outer space? An alien or something?"

I didn't feel like explaining, but I didn't want her to think I was an alien. "I'm from Earth, I'm just not human anymore."

She nodded, knowingly. "You're a vampire."

I was a little shocked. "How did you know?"

"I'm from Jamaica. Our mommas educate us properly in many of the Old World ways."

It was nice chatting with her, but I needed to be moving on. "What's with him?" I asked, motioning to the big lug on the floor.

I felt her heart grow heavy. "My ex-husband. He's bad through and through. Too many years of drugs and alcohol, I guess. Now the only pleasure he seems to get, is beatin' on me and the kids."

"You said ex-husband. So you left him?" I asked, innocently.

She let out a loud sigh. "Yes, I did," she said speaking out loud. "He doesn't live here anymore, but he just keeps coming back. Each time he does, he beats me worse. Once he realized he could only hurt me so bad, he started beating on the kids, too. He knows that hurts me even worse."

"And you've tried the police..." I began to ask? The look on her face told me that was a dead end.

I looked at the sack of shit lying before me on the floor. I quickly scanned his mind and found just what I expected. He was more than capable of murder; he was guilty of it. "What's your name?"

"Delthea."

"Delthea, this man won't hurt you anymore. In fact, after tonight, you'll never see him again. Are you okay with that?"

A shadow crossed her face, but she nodded. "He drives a cab. It's out front. He keeps a loaded shotgun in the trunk." She looked down, embarrassed and ashamed, "Lord knows I've thought of killing him myself many times. I'm a Christian woman though and I just can't bring myself to do it."

I smiled. "Good. You keep your faith and leave this unpleasant business to me. There'll be nobody to blame but me, understand? You couldn't stop me if you tried, so you must not ever feel any guilt about this."

"God bless you, Mister."

That rocked my world a bit. I smiled at her. "Thank you Delthea, thank you."

I stood the dirt bag up and mentally had him walk out the door and to his cab. I turned to leave, when a thought hit me. There was something special about this woman. How often do you run across a human who can communicate telepathically? She seemed to accept my being a vampire and didn't seem overly concerned about it. Besides, she exhibited a real toughness in her character that I liked. I felt I could trust her.

I turned back to Delthea and spoke out loud for the first time. "Do you work?"

"Yes, sir. I'm the assistant manager of a fast food restaurant. I do a fine job, too."

"I'll bet you do, Delthea. How'd you like to blow this town and get a fresh start for you and your boys?"

She was curious, but leery. "Where would I be going, and what would I be doing?"

"How does sunny California sound? I just bought a rather large house there, and I need somebody to run it. There's a gatehouse that isn't being used. It's on a little over forty acres of land in the foothills. I think your boys would be happy there. There's plenty of room to stretch out and be a boy. There are excellent schools in the area, and I'll even provide a car for you to drive."

"What do I have to do? I know nothing comes for free. I already told you, I can't be a part a no..." she stopped herself and looked at the two boys who were staring up at her. "I can't be a part of nothin' bad, mister."

I smiled another of my hopefully reassuring smiles. "I simply want you to run my household. I'll rarely be there, but there's a lot of maintenance that needs to be monitored on an ongoing basis. In addition, I'm planning some new construction that will require monitoring. I need someone I can trust, and I think I can trust you. All I ask in exchange for what I think is a pretty good offer, is that you're loyal to me. If so, you and your boys will be well taken care of."

"I won't ask about the 'if not' part," she said. "I'll need to think about it. I feel like I'm making a pact with the devil or something."

I must have looked hurt, because she immediately said, "Not that you're the devil or anything. It just kinda feels that way, you know what I mean? Oh, never mind."

I smiled at her, letting her off the hook. "I do know what you mean, Delthea. You think about it, though." I opened my wallet and extracted a small stack of one hundred dollar bills, and my new lawyer's business card. "If you decide to work with me, call this man the day after tomorrow and tell him you're accepting a job with me at the house outside of Fresno. I'll talk to him before then, so he'll understand. He'll fill you in on all the details." I looked around. "The house is furnished, so sell what you can here to get some extra cash. You'll only need to bring your personal belongings." I handed her the money. "This will get you out there. Be there within two to three weeks if you want the job. If not, keep the money and forget you ever saw me."

She nodded and took the money.

Ten minutes later, her ex-husband pulled his taxi into a busy gas station. He got out of the car, opened the trunk, and pulled out the shotgun. He began yelling at everyone in sight, and when he had drawn plenty of attention to himself, he placed the barrel of the shotgun a couple of inches under his chin and pulled the trigger. He made such a mess, that the coroner never realized he was running a few pints low.

Chapter 23

I sensed Adrian approaching my room and, before he had a chance to knock, I hastened to open the door. I was excited about all I had learned and was anxious to share it with him. I nearly did a double take when I opened the door and realized the haggard old man in front of me was Adrian. In just a few hours, somehow he'd aged noticeably. His skin looked pale, his cheeks were sunken in, and even his hair had grayed. Could the strain of this ordeal be getting to him, I wondered?

He looked at me for a moment as though puzzled by something, then shuffled slowly past me to a chair and eased himself into it with a thankful groan.

"Come here, boy," he said in a shaky voice, motioning for me to come closer.

I had no idea what was happening to him. Adrian was undergoing some type of rapid aging process, and it didn't take a rocket scientist to figure out that this affliction was in some way related to him being a vampire. Somehow, in all the long months of training, it had never occurred to Adrian or the ladies to warn me that such a thing could happen to a vampire, much less to tell me what to do when it happened.

I knelt beside his chair and tried to keep the deep concern I was feeling from infiltrating my voice. "You need rest, Adrian, and you need to feed. When did you feed last?"

He looked off into the distance and said weakly, "Feed? Feed? Ah, no, sorry I don't have anything for you to feed on."

Now I was seriously concerned. He was clearly confused and needed help of some kind, but I had no idea what I should do or who I could turn to. It wasn't like I could pick up a phone and dial 911. I felt woefully unprepared for this type of situation and it both frightened me and pissed me off at the same time. I couldn't let anything happen to Adrian.

"Is there anything I can get you," I asked?

Perhaps he had some of his special wine in his room? If not, I could always get a 'take-out' meal for him, or let him feed off of me as a last resort.

"Get me? Yes. Yes, you can get me..." his already frail voice trailed off to a whisper and his head lowered until his chin was nearly on his chest. Suddenly his head popped up and, grinning his usual shit-eating grin, he finished, "a partner in crime who isn't so gullible."

Before I could respond, he fell back into his chair laughing and snorting in what I can only describe as a most undignified manner, especially for someone of his advanced years.

"What the hell...?" I asked.

"It's makeup, you boob. I've known some of the people I was meeting with for close to thirty years. I couldn't show up looking exactly like I did when I first met them, now could I?"

He opened his mouth wide, and forming a hook with his right index finger, inserted it and began tugging on his right cheek. I'd seen him do this all too often and I knew it was his way of letting me know I was once again the proverbial fish on a hook. This time, I'd not only taken the bait, but the hook, line, and sinker, as well. In fact, I'd even tried to swallow the darn fishing rod for good measure.

I felt like a total idiot, and even though I knew it'd likely make for a hilarious story some day in the not nearly distant enough future, I couldn't stop myself from venting a bit in the present. "You're an asshole, you know that Adrian? You're a total asshole. Here I was concerned about you, and you took advantage of me. I swear, that's the last time I worry about you...you old jerk wad!"

My juvenile tirade made him laugh all the harder. "I'll never get old as long as you're around, John. Laughter keeps the soul young, and you always keep me laughing."

Anxious to change the subject, I asked, "So, how did your meetings go? Any luck?"

He became serious, and I could tell he was frustrated. "I met with two Senators, a Congressmen, and a Supreme Court Justice, all of whom have had strong ties to the FBI at some point. None of them knew anything about any organized paranormal investigations or vampire hunts. In fact, none of them believed in vampires."

"You came right out and asked them?"

"No, of course not, silly boy. We chatted about politics or, more specifically, my contributions to certain causes they support. Since I was there...well, I took the opportunity to probe their minds a bit. Unfortunately, I found nothing."

"Gosh, there's a surprise. You probed a politician's mind and found nothing."

Adrian smiled. "I stand corrected. I found nothing of interest relative to our purpose. Take my advice, and never trust what a politician says. Only trust half of what you find probing their minds. Sometimes I think they tell so many lies that they lose track of reality."

With a hint of self-satisfaction, Adrian continued, "I do believe my old friends will be a tad more environmentally conscientious in the future, however. They should all discover a new found interest in the development of hydrogen power and putting a stop to global warming."

"Meddler," I said, immediately wishing I hadn't since I knew it could be a sore spot with Adrian.

Adrian had strong feelings about vampires interfering in the affairs of mankind. Although I had limited detail, I knew from tidbits of conversations with Emily and Jasmyna that it had something to do with his maker, who Adrian felt often unjustifiably controlled the outcomes of major historical events. Feeding off of humans was fine and, of course, doing what we needed to do to survive in their world. Meddling in politics or attempting to change the course of mankind in any way was strictly off limits in his book.

"I'd say 'Survivalist' is more accurate. Even our hearty species needs to breathe air, thank you very much. Besides, the cleaner our air is, the better off we all are, right? Now, how did you make out with your lovely Ms. Poole?"

"Well, it's a good thing I came along to ensure we accomplished something besides promoting 'Spare the Air' day to a bunch of over-the-hill politicians. I think I may be on to a little something," I said. I tossed my new favorite book down in front of him, knowing I was understating my find.

In as much detail as I could recall, I recounted my experience at Miss Poole's house. He was particularly interested in the video Ms. Poole had imbedded in her memory and had me go over it multiple times. We surmised that it had been made to convince the FBI that catching vampires was of the utmost importance and worthy of their most vigorous efforts.

"So, the question is," I asked, while pacing around the small room, "where do we go from here? It's very possible our FBI friends are really just pawns in this whole thing. They legitimize the actions taken against us and do the majority of the grunt work. A worthy opponent, indeed, but I don't think the answer to the million dollar question lies with them."

"On the other hand," I continued, "if we could get our hands on this dork Sedgewick for a few minutes, we might be able to get some real answers. Unfortunately, we don't know much about him."

Adrian picked up the book and appeared to study the author's picture for a short time. "Yes, he does look a bit like a whale's penis."

I knew Adrian was making fun of my use of the word dork, but I saw an opportunity that I couldn't pass up, "So, you're an expert on whale penises, huh Adrian? Seen lots of 'em have you? Uh, huh, it's always the quiet ones."

He closed his eyes and sat perfectly still. To this day, I firmly believe he was trying to back time up twenty or thirty seconds, somewhere just prior to the point where he opened his mouth and inserted his whale sized foot. Fortunately, time travel was not in his repertoire of vampire skills, so his ancient old ass was mine this time!

"Hey, don't worry about it, Adrian," I continued, enjoying myself immensely. "I won't tell anyone. Did I ever tell you I had a job circumcising whales before I was in the Navy? Yeah, it didn't pay much but the tips were huge!"

He simply pointed at me in recognition of his slip up, and said, "Touché."

Every ounce of my being wanted to jump up and claim my momentary superiority by doing an end zone dance to beat all end-zone dances, but I forced myself to act like I'd been to this sacred place before. I just wish there'd been somebody else there to witness it.

"One of my companies handles things like this," he said, as he pulled out his ever-handy cell phone and got us back on track. "I'll have them gather everything they can on this...this dork, Sedgewick. We should have some high level information relatively soon, but the really juicy stuff may take a few hours."

"One of your companies? What kind of company handles stuff like this? Do you own a detective agency or something," I asked?

He rolled his eyes, ignoring my questions, and focused on his phone call. A few minutes later, he hung up and said that our best course of action was to get some rest until he heard back. Besides, he wanted to read through the book I'd lifted from Ms. Poole.

Once again, I found myself feeling a bit inadequate, or at least severely under prepared. He knew senators and congressmen and had a company that did spy stuff. I needed to get myself one of these "companies" and some connections higher up than the lady who handles my laundry.

It took eight of the most painful hours I've ever endured, but we finally had what we considered an adequate amount of information on

Dr. Peter Sedgewick. All of it seemed to support our original suspicion that this guy was up to no good; at least as far as we vampires are concerned.

Sedgewick lived on a small estate in Maryland, about sixty miles south of Washington D. C. It had formerly been a tobacco farm, and during its heyday probably had more deaths per year to its credit than the average vampire. Since nobody was hunting it down with an extreme vengeance, the estate doubled as his private research facility. Sedgewick's primary function, at least according to the information we had, seemed to be his role as the executive director of something called the Religious Artifacts & Antiquities Commission. When we read that part, we looked at each other and said in unison, "Templars."

Adrian's plan called for us to wait patiently until nightfall and then make our way onto the estate to investigate. An aerial reconnaissance of the surrounding area was being made, and detailed photos would be available for our perusal in a few hours. Yes, detailed aerial photos. I've got to get one of these types of companies! Adrian politely reminded me that when you've been around for nearly six hundred years, you tend to make a few contacts here and there. When you bring them all together to do research for you, you might as well start a company. How silly of me. Everyone should start their own research company with the capability of providing aerial reconnaissance photos!

My suggested plan of attack was much simpler and was based on the fact that these were not nice people. They kidnap vampires, and do who knows what to them. Plus, it was immediately executable and I was tired of waiting. In my humble opinion, the best approach was to get in as soon as possible, and using our God given vampire talents, kill everybody on the premises. If we found Emily, we'd free her and let her wreak some vengeance too. If not, we'd make someone talk until we knew where she was. Then we'd kill them too.

Adrian wasn't too keen on my "Rambo" style plan as he called it, at least not at first. Admittedly, it wasn't much of a plan, but the only benefit to his was darkness and the fact that we'd know the lay of the land better. In the end, he surprised me by deciding my plan had its merits and that time was the most critical factor. We hopped into his rental car and headed south on Interstate 301.

Sedgewick's estate was not the easiest place to locate. In fact, all we found initially was an unadorned entrance road. From the main road, it seemed to twist and turn back through a mass of thick Maryland foliage, and then disappear into some place that was likely evil and unfriendly to vampire kind.

Fortunately, there was a mailbox by the side of the road, which clearly displayed the address in large gold numbers. Unfortunately, there was not a neon sign that proclaimed a whale's penis named Sedgewick resided on the premises. Admittedly, it was tough without this vital neon sign to guide us, but based on the aforementioned house number we decided we had the right place. We'd know for sure shortly.

We parked off the side of the road about a half a mile past the entrance to the estate, and sticking close to the edge of the tree line, we hiked back towards our objective. I looked at my watch and noted that it was 9:30 a.m. local time. We assumed that we had the element of surprise on our side, since we doubted anyone was expecting us. Our selected time of attack was either great or horrible. Assuming they had guards, they would have had plenty of time to wake up from a good night's sleep, shit, shower, and shave, and even have a hearty breakfast. I imagined them checking their guns twice, then sitting down to wait for us.

During my four years in the Navy, I don't recall reading any military strategy books that suggested attacking at 9:30 a.m. Come to think of it, the only military strategy I could recall involved a destroyer laying a smoke screen, and I think I saw that in an old black and white war movie. Unless Adrian had a smoke canister hidden in his ass, I don't think this strategy was going to work for us. Then again, maybe 9:30 a.m. is prime attack time, and everybody's just been keeping it a secret. And maybe one of us vampire commandos was slightly paranoid and was getting worried we shouldn't be acting on his weak-ass advice after all.

We entered the woods about a hundred yards before reaching the entrance road, hoping to avoid any cameras that might be positioned there to look for smoke screens. Our plan was simple enough. We'd head straight in and look for whatever appeared to be the primary residence. Once found, we'd do a quick recon and evaluate the situation, adjust our plans as necessary, then attack. It was simple, direct and, hopefully, effective.

Fifty yards from the road, we came to a chain link fence. It was deep enough into the tree line that it couldn't be seen from the road, and even we didn't detect it until we were within twenty feet of it. It was approximately six feet high and had another two feet of barbed wire strung along the top. We looked at each other and nodded in confirmation. If there was any doubt about this being the right place before, this removed it. Adrian spoke to me in his silent voice, "Be alert now. The closer we get to the house, the tighter the security will likely be."

I nodded in agreement. An eight-foot high jump is within most vampires' jumping range, so one at a time we leapt over the fence without touching it. If only I could have had this ability back in my old high school gym class...

We'd moved in another thirty or forty yards, when I began to get a sense of some type of electrical or magnetic pulses. It felt as though static electricity was running through my entire body. Adrian didn't feel anything, but silently told me to check it out. As I moved forward it got stronger, but as I backed off it lightened up. I tried moving forward in several other spots, but the same thing always happened. I was puzzled, because I couldn't see anything that looked like it would be emitting an electro-magnetic field. There were no stakes or poles visible, and nothing seemed out of the ordinary with the trees, Adrian waited patiently, letting me work it out.

I began to wonder if it was just in my mind. I approached one more time to be sure, but when I definitely felt the electromagnetism increase, I retreated. Frustrated, I sat down to think for a minute. As soon as I felt the moist earth with my bare hands, they began to tingle. I might be slow, but it didn't take me long to realize what we were up against. Some type of sensor cable was buried in the ground and probably formed a ring around the whole facility. I recalled enough about electromagnetic fields from my Navy days to know we didn't want to break through it. It was probably set to detect an object the size of a man, and to ignore smaller creatures.

I silently explained the situation to Adrian, and he reached down and felt the soil where I'd felt the tingling sensation. He nodded thoughtfully. "I don't feel it, but I trust your senses. Any bright ideas?" he asked.

"Piece of cake," I replied. "Follow me."

To hide the cable in this dense forest, they'd had to place it close to several large trees. They must have felt sure it would be totally undetected, since the tree branches allowed for an easy path over the cable. I simply jumped up and grabbed a fairly large limb of a tree. Then I swung myself up and climbed to the opposite side of the tree and dropped back down. While Adrian followed my path through the tree, I walked back towards the fence and could easily sense the electronic field from the opposite side too. Another hurdle down, but who knew what was ahead?

A cluster of white buildings began to come into view through the thick vegetation, and we slowly worked our way towards them. Finally, we got down on our hands and knees and crawled to a spot behind a neatly trimmed boxwood hedge. The hedge appeared to mark the boundary of the estate's well manicured landscaping, while the area we'd come from had been left in its natural wooded state. As we knelt behind the hedge and took advantage of the protection it offered, we took turns peeking out and surveying the buildings in front of us.

Everything looked innocent enough at first glance. There was a large, well-maintained three-story main house and what appeared to be a sizable detached garage, capable of holding at least four cars. Though not directly attached to the main house, a covered walkway connected the two structures. A small barn or workshop stood approximately fifty yards behind the garage and was painted in the same traditional white with green trim manner as the two larger structures. The grass was well manicured, and from my best guess I'd say it made up nearly an acre of open space around the buildings. It didn't take long to realize that while everything looked innocent enough, it was designed to make it nearly impossible to move between the buildings and the woods without being seen. Careful examination revealed several small cameras strategically located under the eaves of all the buildings.

"Okay, any more bright ideas?" Adrian asked with his silent voice.

I was winging it, now, but I tried to sound confident, or at least as confident as you can sound in silent voice. "Well, we could stay here forever and do nothing, or I could stand up and start walking towards the small structure. You stay put and see what happens. Once whatever is gonna happen...happens, you jump out and kung-fu the shit out of 'em. I'll watch!"

"That's the most ridiculous plan I've ever heard," he replied sarcastically. "I'll walk out to see what happens, and YOU jump out and kung-fu the shit out of them."

"Hmmm, you have a point. Are you just gonna watch, or are you gonna help?"

"It depends on how badly they're whipping your ass."

"Screw that," I said, and stood up before he could stop me. I started walking slowly towards the smallest building, put my hands in my pockets to enhance my casual appearance, and tried to whistle through lips that had inexplicably turned dry. I tried my best to look like I was simply on a stroll in the woods and had somehow gotten off course. I'd made it about six steps when an alarm went off. I looked around as though confused, but kept walking slowly ahead.

Four guards came running out of the small building, and two more out of the main house. They all had Uzi's and were wearing the silliest looking helmets I'd ever seen. They looked like a kitchen colander turned upside down, and covered in foil—like something you might picture a kid in the 1950's would make after seeing one of those corny old space movies.

"Get your hands up," the closest one yelled.

"Get down," yelled another.

I smiled my friendliest smile and shrugged, "Guys, what's all the fuss? Do you want me to put my hands up or to get down? For God's sake, point those guns somewhere else before someone gets hurt."

"Down on the ground," the closest one yelled. I could hear the fear in his voice, and that brought a bigger smile to my face. I was completely surrounded now.

"Get down, sir, or we will shoot," another one yelled above the screeching alarm.

"Okay, okay, you got me," I said, putting my hands in the air. "Do I really have to get down on the grass? I'd hate to stain my new pants. My wife will kill me."

"Get down," yelled the first guard again, panic now emanating from his voice. "This is your last chance." Though I was at best six feet away, he was eyeing me down the barrel of his mini-machine gun. Must not have been much of a shot if he had to aim from this distance.

I shrugged and slowly started to get to my knees. One of them came up from behind me and gave me a totally uncivil shove. Again, my smile widened knowing he'd soon pay dearly for that shove. The alarm stopped, so someone somewhere must have figured everything was under control.

"Okay, Adrian, you can start the kung-fu shit any time now," I yelled in my silent voice.

Adrian was fast. He was very fast. I really did intend to help Adrian since there were six of them, but I would have just gotten in his way. These poor guys never knew what hit them. One moment they were clearly in charge, and the next they were reaching down to close the gaping hole in what had once been their stomachs. His bare hands had cleanly sliced through all of their abdomens, and one by one, they fell to the ground. Groaning in unison, they all tried to hold in their intestines, as if it would somehow prevent their imminent demise.

"Come on," he urged, and we set off at a run for the small building. "Four came out of here, so let's check it first."

He was clearly back in charge now as we headed for the door. It opened silently, and in an instant, we were inside. We found ourselves in a small eight-foot by eight-foot atrium, surrounded by glass walls in front of and to the sides of us. An extremely thick glass door was in front of us, and it probably would have provided a decent level of security if someone hadn't left it propped open. One of the security guards had probably gotten lazy, which is not a good thing when you're in the security business.

Through the glass walls, we could see at least a dozen TV monitors and several banks of controls and switches. Two operators sat with their backs to us, oblivious of our arrival. Boy, were they in for a surprise. Hope they didn't have dinner plans.

We both silently stepped through the doorway, and I hit them with my best James Cagney impression, "Come out and take it, you dirty, yellow-bellied rats, or I'll give it to you through the door!"

We had the guards' attention now, but instead of showing some appreciation for my skill at imitating movie stars, or even reaching for their guns as would be expected, they frantically grabbed for two more of the silly looking helmets. They died before they could get them on.

"What the hell are these stupid helmets for?" I asked. I picked one up and put it on my head as a joke.

I looked at Adrian, and he just stared at me like I was an idiot. "What?" I asked in my silent voice. Again, he just seemed to look at me. Suddenly, he frowned.

"Take it off," he said aloud.

I did.

"What?" I asked again.

"Well, well, I think they've discovered a way to block our mind control signals. Put it back on, and try to talk to me in your silent voice."

I popped the weird looking helmet back on and silently said, "You were pretty good out there...for an old fart."

No response. I looked at him and waited for him to say something. Nothing. I took the helmet back off and tossed it on the ground.

"Okay, we know that's one less weapon in our arsenal," he said aloud, shaking his head. "I guess we'll have to rely on speed and cunning."

"Okay by me," I responded, "but what are you gonna use?"

"Bite me, Junior. So, where do we go from here?"

I looked more closely at the monitors and found exactly what I wanted. One of the monitors clearly showed an image of Emily, locked in a cage, with one of the weird helmets attached to her head. As happy as I was to see her alive, seeing her caged and cuffed really pissed me off.

I pointed to the screen and said, "There."

He looked at the image for a few seconds, and I knew he was taking it all in. As pissed as I was, I felt sorry for anyone who got in his way.

"Yea, but where's there?" he asked, looking at the other monitors for a clue.

"Good question. The main house, maybe? I don't know. This seems to be the guards' control room. Doesn't seem to be much else here."

"The main house is as good a place to start as any. Let's go, but be careful."

I was just about to stay something clever like, "After you, Grandpa," when a noise behind me caught my attention. I turned in time to see a hidden elevator door slide open, revealing a bored looking guard with a cup of coffee in his hand. Seeing me, he reached for the button to close the door, but he was too slow. Way too slow.

I grabbed his coffee and his throat simultaneously and pulled him from the elevator, being careful to keep my foot in the doorway so it wouldn't automatically close. I looked him in the eyes and for effect took a sip of his coffee. Not bad, but I prefer French Roast when I'm on a killing spree.

"Where's the girl?" I asked, trying to act like I did this sort of thing every day.

He gagged, and I realized I was holding his throat too tight. Oops. I loosened my grip a tad and repeated my question. "Where's the girl?"

"Da-Da-Da, she's down," he gasped. "She's in a cell in the underground facility. Please don't ka-ka-kill me!"

I pulled him closer, so that our eyes were about six inches apart. "What's your name?"

"Bo-Bo-Bobby. Bo-Bo-Bobby Davis," he stammered.

Okay, Bo-Bo-Bobby Davis," I stammered back, "I can envision a scenario where you actually live to talk about this. The odds are pretty slim I admit, but if you do everything I ask, you may just survive a run in with not one, but two very nasty vampires. Do you understand me, Bo-Bo-Bobby?"

"Ye-Ye-Yes, sir. I'll do anything you a-a-a-a-ask."

"Good. Now, what's the best way for us to get to her?"

Bobby quickly warmed to the task. "Ta-Ta-Take this here elevator down. There's one gu-gu-guard at the door. His name's To-To-Tony and he's a je-je-jerk from New York. You'll see lots of pi-pi-pipes and stuff running along the walls. Go down the ha-ha-hallway to the left. It leads to a laboratory under the ma-ma-main house. About halfway to the ma-

ma-main house, you'll see a big observation window. She's insi-si-side of the observation room. It's where we used to keep Vir-Vir-Vir-Virgil."

Virgil? This was an interesting bit of info. "What's holding her in there? Is she drugged? Tied up? What?"

He seemed proud for a minute, and almost boasted, "She's in a ti-ti-titanium cage. Evidently even you demons aren't stro-stro-strong enough to bend ti-ti-titanium ba-ba-bars. And her hands are cuffed with ti-ti-titanium handcuffs behind her back, so that she can't take her helmet off. Otherwise she might be able to trick a gu-gu-ard into helping her."

The thought of Emily in a cage was pissing me off to the point where I wanted to pop Bo-Bo-Bobby's head like a pa-pa-pimple, but I needed more info. "How do I get her out of the cage, Bobby?"

"Ga-ga-gosh," he pondered, seeming to rack his pea sized brain, "I never thought about getting someone out. We're usually concerned with ke-ke-keeping them in."

"Think Bobby, your life might depend on it." I tightened my grip on his throat just a wee bit tighter.

It's amazing how the fear of death works. Suddenly, his eyes lit up and he ventured a guess. "I think Do-Do-Doc Sanchez knows the combo. She was down there in the second observation room when I came up." His brow furrowed, "She's ni-ni-nice though and I'd hate to think I caused her any ha-ha-harm."

"No worries, mate," I assured him. "Now where's this second observation room?"

He looked at me like I was the idiot. "It's ne-ne-next to the first one, of course. It's where they observe those that are working on the de-de-de-demons."

Of course, it's where they observe those who are working on us demons! What was I thinking? This place was making me crazy, and fast.

"I think we have enough," Adrian said. He took our new friend by the shoulders and looked Bobby in the eyes, planting something deep within him. I wondered what, but didn't have time to ask.

We headed down the elevator, and Bo-Bo-Bobby's directions were spot on. The door slid open and To-To-Tony, the jerk from New York, died instantly.

We hurried down the hallway and came upon a series of thick glass windows. The door to the first room was open, and I spied an attractive young Hispanic woman in a white lab coat sitting at a desk working on a computer terminal. I was directly behind her before she realized someone else was in the room. She turned with a heavy sigh to see who had the audacity to disturb her work. She gave me a puzzled look, and when I gave her my most dastardly smile, the realization of her predicament set in. I put one hand on her shoulder, holding her firmly in place. I reached out with my foot and pulled another chair over, placing it directly behind hers. Sitting down, I wrapped my arms around her and hung my chin over her right shoulder. Tenderly, I pressed my cheek against hers. She sat perfectly still, but her racing heart betrayed her.

Through the observation window, which Bobby Davis had informed us was used to "observe those who are working on us demons," I saw Emily standing quietly in a cage, with her arms seeming to hang casually behind her. My heart ached at the sight of her, though I noticed she didn't seem to be distressed in the least. In fact, she was just standing there looking a bit bored, as though she was taking everything in stride.

"Hello, Dr. Sanchez," I said in a voice more calm and matter-of-fact than I felt inside. "I believe you've been observing a friend of mine and I've come to get her. Would you be so kind as to open her cage?"

"I can't," she whispered, her body trembling in fear.

I pushed my view of hell into her mind and heard her gasp. I then switched to an image of a pack of bloodthirsty werewolves ripping her naked body to shreds. I should have used vampires, but I'm still new at this stuff, and sometimes I forget to use the right monsters. It did the trick, though, and that's all that mattered.

"No", she gasped, and her whole body began to convulse in such primal fear, that she nearly passed out. I made a mental note to myself to go lighter on monster images next time.

I tightened my arms around her and lifted her to her feet. I slowly whispered in her ear, "Open the cage, Dr. Sanchez. Open it now. Or, I'll be forced to throw you to the wolves!"

I released her and she stumbled out the door, through the hallway and into the observation room holding Emily. She fell to her knees and, trembling, began to push some buttons on a cleverly hidden keypad.

Emily looked at me and didn't seem the least bit surprised. "It's about time. I was getting hungry," she said matter-of-factly.

As the door popped open, I reached in and grabbed her. "A simple 'thank you' will suffice, my dear. Is this the new hat style in New Orleans this year?" I asked, as I popped the silly helmet off her head and tossed it on the floor."

Turning to the still trembling Dr. Sanchez, I asked, "The handcuffs, Doc? How do we get the handcuffs off?"

"Only Dr. Sedgewick has a key to the handcuffs." I knew she wasn't lying by the look on her face, so I turned to Adrian.

"Well?"

He put his hand on Doc Sanchez's shoulder and gently pushed her towards Emily. "Drink Emily, you may need all of your strength to get out of here. There may be more guards waiting upstairs."

"I'll be fine for a while," she responded, and we all knew what she meant. She'd yet to reach the hunger point where she was willing to kill someone who wasn't dying.

Adrian looked at her hard for a few moments, then again pushed the good doc towards her. "Drink, Emily. It's okay."

His message was clear, Dr. Sanchez might not be dying of natural causes, but she was going to die. Emily understood, and with her mind now free to manipulate her victim, she mentally pulled the doctor to her. Looking into her eyes, Emily sent her a message that made the young Ms. Sanchez visibly relax and roll her head to one side, opening a clear area for Emily to chow down.

While Emily dined silently, Adrian reached down and grabbed the helmet. Tossing it to me, he said, "Take this and Emily and go out the same way we came in. There's some unfinished business down here that I need to take care of. Don't worry about the handcuffs; you'll get them off easily enough on the outside. Now go."

I immediately protested. "No way, Adrian. Either we all stay and finish this together, or we all leave together. Emily and I can handle..."

"Damn it, John, do as I say," he snapped, cutting me off. He was more serious than I'd ever seen him. He looked at me and must have seen the shock and hurt he'd inflicted, because he immediately lightened up. "I've been in much worse situations than this, and survived to tell about it. This may be our only opportunity to gain valuable information about our adversaries, and there's still Sedgewick to deal with. Please take Emily out of here and meet me back at my place in Napa. In fact, I'll be at least a day or two, so take my plane and send it back for me. There are a few more people I need to talk to, now that we know more about who we're dealing with. Now go on, get out of here."

I started to protest again, but Emily stopped me. "Let's go, John. Adrian will be fine. Do as he says."

Part of me was disappointed that she took his side, but then again, she had known him for over a hundred years longer than me. She had total faith in him, and I guess I should too. I grabbed her by the elbow and we headed off down the hall. "Be careful," I called out, looking back over my shoulder. Adrian didn't respond, as he was already hard at work. He was holding Dr. Sanchez by the shoulders and looking deeply into her big brown eyes.

Chapter 24

We'd been back in California for two full days before Adrian decided to once again bless us with his presence. It felt odd to be in his home without him there, even though I'd spent so much time there and the staff welcomed me back like their returning prodigal son. Knowing he was back safely was a relief. My ego was still bruised at having been sent back early, but I knew I'd get over it in a decade or two.

My strategic retreat with Emily is hardly worth mentioning. We simply left the way Adrian and I had come in, and we encountered no resistance. I grabbed a couple of extra space helmets in case there were different models and did some quick damage to the equipment in the security control room. I also removed the chair that one of the guards had used to hold the door open, and let the door close behind me. I figured someone would be left trying to figure how we got in without busting up the door. Perhaps they'd even wonder if it was an inside job. I'd only been at this game for a few hours and already I was getting pretty good at it, in my ever humble opinion.

As we passed the bodies on the way to the fence, Emily hardly gave them a second glance. I guess she'd already accepted that someone would have to pay the price for our admission. We could have been nice and left the car for Adrian, but I figured he was smart enough to boost a car if he needed to. The way I saw it, he'd decided to send us away, so he could figure out a minor detail like transportation on his own.

The flight crew didn't have the tools to cut through Emily's handcuffs but promised to have the appropriate saw waiting when we landed. She didn't seem to mind, accepting this with nothing more than a small shrug of her perfectly shaped shoulders. Her ability to remain calm regardless of the situation always amazed me. Of course, I made the necessary sleazy comments about her being in handcuffs and it turning me on, and she responded with the obligatory roll of her eyes and heavy sigh. Adrian's plane was well stocked with our kind of food, so we feasted. Though she'd snacked on Dr. Sanchez, she proved to be one hungry gal, as she wasted little time slugging down several bottles of Adrian's best non-alcoholic stuff. For desert, we curled up together on a seat that reclined and took turns nibbling on each other.

Adrian, Emily, and I met in his library shortly after his return. Having had an adequate dose of Emily, and knowing she was once again safe and sound, I was in very high spirits. Adrian, in his sensible and direct way, brought me back to reality.

Standing in front of his oversized fireplace with its imported marble mantle, hands clasped behind his back, Adrian began, "I find the current situation most worrisome. As I've said before, in all my many years I've never seen an attack of this sort on our kind. Of course, there have been several churches and other esoteric organizations of limited power that have attempted to eradicate us in the past. Most of their efforts amounted to little more than a minor irritation. This time, however, I fear we're up against a whole new beast."

"I agree," said Emily. "They have sophisticated tools, like their silly little helmets, and they've even managed to get the United States government involved. That means nearly unlimited resources can be brought to bear against us."

"All true," replied Adrian. "However, my concern runs deeper than that. In the past, all efforts were focused on killing us. This time, they wanted at least some of us alive."

"Sure," I piped in, "they probably wanted Emily to tell them everything she knows regarding the whereabouts of other vampires. Once they pumped her for all the information she had to offer..." I left the thought hanging there, not willing to say what they'd likely have done to Emily. I looked at her and all she did was raise her eyebrows to acknowledge the thought.

"Actually, I'm afraid there's more to it than that," Adrian said. "I know you didn't want to leave me behind in Maryland, John, but I sent you back early for a reason. I needed to totally focus on each person's thoughts and to be able to tie them all together in the end. Your planning worked to perfection, and we accomplished our primary mission, which was rescuing Emily. I had a secondary mission, however, which was to gather as much intelligence as I could. Perhaps if my mental faculties were stronger, I could have maintained the needed level of focus and kept you by my side. For that weakness, I apologize."

There was nothing wrong with Adrian's mental faculties. As he spoke, I realized that even though Emily and I could have been a slight distraction while he was heavily into reading people's minds, he was mostly trying to massage my bruised ego. I had too much respect for him to allow that to happen.

"Don't be silly, Adrian. You were right to send us back. As you said, the primary mission was accomplished and I should have been smart enough to understand you needed to follow through on a couple of things. So, what else did you find out?"

"As I figured, several different people hold, or in several cases I should now say, held, a different piece of the puzzle. It seems that only Dr. Sedgewick understands the plan fully. It's too convoluted to explain to you how I pieced it together, but in my opinion, the plan isn't about trying to kill us, but rather to learn how to control us!"

Emily and I both gasped. We didn't have to be told that controlling even one vampire could be a pretty powerful weapon. Controlling several would be huge.

"We know that they are, or at least think they are, controlling Virgil. He led them to you and Jasmyna," he continued, indicating Emily, "and without the aid of a timely phone call, she too might have been taken captive. Now, Emily, we need you to tell us exactly what happened to you, and please don't leave anything out."

Emily took a deep breath, and began, "I was walking home, and a van pulled up from behind very quickly. I immediately sensed danger, but as I turned towards the van, they shot me with some type of electrical stun gun. Before I could shake off the effects, Virgil leapt out and knocked me to the ground. He pulled my hands behind my back and while he handcuffed me, they popped that damned helmet on me. I fought back of course, but between Virgil's strength and not being able to use my mental powers, I didn't have much of a chance. They shoved me into a cage, similar to the one you found me in, but much smaller of course."

I trembled with anger and silently vowed I'd get even with Virgil someday.

"This may be my pride talking," Emily continued, "since it sounds like I was taken so easily, but I really think the whole thing was well rehearsed. It was carried out with military-like precision, and though everyone except Virgil was scared, they didn't waste a move.'

"Trust me," Adrian said, "you're no easy mark. What you experienced was well planned and rehearsed many times. Several people I 'interviewed' considered your capture to be a major win for them. Please continue, my dear."

"Well," Emily continued, "they took great care to keep my hands away from my head. They were very aware of the importance of keeping that helmet on me so I couldn't use my mental powers on them. With my hands cuffed behind me, I couldn't reach the chinstrap to take the damn thing off. The more I struggled, the more they zapped me with that damned stun gun. When I could smell my flesh burning from it, I decided it was time to chill and wait for them to slip up, or for something to happen that worked in my favor. Of course, I always knew the cavalry would show up to rescue me at some point!"

She paused for a moment to collect her thoughts and finally continued. "I was in the van for several hours, at least the better part of a day. We headed north, until we arrived at the place you found me. Virgil personally transferred me to the larger cage, and I was locked in it until you rescued me, Adrian."

"Adrian? Hey, what about me? It was my plan, you know," I asked, pretending to be hurt.

"Oh, were you there too?" she asked, scratching her head as though confused. Then she smiled at me and said in mock sincerity, "Oh gosh, how could I have forgotten all ready? It's only been about fifteen minutes since you reminded me for the hundredth time that you came to my rescue. Yes, John, you're my hero and I'll be eternally grateful."

"Okay," I said, raising my hands up in front of me. "I was simply trying to bring to light a few key facts, but if my input isn't appreciated..."

Adrian couldn't suppress a smile at our verbal sparring, but urged her to continue her story by asking, "Once you were in the facility, what happened next, Emily?"

Emily shrugged, "Not much, really. I think they were too afraid of me. The guards walked on the far side of the corridor when they passed the room I was in, and wouldn't make eye contact. I wasn't even asked any questions. It's all kind of odd, really!" She seemed puzzled thinking about it.

"Wait a minute," I piped in. "If they weren't going to quiz you, why the hell did they kidnap you?"

"That's a good question," Adrian responded. "I think you're right, Emily, they were deathly afraid of you. I had one of my labs look at the helmets you brought back, and they were actually quite impressed. It seems they have come up with an electronic method of blocking telepathic communication. They all wore the helmets for protection and kept one helmet on Emily for safety's sake. They have a healthy respect for the power of our minds."

"Guess they should have had more respect for the power of our bodies," I sneered, feeling pretty cocky about the ass whipping we'd delivered. "We tore through that place pretty damn easily."

"It was too easy," Adrian stated.

"What do you mean, too easy? Are you thinking we were set up or something?"

"No, but I have some experience with prisons and such, dating back to the days when castles and fortresses were actually somewhat effective. The technology has changed, but certain key components haven't. I believe that facility was designed primarily to keep someone in, not to keep someone out."

I sat up straight, "You're right, almost all the monitors were focused on the inside rooms of the facility. And the elevator guard was at the bottom of the elevator, not the top."

Adrian shrugged and responded as if he were talking to a child, "Yes, of course, I'm right! So, boy genius, what's all this tell us?"

"What does all of this tell us?" I asked very slowly. It was a thinly disguised stall tactic, but it was all I could muster at the time.

"That's what I asked, Sherlock. What can we deduce from the facts that have been presented here?"

Deduce? What can we deduce? I was on the spot and had to think quickly. Well, we can deduce...nothing. Damn, what the duce? I couldn't deduce. I had nothing. Zero. Zip. Nada. I hate having nothing. Luckily, Adrian was on a roll and his impatience with my inability to deduce anything saved me from saying I could only completely deduce that I couldn't deduce anything.

"Why, it's obvious," he began, answering his own question, "that they didn't expect anyone to come and rescue Emily. They probably base a lot of their information about us on Virgil. Of course, we all know he's something of a lone wolf, but they don't. Since he's all they have to base their knowledge on, they assume he's the norm. To them, Virgil's an average Vampire."

"Damn," I piped in, "that's just what I was going to say! Well, except for the 'lone wolf' part. I was leaning more towards a horse's ass!"

"Lone wolf? Yes. Horse's ass? Definitely. I think he's just a big chicken shit though, if you ask me," Emily offered, with a rare hint of emotion in her voice.

"Well, since we're off on a rather strange animal tangent, might I suggest that hopefully he'll be a very 'dead duck' before long. At least he will be if he crosses paths with any of a number of very pissed off vampires," added Adrian, joining in on the fun. "Seriously, though, my point was that they are using him as their reference point. They assume that we're like him."

"Awe geez," I muttered as another thought hit me. "That means they think we're all a bunch of inbred idiots with serious hygiene issues. How embarrassing is it to be us right now? Well, after what we did, they probably won't make that mistake the next time."

Emily turned to Adrian, "Will there be a next time?"

"I'm afraid so," he said, pulling a cell phone from his pocket and looking at it. As if on queue, it rang. Actually, it didn't ring. It played the theme from the old *Dark Shadows* television show, which I can only assume is a part of Adrian's twisted sense of humor. He popped it open and pressed it to his ear.

After a few moments of listening, Adrian grunted an appreciative sound into the phone and hung up. He immediately picked up a remote and turned on the TV to a national news cable station. They were talking about an exploratory space trip to Mars.

"Okay," I began, "this is interesting, but..."

"Shhhhh," they both hissed at me in unison.

The story on the television changed.

"In what can only be described as shocking news today," began a female anchor, "an apparent suicide has taken place in Washington D.C. At approximately 2:00 p.m., today, Dr. Constance Sanchez entered the downtown office of her boss, Dr. Peter Sedgewick, the renowned art historian and recently appointed Director of the newly established Religious Artifacts & Antiquities Commission, and fatally shot herself. Based on a note left behind, it's believed that Dr. Sanchez, a long time co-worker of Dr. Sedgewick's at the Commission, had a personal relationship with the Director outside of the workplace and that relationship had soured. We'll update you as more details become available."

Adrian clicked off the TV and turned to face us. It was painfully obvious what he'd done, but he didn't seem at all pleased. Being far less cool than he, I couldn't suppress a laugh.

"I can't believe you, Adrian, why didn't you tell us you'd programmed the good doctor to kill herself and make the, er, bad doctor look bad? That was a stroke of genius."

"Genius? No, I'm afraid it might have been one of my less intelligent moves. It's always better to know who your enemies are. I'm afraid the Templars, or whoever is running Sedgewick, will simply find a replacement for the good doctor, or as you say, the bad doctor. I'd hoped to catch him home and maybe put an end to all this, but unfortunately he wasn't at the estate when we broke Emily out. I had to settle for sending him a message, or a warning really, through Dr. Sanchez."

Pacing back and forth with his hands clasped behind his back, he continued, "My concern is that now, whoever runs Sedgewick knows we're on to him. Thanks to my shenanigans, he may have just outlived his usefulness. I'm sure his research is well documented within his organization and someone will step up to fill the void if he's eliminated. At some point, someone will come looking for us. Hell, I may have started a war by killing so many of their members, plus Dr. Sanchez. From all the information I gathered, she was considered one of Sedgewick's most trusted allies and was responsible for the development of their protective helmet."

"No, Adrian," Emily said flatly, "they started this mess. We know they've manipulated Virgil, and I was their next experiment. This is firmly on their shoulders, not ours."

Adrian sighed. "You're absolutely right, my dear. I just hate to see some type of war started, especially after all this time. We need to figure out a way to prevent this from going any further. No good can come from it I tell you, no good at all."

A thought occurred to me, and I asked, "What other information could Virgil have given them? We know he ratted out Emily and Jasmyna, and to some extent, me. Is there anyone else he could hurt?"

Adrian nodded. "I've already alerted the others of our kind. They're taking precautions. I'm afraid our friend Virgil has become 'persona non grata' throughout the entire vampire community."

"Ah, an all vampire alert!" I exclaimed. They gave me a puzzled look.

"You know, like in *101 Dalmatians*? An 'all dog alert'? Pongo and the gang to the rescue?"

Nothing. No response at all. They continued to stare at me like I was crazy. Obviously, they weren't in touch with their Disney side, so I quickly changed the subject. "What about you, Adrian?" I asked, clearing my throat. "Does Virgil know where you live? Surely, he must know something about you."

"Yes he does, and I've taken precautions too. In fact, all of us are leaving here tonight. Until this thing settles down, we can't stay in one place for too long."

"This really sucks," I said, as the realization of our predicament set in. "That bastard Virgil has ruined everything. I'm supposed to be out hunting, not getting hunted!"

Adrian smiled. "We've been hunted for as long as I can remember, John. They just weren't this good in the past."

"Gee, that's comforting," I said, whining just a bit too much. To cover, I continued in obvious jest, "Now I keep expecting someone to pop in here and zap the hell out of me with one of those little stun guns they used on Emily. If they try to cuff me, I'll gnaw through my own wrist before I let them cage me for their evil experiments."

Emily held up her index fingers and pointed them at me. Wiggling them, she started making little "Zap, Zap, Zap" sounds. I stuck my tongue out at her and Adrian shook his head in mock exasperation.

"Okay, so what's the plan?" I asked, rubbing my hands together as I warmed to the task of planning our next moves. "We can't run forever. I know I'm not a million years old like you two, and I'm just an inexperienced young pup when it comes to the ways of our kind, but I think some good old football strategy applies here."

"Football strategy?" they asked in unison.

"Sure. Sometimes the best defense is a really good offense. Then again, it might be that the best offense is a good defense? I mean a really good offense can get pretty defensive at times."

I'd started out with a clear idea of what I was going to say, but my mind was working on a plan so fast that I now had no idea what was coming out of my lips.

"That's exactly what I've been thinking," Adrian cut in, pounding his fist on the mantle.

"Really?" I asked, interested to see where my ramblings had taken him?

"No, but I couldn't stand hearing you blabbering on like that. I was simply trying to get you off the hook!" He paused momentarily for effect, and then burst out laughing. "You're so damned gullible, John. I love it. You definitely keep things interesting."

I grunted in disgust, and pretended to scratch my right eye with my right middle finger.

"Actually, I do believe you're on to something, John. We're going to go Dracula on them. A very offensive defense, as I'm sure you were trying to say."

He had a nasty twinkle in his eye and a wicked grin on his face. If that look meant anything close to what I thought it meant, for the first time in a long while, I felt we had a chance.

Chapter 25

Since our plans called for laying low for a few days prior to meeting up at one of Adrian's hideaways in Arizona, I decided to head to my new home in the foothills east of Fresno. Adrian had teased me for buying it, since during several of our long conversations about my childhood, I'd done a pretty good job of talking trash about the area. It's funny how things change, but it felt kind of good to be going home. Besides, the city had grown substantially since I'd lived there and it hardly seemed like the same place. The high crime rate that remains in parts of the city actually works in my favor.

Delthea had decided to take the job and had already arrived with her boys. The place was too new for anyone to know about, and I was anxious to get a safe haven of my own established. As soon as I nailed down a few details at the house, I'd start working on putting together my own Company. I know Adrian has been around since the invention of dirt, but I couldn't shake my petty jealousy. I, too, would have my own Company.

I knew immediately upon arriving at my new home that my male intuition had been correct once again. Delthea was perfect for the job. The house was just over six thousand square feet and sat in the middle of a forty-acre site. The price had been right, so I had no problem investing in a few improvements. Delthea made some great suggestions, and I knew she had my best interests at heart.

Early on in my training, Adrian had insisted that it was imperative that I have the ability to escape from my houses should they ever come under attack. Recent events had proven this to be good advice, as Jasmyna had used just such a route to safely exit her home in New Orleans. I'd barely begun to discuss this with Delthea, when she presented me with some plans she'd drawn up. She was way ahead of me.

First, she suggested we convert ten to twelve acres of the property to vineyards. This would lend credibility to her plan, as well as produce income for the property. Though I knew nothing about growing grapes, I had a pretty good connection in Adrian, now, so I agreed. A contractor would be brought in to establish a working vineyard as soon as possible. It would take a few years to begin producing, but time wasn't a huge concern for me.

According to her plans, a portion of the house's basement would be converted into a wine cellar. Under the guise of developing a way to stock the wine cellar with barrels of wine, a small underground tunnel, or passageway, would be built between the new wine cellar in the house, and an existing outbuilding, which had originally been designed as a large multi-purpose garage and repair shop. This building would be converted into a winemaking and storage facility. It was actually a fairly well laid out repair shop, and already had what is commonly referred to as a grease pit for working underneath vehicles. An automobile or tractor can be driven onto a couple of heavy-duty metal ramps that extend across the open pit, and a mechanic can shimmy down a ladder and work comfortably underneath the vehicle while standing upright. Similar arrangements are often used for changing the oil in a vehicle.

According to her design, a barrel of wine would be able to be lowered into the pit and placed onto a small trolley cart, which would be on a handy little trolley track. The door to the tunnel could be opened, the cart hooked to a cable, and then the whole thing could be pulled slowly through the tunnel to the wine cellar in the house. Empty barrels could be returned using the same process in reverse. They'd be loaded onto the cart in the wine cellar and unloaded in the winemaking/storage facility.

Of course, none of this really mattered since I didn't drink wine, especially by the barrel full. It simply provided a reasonable excuse for building a nifty little escape tunnel between the house and the outbuilding.

A different construction company would build a second "drainage" tunnel. Running between the pit and a fishing pond located at the back of the property, which would ensure that I had multiple options. I approved her design on the spot and thanked her for taking the time to develop such an elaborate scheme on my behalf. I was rewarded with a genuine blush and a pop on the shoulder.

Delthea was also making arrangements for a live-in housekeeper and gardener. She'd volunteered to do the cleaning herself, but after I gave her my own lengthy list of tasks and chores to do, she agreed to bring in some hired help to handle the brunt of the housework. Again, thinking of my safety, she insisted we add two small apartments over the detached garage for the new hired help to live in. The living accommodations would be deducted from their salaries.

I was surprised when Delthea informed me that we had a female ghost living with us, though in her opinion there was no danger. We chatted about the supernatural for a while, and I realized she knew a lot more about many subjects than I did. Remembering my experience seeing a ghost in New Orleans, I had no reason not to believe her. Although I kept an eager eye out for our supernatural visitor during this stay, I wasn't rewarded with a visit.

To my surprise, I found I really enjoyed spending time with her boys, though I noticed she kept an eye on me the first day or two. Not that I blamed her, since she really didn't know me that well. I recognized that it took a leap of faith on her part, and I vowed to myself that I'd never let her down. I'd protect her boys with my life.

My experience with children was limited, since Susan and I never conceived. Perhaps I was too wrapped up in my petty little life to fight for having children of my own, but now I realized what I'd missed out on. The boys, Anthony and Marcus, who were seven and five respectively, were hilarious. They laughed at everything; especially bodily functions like burps and farts, and they could have as much fun playing with an empty box as with a video game. I think their sole purpose in life was to make me laugh, and they were good at it.

Delthea cautioned me that there might be a little bit of hero worship going on, since I was the new male figure in their lives, so I had to be careful. Still, you've got to love kids who can change the words from "Old McDonald Had A Farm", to "Old Delthea Has A Big-Butt." I did notice the song got both boys a pop on the back of the head, so I haven't tried singing it myself yet...at least not out loud.

I was determined to treat her boys like my own, at least from a financial standpoint. In fact, I insisted that they have all the privileges money could buy. They'd participate in sports, cub scouts, music lessons, or whatever they wanted. College wouldn't be a problem, providing they did the work to get in. Perhaps from a survival aspect I was buying her loyalty, but I really enjoyed sharing things with her and the boys. They appreciated everything I did for them so much, that I wanted to give them the world. Killing her husband had granted her freedom from a living hell, but that wasn't enough. I wanted her to feel like she'd moved up to heaven.

By my reckoning, Delthea was the first person in my Company. I want her properly motivated, and simply being free of her ex-husband wasn't enough to keep her motivated at a level that suited me. It's like having a job. Sure, if you're out of work and finally land a job, initially you're stoked just to be working again. But that wears off. Long-term motivation requires more than being free of danger; she needs to know that she is important and that I value her efforts. It's actually true, so it's not a stretch in the least. It's just important that she always considers being with me her best option.

Chapter 26

Comfortable that the new house was well taken care of, I headed down to Arizona. Adrian had a safe house there, and we'd agreed to meet to finalize our plans. I was missing Emily and looked forward to jumping her ancient but lovely bones once again.

Adrian's highland hideaway was about twenty miles outside of Flagstaff. When he said it was in Arizona, I assumed it was in the desert and expected to see the usual desert fare; saguaro palms, sun-baked cow skulls, and endless miles of sand and dirt. His cabin was surrounded by lush vegetation, and the terrain resembled a forest more than a desert. I commented on the fact, and Adrian patiently explained that we were in Northern Arizona, and the terrain I'd envisioned could be found farther south. He also suggested that I get out more.

My reunion with Emily was all I could have hoped for. As anxious as I was to put Adrian's plan into action, I wanted to enjoy every moment with her. The concept of living for centuries was hard to get used to. Patience might be a virtue, but it doesn't satisfy the burning down below. I still wanted immediate satisfaction, and Emily happily provided it.

Sitting on the deck under the largest moon ever to cross the night sky, I asked Emily and Adrian about ghosts. I felt silly bringing it up, knowing I was opening myself up for some good-natured teasing, but eventually I got the desired outcome and we had a lively discussion on the subject.

I started by breaking one of our long, comfortable silences, "Oh, by the way, did I ever tell you guys I saw Casper?"

"Casper?" Emily asked.

"Sure, the friendly ghost. He said to say, 'Hi'."

"Here we go again," said Adrian, shaking his head. "Okay, so what's the punch line?"

"I'm serious. Not about Casper but about ghosts. I think I saw one in New Orleans. It was the night I went out with Virgil. Delthea says we have one in my new house. I think I believe her, though I haven't personally seen it."

"Ghosts are all over," replied Adrian. "Interesting that you have one at the new house, though. I didn't think it was that old from the way you described it. Generally speaking, you find them in older buildings. Occasionally, they occupy a new building that was built over their old space. Your house was probably built over an old Indian burial ground, and now your television's going to suck you into some giant void."

"Happens all the time to rookie vampires," chimed in Emily.

"So, what the hell are they?" I asked, ignoring the ridiculous part of their answer.

"Ghosts," they replied in unison. Have I mentioned that I hate them sometimes?

"Let me rephrase my question," I said with mock exasperation. "What exactly are ghosts? As a human, I didn't think they existed."

"Ah, but you didn't think vampires existed, either, did you? Let me see if I can explain their existence in simple terms..." Adrian, ever the teacher, began.

"Better make it very simple terms," interjected Emily, wrinkling her nose at me.

I glared at both of them. "Never mind. You probably don't really know anyway."

We sat quietly for about thirty minutes, absorbed in our thoughts and staring at the shrinking moon.

"Ghosts are simply confused souls," Adrian began, as though he'd never stopped talking. "They've died, but they don't know it. Perhaps I should say they don't accept it. It's rather sad really. Time has no meaning, other than here on Earth, so they generally stay and relive some portion of their life, over and over again. You may be too young to remember record albums, but it's kind of like when you'd get a scratch in one of them. The same small segment just kept repeating over and over, until you move the needle on. I've tried talking to them several times, but they don't really listen. They are in a state of confusion."

"I've helped a few cross over," piped in Emily. "It's so sad. They cling to their silly human existence, instead of crossing over to the wonders of the other side."

"You've helped ghosts?" I asked intrigued. "You mean you can talk to them?"

Emily shrugged and said, "It's more like talking at them, than to them. Their thoughts are all jumbled, so you pretty much have to yell at them to get their attention. Then you have to make them understand they're dead and they need to go to the light. Some do, some don't. Either way, they're nothing like the ghosts you read about in books."

I was very interested. "So, they don't really haunt people?"

"Not really," Adrian explained. "They're too lost in their own situation to effectively haunt someone. I don't think they have the mental capacity to organize a plan. They may rattle some cabinet doors, or break a glass for attention, but they can't plan an elaborate or detailed haunting. Werewolves, now, that's a different story."

"I'm not biting, and the pun is intended," I said.

Adrian chuckled. "If vampires and ghosts are real, why not werewolves?"

Still not willing to be made to look foolish again, I said, "And mummies?"

Adrian sat up on one elbow, and warmed to the conversation. "Actually, mummies do exist. In ancient Egypt, they mummified royalty and those rich enough to afford it. This is a well-documented fact, John. I promise I'm not making this up. You should watch The Discovery Channel more often. Or, get daring someday, read a book."

I looked at Emily, knowing I was being had, but she was no help. She simply nodded and piled it on. "It's true John. There really were mummies. Actually, I should say that there *are* mummies, since some of them are still intact after all this time. Of course they don't come back to life or anything cool like that, but they do exist."

I'd let them have enough fun at my expense, so I said, "Okay, back to the werewolves. Were you serious about that, or just pulling my leg?"

"Nope, they definitely exist. Their numbers have dwindled significantly through the years. Progress hasn't been kind to them. They simply aren't as intelligent as we are. More like wild beasts, I guess. Virgil would have made a much better werewolf than vampire."

I was amazed. "How come nobody knows about this?"

They both laughed, and Adrian said, "Of course, people know about this."

Not to be put off, I continued, "As a recent human, I thought they were just myth and legend. The only people who actually believed in this stuff were considered kooks."

"There's a lot of information you aren't privy to as a regular run-of-the-mill human. The humans that run things, and I mean really run things, keep the flow of information limited." Adrian was on a roll, and I didn't dare interrupt him. "The Templars have known about us, as well as several other groups, for centuries, yet they don't share the information with the general public. They even hide their own existence. Knowledge is power, and they live for power. They control more than you'd ever believe."

"Like what?" I asked, unable to control my curiosity.

"Like the media, for instance. They control several of the major newspapers and television stations, indirectly run many major corporations, and control major pieces of the government, including the military."

"Come on, Adrian" I challenged, "surely you're joking? You sound like one of those conspiracy theorists."

Adrian sighed but didn't smile. "I'm afraid not, my boy. I know I sound paranoid, but it's true. America was an experiment. The Templars, operating from within the Masons and the Rosicrucians, controlled most of Europe. Still do, in fact. Remember, much of the nobility throughout Europe secretly belonged to these groups at the time. As the American colonies were developing, they saw an opportunity to establish a better way of running a country. They'd experimented throughout Europe, starting in the fifteenth century, but met with little success. Keep in mind, though, that they can't and don't control everything. At best, they control key positions, so there are always flaws, imperfections, and the occasional wildcard thrown into their best laid plans. Their worst failure was in France, which still hasn't recovered. The United States is their crowning achievement, at least to date. From here, they can control most of the world, all in the name of democracy and human rights."

My brain hurt. "So just how is it that we're gonna beat these guys again? They sound like they're everywhere."

Adrian smiled. "They're human and therefore flawed. They don't trust one person at the reins, which in turn forces them to keep things fragmented. Their controlling body is a council. As far as vampires are concerned, I believe many of them don't care about our existence, or they place little importance on it. At least they haven't cared enough to make us a priority. Obviously, there's a branch or group that does care, seemingly more of late, and that's what we'll focus on. Since knowledge is power, I doubt they've freely shared knowledge about us throughout their organization, or maybe even with the entire council."

"So," I said, catching on, "all we really need to do is focus on the branch that's interested in us, and forget about the rest?"

"I hope so," he replied. After a long pause, he continued, "We're breaking new ground here. Something, and I'm not sure what, has caused an increased interest in us. It could be one individual's curiosity, or some grand scheme we don't know about. Whatever's happening, we'll just stick to our plan and see how it plays out."

"When do we start," I asked?

A dark shadow crossed his face and his eyes narrowed. "My best guess is two days from now. We head back to Napa tomorrow, separately. Get plenty of rest and nourishment. Once it starts, it'll be all or nothing. I don't expect us to be able to relax for quite some time."

We sat quietly for a few minutes mulling over the upcoming events. I decided to ask Adrian about his origins for the hundredth time. All he could do was say no and make fun of me for the millionth time.

Using a new tactic, I said, "So Adrian, we're heading into a lot of danger. Some of us, especially those who are old and feeble may not return. Perhaps there's some information about your life you'd like to share?"

He sighed heavily. "Yes there is, John. I guess this is as good a time as ever to tell you that I'm a vegetarian. When you think I'm drinking wine, it's really V8 juice!"

"Aw, come on, what's the big secret?" I asked.

Both he and Emily chuckled. "There is no big secret. We just like irritating you," he said.

"I bet you have something to hide," I continued, not willing to give up too easily. "You were a criminal or something, weren't you? Wait, I know. You taught ballet at a girl's school in France, right? No, no, I've got it. You were an accountant, or better yet, a tax collector. Yea, that's it. I'm sure they've been reviled throughout history, so that's gotta be you. Adrian, the IRS agent."

Obviously, I was just trying to needle him, but suddenly he sat up straight and looked at Emily. They both started laughing.

"What are the odds?" he asked her, shaking his head.

"I told you," she replied. "Our boy is one of the luckiest creatures I've ever seen."

Turning to me, Adrian said, "Okay, okay, you've got me. I'll tell you my boring story, but then you've got to shut up about it. Agreed?"

I was excited, now, feeling that I'd finally earned a right to privileged information. "Agreed…"

He cleared his throat to begin, but I interrupted. "Mr. Tax Collector!"

He gave me the finger, and then looking into the distant sky as though it held the answers to life's puzzles, he began his tale. "I was born in the year 1420, in a small town in Hungary. It was a beautiful place, really, and my childhood was actually quite nice. We weren't royalty, but my father was an educated man of some stature. As such, we were afforded most of the luxuries of the day.

"Having successfully navigated the many hazards a child faced in those days, including the occasional whipping from my maternal grandmother, I attained the ripe old age of ten. It was during my tenth year that I was sent to Italy to study religion. I was, you see, destined to become a priest in the Catholic Church. In fact, I was named after a Pope, Adrian IV, who some two hundred and seventy years earlier had shown favor to my ancestors. I should point out that I was not the first child in my family named after the good pope. By my count, I was the thirty-second. Obviously, my family didn't forget a favor!"

"What the heck did they do for this guy?" I interrupted.

"That's the odd part," he said shaking his head. "None of my family were even sure anymore. Oddly enough, though, he was from Britain, and we tended to be fair skinned. My guess is that there was some sort of hanky-panky going on, though back then, we were never allowed to even suggest it. Regardless, we were taught that we owed our standing, which included a fair sized chunk of property, to Adrian IV."

"So how'd you get from priest to tax collector," I asked.

Adrian stared at me until I made a motion of zipping my lips.

"As I was saying, I headed off to Florence to study religion. Now, you need to understand something about religion in that day. I'll try to make it simple, but it was incredibly complex, even for one who lived in the middle of it.

"Many of those going into religion became monks. Basically, they cut themselves off from the world and lived a simple life. Others became priests, who of course were active within the local communities. Finally, a select few became politicians. Not in the same way that you might think of, but in a manner of serving the greater good of the church, which was then a very politically oriented organization. For centuries after the collapse of Rome, the Church filled an organizational void, if you will, in the structure of Europe.

"Although I was an eager learner, I soon realized I didn't have a deep enough dedication to God to become a Monk. In fact, I also realized that I didn't feel strongly enough about the masses of people to want to go and care for them the way a priest needed to. And then, at the ripe young age of fifteen, I discovered the gentler sex."

I couldn't suppress a laugh. "Kind of late to notice the opposite sex isn't it?"

Once again, I got the evil eye for interrupting.

"Of course, I knew they existed, I just didn't know how good they felt lying next to you on a cold night. I was traveling with my mentor to Austria, and we stayed the night at an inn. It was cold, and as I was just beginning to doze off in my room, a pretty young girl that I'd seen in the dining hall snuck into my room. We lay there looking at each other for a few minutes, me having no clue what to do, and her probably wondering if I was an idiot. Well, with her guidance, we finally got the deed done. In fact, we got it done three times. Needless to say, I was hooked. The trouble was, I'd found the greatest joy in life, and I couldn't tell anyone.

"I spent six months thinking about a lifetime of continually wanting to break my already broken vow of celibacy, and decided against it. I couldn't get the girl out of my head and I was walking around in a constant state."

"A constant state?" I queried, confused by his wording.

"I was constantly in a state of arousal. I was horny all the time. I had major wood. Got it?" he asked, frustrated by my interruption.

Picturing a horny Adrian at fifteen was hilarious to me, but I decided to tuck any related jokes away until later. I needed him to continue with his story, and if I interrupted again, he might take a fifteen-year intermission. Once again, I made a motion of me zipping my lips.

"Anyway, I confessed my transgressions," he continued, "and was promptly sent back to Hungary. There, they decided to take advantage of my education and I was first sent to work for the great Sigismund as a junior diplomat and translator at the Diet of Iglau, where he was acknowledged as regent of Bohemia."

"Huh?" I queried, intelligently. I was lost.

"Let's just say it was the coolest meeting to be at in 1436. Lots of important people floating about, making important decisions and policies."

"Ah yes, of course," I agreed, nodding. I had no freakin' idea what he was talking about, but I wasn't going to look stupid again.

"Well, one thing led to another, and as I moved up the chain, I began to work for Mihaly Szilagy, a Hungarian governor for King Ladislas V. My main job was negotiating with our industrious German immigrants, who occupied several towns and villages in the region. It was exciting work, but there seemed to be endless unrest. I've always been good with numbers, so I was what you'd consider today a tax specialist. Unfortunately, the King died in 1457, and the crown was passed to his young nephew, Matthias.

"Mihaly was pretty tight with our friend Vlad Dracula, which is how I became involved with him. Of course, I knew his reputation as Vlad the Impaler, the brutal prince who ruled his lands by taking advantage of the pointed end of a stake. Vlad had been wreaking havoc on several German towns, and it became important to Mihaly and King Matthias that he cease his aggressions."

Adrian looked at me suspiciously, and explained in English, "They wanted Vlad to take a chill pill. Ease up on impaling Germans for a while. Vlad was Prince of Wallachia at the time, and he had a major hard-on for the Germans."

I nodded, showing him that I was tracking with him so far.

"Anyway, they sent Benedict de Boitor, one of the brightest guys around, to negotiate with Vlad. Now you need to understand, Benedict was one sharp cookie, but dealing with Vlad was always a total unknown. One minute he was rational, the next he was staking you, your family, and everyone you'd ever known for some silly reason. Vlad was totally unpredictable."

Again I nodded, assuring Adrian that I was no dummy, even though I was mostly lost. History lessons had always put me to sleep. Though he didn't say anything, I think he recognized he was losing me a bit.

"When Benedict got to Vlad's castle in Tirgoviste, Vlad invited him to dine in a courtyard decorated with dead and dying bodies hanging from stakes. Imagine mutilated body parts everywhere, the stench of death all around; we're talking nasty beyond belief. In front of the head table is a special stake. Vlad calmly indicates the stake is for Benedict. Instead of panicking, Benedict wisely answered that if that staking him was Vlad's will, then it couldn't be wrong since he was a just and wise ruler."

Now the story was getting interesting, and I was totally in to it.

"Old Benedict probably thought he was a goner at this point, but to his surprise, Vlad started laughing and said, 'You're all right, Benedict. If you'd screwed up your answer, you'd be demonstrating a Hungarian pole dance for us right now."

I was beginning to get the feeling that Adrian was over-simplifying the story for my benefit, but I wasn't complaining since I actually understood him for a change.

"Not only did Benedict escape with his butt hole intact, but Vlad showered him with gifts, like a new six-horse power carriage with the latest spoke wheels, lowered in the front, jacked up in the back and painted candy apple red. Of course, he also insisted that all future diplomats have the same skills as Benedict."

"Okay," I began, knowing that he was now having great fun with history at my expense, "and this is important to your story because...?"

Adrian sighed, and shook his head. "Patience, I'm getting there."

I held up my hands, "No rush."

Emily giggled.

"Well, needless to say, Benedict's successful mission was quite the story back in Hungary. Unfortunately, we needed to send someone back a few weeks later. Since negotiating tax rates was involved, yours truly was elected."

Now I was beginning to understand.

"I think I received more advice on how to stay alive, than I did on what to negotiate," he continued. "When I arrived, I too was treated to a banquet. Determined not to slip up, I answered every question as humbly and honestly as possible. Things were going well until they brought in a young girl, maybe sixteen or seventeen, and a finely dressed gentleman who appeared to be in his early forties. Vlad told me the gentleman and his servant girl were guilty of plotting against him, and asked me what their punishment should be. Obviously, he was asking me to sentence this frightened young girl and her master to death.

"I explained to him that I was a mere diplomat, and that such decisions should be left to wiser and more just men, such as him. I'd hoped it would satisfy him, but it didn't. He pressed the point, wanting to know if I was partial to his enemies. I knew everything was falling apart, and I could sense his mood turning dark. Deciding that the girl and her master were dead either way, I said, 'Lord, though I have not been privy to the details surrounding this case, I know you would only speak the truth about their guilt in this matter. Though I would never presume to take such a liberty, it seems you've asked my honest opinion here. Therefore, they, by nature of their crimes, are guilty of opposing your sovereignty and must die. Though I'm no expert, I believe the proper method of punishment would be impalement."

I realized I'd been holding my breath, and I let out a heavy sigh. No way was I interrupting Adrian now.

"This seemed to appease him for the moment, and he signaled to several of his henchmen. They grabbed the girl and unceremoniously threw her on one of two waiting stakes. She screamed for a few seconds, but I think it pierced her heart, because she quickly went silent."

"Vlad walked over to her and, taking his knife, sliced her throat. He held his golden goblet under the cut, and filled his cup with the young girl's blood. I knew he was making a point, and for a brief moment, our eyes met. It's amazing how much you can think about in a matter of seconds, especially when you're staring into those two black portals to hell that were his eyes."

"I wanted to vomit, but I knew my life depended on my next few moves. If I failed, I would die too, likely in the same manner as these two poor souls. Of course, someone else would have to come to this living hell and try to negotiate the same treaties. On top of all that, there were thousands of innocent German lives at stake."

"I looked at his henchmen and nodded towards the gentleman, then the stake. I felt especially pained, because this fellow just stood there smiling at me. I knew that he'd probably assume I was condemning him to the stake, so that I would live. He had to think I was the scum of the earth.

"I believe Vlad's henchmen were surprised by my move, but they looked at Vlad and he nodded his consent. They grabbed the still smiling man and threw him belly first on the second stake. Everything was a blur now, since I was witnessing the first death that I was directly responsible for. Still in a daze, I picked up my cup and a knife and walked over to the man. I'd come this far, and I needed to finish it. I lifted the man's head and to my surprise, he was still smiling at me. This shocked the hell out of me, but I took my knife and sliced at his throat, thinking maybe I'd ease his misery."

Adrian was no longer with us. I could tell by his voice and the look in his eyes that he was reliving the moment. I wondered how many times he'd suffered through this over the centuries, and I understood why he's been reluctant to share his story.

"Imagine my surprise," he continued. "When my first attempt at slicing his throat was not successful. I made a second attempt, and got a small trickle. Vlad had cut through the girl's throat like butter, but I was struggling. Obviously, there was a trick to slicing throats that I wasn't privy to. Anyway, I'd managed to get a trickle flowing on my second attempt, so I held my cup up to it and let some dribble in. When I had a swallow or two in the cup, I turned to Vlad and raised my cup. For the first time, Vlad smiled and returned my salute. At the same time, we both drank."

"Imagine my surprise when my freshly impaled victim, he of the recently sliced throat, began to laugh again. With a mighty twist of his body, he snapped the wooden stake off a foot or so in front of his body. Vlad's henchmen were too shocked to move, and the Prince just stood there staring in disbelief."

"This 'gentleman' stood up and pushed the rest of the now broken pole into his stomach, then reached around and with one mighty tug, pulled the pole out through the back. It must have hurt like hell but he just smiled. Then, he pointed at Vlad, and said, 'So, you are the great Vlad Dracula? Vlad the Impaler. I expected so much more out of you. You're nothing but a common tyrant, whose time is short.

"'What manner of black magic is this?' screamed Vlad, a touch of hysteria in his voice, and no longer appearing quite so menacing.

"This amazing gentleman just laughed at him, and then brain freezes everyone in the courtyard but me.

"'So,' he asked me, rather nonchalantly, 'what do you think of my blood?'

"I was terrified and ready to faint. He looked at my cup, and said, 'Go ahead, and finish it.'

"I wasn't about to argue, so I gulped down what was in the cup. To be honest, I'd only pretended to drink the first time. Blood had entered my mouth, but I had let it flow right back into the cup. This time, out of a totally new fear, I drank. As soon as the blood entered my system, I got a jolt. I'm sure it was much like when you bit Jasmyna, John."

I nodded, remembering that initial feeling of strength, "Yes, it was a heck of a jolt."

"He took me by the hand and, turning serious, asked me to go away with him. He'd seen something in me during our short encounter, and he wanted to share his magic with me, if I was interested. I was incredibly pumped up on his blood, so I agreed. We left Vlad's court, with all of them still staring off into nothingness. I'm sure later they wondered what the hell had just happened. Back in Hungary, when I didn't show up, they simply assumed I'd failed one of Vlad's tests."

Adrian stopped talking, and we all sat for a few minutes. As usual, I was the first to break the silence.

"Okay, so what happened next?" I urged. "Your maker, my great-grandfather, who was he? Is he still around? How old is he?"

"Oh, he's around," Adrian said as he exchanged a look with Emily. "Someday, when this is all over, I'll tell you all about him. For now, suffice it to say that while I love him dearly, we don't see eye to eye on a lot of things. I suppose ours is a lot like many parent-child relationships. We're just different. Even after all these years, and countless arguments, we don't agree on many important things."

I was still curious and asked, "What's so important that you can't agree on? Is it the way you feed?"

"John," Adrian smiled at me, "that's enough for one now. Give it a rest. I promise I'll tell you more after this mess is cleared up. Relax, there'll be plenty of time for you to learn your history."

"Okay, but can you at least tell me his name?"

Adrian's eyebrows raised a notch, and he smiled. "Actually, he's gone by many different names, much like the rest of us. The only difference is that his names have been better known around the world. At different times, just to name a few, he's been known as a Marquis, a Count, a Duke, a General in the Army, and of course in the early days of the United States, both a congressman and a senator.

"Wow," I said, amazed. "I'm no expert, but it doesn't sound like he's got the whole "low key" thing down very well, does he?"

Adrian smiled, but it wasn't a pleasant one. "No, he has never been into laying low. Just the opposite, though he's always hidden his true identity. He's been several other prominent figures throughout history, but enough about him. We've got work to do."

"One last question," I said pushing my luck. "Since he was a count and a duke and all that, does this mean I'm some type of royalty now too?"

Emily answered for him. "Yes, John, it means you're a royal now. You're a royal pain in the ass!"

For some reason they found this greatly amusing.

Chapter 27

Once again, Adrian's prediction came true. The evening after we returned to Napa, his house was the target of an FBI raid. It was done quietly, but effectively. Twenty-two agents, wearing the now familiar "anti-vampire" helmets surrounded his house. With military precision, they worked their way inside his home.

Bursting in full of anticipation, they were disappointed to find nothing more than an exceptionally well-appointed domicile. Only they could say what they were expecting to find, but I doubt it was what they found. No vampires hanging from the ceiling, no drained bodies littering the floor, and for all intents, no evidence of vampires at all. Several hours of searching turned up nothing of consequence. Adrian's trustworthy staff, who revealed nothing more than puzzlement at all the fuss, were put in a van and transferred off the property.

While they searched, we waited patiently in the vineyard. When he felt the time was right, Adrian attacked first. It was a simple strike. One agent, picked at random, simply disappeared. It took nearly thirty minutes for them to notice, and then they seemed more puzzled by the disappearance than concerned.

Next, it was my turn. With the stealth of a Ninja Turtle, I took a second agent. Careful to leave no trace, I ensured that he simply vanished from the face of the earth.

Emily volunteered to grab a third agent, but Adrian was satisfied with two. In reality, I think he'd have preferred a third but knew Emily never killed unless someone was already marked for death. While we hadn't technically killed our hostages yet, their future didn't look very good if we stuck to our plan. He didn't want Emily to have to make that particular choice, at least not yet.

I wanted to stay and watch them go nuts when a second agent came up missing, but Adrian insisted we move on with our plan. We loaded our unconscious hostages into a rental van we'd acquired for the purpose and headed south.

In 1959, Adrian had acquired a wonderful old Victorian just off

Grand Avenue in Alameda. He was sure Virgil would remember it, since it was one of the few places he'd allowed Virgil to visit him. If Virgil knew about it, we had to figure our FBI friends did too. Though he'd kept it staffed and perfectly maintained, Adrian hadn't been to the house in nearly thirty years. If the bad guys knew of its existence, it would definitely implicate Virgil.

Sure enough, we found two cars with special agents watching the Alameda house. Waiting until the dark of night to cover our moves from prying eyes, we snatched two more agents from one of the cars. The unconscious bodies were beginning to pile up in the van.

The next stop was my old house in Vintage Oaks. I'd argued with Adrian about this briefly, but he felt sure they knew I still owned it. Even though I hadn't lived there in well over a year, he expected that they'd be keeping a precautionary eye on it. As usual, he was right.

It felt odd to see someone watching "my" house, even though I hadn't thought of it as my house in a long while. I could understand them watching for Adrian, since he was a big-time vampire from back in the day. But, why me? I was a real nobody. I'd even made it a point to inform my red headed friend, Miss Leslie Denise Poole, that I was nobody special. So why were they interested in me? I suddenly felt very uncomfortable knowing that I was a major player in this deadly game. I was somebody's enemy. Yikes!

We snatched two more agents from the detail in front of my house, and now we were up to six. We headed back to the Napa property, and parked behind an old barn about a half a mile away from Adrian's house. It too belonged to Adrian, but was active only during the harvest season. We'd watched them search it on their way in, and finding nothing but farm equipment and dust, they'd moved on to the main-house. Now we took up residence, and quickly set up shop.

Emily stayed behind, and keeping an eye on our still unconscious hostages, began preparations for phase two of our plan. Adrian and I cautiously headed through the vineyards to the main-house. Activity was high, presumably because they couldn't find their missing agents. By now, they might also realize that agents were also missing from Alameda and Vintage Oaks. That would be fine with us, since it was actually part of our plan.

Snatching a human is generally not very difficult for a vampire, but these humans were on high alert. It was imperative to our plan that no warning could be signaled from our victims. They just had to disappear off the face of the Earth, at least temporarily.

We managed to grab four more agents over the course of the next hour, and cart them back to the barn. That brought our total to ten, which Adrian assured us was satisfactory for our purposes. The time for dirty work had arrived. It was time to "Go Dracula" on them, as Adrian had said.

For those of you who don't know about the real Vlad Dracula, I'll attempt a quick history lesson. No, he was not a vampire as I learned when Adrian shared his own story. Compared to him, however, we're saints. He was humanity at its worst, a homicidal maniac, responsible for many thousands of deaths. This guy ranks up there with the likes of Adolf Hitler, Joseph Stalin, and Saddam Hussein.

Like most people, my familiarity with Dracula came from modern movies, and I always assumed he was a figment of Bram Stoker's imagination. Adrian, who had first-hand knowledge of this character, set me straight on the drive back to Napa.

According to Adrian, Vlad Dracula was born in 1431, the second son of Prince Vlad Dracul. The letter "a" on the end of Dracul, simply indicated he was the "son of" Dracul. He spent his early years in Hungary and Wallachia, which was somewhat ruled by Hungary. At the ripe old age of eleven, he and his younger brother, Radu, were sent to live with the Turks. Basically, they were hostages of the Turks. The general idea was that, as long as the Turks held two of his sons, Drac Sr. would stay in line. According to Adrian, this was a fairly common practice back then. Though they were officially hostages, they were treated much the same as the local royal rug rats. They went to school, were taught proper etiquette, and often even received military training.

Well, in 1447, old Drac said to hell with his younger two sons and went to war anyway. Both he and his oldest son, Mircea, were killed for their effort. Now it seems that the Turks would be perfectly within their rights to kill the two young boys, but for some reason they didn't. Adrian claims that rumors of the day had young Radu, who was a reasonably handsome young man, and the Ottoman Turk Sultan Mehmed, had a little something going on.

The Turks decided to release Vlad Dracula, now a manly sixteen year-old, back to Hungary, where he could continue the studies expected of a young noble. Doing what every young boy fantasizes about at the age of sixteen, rather than studying Latin, that is, he attempted to assume control of Wallachia. Actually, he was successful, but only for a few months.

In 1456, now a much smarter and more determined young man, he assumed control of Wallachia again. This time, he reigned for about six years. It would be a bloody six years, and it was during this period that

Adrian had his encounter with him. It was also the period that Vlad
Dracula earned the nickname, "Vlad the Impaler."

He ruled his land brutally, but effectively. If you broke the law, you
were impaled on a stake. No warnings, no second chances. One of his first
tasks was to hold a huge celebration for all the local vagrants, ruffians,
and other assorted law-breakers. He lured them into a courtyard with
the promise of an awesome keg party, and then he locked all the doors
and burned the joint to the ground. He had effectively reduced crime
by a significant amount in one fell swoop. I understand the Democrats
attempted a similar feat with the Republicans during the Clinton years
but had trouble getting the fire lit.

Anyway, when young Vlad determined that some of his local leaders
weren't taking care of their subjects, they too got a slow ride on the
stake train. Much like the crosses we hear about in Christ's time, these
human decorations-on-a-stick were placed in the open for all to see
and enjoy. If you were lucky, you got a pointed stake and a quick death.
If Vlad was having a bad hair day, you got a rounded-off pole, lightly
greased, aimed up the poop shoot. He fully realized the psychological
effect this had on people and used it to his advantage. As brutal as he
was, the country actually began to prosper.

In 1461, Sultan Mehmed decided he'd had enough of Vlad who
wasn't paying the proper tribute to the Turks. He began by attacking
Vlad's ports, and in 1462 he set out in earnest to teach this young
Wallachian prince a lesson. Now, it's important to understand that
this was not a very even fight. Vlad had about 22,000 foot soldiers and
8000 cavalry. Mehmed had an army of 300,000, including a 4,000-man
cavalry unit headed by none other than Vlad's dear little brother, Radu.
I'm guessing that he and Mehmed still had it going on, but wonder how
he led the cavalry since he probably had trouble riding a horse most
of the time. Hey, those long war campaigns get lonely when you're a
Sultan...

What do you do when you're outnumbered ten to one? You go
"Dracula," which is exactly what Adrian had us doing now! Dracula knew
every inch of his countryside, and he made Mehmed pay every step of
the way. He also knew that an army that size required a ton of logistical
support, including whores, cooks, whores, camp workers, more whores,
a multitude of other camp groupies, and a few more whores. Did I
mention they brought a bunch of whores with them?

Wisely, Vlad never faced them directly. Instead, he darted in on
quick raids and continually attacked their flanks. Every night, sentries
disappeared. Rarely did anyone who separated from the hoard ever show

up again. He scorched the earth in front of Mehmed's army, and as they slowly moved forward, they found not a single living human or animal. All the wells were poisoned. Criminals avoided demonstrating their pole dancing skills by being sent into the Turk camp as assassins, and diseased whores gained Vlad's favor by spreading their various sexually related illnesses among the Turks. Needless to say, Mehmed's trip to Tirgoviste, Vlad's capital, was less than pleasant, though I understand t-shirts advertising, "Wallachian Girls are Easy" were quite popular among the troops.

As was the custom of the period, as Mehmed closed in on Vlad's capital, he sent several emissaries ahead to accept the upstart Dracula's surrender. Figuring that since the yellow-bellied chicken hadn't shown his face yet, and there was no reason to believe he ever would, it was pretty much over with. Conventional wisdom of the day would have had Vlad battling him as far from his capital as possible. Vlad was far from conventional, however, and Mehmed's mind would soon be changed.

About forty miles from Tirgoviste, Mehmed and his army came to the Valley of the Dead. It was foggy the morning they set out through the valley. As the fog burned off, they found themselves surrounded by thousands of staked bodies. Every sentry and soldier that had disappeared was there, hanging from a stake, body rotting in the rising sun. Strategically staked across the road, sending a clear message to Mehmed, were the emissaries he had recently sent. Vlad's response was clear; there would be no surrender.

So, what did the good Sultan do? He did what most sane men would do. He simply turned around and went home. I like to imagine him standing there in the Valley of the Dead, the stench of thousands of dead bodies all around him. The trip had been hard, the land was all burned up, there was hardly any water to drink, everyone had sores on their peckers, and he was facing what was clearly a madman. I think he looked around and said, "Screw this!" or the Turkish equivalent, anyway.

So what happened to Vlad? Well, later that year he was overthrown from within Wallachia and imprisoned in Hungary, and good ol' Radu took over. Radu ruled until 1475, when Syphilis got the best of him and he died. Despite the fact that Vlad had spent the majority of his time in prison impaling spiders and roaches, the King of Hungary decided to reinstall him as the ruler of Wallachia. He ruled again for the third time, until the end of 1476, when he was killed in battle. His severed head was sent first class to Constantinople in hopes of relieving thousand of old soldiers from the nightmares they'd had since the "Great Wallachia Campaign." Yes, I'm making that part up.

Now that you know more than you could ever have wanted to know about the real Dracula, you're probably wondering what that has to do with our current situation. Well, per Adrian's plan, we were planning a strategic retreat, or an offensive defense. We couldn't stop them, but we could make them think twice about whether or not pursuing us was worth it.

Adrian, Emily, and I set to work. It was a gruesome task, but this was war. I'm talking real life or death stuff. We needed to strike a significant blow and to send a clear message with one action. I was concerned about Emily, who cared so strongly about humans and their souls, but she set about the task at hand with a determination I'd never seen in her before. When we were finished, Adrian insisted on doing the last dirty deed. He took a five-gallon can we'd filled with blood, and left a bloody trail back through the vineyard to the main house. When he finished leaving this "trail of bread crumbs," he met up with us, hiding in the loft of a neighbor's barn with our binoculars focused, waiting to see if ten presumably good men had died for nothing.

As expected, one of the agents found the trail of blood. They had no idea it been poured heading into their direction, and not away from them. They assumed someone had been injured and was being carried away. In minutes, the alert was sounded and a large force followed the trail, eventually encircling Adrian's barn. They were clueless as to the grizzly site that awaited them.

We noted that they all wore their funny little helmets for protection, yet none seemed too anxious to enter the barn. Warnings were called out, threats made, and finally one brave man was sent to open the doors. What they found caused several to turn and vomit. Ten of their compatriot's decapitated bodies were impaled on vineyard stakes, which we'd arranged in a loose semicircle around a pile of heads, which had in turn been neatly stacked in a small pyramid. Stacked next to them in a similar pyramid, as if to display their worthlessness, were ten of their silly little helmets. These were men from three different sites, so our hope was to make it appear as though we could be anywhere and everywhere, at any time.

Not needing to see any more, we made our way back to the van and started the long drive back to Arizona. We took turns driving, and most of the time passed in silence, all of us deep in our own thoughts. I caught myself wondering if we'd simply committed murder ten times over. Had the lives of ten humans been wasted? It was depressing to think about, so I tried to think positively. I found I was okay with the killings as long as I could internally rationalize that it was for a purpose and my continued existence was a good enough purpose for me.

To help matters, Adrian handed me a small bag of badges he'd collected from the dead agents. He asked me if I noticed anything odd, and after a quick examination of one of the badges, I replied that it looked fine to me, though I had no idea what a real FBI badge looked like. Next, he had me look at all of them together and the lights began flashing in my pea-sized brain. The numbers on the badges were sequential, all within a few digits of each other. The spread of numbers was less than forty for all ten of these guys. What was the possibility that all ten of these guys had joined the FBI at the same time? Slim to none in my book, so obviously the FBI bit was a cover. For some twisted reason, that made me feel better about their deaths.

Pulling into the garage of Adrian's Arizona house, I muttered without thinking, "Home at last, home at last. Thank God Almighty, we are home at last." My play on Martin Luther King Jr.'s famous words didn't go unnoticed.

"Did I ever tell you that Martin Luther King Jr. was a vampire?" Adrian asked.

Shocked, I replied, "No, you didn't."

"Good, 'cause I would have been lying to you. He was a very good man, though; too bad the humans killed him. They tend to do that to their best."

Emily smiled for the first time in a long while. "You are so gullible, John. What are we going to do with you?"

Happy to sense an upturn in the general mood, even if I had to be on the receiving end of their jokes, I hugged her, and nuzzling my face through her long hair and into her neck, I whispered, "I can think of several things you can do with me."

Adrian yelled from down the hall, "I heard that. Get a new line."

Emily chuckled, and hugged me back tightly.

Chapter 28

We were lying in bed after passionately making love, each of us having taken turns satisfying the other's needs, and then marveling at how these unselfish acts brought as much joy and pleasure to the giver as to the recipient. Emily's head was on my chest and her fingers were tracing little circles on my stomach, when I got the sudden feeling she had something on her mind.

"Are you okay, my love?" I asked, concerned the activities of late might be having an impact on her.

"Yes, I'm okay. Actually, I'm concerned about you," she replied.

"Me?" I asked, more than a little surprised. "No need to worry about me. I'm okay with everything we did. I'll admit that seeing those fake badges helped."

"No, John, it's not that. It's us."

"Us? As in you and me?" Panic started to set in. I couldn't lose Emily.

"John, do you remember our conversation in Cabo? The one about us seeing other people?"

I sat up and took her hands in mine and kissed them gently. "Of course I remember that conversation. I have your permission to 'get some' whenever I feel the urge. Well, I'm happiest making love to you and I haven't had the urge to be with anyone else. Emily, you're really all I need right now. Why would you be concerned about us? Have I done something wrong?"

She removed her right hand from mine and caressed my face. Instead of the look of joy one would normally expect from someone who you'd just expressed your love to, I saw only a look of deep concern and sadness.

"It's not that you've done anything wrong, John, you're just making our relationship too exclusive, and that's not healthy for our kind. You're treating our relationship like a human relationship, but we're not human. I do love you, John, and if we were human, I'd probably want to be married to someone just like you. Again, we're not human. We're vampires!"

I was speechless.

"You need to go spread your wings a bit. Enjoy your gifts. Remember when you showed up in New Orleans? You wanted to cut loose and live it up."

Dropping her voice down to sound more like mine, she continued, "Nothing with two legs and a pussy is going to be safe when John Steele is around."

I didn't laugh or even smile. I was beyond speechless, and I was reeling from a deep sense of rejection. Part of me knew what she was saying made sense, but I was too numb from the pain to think it through. I did what any other guy in my situation would do, I got up and started getting dressed.

"John, please don't go. We need to talk. I said I love you, and I do. I expect us to be making wild and passionate love for centuries to come. Please stay."

I finished sliding my t-shirt over my head and walked over to the bed. I took her face in my hands and bending over, kissed the top of her head.

"I love you too, Emily. I'm fine. I just need some time to think." With that, I turned and left the room.

Sitting out on the back porch, staring into the night forest, I tried to get my emotions under control. I loved her and hated her at the same time. Part of me felt foolish, and part of me was angry. I put my face in my hands and let out an audible groan.

"What's the matter?" a voice from behind me asked. "Have some bad Mexican food?"

Adrian was making a joke, but I didn't feel like laughing. At a gas station just over the Arizona border, I'd feasted on a young Mexican lad. He looked like trouble, and when I scanned his thoughts, I realized he was guilty of multiple murders. He'd hitch a ride, and then rob and kill the unsuspecting good Samaritans. Naturally, I offered him a ride with us and he got more than he'd bargained for.

Adrian pulled up a chair and sat down beside me. I loved Adrian, but I preferred to be alone at this moment.

"Love hurts, John. It's a bitch, but love hurts. I've known Emily since the day she made The Choice. She's never loved a male vampire the way she loves you. However, her experience informs her that a monogamous relationship won't work for our kind. I've never seen it work in all my years."

"I know, Adrian, I know. It's just that Emily makes me feel so special. I've never felt like this with another human being..."

I caught my mistake and looked at Adrian. The depth of sadness his eyes displayed was so moving that I knew his heart was breaking for me.

"Okay," I said. "I get it. We're not human beings."

"John, this is not as complicated as you might think. I know how Emily feels about you, and I believe you two can carry on as you have for as long as you'd like. She's just trying to ensure the relationship stays healthy and ensure you understand that you're both free to have other partners. If you choose not to do so, that's your business. You just can't expect her to do the same. Can you live with that?"

I needed to think this through, but I didn't feel like being part of a one-sided relationship. Oddly, I didn't feel jealous at the thought of Emily being with human males.

"I think I'll be fine, Adrian, I just need some time to noodle it over."

"Then time is what you'll have my boy. You have all the time in the world."

Chapter 29

After a week of planning and re-planning and then more planning, Adrian
and I set off in different directions. He was heading to Mexico City to
meet with a contact he had within the Templars. We'd received some
information from Adrian's vast network, and the initial information
indicated that our good friend, Dr. Peter Sedgewick, was in fact the
driver behind the Templars' increased interest in us. Adrian's plan was
simple and direct. He would try to make contact with a senior individual
in their organization, and then he'd negotiate a truce. We simply wanted
things to return to normal, whatever that meant.

I was headed off to Washington D.C., for another date with my
new best friend, Miss Leslie Denise Poole. Now that the FBI, or who
knows what other government agencies were involved, there was no
way of knowing whether or not negotiating a truce with the Templars
would make them back off. Now that they were involved, were we stuck
with them on our trail? It wasn't good enough to get the Templars off
our backs; we wanted to ensure that the government would leave us
alone, too.

It was impossible for us as outsiders to know how deep the
connections ran between the two groups. Our guesses ran the gamut
from the Templars being totally in control of several major intelligence
agencies, to a more realistic guess that they were simply well connected.
Very well connected. Specifically, we were interested in what was going to
happen in the FBI's Paranormal & Psychic Investigations Department.
We knew we'd done a lot of damage in Napa and were reasonably sure
a lot of people weren't happy with us. The news had been oddly silent
about any "incidents" in the Napa area, and we'd expected to at least
read that a drug bust had gone bad or something, considering all the
commotion.

Tracking Ms. Poole down was a simple matter, especially since I'd
been to her house before. To my surprise, I found that she'd installed
an alarm system, so something had her spooked. It could be that she
was simply worried about generic trouble, like burglars, prowlers, and

peeping Johns. I refused to take this change as a coincidence, though, as there was just too much craziness going on. The last thing I needed to do was to walk into a vampire trap.

Rather than risk setting off an alarm that I had no idea of how to beat, I went back to my car and waited. My patience rapidly wore thin, and I almost gave up and went looking for her. Luckily, at 8:35 p.m., just as I was reaching for my keys to start the engine, my hot little redheaded friend showed up. She pulled into the short driveway and began unloading groceries from the trunk of her Saturn. Unnoticed, I got out of my car and ambled down the street in the general direction of her house. I'm a world-class ambler, by the way.

I slowed and watched as she struggled through the front door with several plastic bags, all filled with goodies that would make me puke up a lung. I moved quickly up the driveway and grabbed the last couple of bags, then closed her trunk quietly. I walked in the front door with her supplies and decided to impress her with my Desi Arnaz imitation. Really working the Cuban accent part, I called out, "Lucy, I'm home."

I must not have nailed the accent part, because she immediately dropped the bags she was holding, fumbled with her purse for a full five seconds, then extracted her service revolver. Trembling, she aimed it in my general direction. Come on now, it wasn't that bad!

"You!" she nearly screamed, then rambled on excitedly. "John Steele. You're a vampire, aren't you? I knew it. Part of me always knew it, even though the evidence pointed against it. Now, you're here to seek your revenge, aren't you?"

Quick thinker that I am, I realized that I had a choice here. I could play bad-ass and use pressure to get the information I needed, or I could work this and see where it went.

The first choice was just too easy and not much fun, so I chose the latter. I smiled at her, and said, "Leslie, my dear, if I was here to hurt you, do you think I'd be carrying in your groceries?"

She must be a pretty good shot, because she found no reason to hold the gun still, or to assume the standard shooter's stance, peering down the gun sight at me, one eye pinched shut and the other boring a hole in my demonic black heart. No, she had both eyes wide open, and was staring at me like I was a vampire or something.

"Leslie? Hello. Earth to Leslie. Come in Leslie."

She blinked. Not a huge response, but I could tell my charm was beginning to work its magic.

"We need to talk, Leslie. Why don't you put the gun down so we can have a nice little chat? It wouldn't do you any good anyway. Bullets can't hurt me," I lied. I had never been shot, but I figured if I could survive a near decapitation, I could survive a bullet. I bet it hurt like hell, though, and I didn't want to find out tonight. I cranked up the wattage on my smile, hoping it would be better received than my Desi imitation.

"My God, you're going to kill me, aren't you?" she asked, trembling.

"No, Leslie," I said seriously, but still smiling. "I'm here to talk with you, not to hurt you. Too many people have already been hurt. Why don't you put that silly gun down now, so we can talk? Better yet, keep it if it makes you feel safer. Would that be better? It's useless, but I want you to feel safe. I'm not here to hurt you, really."

No response, so I continued to coax her, "Let's get these groceries put away before something melts."

"Oh, God," she pleaded out loud, but obviously not pointed to me. "How did I ever get involved in all this crap? All I ever wanted to do was be a good FBI agent. I don't want to die. I'm too young."

I was surprised to find my heart going out to her. She was really scared, and obviously in over her head.

She continued rambling and began sobbing, "I mean, I know I'm not the best agent, and I know Peter let me in the group because he thought he could get me into bed, but I really wanted to make a difference. How did this get so screwed up? Mom was right, I should have become a travel agent instead of a FBI agent..."

"Leslie," I said in a loud voice, "the groceries?"

She looked startled and a little puzzled. "The groceries?"

"We need to put the groceries away. You know, before stuff melts. You can continue telling me about yourself, but we really should get this stuff put away." I hoped focusing on a simple task would calm her.

Now she looked really puzzled. "The groceries? You mean you're really not going to kill me?"

"No, dear, I'm simply here to chat. Believe it or not, we don't just go around killing people. Well, I guess sometimes we do, but not all the time. That's not the plan this time, though. I'm here to chat with you. Good golly, can we just get these things put away so we can chat comfortably?"

She slowly lowered the gun, looking at it for a moment as though considering her options. She took a quick look back at the reassuring smile on my face, and then with a heavy sigh, she put the pesky little pistol back in her purse.

"You're right, it probably wouldn't do any good anyway."

I was tempted to jump into a karate stance and yell something about falling for my evil trick, but I used my better judgment for a change and refrained. She wasn't ready for me to turn up the charm and humor quite yet. Instead, I carried the bags into the kitchen, and began emptying the contents onto the small table.

"You worked late tonight. Have you eaten?" I asked.

"Yes, I always eat before I shop. It keeps me from buying junk food. I'm being rude though, have you eaten? Are you hungry?"

"No, I'm fine," I replied. "I sucked a few of your neighbors dry while I was waiting for you."

Her eyes got huge, and I heard her gasp.

"I'm kidding, Leslie," I laughed. "Jeez, where's your sense of humor?"

She let out a sigh of relief, and then I noticed a slight smile cross her lips. "You had me going for a minute. Please, please, please, don't kill any of my neighbors. I couldn't handle it. But there is a dog next door that won't shut up..."

I pretended to spit something out of my mouth, and said, "Yuck, dogs. The fur gets all caught up in your throat and then you get that urge to lick your own balls, which can really be embarrassing in public. I'll pass. Sorry I can't help there."

She shook her head, as though clearing her mind. "I'm sorry, I just never thought I'd be in my kitchen, putting away groceries, and talking to a real live vampire."

"So, then, let me get this straight. You're okay with the idea of being in your kitchen, putting away groceries, and talking to a real *dead* vampire?"

Her smile broadened, "Well no, of course not. I mean yes...Oh, you know what I mean. Wait a minute you're teasing me! I can't believe it. I'm not sure I like this, a vampire and a smart-ass. You're supposed to be evil, not nice and funny."

"I'm supposed to be evil, huh? Well, just to show you how wrong you are about me, let's see how you like this," I said. Pulling her into my arms, I gave her my best kiss. At first, her lips were stiff and tight. I almost let her go, feeling both embarrassed and rejected. To my good fortune, her mouth opened slowly, and I felt her warm to the task. The kiss lasted a full eleven and a half seconds, and then she suddenly pushed me away.

"What are we doing?" she gasped. "This is crazy!"

I nodded, slightly puzzled at my own action. I sure hadn't come here intending on kissing her. Somehow, I found myself really liking her. I could sense that she was an extremely decent person, and the world had too few of them. She truly wanted to do right by the human race. Although she appeared stiff and formal like you'd expect from a well-trained FBI agent, on the inside she was just another vulnerable soul. Besides, she still smelled as good as the first time we'd met in San Francisco.

I looked at her, and said, "I'm sorry, I had no right to do that."

She pulled a chair out from the table and sat down. "None of our data indicates any real sexual impulses or desires on the part of your species. We know you don't change into bats and fly in to young girls' rooms, like in the movies. So, why did you kiss me, and why do I have this weird feeling we've kissed before?"

I sat down across from her and looked her in the eyes. "I'm not sure why I kissed you. To be perfectly honest with you, I think I kissed you because I'm attracted to you. You make my thing sing. Oh, I almost forgot, we did kiss once before."

She looked shocked, "Attracted to me? How so? Is it my blood type or something? What's it have to do with singing, and what do you mean we've kissed before? Trust me, I know who I've kissed, and you're not on the list."

I blushed at her directness and realized she wasn't looking at this in the normal man-woman way.

"That's a lot of questions, but let me see if I can cover them all. Attracted to you, and how so? Well, how about in the 'I'd like to jump your bones and rock your world' kind of way. It has nothing to do with your blood type, but I will admit I like your perfume. Never mind the singing part, that's just me, being a guy. Anyway, I said I'm sorry, and I am. I guess I just thought I was overwhelming you with my charm, and well, you know..."

Her eyes got big, and it was her turn to blush. "Okay, but you still didn't answer my other question. What do you mean we kissed before?"

"Is it really that important?" I asked, now embarrassed by my silly prank the first time we'd met.

"Yes it is, at least to me. Whenever your name came up at work, I felt this remarkable urge..."

"Yes?"

"Oh," she said, suddenly looking a bit embarrassed. "I guess it's not that important after all. Just silly girl stuff."

"Okay," I sighed. "It's confession time. We did meet. You were trailing me from Cabo to San Francisco."

She looked puzzled. "Yes, I was supposed to follow you after you split off from the vampire Emily Durant in Mexico, but you did nothing to warrant further investigation."

"Actually, I did do something. You followed me to a hotel, where I snatched you from the hallway. You tried to block my mental probe by reciting something over and over again in your head. I kissed you to distract you. It worked. Then I interrogated you and planted a few suggestions in your subconscious mind, then 'suggested' that you forget the whole meeting."

"Wait a minute, just what suggestions did you plant?"

"Well, I don't remember exactly, but it had something to do with making you horny every time my name was mentioned. I think I also suggested that you mistrust anyone who considers me a serious threat."

"You rotten bastard! Now I know why I nearly went nuts thinking about you...in that way. Every time we talked about you, I ended up getting into an argument with someone."

"Well, it gets worse."

"Worse?" she nearly screamed. "How can it get worse?"

"Well, I figured that you were actually a nice young lady and you'd be better off not working for the FBI. So I suggested that you'd quit next summer and decide to teach underprivileged children, and you'd be happy doing that for the rest of your life."

"Teaching underprivileged kids?"

"Sure, why not? I suggested that you'd be happy the rest of your life, so it wasn't that bad."

She shook her head slowly, and I could tell she was amazed at hearing her potential future. "Can you fix me, John? I love being an FBI agent and it's what I want to do. It's my choice for a career, and believe it or not, I've worked very hard to get where I am."

"Of course I can fix it," I said, though I had no idea if I actually could. "In fact, most of that would probably never happen. It was so far out in the future, the hypnotic effect would have probably worn off. Did you really get hot thinking about me?"

"No, you made me sick."

"Come on, 'fess up. You got hot didn't you? In fact, I'll bet you want me right now," I teased.

"I want you all right. I want you out of my house, and I want you out of my life."

I wiggled my fingers at her, as though I were hypnotizing her. "You will fall madly in lust with me and satisfy my every sexual desire," I said, with my best Vincent Price imitation, though it probably came out more like a bad Ricardo Montalban. Jeez, I suck at imitations.

A smile jumped onto her face. "I can't believe it, you're such a goofball. You're supposed to be all evil and nasty, not funny and cute. You keep talking about sex. Are you still capable of doing it?"

"Sure, I can have sex. Of course, first we need to sacrifice three cows, two horses, and a pig to our love goddess, Vampirella," I joked. "Silly girl, of course I can have sex. So, you think I'm funny and cute, huh?"

"No, I misspoke. I think you're ugly and you smell bad. We didn't know that you still function like us sexually. We knew the subjects in New Orleans lured their victims in with promises of sex, but we didn't think they were capable of following through."

Confused, I asked, "Why would you think we couldn't follow through? My sex life is better now that when I was human. For the record, the ladies don't just offer sex. They offer a feeling of being loved to those about to die. It can be sexual, but it can be simple tenderness and understanding, too. I've seen them just hold someone's hand as they cross over, if that's all that's needed."

"But you don't produce children, at least not in the human manner, right? We figured you'd somehow evolved away from the basic need for the human form of reproduction."

I shrugged and replied, "I can see your point, but sex isn't just about producing children. It's also about pleasure. It's about intimacy. It's about two people sharing a connection in a special way."

"I never thought of it that way."

"What, sex as pleasurable? Or us using it for pleasure?"

"Either, I guess," she said looking down, embarrassed.

"Can I make a suggestion?" I asked.

"No, but I have a feeling you're going to anyway."

"Take a leap of faith, and go to bed with me, Leslie. Consider it research. I promise not to hurt you...too much." Yes, I smiled and winked at her when I said that. "Besides, we have a lot to talk about, and right now my mind is too full of sexual thoughts about you to think straight. I can't focus on the important stuff."

"You're serious? Just like that, you think I'm going to sleep with you?"

"No, I didn't say anything about sleeping. You look like someone who snores, so I'd have to know you much better to sleep with you. I just want to have sex with you. Go on and take a risk, Leslie. Be the first girl on the block to knock boots with a real bad boy!"

She stared at me for several long seconds, and then said as though there were an invisible third person in the room, "Oh, my God, I think I'm going to do it. I'm going to go to bed with a vampire!"

She stood up, and shaking her head as though still bewildered at her own reaction, she took my hand. "The bedroom's this way."

I didn't need coaxing. I followed her into her room, and closed the door behind us.

Chapter 30

Sex with Leslie was wonderful. It was a lot different than being with Emily to be sure, but still wonderful. Emily was a tiger, wild and dangerous. Leslie was a kitten, tender and cuddly. What Leslie lacked on the experience side, she more than made up for with her willingness to learn. This was the first time I'd been with a human since becoming a vampire, and I was thrilled with the outcome. Adrian had warned me that our superior strength and stamina could be an issue if we weren't careful, but I felt our first little romp was a total success. I based this not on scientific evidence, but on the fact that neither of us could quit smiling, or kissing, or touching each other. I think that's a good sign.

Still amazed at being in bed with such a stud, Leslie giggled, "I can't believe I had sex with a vampire."

"I can't believe I had sex with a FBI agent," I giggled back.

That made her accidentally snort, which made us both start laughing. Finally, catching her breath, she buried her head in my chest and said, "Okay, John, you came here to talk. If you've cleared your mind of all the sexual thoughts, let's talk. What's up?"

I caressed her hair and kissed the top of her head. No use beating around the bush at this point, so I said, "I need to know everything, Leslie. I want you to rat out your whole group. I hate to ask this of you, but I must. We need to know why you're after us."

She didn't say anything for almost a full minute, then asked, "Is there going to be more killing?"

"I can't make any promises, but I can tell you there's no desire to continue this war from our side. If you tell me what I need to know, we can greatly reduce the chances of there being more killing. For starters, what do you know about the Knights Templar?"

"The Knights Templar?" she asked, sounding puzzled. "I think I remember them from a history class. They were crusaders, right? Now they have drinking clubs for old men all over the place."

"Right, the Templars were formed during the Crusades. The drinking clubs you're thinking about are probably the Masonic Lodges.

That's a common mistake people make, though," I said suppressing a smile at the memory of my similar blunder. "I need to know what you know about them now. I'm talking about the modern Templars. I'm talking about your friend, Dr. Peter Sedgewick."

"Peter? Peter is...a Templar? What on earth has that got to do with anything?"

"Yes, we're reasonably sure your friend Peter is a Templar. They've been around for a thousand years, most of it as a secret organization. Centuries ago, they rose to great power, and then when it benefited their purpose, they went underground. They're very powerful and have their dirty little paws in everything. I can give you all the details later, but we know that they, through Peter Sedgewick, were using your agency to their advantage."

"But why?' she asked.

"We believe they want to know more about vampires, so they can control us. They can't, of course, but to them we must represent too much power for them to ignore."

Leslie sat up and looked at me. I could see the wheels spinning. "I always felt there was something going on that wasn't in the open. So, we were pawns, huh? Those agents that nobody knew died for this Templar group?"

"Nobody knew?" I asked.

"Yes, we heard several agents died, but we never got a list of names. Nobody seems to know who it was that died."

I told her about the badges, and how they were all within a few numbers of each other. She agreed this was nearly impossible and concluded that they probably weren't real agents after all. It got her a little bit pissed off to think of someone imitating an agent in an official capacity. Still, she wasn't pleased that so many humans had died.

"Yes," I said sitting up and taking her hands in mine. "I'm sorry we had to kill so many of these humans, Leslie. Our kind has lived in the shadows for centuries. We have no desire to rule the world, or anything like that. Yes, we kill some humans, but it's how we survive. Some, like Emily who you kidnapped from New Orleans, only kill humans that are already dying. Others, like Virgil, are a menace to all society, both human and vampire. He needs to be eliminated. In fact, given the chance, I intend to eliminate him myself."

She shivered at the mention of Virgil. "He's one sick and scary individual, a real monster. We thought all vampires were like him."

"No, he's an anomaly, at least from my limited experience. How'd you hook up with him anyway?"

She looked thoughtful for a minute. "Actually, he came to us courtesy of Peter. Our unit was formed when he showed up. According to Peter, he volunteered to help us if we'd help him eliminate the rest of the vampires. We recorded his every move and he taught us a lot. The main lesson though was never to trust him. When he comes in, we make him stay in a cage at Peter's place."

"Yes, I believe I've seen it. It's where you were holding Emily?"

"Oh, so you were involved in that too?"

"Yep, I was there. Emily is very special to me, and I'd die before I let anyone hurt her."

There must have been one of those tones in my voice that only women understand, because I clearly saw a "look" cross Leslie's face, though even with my enhanced vampire skills, I couldn't tell exactly what it meant. I'm probably better off not knowing.

"I need to know everything your unit worked on, Leslie, at least relating to vampires. Do you have transcripts, or something I can get a copy of?"

She looked thoughtful for a moment, then replied slowly as though thinking carefully, "Yes, of course there are some transcripts. But, other than the fact that we had great sex, and it may save a few hundred lives, why is it I should share them with you, again?"

It was a good question. "Look, Leslie, I'll be honest. This is going to be a bit of a one-sided deal. I, or I should say we, want to restore the balance. Most of what Virgil told you is wrong. You picked the wrong guy to educate you on vampires. By knowing what you know, we can protect ourselves. Once we're comfortable that a bunch of humans with space helmets aren't going to come looking for us, we'll leave the FBI alone."

"So, basically, we opened a can of worms we shouldn't have. We need to close the lid and forget we ever opened the can?"

"That's a good way to put it, kind of a Pandora's box, if you will."

She looked down for a few seconds and then reached up with her thumbs and forefingers and playfully tweaked my nipples. "So, what happens to us, my demon lover? I suppose I get you the information you want, and you fade away into the night never to be heard from again? Then a year from now, I end up teaching underprivileged kids for some unknown reason."

I reached up and tweaked her nippers back. "Silly, girl, you're not going to get rid of me that easily."

She smiled and threw her arms around me. "I still can't believe I'm in love with a vampire."

"Whoa, girl, let's not use the 'L' word just yet. Let's just say we're very, very fond of each other. After all, you're a pillar of goodness and strength in the human world, a real live agent with the Federal Bureau of Investigation. And me, well, I'm a disgusting creature of the night."

"Creature of the night?" she giggled. "You've been reading too many vampire novels! Tell me you love me. Come on, tough guy. Lie to yourself if you must, but I want to hear those magic words directly from your lips."

I kissed her and whispered, "I like you."

"Not good enough. Try it again."

"Leslie..."

"Hey," she giggled, "I know we're not going to get married and have ten little kidlets running around. I know the differences between us better than most. I want, no, I *need* to hear this, John. Even if it's just for this moment in time, I really need this. Say the words, John..."

I'm easy, but not that easy. I rolled her over and gave her a deep kiss. Looking her directly in the eyes, I made a vow to her. "Leslie, if you help me with this, you'll be doing a very good thing. In return, I'll help you in your work at the FBI. Think about it. I can go places and do things no human can. I'll be your very own secret weapon."

Her eyes lit up, and she got up on one elbow. "Really? You'd actually work with the FBI?"

"No, I'll work with you. The FBI doesn't have to know I exist. I'll do your bidding, and your bidding alone."

I held out my hand, and asked, "Deal?"

"Deal," she said, "as long as you say those three magic words."

"I lust you."

"Nope"

"I need you"

"Yes, you do, but that's not it either."

Knowing I was whipped, I caved in. "Okay, okay, I love you, Leslie. If I were human, I'd want to marry you. I'd want you to have my babies. I'd breathe every breath, wanting only to be with you. You'd be my everything..."

"Hey, hold on there, fang face," she interrupted. "Don't get carried away, now. You were a good time and all, but what's all this 'love' stuff? Can't you just accept that what we had was simply sex, and move on?"

I was confused at first, then realized it was her way of embarrassing me for a change, thus shifting the balance of power over to her where it belonged.

Shaking my head, I said, "Now that our business is concluded and I've been made to look the fool, how do you suggest we celebrate?"

I was only too happy to comply with her celebration request, although I began to wonder if Adrian was right about us having an advantage in the stamina department...

Chapter 31

I returned to Arizona a changed vampire. I'd made love to a human and I actually had feelings for her. However, I found my feelings for Emily were unchanged. Normally I'd be considered a low-life, two-timing son of a bitch. Oddly, this was all somehow okay.

I was pleased to find that Jasmyna had joined up with our little gang of troublemakers in Arizona. It was great to see her again, and I knew her ability to look at problems in a logical way would be an asset to our planning. Also, having her close made me feel like she was safer, even though there was no real logical reason for thinking that. She'd been taking care of herself for centuries, and there was no obvious reason to believe she couldn't keep right on taking care of herself. It was probably just remnants of my human male ego. I seemed to have a lot of that going on.

Adrian's trip to Mexico had been relatively successful. He'd met with some individuals known by him to be Templars. They'd listened to his request to meet with a senior member of the organization and seemed to understand the urgency. They definitely understood the threat. A signal was arranged, which would let us know if the meeting was on, and if so, when and where.

Before engaging these contacts in conversation, Adrian had secretly probed their minds. The information he acquired was interesting, but there was no way for us to know if it was accurate, since it could have been the organization's internal cover story. If it was accurate, then it seemed the evil Dr. Sedgewick was thought of as a bit of a loose cannon. While outwardly many senior Templars supported him, privately they thought he was an egomaniac, who was only out to take care of himself.

It seemed that many insiders thought there was more to his research than simply investigating vampires. Most felt they had plenty of information on us, and most really considered us little more than a nuisance. Since our motives weren't typically political or social, we were not considered a threat to their plots and schemes.

Adrian was pleased with the outcome of my meeting with Leslie.

She'd downloaded volumes of information and transferred it to several CDs. Emily and Jasmyna began pouring over the data almost as soon as I walked in the door and would soon have a clear idea as to the extent of the information Virgil had shared with Sedgewick's team.

Virgil was another loose end that needed to be dealt with. We had no idea where he was, and none of us would feel safe until he was permanently out of the picture. Thanks to Adrian, the entire vampire community was keeping an eye out for him. So far, we'd heard nothing back.

My second night back, I was on the rear deck, relaxing in a far too comfortable chaise lounge, looking up at the bazillion or so stars that were winking back at me. Whenever I have a lot on my mind and I start taking things too seriously, I find it helps to look at the really big things in nature. By that, I mean something like the stars, the ocean, or perhaps a mountain. I can look at them and realize that they've been there for thousands of years, and will continue to be there for thousands more. My problems represented one little wrinkle in a speck in time. Even as a vampire, my time in existence would be short compared to the hundreds of thousands of years it takes for a river to cut a canyon, or a mountain range to form. Am I a philosopher or what? Sometimes I scare myself.

Emily, taking a break from reading the voluminous information Leslie had provided, was pretending to be impressed with my "big world-small problem" philosophy. She'd already found out a lot from the data Leslie had provided and was beginning to develop some theories. I found it odd, but both Emily and Jasmyna were very competent with computers and modern technology. Hell, they were almost geeks.

"So, just how was it you convinced this human, Leslie Poole, to give you all this great information?" she asked with just a touch of fake jealousy in her voice.

"What do you think?" I replied, as though it were the most natural thing in the world. "I turned on the ol' John Steele charm and I had her eating out of my hand."

"The ol' John Steel charm, huh? Let's see, that means you probably tripped going in the door, said absolutely all the wrong things, and drooled while staring at her breasts like a horny schoolboy. Then, I'm sure you provided her with the worst sex she's had since high school, and left without so much as a thank you."

I knew Emily was teasing me, but also letting me know it was okay to sleep around. A little. "Hey, I had her begging for more. When we were through, she got on her hands and knees and called me 'Master'."

She leaned over and kissed me, and said, "So what do I get if I call you Master?"

I purred in her ear, "Anything you want, baby."

She let out one of her wicked giggles, and whispered, "When this is over, how about we spend a whole week naked in your new house outside Fresno? Just you, me, some candles, and plenty of massage oil."

Is this woman incredible or what? "Sounds good to me. I'll get the candles, and you bring the oil," I whispered back while nibbling her ear. Suddenly, an alarm went off.

"How'd you know I bought a house outside of Fresno?" I asked, puzzled. "It was supposed to be my first safe house. Guess I blew that one. Damn."

She shrugged. "I read it in the documents you brought back. I'm sorry; I didn't know it was a secret. Then again, if the FBI knows about it, it's not much of a secret, is it?"

Double damn. I'd bought the house under my real name, John Steele. Adrian and I had assumed it was good for several more years. Not expecting the FBI to be tracking me, they'd more than likely tracked the transfer of funds. So much for my first safe house being safe.

"It's not your fault," I said, still bummed. "I should have switched to a different identity. So, what did they say about it?"

"Not much, really. The data I read is weeks old, but they think you're simply in cahoots with us, since you can go out in the daylight. I didn't see anything that indicated they'd identified you as a full-fledged vampire. They probably think you're a wanna-be."

"Shit," I exclaimed, sitting up. "Does Virgil know about the Fresno house? Does he know I'm still alive?"

Emily thought for a second. "Not that I've read about. I still have a lot of information to cover, though. Guess I better get back at it. Are you concerned Virgil will come after you there?"

"No, I'm not worried about me. I'm worried about Delthea and the boys. I better call her."

Chapter 32

I called the main house number three times and Delthea's cell phone four times in the span of about fifteen minutes. No answer. Adrian saw the concern on my face and sought to console me.

"You have no proof that Virgil even knows about your safe house. Let's finish analyzing the data you brought and then make a decision. There could be any number of reasons that your humans aren't answering the phone."

"Yea," I said, shaking my head in disgust, "like they've been munched by that monster. Adrian, I brought them all the way across the country to get them away from a hellish situation. If all I did was feed them to Virgil, it'll kill me. They deserve better than him. I need to go there as soon as possible."

"Don't be ridiculous. There's still a war going on out there. We need to stick together until this thing is resolved."

"There's a simple way to get an answer," I said, wishing I'd thought of it sooner. I picked up a cell phone and dialed Leslie's number.

She sounded surprised to hear from me, since I'd told her not to expect many phone calls. I got straight to the point. "Leslie, does Virgil know about my house outside of Fresno? In fact, does he know anything about me?"

She hesitated, and I wasn't sure if it was to think, or because she was embarrassed. "I think it might have come up, John."

"You think? I need to know Leslie. There are innocent lives at stake."

"Peter pretty much gave Virgil everything we had on you, Adrian, and the two New Orleans ladies. Information relating to you guys was always one of his biggest bargaining chips. I'm really sorry if..."

"I gotta go," I said cutting her off and hanging up.

I turned to Adrian, and said, "He knows. Leslie just verified it."

"How much does he know about you?"

"Enough. They may not know I'm a vampire, but he does. He knows the address of my safe house and knows I can get around in the daylight.

He may be amazed that I recovered, but then again if he knows you were involved, then he probably figures anything's possible. I'm sorry Adrian, I've got to go to Fresno."

This time he didn't argue, he just nodded.

Chapter 33

The drive to Fresno from Adrian's Arizona hideaway should take a sane man about nine or ten hours. I did it in a little over seven. The 'vette performed marvelously, but at the time I hardly noticed. I'd driven south to I-40, zigzagged across I-15 and CA-58, then up CA-99 to Fresno. Once back in familiar surroundings, I eased up a bit, and taking CA-41 North, headed to what was to have been my first safe house.

Taking the winding foothill road that led to the house, I found myself wishing I'd come up with a plan. Seven hours of driving had produced nothing more than a stronger desire to kill the SOB if he'd touched Delthea or the kids. At the edge of my property, I pulled off the road and stopped. I couldn't see the house, but I could see the gated entrance.

I quickly sucked down a container of blood that Adrian had sent along, and couldn't resist a smile at my friend's ingenuity. He'd found a food warmer that plugged into a car's cigarette lighter, and packed it with several varieties of blood. I appreciated his thoughtfulness, but right now, the variety of blood I was most interested in was Virgil's.

I decided to try calling one more time and dialed Delthea's cell. No answer. I dialed the house as an afterthought and was surprised to hear the phone picked up.

"Hello," I said. "Delthea, is that you?"

"Sorry, bro," Virgil's all too familiar drawl hissed at me. "That there colored lady, what'd you say her name is? Well, she ain't a gonna be answerin' this here phone no time soon. Seems she done misplaced most a her blood. Now where'd it go? Oh yea, I guess I done drunk it all up. Sure was tasty."

"You bastard, "I said seething. "You're dead."

He cackled and replied, "Yer dead too, ya damn fool. All a us vamps is dead, or din't them woman folk tell ya? I thought I done kil't ya for good, but ya snaked outta it some how. Well, ol' Virg won't miss this time. Come on home, boy, I'ze waitin' fer ya."

"I'll be there tomorrow," I said, and hung up the phone. The way I figured it, I'd either bought some time or the element of surprise.

Chapter 34

When planning a sneak-attack on an extremely nasty vampire that's camped out in one's own home, it helps to know what you're doing. I suddenly realized just how limited my experience was in this area. Adrian and I had pulled off a successful raid in Maryland, but that was probably more luck than skill. No amount of playing army as a kid, watching A-Team reruns, or reading Dirk Pitt novels can prepare you for the real thing.

I considered the direct approach. I could simply drive up and park in front of the house, then yell for him to come out and fight like a man, er, a vampire. Of course, he'd come out and simply remove my head again. Probably not the best option if I really wanted to continue my existence.

Thanks to Delthea's ingenuity, I was investing in a pretty complex escape route. Obviously, if it could let me out in an emergency, it could also let me in. Unfortunately, it was far from finished. Construction on the new wine cellar was progressing, but the link to the pond hadn't even been started yet. The benefits of this elaborate tunnel system were becoming more obvious to me, but my timing was bad. Thinking of Delthea's efforts on my behalf made me more resolved to avenge her killing.

Somehow, I needed to sneak up on him, but how? Even if I could creep from tree to tree, sneak in an open window, and tiptoe through the house, his vampire senses would pick me up. We can sense each other from short distances, so my task was made even more difficult. If I could sense Adrian or Emily as soon as they walked into a room, I had to assume his senses were more finely tuned than mine, and he'd pick me up as soon as I entered the house. With my luck, he'd probably know I was there before I sensed him, which lowered my chances even more. Crap.

In the end, I decided to take the direct route. I guess I'm not much of a sneaker. I figured confronting him directly took away the advantage of surprising him, but it also lessened the chances of him surprising me.

If he somehow got the drop on me, I stood no chance. Just because I planned to confront him directly, however, didn't mean I had to fight fair. I deserved some advantage for being such a nice guy. I decided a gun would do nicely. I was going to shoot the bastard. It wouldn't kill him, but it ought to slow him down a notch.

Acquiring a gun on short notice is typically not very easy. This is when it really helps to be a vampire. Driving back in the general direction I'd come, I passed a small diner with a California Highway Patrol car in the parking lot. Perfect. I parked next to it and waited. Fifteen minutes later, the world's largest highway patrolman came out, toothpick firmly clenched between his gigantic pearly whites and his John Wayne swagger down to perfection. Five minutes later, I drove away with his personal 9mm Beretta and three spare clips. For the rest of his life, he'd never figure out where he misplaced his favorite handgun.

After ensuring my new equalizer was ready for action, I headed back to the house. I pulled up as close to the front door as I could and, as I exited the car, I carefully tucked the gun into the waste band in the back of my snug fitting jeans. Jeans are one of life's greatest pleasures, and I was hoping to go on enjoying them for a few more centuries. Anyway, I'd already pulled my shirt out so it would conceal the bulge, just in case he got behind me. Deciding to be subtle, I reached in the open car window and laid on the horn for a few seconds.

"Come out, come out, wherever you are," I yelled, scanning the façade of the house for any signs of Virgil.

The front door slowly swung wide open, but there was no sign of Virgil. I guess this was my invitation to the dance.

I carefully proceeded up the brick walkway, my senses as sharp as I could tune them. A monster was on the other side of the threshold, and caution was definitely the word for the day. When I reached the open doorway, I stopped and peered inside. It seemed darker than I remembered. I tried to sense his presence but came up empty. I took a deep breath and entered my house.

The downstairs consisted of several large rooms, all arranged around the central foyer. It had a stately feel to it, which is probably why I was originally attracted to it. To my left was a large formal living room. It had been so nicely decorated, I almost hated to enter it. It looked like the kind of room my size twelve feet and I would be better off staying out of. From this room, moving towards the back of the house, there was a formal dining room, then a large kitchen with a huge fireplace and informal dining area. I knew this is where Delthea and the boys enjoyed most of their meals.

To the right was my office. Not that I'd really used it much yet, but it was my favorite room in the house. It looked like a library with its heavy wood bookcases, large fireplace, and overstuffed chairs. Above the polished wood wainscoting, the walls were covered in a dark green fabric and contained several small paintings. These mini-masterpieces were meant to inform visitors that the owner of this abode was the most-manly type of man, a hunter of ducks and foxes. Perhaps I didn't hunt the poor little foxes depicted in the paintings, but I am in fact a hunter, a hunter of humans. Unfortunately, at the moment I felt more like the fox.

Along the right side of the foyer, about halfway through the atrium, a wide staircase began its rise. It gently curved to the left as it rose, ending on a second floor landing. Several oversized paintings had been meticulously placed along the stairway walls since the last time I'd been here, probably by some local decorator, whom Delthea must have hired. They looked good hanging there, even to my untrained eye. Too bad I'd never be able to tell her so.

I was wondering which way to start looking, when I heard a door slam upstairs. That answered several questions. First, he was upstairs. Second, he was going to screw with me. Not good answers.

I took a deep breath and started up the stairs. Suddenly, sensing him close by, I stopped in my tracks. He was close, very close. I was looking up at the landing, trying to see which direction he was in, when something caught my eye. It was a strand of string, hanging over the balcony. Puzzled, my eyes followed it upwards. It was tied to the doorknob on the upstairs bathroom door, which was now closed.

Realization hit me with incredible force, much like the proverbial ton of bricks. The simpleton had tricked me. He'd rigged a line so that he could slam an upstairs door from downstairs, which meant he was somewhere behind me.

Virgil hit with an even more incredible force. I never heard him coming, which gives some idea of his prowess at these types of games. The guy is good. He simply snuck up behind me while my attention was on the upstairs landing, and punched me in the back of my melon. I was knocked nearly unconscious.

I wish I could report that I put up a valiant fight, but Virgil's first punch had stunned me so severely, I didn't stand a snowball's chance. Knocked off balance and my world spinning, he quickly and unceremoniously dragged me back down the stairs and to the middle of the foyer.

He dropped me on my belly and twisted my arms behind my back.

I heard a loud snap and realized I'd been handcuffed. I pulled hard on them, panic setting in quickly, but it was useless. He had me.

"Titanmium," he mispronounced with a laugh. "I borrowed 'em from them FBI folk. Try if 'n ya want, but they're strong uns."

"You're in big trouble Virgil. You're making a big mistake here. I just came to talk to you," I lied out of desperation.

He held the recently acquired 9mm in front of my face and said bitterly, "You gonna do yer talkin' with this?"

I felt like a kid getting caught with his hand in the cookie jar. "That? That wasn't for you. Come on, Virgil, even I know a gun can't hurt you." I hoped he'd fall for my line of bullshit.

Nothing doing.

"Bullshit," he spat. "You was gonna pop me one and I hates gettin' shot. Don't lie ta me. Yer dead either way."

"Come on, Virgil, why else would I come here alone? Obviously, I'm no match for you physically. I came to see if I could get you out of hot water with the rest of our kind. I came to talk, not to fight. I may be your only chance."

"You came alone?" he asked, suddenly looking around the room with interest.

Pleased that he was still talking and not disconnecting my parts, I said, "Of course I'm alone."

"Then who's that?" he asked nodding in the direction of the front door.

I was caught off guard for a second when, suddenly, I too felt the presence of another of our kind outside the door. I started to speak, but was dumbfounded when the entire front door blew in off the hinges, slid across the floor, and landed about three feet from your favorite hero. Uh, folks, that would be me.

There, standing tall and looking imposing as hell, was Adrian.

"Virgil," his voice boomed. "It's time to pay for your crimes."

For the first time ever, I saw terror on Virgil's face. He let out a slight whimper, and began to back away. Obviously, Adrian could be a badass when he wanted to be. That's my grandpa!

For a brief moment, I thought it was over without a fight, but then Virgil surprised me. He let out a battle cry, the likes of which I hope to never hear again, and rushed at Adrian. Adrian never flinched. He simply imposed his will on Virgil, using his powerful mind as his weapon of choice.

Though it was aimed at Virgil, I caught the overflow and it nearly knocked me unconscious. Virgil stopped five feet from Adrian and, dropping my recently acquired gun, grabbed his head. He twisted violently and fell to one knee. Making an obviously painful attempt, he once again turned towards Adrian and prepared to attack. Adrian gave him the whammy once more, and he never fully made it to his feet. He fell forward, hands pressed over his ears, and landed flat on his chest. Actually, Old Virg kind of bounced, now that I think about it. Ouch. He lay there whimpering and kicking the floor with his right foot.

Adrian turned towards me and, shaking his head, said, "I see you had him right where you wanted him?"

"Another thirty seconds and he was toast."

"Uh, huh. Guess I should leave then?"

"Well," I said rolling over to expose the latest accessory to my wardrobe, a pair of highly polished titanium handcuffs. "Since you're here, you might as well help me out of these handcuffs. What are we gonna do with him?"

As soon as I said it, Virgil jumped to his feet and ran screaming into my formal living room. The way he was running, I doubt he was concerned about bumping into my expensive furniture with his size-fourteen shoes.

"He won't get far," Adrian said, while rolling me over to get a good look at my handcuffs. "Goodness," he said, while giving them a none-too-gentle tug. "These are some good ones. We'll have to get someone to cut them off."

"Or, we could get the key," I suggested, nodding in the direction Virgil had left.

"Will you be okay?" he asked, standing.

"I'll be better when I know he's been taken care of. Go get him."

Just as Adrian turned in the direction Virgil had departed, our good buddy jumped back into the room. He was wearing one of the silly looking little helmets we'd seen our FBI friends wear. Adrian had so thoroughly dominated him, that I initially didn't realize the gravity of this new situation.

"Time fer you to die, old man," he spat, crouching into a fighting stance.

Adrian didn't seem overly concerned, but assumed a fighting stance too. For several seconds, neither said anything, they just circled around a poor handcuffed vampire who happened to still be lying on the floor, wishing he were someplace else.

"Why, Virgil? Why have you turned against your own kind?" Adrian finally asked.

"My kind? That's a real laugher. Ya'll never liked me. I kin tell. Jus cuz I ain't all fancy pants like junior here," Virgil said, indicating me.

"My pants aren't so fancy, Virg," I interjected. "They're just jeans. I mean they do fit rather nicely and show off my rear to its best advantage..."

"Shut up," they both yelled simultaneously.

I can take a hint. I closed my yap and lay there watching, waiting for Adrian to kick his hillbilly ass.

It's funny, but real fights are never like in the movies. Nobody choreographs each move, and they're generally over much quicker than you'd think. This fight was no exception.

Virgil suddenly leaped over me, and tackled Adrian. They rolled to the ground and both let out inhuman growls. I think if Adrian had been able to use his martial arts skills more, it might have come out differently. But Virgil knew fighting; it was his life. Rather than allow Adrian to use his kicking and punching skills, he turned it into a wrestling match. It was pure strength against strength, and this was the only way the advantage could be tipped towards Virgil. He's pretty smart for someone who's so dumb.

They rolled around, ripping and clawing at each other for a few seconds, but Virgil ended up on top with his hands at Adrian' throat. Blood and spit were coming out of his mouth as he ranted incoherently. He was in such a pure state of rage, that I almost expected him to explode. I needed to do something, but I didn't know what.

Looking around, I saw the gun on the floor and decided it was my only chance. I scooted, twisted, and wiggled my way over to it, then rolled over on my side so I could grab it. I grasped it firmly in my right hand, and rolled over once more so the gun was facing the two embattled monsters.

Have you ever tried to fire a gun behind your back, lying on your side with your hands cuffed, and knowing that the shot had better be a good one? If so, you're crazier than me. Let me tell those of you who haven't tried it, it isn't easy! I took careful aim and shot Adrian in the thigh. Damn.

I adjusted the angle a bit higher and shot Adrian again about three inches from the first spot. Double damn. Luckily, neither shot seemed to faze him, but this wasn't working out so well. I over adjusted and put a bullet hole in my wall. At this rate I'd be out of bullets soon.

My fourth shot found its mark. I hit Virgil in the right shoulder. He didn't seem to notice either. Damn. Maybe bullets don't hurt us? I fired again and I saw a small hole appear in his side, but again it didn't seem to bother him. Getting a bit pissed now, I fired again. Though Adrian will always say my sixth shot was pure luck, I will always argue it was totally planned.

I hit the helmet in the exact spot it connected to the chinstrap, and it flew off of his head. Just for a second, I saw a look of confusion cross his face, then panic. His hands flew off of Adrian's throat and, once again, he grabbed his own head. Adrian didn't need more than a second to regain the advantage. Virgil closed his eyes and began screaming in agony, all the while using his feet to push himself butt first towards the opening where my front door was supposed to be. Finally, a foot short of the opening, he curled up in a ball and rocked back and forth. I can only imagine the hell Adrian was mentally inflicting on him.

Adrian got to his feet and, rubbing his throat, walked over to Virgil. With one swift move, his hand knifed into Virgil's chest cavity and grabbed his still beating heart. Virgil stopped making noise and looked him in the eye. With a sharp tug, Adrian ripped his heart from his chest and held it up for him to see. It was the last thing Virgil would ever see, as his eyes glazed over and his lifeless body slumped to the floor.

Adrian looked at the heart in his hand for a second, and then dropped it with disgust onto the floor next to Virgil's body. He leaned over and wiped his hand on Virgil's shirt, then turned to me.

"Nice shooting, Tex, where'd you learn to do that?"

Glad to be the hero for a change, I began to boast, "Well, when I was in the Navy, we had to qualify with a .45-caliber automatic. It's a little different, but..."

"John?"

"Yes, Adrian?"

"You shot me in the leg. Twice."

Oops, I'd gotten caught up in the moment and forgotten my first few misses.

"Hey," I began in my defense, "you ought to try shooting a gun with your hands tied behind your back. It ain't easy, you know."

"It isn't easy. Ain't, ain't a word. You managed to shoot me twice, though, John. Not once, twice. I can't believe it. I'm fighting for my life, and you decide to help me, how? By shooting me. By the way, it hurts like hell in case you're interested."

"Come on, that last shot was a great one. Did you see the expression on his face when he realized his helmet was gone? I wish I had a picture of it."

"Yes, I saw it. I saw it from about six inches away. I'm still amazed you didn't hit me a third time. What a lucky shot."

"Come on, help me up. Of all the ungrateful people, I'm telling you. I save your life with the shot of the century, and all you can do is complain about a couple of near hits. Luck had nothing to do with it. Buffalo Bill would have been proud of that shot, that's how good it was."

He helped me up but kept shaking his head. "Buffalo Bill, my ass. He never shot Annie Oakley. I still can't believe you shot me. Not once, mind you, but twice. You suck. Give me that gun before you hurt someone else."

The phone rang in the atrium and interrupted our argument. Adrian picked it up and with a shrug, held it up for me to talk. "Hello?"

"Mr. Steele, is that you," Delthea's familiar voice asked.

"Delthea, you're alive," I exclaimed. "Thank God. Are the boys okay?"

"We all fine, Mr. Steele, but you gotta get outta there. Fast. There's something evil lurkin' about. I sensed it two days ago, so me an the boys up and left. We're visiting the most magical place on Earth. You know what I'm saying, Mr. Steele?"

I wanted to laugh, partly at the joy of finding out she and the boys were alive, and partly because of her attempt at explaining her location in code. I was impressed with her sensitivity to danger, though. "I understand your location. I hope the boys have a good time. And you're right, dear, something evil was here."

I looked at Virgil's slumped over body and continued, "It's gone now. It's gone for good. It's safe for you and the boys to come home whenever you're ready." I hesitated for a second and then continued, "If you still want to, of course. I never intended for you and the boys to be in harm's way. I won't hold it against you if you don't come back."

She chuckled. "You ain't getting' rid of us that easy. We're all family now. These boys think you're the greatest thing since sliced bread. No sir, a little upset like this ain't gonna make us leave. We'll be back tomorrow night."

I smiled at Adrian who'd heard the whole exchange and was smiling too. "Come on home, Delthea," I said into the phone. "Come on home."

Chapter 35

Adrian received the high sign from his Templar contacts, so the meeting was on. It would be held in Jackson Square, back in the French Quarter of good ol' New Orleans. We were to meet out in the open, in the middle of the afternoon, with three senior officials from the Templar organization. The desired outcome of this meeting from our perspective was a truce between them and the vampire community. We could only hope their desire was something of a similar nature. I had the distinct feeling of having come full circle. The last time I'd visited Jackson Square, I'd stumbled through as a dying human. Now, I was hoping not to become a dead vampire.

We'd decided that Adrian and I would meet the Templars, while Jasmyna and Emily watched from a short distance away. It was easy for them to change their appearances, and they quickly made themselves blend into the surrounding crowd. If anything went wrong, it would be their turn to rescue us. I had total faith in these two wonderful women. Knowing they were backing us up gave me a strong sense of confidence that no matter what, the situation wouldn't get out of hand.

Adrian and I strolled in at the appointed time and stood under the statue of General Andrew Jackson, hero of the Battle of New Orleans and the seventh president of the United States. His nickname was "Old Hickory," and I'm sure I'm not the first to wonder if he'd gotten it from his wife, Rachel. We wore casual clothes, attempting to blend in with the locals and tourists that filled the square. My instructions were clear. No matter what, I was to remain silent. Adrian had pressed this point so many times that I'd actually been forced to pinky swear that I'd keep my mouth shut.

Sure enough, three gentlemen in suits walked up to us. Obviously, they weren't into disguises or blending into crowds. I could easily sense the fear in them, and I'm sure Adrian could too. Though it was obvious who we were, one of them asked us our names.

Adrian replied dryly, "Mr. Smith and Mr. Jones. Let's get down to business, shall we? After centuries of peace, you decided to openly attack us for some reason. In fact, you kidnapped one of my friends. We rescued her, but several of your kind died, brutally I might add, during the rescue. You also invaded my home in Napa, which I consider a personal affront. Again, ten more of your kind died brutally as a result of that poor decision. Is this going to go on? Are you through losing people yet? Our patience has reached its limit."

I wanted to smile, because Adrian had come off just as we'd planned. He made the clear distinction between our "kinds," and had made it obvious that we'd won each battle. He'd also made it clear that we were in no mood for any more foolishness. I should point out that, even though he was doing the talking, they were probably wondering just who the bad ass next to him was.

One of the Templars responded with an obviously well rehearsed line, "I'm afraid that mistakes were made. You and your kind are no longer of any interest to us. You have our most sincere apology for any trouble we've caused. We fully understand that you have no reason to believe us, so another has come who believes he can convince you that we speak the truth."

Suddenly, I felt the presence of another of our kind. Adrian must have sensed it, too, as I saw him stiffen slightly. It's difficult to describe the feeling we get when we sense another vampire's presence. It's kind of like "the Force" in the *Star Wars* movies. You just feel it. The Force, if you will, was strong in this new presence. Stronger than any other I'd ever felt.

"Is my word good enough?" said an approaching stranger, who was clearly the strong new vampire presence. He was slightly shorter than Adrian, but he carried himself very tall. He had a distinguished air about him and could easily have passed himself off as a CEO or senior politician. In fact, he looked vaguely familiar.

Switching to his silent voice, so only the three of us could hear, Adrian responded, "Hello, Father. I should have known you'd be involved in this somehow. But why attack us, and why with the aid of these human foot soldiers?"

The gentleman responded in kind, the hint of a smile appearing ready to appear at any moment, "Hello son, I've missed you, too. Actually, for a change, I'm not responsible for this one. Well, at least not directly, anyway. I'll admit it's my mess to clean up, however, so don't you worry about a thing. Long story, as you'd expect."

Adrian shook his head, "But Templars? Why in God's name are you involved with this scum? And why have they attacked us?"

The stranger nodded in the direction of the three suits and said with a certain degree of pride, "This scum, as you put it, is the cream of the human crop. Each one is specially selected for service to their cause. I've worked with them off and on for nearly a millennium now, and as far as humans go, they're quite a useful lot. That's no concern of yours, though, and it's not why we're here."

"Oh," Adrian interrupted, obviously taken aback. "They aren't why we're here? Then pray tell, Father, just why is it we *are* here?"

"We're here because of an idiot named Peter Sedgewick. Yes, he's a Templar, and I suppose he did start this ruckus using his position within the organization. However, I believe I was his ultimate target. Somehow, my friend Sedgewick figured out that I'm a vampire. He and I have never seen eye to eye, and I believe he thought he could develop a way of getting the upper hand on me. He stumbled across Virgil and figured he could use him to gain information on the weaknesses of all vampires, including yours truly. A useless attempt, of course."

"So why'd you let Sedgewick come after us," Adrian asked?

"Ah, that sneaky little bastard. I clearly underestimated him as a serious threat. I always thought of him as somewhat of a minor irritant, and not as a true enemy. Anyway, I was in Australia and a little out of the mainstream information flow. Once I realized what he was up to, I immediately returned to the States. By the way, Adrian, you did a nice job in Napa. Did I detect a little bit of our old friend Vlad Dracula's methods being put to use? Still quite effective I must say. There were a great many of my Templar friends who were really shocked by your heartless brutality, and this isn't an easy group to shock."

I had a million questions, but with my strict gag order, I remained quiet. So this was my great grandfather, the vampire nobody seemed to want me to know much about. I'll be damned if he didn't look familiar, though. He cut an impressive figure, even when standing next to Adrian.

"Yes," Adrian responded flatly, "we did go a little bit Vlad on them. It worked for him, so I figured it might work for us. So what now? We have the word of these three goofballs that the Templars will back off of us," Adrian said, indicating the three gentlemen standing nearby, trying desperately to control their fear. "But what about the government agencies they control, and what about Sedgewick?"

"Already taken care of," the gentleman said. "I've had every agency we work with locate and destroy every scrap of information on you, Emily, Jasmyna, and young John Steele here." With that, he turned and looked at me for the first time.

"Hello, John," he said out loud, as though I couldn't hear him in silent voice.

I assumed the gag order was lifted, at least enough for me to be polite. I responded in silent voice with a simple, "Sir", and a nod of my head. It had worked in the Navy, and I hoped it was appropriate here.

Switching to silent voice, he said to me, "I understand you've had quite an adventurous time since you've joined our little family. It's time we got to know each other a little better; let me prove to you I'm not the feeble minded old fool that I'm sure Adrian here makes me out to be. Tonight, I'd like for all of you to join me for dinner."

Turning to Adrian before he could decline, he said, "I really must insist, Adrian. There's still the little matter of Sedgwick to...handle. Might be some fun in it if you play your cards right. I'd like Jasmyna, Emily, young John here, and you to meet me at my place in Baton Rouge for supper. Let's say 5:30 a.m.?"

With that, he smiled, nodded, and turned on his heel. I couldn't help noticing his walk exuded more confidence and purposefulness than any I'd ever seen. His Templar buddies had difficulty keeping up.

Chapter 36

Frankly, I was a little surprised Adrian accepted the invitation, especially without putting up much of a fuss. Of course, the ladies both saw and heard everything that had transpired and when we met briefly afterwards, they were more concerned about what to wear than whether or not we should attend. Evidently, formal attire would be required, so the rush was on to acquire acceptable attire for everyone.

I stand corrected, since it seems the rush was on to find something acceptable for me to wear. The ladies had closets full of formal gowns waiting to be worn, and Adrian had his "formal dinner attire" waiting back on the plane. Excuse me, but who in the hell travels with formal dinner attire besides James Bond or a television game show host? Since leaving Susan, I'd become more of a jeans and t-shirt type of guy. My boring old suits were retired long ago and none of them fit the "formal" standard set by Adrian anyway. Besides him, I don't know one single person who owns, much less travels with, formal dinner attire. To the new and improved me, formal attire means a nicely tailored sports coat, which can be thrown on in an emergency. Like oh, maybe, the President is coming to dinner.

Needless to say, phone calls were made, favors were called in, money was passed out like candy, and John Steele acquired his first tuxedo. A local tailor worked his little fingers to the bones through the early evening and into the night, and I emerged looking like a million bucks, or roughly the cost of my new monkey suit. I even acquired a pair of the shiniest black shoes you've ever seen, which scared the hell out of me because I knew their first major scuff was just around the next corner, and Lord knows the evening would be ruined if one of my shoes got scuffed.

Since "supper" was at 5:30 a.m., we departed New Orleans at approximately 4:00 a.m. in Adrian's limo. Now I'll be the first to agree that Louisiana doesn't play by the normally accepted dining rules, but 5:30 a.m. seems an odd time to eat anything except breakfast. Fortunately, Adrian's limo was properly stocked for its current passengers, so we were able to have cocktails in route.

There was no traffic to speak of on Interstate 10 at this time of the morning, so the roughly eighty-mile trip to Baton Rouge seemed to fly by. We made it to town fifteen minutes early, but Adrian had the driver circle around town a bit, so that our official arrival would be precisely at 5:30 a.m.. I'd never seen my three companions acting so odd, as though they were somewhat concerned but anxious at the same time. I didn't sense any fear on their part, just apprehension.

It was still dark when we pulled up at our destination, but I could tell it was an old Greco Roman style building, which for some reason didn't resemble a house at all. When the limo pulled around back and we exited the car, I realized that this wasn't someone's private residence after all; it was a damned funeral home! I started to comment to Adrian, but he silenced me with one of his patented looks.

We were met at the door by another vampire, who simply bowed formally and bid us to enter. He was a large fellow, who looked like he'd be more comfortable in a football jersey than the formal attire he was wearing. Though he hardly seemed to notice me, I felt a strong bond with him already. Without a word passing between us, I knew he was a jeans guy too.

Our linebacker friend led us to a very formal dining room, which was filled with expensive looking antiques and hardly seemed suitable for a funeral home, unless a vampire owned it of course. It seemed our host had acquired a pair of linebackers, as another equally large vampire in formal attire was waiting to serve us drinks. To be honest, this whole scene was freaking me out a bit. I felt like I was taking part in an elaborate exhibition or play, but I didn't know what my role was.

Once drinks were served, our host made a grand entrance and walked around shaking hands and hugging everyone like they were his long lost family, which I guess they were. He shook my hand, then let out a huge laugh and pulled me close for a heart felt vampire hug. I guess we'd officially bonded.

"Sit, sit, please, make yourselves comfortable," he said. "Supper will be served shortly but we have some business to attend to first, which unfortunately can't wait."

I noticed there were actually name placards in front of certain spots, so someone had taken the time to figure out a seating chart. I found mine and took my seat, bummed I wasn't next to Emily. When we'd all been seated, our host walked to the front of the table and placed his hands on the back of the single chair at the head of the table, where I assumed he'd take his position as the event's host. He looked at his watch and smiled.

"My dear family members," he said in silent voice, while pulling the chair at the head of the table out and to the side about five feet, "I've brought you here tonight to introduce you to a special guest. As a favor to me, I'll ask you not to speak until the appropriate time." With this, he smiled and winked at all of us. I was totally lost, now.

Speaking out loud, he said, "Ladies and gentlemen, it's my privilege to introduce to you, Dr. Peter Sedgewick!"

The curtain was pulled back by one of the linebackers and the man I'd seen on the cover of Leslie's book entered the room to a very brief but polite applause. He looked like the same pompous ass depicted on the book cover. Initially, I thought my senses might be failing me, or perhaps it was the fact that I'd never been in the midst of so many of my kind. I closed my eyes and refocused my energy on the gray haired prick entering the room as though he owned it. Damn, Dr. Peter Sedgewick was a vampire!

Our host held up his hands and said warmly, "Dr Sedgewick, the floor is yours."

With great flair, Sedgewick walked to the head of the table and began, "Fellow vampires, I know that just a few short weeks ago I thought of you as my enemies. I'll admit I was jealous of your power and thought vampires a menace to society. But now," he said, raising his hands and looking at them as if for the first time, "I realize what we are truly capable of. My friends, we are gods. We are meant to rule the world!"

Sedgewick, standing at the end of the table, put both hands on it and leaned forward for emphasis. "My good friend and our dear host has shared his blood with me, and allowed me to make The Choice. Why were we given this tremendous power, you ask? It is our destiny to lead the sheep of the world. We are the good shepherds, my friends, and by God they WILL do our bidding! With my leadership, we can take over every government, country by country. We'll start with the United States, then England, Germany, Russia, and beyond!"

He stopped to think a second, and then added, "Screw France, they can wait 'til last."

Back on his soapbox, Sedgewick pounded his fists on the table and asked, his voice rising to a fevered pitch, "I need to know, my brethren, can I count on you? Are you with me?"

The room was silent for a minute and suddenly I began to feel a bit dizzy. I immediately realized it was just the now familiar feeling I get each morning as the sun rises in the east, telling all good vampires its time to be in their coffins. They'd picked the damnedest time for this meeting, clearly forgetting that it wasn't the best time of day for yours truly. I sat up straight and focused like Adrian had taught me so that I wouldn't succumb to the sun's pull and, soon, my full focus returned. I didn't want to miss any of this excitement. Were my new family members really buying into this guy's line of crap?

Sedgewick had finished his sermon and now stood quietly waiting for our answer. He looked from face to face, as though challenging anyone to do anything other than agree with his world domination plan. Then, as though someone had thrown a magic switch, his eyes rolled back in his head, and Sedgewick passed out. Technically, I suppose I should say that he fell asleep, which as I know all too well happens to new vampires. Standing at the end of the table and leaning forward as he was, put him in the perfect position to make the event extra special. He dropped like a sack of shit, but his chin caught the edge of the table, making a rather loud cracking sound as his head snapped backwards. I'm no expert on world politics, but I believe it could be considered quite an unceremonious exit for the future leader of the world, dropping down and banging his chops as he did.

There was a moment of stunned silence, then to my surprise the entire room burst into laughter. Even my new linebacker friends, who had been totally stoic up until this point, couldn't help chuckling. I wasn't quite sure of what to make of it at first, until I realized this whole event had been staged for our benefit. It was vampire humor at its best!

Adrian was nearly in tears and asked nobody in particular, "Did you hear his chin hit the edge of the table?"

"Hey, John," our host asked, between gasps, "do you know why Sedgewick wanted to rule the world?"

I shook my head, knowing I wasn't going to get a serious answer. The others knew the answer and started laughing before he could choke it out himself. "He always wanted a job he could really sink his teeth into!"

Jasmyna was doing a pretty good imitation of Sedgewick's voice and pounding her fists on the table, "Are you with me, my brethren?"

Once again, everyone burst into laughter, and several of his other lines were repeated for the benefit of all, and they all seemed to get funnier each time.

"I still loved it when his chin hit the edge of the table," said Adrian, shaking his head and wiping away tears of laughter. "Perhaps Sedgewick just set his 'ghouls' a little too high!"

"His ghouls too high?" asked Emily, shaking her head in disbelief. "That's horrible. Now I know you've lost it, Adrian!"

Finally, our host turned to his two henchmen and said, "Gentlemen, please get this piece of feces out of my dining room and prepare the oven. Once we've witnessed this future world leader's demise, we'll have ourselves a nice supper."

Sedgewick's slumbering body was picked up and unceremoniously carried away. Ten minutes later, carrying fresh drinks to "toast his roast" as our host joked, we were all invited down to the crematorium where, with the fire amply stoked, our dear friend, Dr. Peter Sedgewick, met his demise. When we heard a single scream emitted from the fire, we all raised our glasses and pretended to scream back. This may seem a bit twisted on our part, but it left no doubt in any of our minds that Sedgewick and his world domination plans had gone up in smoke.

Back upstairs, the real party began and I must say I had a wonderful time. Adrian had multiple bottles of his favorite vintage, Emily and Jasmyna took their leave for a few minutes to help a very sick homeless man cross over in one of the funeral home's private viewing rooms, and I found a multiple murderer waiting for me in another. Our host had thought of everything, and made everyone comfortable.

It was nearly noon before we stumbled out to the limo, drunk on fun, promising to get together again soon. I wanted to fall asleep on the way home, but I knew my compatriots were in too lively of a mood. I'd likely wake up naked along the highway or in some other equally embarrassing situation. I looked at my new tux, and for the first time appreciated it and the small part in which it had played. Yes, the whole event had been overly elaborate, but it was for a good cause. We had closure. When you have all the time in the world, why not do things a little bit elaborate from time to time?

Chapter 37

Compared to my recent adventures, the past few weeks were somewhat boring. Nice and peaceful and boring. I think a little bit of boring can be a good thing sometimes. We all returned to Arizona for a few days, and while we relaxed, Adrian and the ladies began to educate me about my great grandfather and a few million other vampire related things. Seems he's quite a character and has influenced many world events over the centuries, which is a major issue with Adrian. It's obvious they all love him, but as with many family relationships, they simply disagree on a great many things. They definitely respect him, and while they all agree I need to spend some time with him, they want it to be in the future. The far distant future!

Emily and Jasmyna decided not to return to the house in New Orleans, at least for a few decades. They loved the old house, and couldn't part with it for good. They, too, had multiple identities, so they'd simply sell it back and forth a few times over the next few years until a paper trail made it appear it was no longer connected to them. Although all government records related to our existence were to be erased, the ladies felt it was prudent to move on to one of their other locations. Seems they had an itch to return to Savannah and a lovely old Victorian they owned there.

I, too, felt that my house outside Fresno was compromised, but decided to keep it. Adrian would purchase it through a corporation he owned and transfer it back to me under a different name. Delthea and the boys would continue to live there, and I'd visit on occasion. Every time I entered the house, I felt like Virgil's ghost was there, especially since his remains, minus his heart and his head, were buried out back. It was kind of creepy.

Speaking of ghosts, I finally met the ghost in my house. Met isn't the right word, since this ghost pays no attention to humans, or vampires for that matter. I was sitting in my office one evening, when I felt a chill. I looked up in time to see her drift past. A very cool experience, and one I'll cherish.

Delthea's sure the ghost's earthly remains are buried around the property somewhere, and she wants to do a séance to find out why she's still there and where she's buried. She thinks a decent Christian burial will do the trick. I'm tempted to try Emily's method of yelling at the ghost to get her attention, then directing her towards the light. Delthea's so caught up in it all that I don't want to spoil her fun. In fact, I have a few ghost related pranks up my sleeve that I'm saving for Halloween. The boys will love them, but the way Delthea can slug, my shoulder will likely pay a stiff penalty.

There was one more personal loose end I needed to wrap up in Fresno. I looked up old Victor Ramsey, the pervert who'd tried to abuse me when I was a kid. He lived by himself in a rundown apartment and, amazingly, still taught Sunday school. Sitting in the back row of his church on a foggy Sunday morning, I sat and watched what now appeared to be a tired old man, sitting a few rows from the front. Watching him, I felt a chill run down my spine, as though he was the monster and not I. Entering his mind, I was sickened by what I found. The man had abused many children throughout his life, and the desire still burned deep within him. A few minutes later, as the choir began a slightly off-key rendition of "Amazing Grace," Victor Ramsey stood up and clutched his heart. Everyone assumed he had a simple heart attack, but Victor died envisioning a twelve-year old image of me, squeezing the life out of his still beating heart.

Oddly, the combination of dealing with Victor Ramsey and getting to spend time with Delthea's boys had a profound effect on me. I realized that I loathed child abusers and that the world would be a better place if some of them ended up missing. I still struggle with the idea of killing innocents but wondered if I could kill a child molester guilt free? Opportunity knocked one evening, and I didn't have to wonder long. I'm happy to say I have no problem there. I was pleased to learn that in an effort to assist my cause, a law was passed requiring convicted sex offenders to register their addresses. How thoughtful and convenient, for me!

Staying true to my word, I returned to Washington D.C. to assist Leslie in her fight against crime. She'd transferred out of the Paranormal & Psychic Investigations Department and was assigned to a new drug enforcement task group that was being formed. Her new assignment would require her to work undercover in the Chicago area for several months. For three wonderful weeks, though, her new team was training in D.C., so we got to spend a lot of time together.

Leslie was pleased, since according to her, this was the first time her schedule had been normal in years. Every evening, she was home by 6:00 p.m. She ate and then we'd make love. We'd watch a movie or go for a walk, then make love again. She'd fall asleep with her lovely head of red hair on my arm, and I'd lie there and just enjoy looking at her. For a human, she's pretty damn hot. In the morning, she'd head off to work, and I'd head off to feed and sleep. Ah, the domestic life.

When it came time for Leslie to move on to Chicago to begin her assignment, I decided to tag along, at least for a while. I took a furnished apartment there, so I could remain close to Leslie and took advantage of my free time to scope out a new city. Eventually, I might buy something if the market's right, but I'm in no hurry. In a city this size, there's an abundance of food. To my surprise, there's also an abundance of drugs. With my particular skill set, dealers are easy enough to discover. In my nightly prowling, I find so many leads for Leslie that her co-workers are beginning to think she's either psychic or connected to an insider. For once, she's a star at work, and I'm happy for her. She's doing the world some good, and I believe I'm doing her some good. When we're together, things are very good. So, considering how "good" everything's going, I guess I'd have to say that my decision to return as a vampire was a good one. All things considered, I guess I'm better off...undead!

Note: Eighteen months after my visit to Susan, she passed away. Nobody noticed me standing at the back of the funeral, but I was there. It was lovely, as far as funerals go. Nice ceremony, a decent turnout, many kind remembrances, and an unusually large quantity of flowers...

Made in the USA